The Ascension
Book One

The Last Incarnation

Copyright © 2005, 2011 Joseph A. Giunta

ISBN-13 978-0615540702
ISBN-10 0615540708

All rights reserved. No part of this publication may be reproduced, stored in a retrieval system, or transmitted in any form or by any means, electronic, mechanical, recording or otherwise, without the prior written permission of the author.

Printed in the United States of America.

The characters and events in this book are fictitious. Any similarity to real persons, living or dead, is coincidental and not intended by the author.

Cover Illustration by Henning Ludvigsen.
Interior Illustrations by Henning Ludvigsen.

Brick Cave Media
brickcavemedia.com
2011

For my wife Lori
and my daughter Ada.
Thanks for putting up
with my obsessive behavior.

For my beta readers,
Nelson Sperling, Deb Bozek
Jen Castillo, Scott Macy
and Karen Miller.
Thanks for helping me
produce a quality story.

For my friend and cover artist,
Henning Ludvigsen.
Thanks for giving my work the
professional look I've always wanted.

And finally...
Thank You, Reader,
for allowing me the chance
to tell you this tale.

By J.A. Giunta

THE ASCENSION
Book One: *The Last Incarnation*
Book Two: *The Mists of Faeron*
Book Three: *Out of the Dark* *

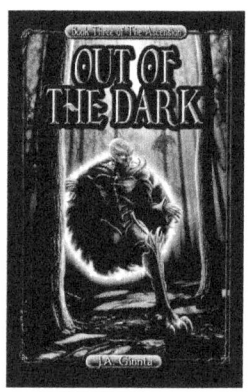

THE GUARDIANS
Book One: *Knights of Virtue*

* Forthcoming

Foreword

The biggest question I'm asked, regarding this book, is why did I feel the need to revise it before the trilogy was complete? Suffice it to say that I know a lot more about writing and the publishing industry now than I did two years ago. I don't mean to disparage self-publishing or the POD (print on demand) industry, but at the time this novel was first printed, I had no idea what I was doing beyond wanting to see my manuscript in print. I say manuscript, because it was a first draft at best.

I wrote this novel over ten years ago and hadn't given it a second look until the beginning of 2005. A friend was looking to self-publish a work-related book, so I looked into it as well. I thought it would be great to see my novel finally in print, to have it somewhere on a shelf or pass it out to family and friends. In that respect, self-publishing and POD are truly ideal. I did some research and found what I felt was the best. To be honest, I was expecting to be turned down, because I knew the book needed work. When I first wrote it, I got lazy toward the end and just wanted it done – so I could send it off to publishers right away! Live and learn.

I was surprised, to say the least, when I received a positive response, that my book was finally going to be published. I hurried to do some final editing, make some name changes here and there with global find and replace, then shipped it off to the publisher. It didn't really dawn on me what I was doing until I was nearly finished writing the third book in the trilogy... destroying any hope of ever having these books printed by what's commonly known as a "traditional" publisher. A few months of intensive research, speaking with published authors, agents and publishers, left me with two choices: discard all that I'd done and start a new series or go back and make this trilogy the absolute best that I can, self-published or not, and do right by those few who had purchased my books. Well you know which one I chose.

I didn't just go back and revise this novel, fixing all those glaring typos that appeared in the first. No, from top to bottom, I rewrote the book. I used every little tidbit of advice I could find during my research. I may not have succeeded in creating the best fantasy novel that's out there, but I did write a book I can be proud of, something I could show to anyone in the world without stumbling over explanations. No more public domain clipart, either. Henning is one of the best character artists in the world. I couldn't have asked for a nicer guy to give my writing a face, because people *do* judge a book by its cover.

So the answer to that big question is, I did it for you, the reader. OK, I did it for myself, too. Being a writer is synonymous with being selfish. I hope you enjoy the changes and don't complain overly much when I rewrite the second book as well, because the third won't be out until I do. It will just have to remain here on my desk, a first draft among many, waiting to be shaped into a book you deserve.

J.A. Giunta

The Last Incarnation

J.A. Giunta

Alixhir
DARLEMAN
Geilon-Rai
Eternoll
Laurenthos
GAEBRIDON RANGE
Systeria
LUMINTOR

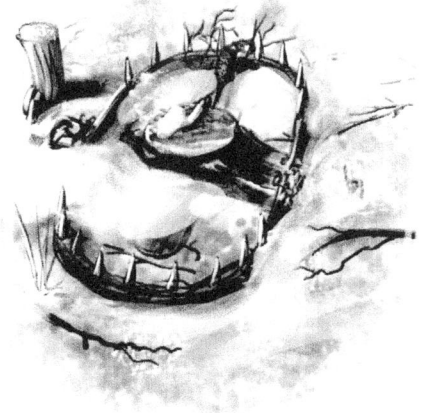

– 1 –

It was winter in the forest of Darleman, where Daroth led his son through fresh snow. It was bitterly cold that early morn, with ice clinging to the leafless trees and hanging down from their outstretched limbs. The rising sun reflected off each icicle and set them alight with a glittering brilliance.

"This is my favorite time of year," Daroth said, a trail of frosty breath accompanying each word. "The crunch of snow underfoot, the brisk morning air... it reminds me of home, in Astor." He looked back over his shoulder to Barr. "After we set these traps and check the others, maybe we can do a little ice fishing. It'd be nice to have something to eat besides hare and potatoes."

"I like potatoes," Barr said and trailed a stick through the snow, lost in some daydream like any other eight year old boy.

Daroth shook his head and looked back to the path in quiet. As he had done every day for the past month, he wondered if moving them out of Alixhir was the right decision. He had sacrificed their comfortable home for a dilapidated cabin outside the city walls, far away from both family and friends.

I had little choice, he thought. *With the way Barr was acting and others taking notice, it was either flee or face the Guardians.*

Concern marred Daroth's brow, as he glanced back at his son. Barr had lustrous curls a chestnut hue and deep earthen eyes that sparkled when he smiled. His nose was straight, offset by dimples in both cheeks, and a delicate chin rounded off his pixyish charm. Barr stood out as a beautiful child. Shorter than other boys, by at least two hands, he was also much slighter of frame. It wasn't that Barr lacked strength, he was just noticeably smaller than other children. For one that already drew undue attention, the recent change in Barr was both cause for alarm and reason for their leaving.

"We'll set one over here," Daroth said and knelt.

He placed an iron trap near a tree with its bark scratched away, pulled wide the jaws until they clicked into place. With practiced care, he took the securing chain and wrapped it once around the tree before driving a spike through two overlapping links and deep into the frozen ground. Daroth concealed the chain and iron jaws with snow before tying his feather marker to a branch. Anyone with business in the forest would know to stay clear of that tree.

"Mine next?" Barr asked.

"Just so."

Daroth tousled his son's hair with a meaty hand. A rugged woodsman and former mercenary, Daroth was a large fellow by any standard. He towered over Barr, cast a shadow twice as wide, but smiled down on the boy with pride and affection. He just assumed Barr took after his natural father, a man neither of them had ever met.

They continued on through the trees, off the deer path and down past a frozen stream. Daroth pulled a brenyn root from an inner pocket and chewed the bitter juice from its stem. From the corner of his eye, he saw Barr stop to forage for a piece of black root and catch up while chewing its stem.

"How do you know that's not poisonous?" Daroth asked. He knew the root was harmless and would have reached for some himself had he known it was there. "Or that there was any, for that matter?"

Barr shrugged. "I don't know." He was silent for a moment, as they rounded a dense grove. "Can we visit uncle Therol tomorrow? I promised I'd return his book when I finished with it."

"I'll take it to him." Daroth looked intently about, searching for any trace of boar.

"Would you ask him for another?" Barr asked and quickly added, "Or a few? I read the last one four times–"

"Place yours here."

Barr was standing ten paces behind. "Shouldn't we put it here? The snow is lighter by this tree, and there's score marks on the backside of that rock."

Trapping little more than a month, and already he thinks he knows better. Daroth shook the snow from his furs, fighting the urge to grin. *Boy learns faster than I ever did.*

"You know the agreement."

With a laugh, Barr knelt and pulled a trap from over his shoulder. "I know," he replied and worked at setting the iron jaw in just the perfect spot. "I can place my traps wherever I want, but if they don't catch anything, I chop wood for a week."

"When I was your age," Daroth said, "I chopped wood *every* day. You should consider yourself lucky."

Covering his trap with torn bark and bits of tinder, Barr was focused on the work at hand. When he finished and stood, wiping snow from his legs, he tied a marker to the tree and gave a smile that warmed Daroth's heart.

"I ever tell you how proud you make me?" Daroth chuckled and pulled Barr close.

"All the time."

They walked deeper into the forest, beyond the grove and checked a few empty traps. Though the lack of prey was disconcerting, Daroth tried not to let it show. Game had been scarce the past few weeks. Aside from laying traps, Daroth would normally spend the better part of a day hunting by bow, but there was less each day to catch.

"We're not doing so well," Barr noted.

"It would be nice if Hearn would put a deer in our path, eh?" Daroth mused. "Venison for a week, sell off the antlers, have a new pair of boots made for you."

Things will get better, Daroth told himself. *If all else fails, I can take up with my brother and ruin my eyes as a scribe.*

It wasn't an encouraging thought.

"Some fishing will do us good," Daroth said and kept walking. "A few snapper and a warm loaf –"

Daroth couldn't hear Barr's footsteps behind him, turned and saw the boy frozen in place. He softly called to Barr as he approached, careful not to startle him from whatever waking dream had taken hold. A vision of fire and broken furniture flashed in Daroth's mind, reminder of the last time he had shaken his son awake.

The boy's eyes stared ahead, as if watching some distant scene unfold, narrowing and widening with emotions written plainly in his young features. Fear tensed his body, set little hands to clenching, and his mouth gave rise to a silent cry.

"Barr," Daroth said firmly, his hands on either arm. "Are you all right?"

"Take your hands off me, young man!" Barr snapped, looking as if he didn't recognize his own father. His eyes then softened and rimmed with welling tears. "Dad, I'm sorry. I didn't mean..."

Hugging him close, Daroth let the boy cry. "It's all right. You're fine now. It's just you and me here, no need for worry."

We're not in Alixhir anymore, he thought, reassuring his own wavering resolve. *There are no Guardians in the forest, no friends to point them our way. We're safe here.* He hugged Barr tightly and let him go. *We're safe.*

It made no difference Daroth had never met one of those dark hunters in his thirty-two years. He'd known plenty who had. The mere mention of Guardians was enough to grip his heart with dread. During his time as a mercenary, he'd heard all too many stories of the knights in gilded armor and dark robes. Guardians served but one purpose, to hunt and destroy all turners. Wielding a magic their own, they could hunt a man across any terrain and would never cease their chase once the scent of *furie* had been made. They were fanatical in devotion and swift in their task.

There was no doubt in Daroth's mind that Barr had the *furie* and that nothing would keep the boy safe but a fair distance from prying eyes. More than just honoring a promise he'd made to his dying aunt, to raise the infant boy as his own, Daroth had quickly grown to love Barr more than any one or thing in this world.

A snap and a yelp echoed through the trees.

"That's from straight ahead," Daroth said, more to himself. "Wolf by the sound of it. Barr, I want you to stay right here until I get back, alright? You don't move from this spot."

Barr had been witness to more than a handful of dead prey, visibly squirmed the first time they had caught a fox. Daroth wanted to spare his son from seeing an animal have its throat cut. He thought it too soon for such a grim lesson. The wolf would be too wounded to set free, its leg snapped and useless. Unable to hunt, the poor creature would surely starve. Daroth intended to do the wolf a mercy and spare it a prolonged death. Though he could collect a bounty for its hide, he preferred to stay away from the city.

"Dad," Barr said with concern in his eyes and took hold of Daroth's arm. "Don't go. Let's go fishing. We can come back for it later. Please?"

"There are times when things need doing that we may not want any part of. But if it's the right thing to do, and we're able to act where others can't..." He gave Barr a reassuring pat on the shoulder. The wolf continued its pained cries. "It'd be cruel to just leave it be when we can end its suffering. Don't worry, we'll be fishing before you know it."

Leaving little room for argument, Daroth nodded and moved ahead. While rounding the hill, he reached for the long dagger at his waist and loosened it in its sheath. He wanted to end this and return to Barr without delay. The sooner they could put this behind them, the sooner they could get their poles and head to the frozen lake. As Daroth passed beyond a copse of thin birch, the trapped wolf came into view.

What in the blazes...

It was the largest wolf he had ever seen, looked more horse than canine for all its size, and stood but a few hands shorter than himself. With a coat of midnight black and tremendous muscles rippling beneath, the wolf looked a monster born of nightmare, a child's fear taken shape from the dark. Its teeth were finger-length daggers of yellowed bone, and its feral eyes glowed a luminous green.

It was all Daroth could do to keep from dropping his blade and running in fear, let alone calm the rapid thump in his chest. He wanted nothing more than to get away, to snatch up Barr and run as fast and far as his legs could carry them. Frightened but still in control of his reason, Daroth looked down at the iron jaw deeply imbedded in the wolf's broken foreleg. He wondered if the jaws and chain would hold or if the wolf would give chase, should it somehow break free.

Dark blood pooled in the snow, a growing halo of crimson about the trap. The wolf growled at him, looked ready to attack, and eyed the long knife in Daroth's hand. Under any other circumstance, he was sure he would already be dead. There was no getting close and no turning back. He couldn't risk the creature breaking loose and coming after them. Broken leg or no, the wolf was no ordinary animal. That such a monster roamed free in his forest made Daroth keenly aware of how close Barr stood waiting all alone.

He quickly surveyed the area and caught sight of a branch that would do. He sheathed his dagger and took hold of the icy limb. With a growl of his own, he wrenched its length from the tree with both hands, and breathed heavy as the wood tore free. His breath frosting the air between them, Daroth faced off against the snarling wolf.

He swung with all his might and struck a solid blow against its head. The wolf dropped with a sharp cry and laid still, with only the rise and fall of its chest to give tell it yet lived. Again and again, Daroth let fly the branch, raining powerful strikes for good measure. Through no fault of its own, the wolf had become all that was wrong in Daroth's life, all that threatened his happiness and made Barr's future uncertain. By the time Daroth's fear and anger had subsided, burned away with each terrible swing, the wolf remained utterly still.

Tired and shaking from the exertion, Daroth let fall the bloodied wood and dropped to his knees. His hands wet with blood, he reached out and took hold of the trap, pulled wide its jaw and tossed it aside. He tried cleaning his hands in the snow, but there was no helping how gruesome he looked. Getting to his feet, Daroth wanted only to leave. He planned to come back later to skin the wolf and reset the trap. For now, all he could think of was returning to Barr and heading home – at least until he spotted the medallion.

What animal wears a medallion? Daroth wondered and slipped the necklace from around the wolf's head. The medallion itself was a palm-sized circle of iron, embossed with four interwoven ovals. *I've seen this before.* He stood and recalled the image from many years ago, a ruined temple in the Emyr campaign. *A holy symbol? This monstrosity belonged to a priest?*

Jaws clamped shut on Daroth's leg.

He cried out from the explosion of pain, threw wide the medallion and fought to remain standing, as the bones of his left thigh were ground to dust in one bite. The wolf's growl reverberated through Daroth's entire body and caused a sickening wave of nausea that spilled the contents of his stomach. The wolf let go its hold and limped back.

Hurts a great deal, does it not? a voice in Daroth's mind taunted. *Your contraption was far worse.*

Sick with a sudden fever, covered in sweat and nearly blind with burning pain, Daroth was certain he was poisoned and hallucinating. He watched on as a beryl nimbus encompassed the wolf. The bones of its foreleg snapped into place and became whole. Muscle stretched back across the deep gash, mended once more, and the jagged edges of its fur closed with no sign of injury.

In but moments, the wolf was fully healed.

Unable to stand any longer, weariness won out, and Daroth fell back to the cold ground. His head struck a rock with a horrible thump, wetting the snow with a spray of blood that commingled with the wolf's. The fall itself should have killed him, but a force of will not his own fought to keep him conscious. Daroth could feel the presence of another in his mind. It toyed with him like a cat pawing a helpless mouse, letting him know that he had lost all control.

I could save you, the voice offered, *leave you to become one of us. Would you like that?*

"No." Daroth blinked slowly, fought to stay awake. "What are you?"

Breath came to Daroth in shuddering gasps, as the creature moved closer to his throat. Its breath was hot, rancid with coppery blood, and set the hair on his neck on end.

What are you? the voice asked in turn. *Are you worthy? Are you a hunter, or are you game?*

Daroth thought he was going mad, the voice in his mind taunting and prodding, enjoying his pain. He could no longer feel his legs, but his head throbbed with each shallow beat of his heart.

His thoughts turned to Barr, and a cold fear began to gnaw at his middle. Greater than any concern for Barr's safety was the overwhelming guilt of having failed as a father. He had tried his best to keep Barr from harm, did all that he could to give the boy a family and a home, but his efforts would all be for naught.

"I'm sorry," Daroth said to his son.

Not good enough, the voice sneered.

Then came the laughter, deep in Daroth's mind, that foretold of his coming doom. He felt the heat of its breath upon him once more, as the wolf moved in close and blocked out all trace of the sun.

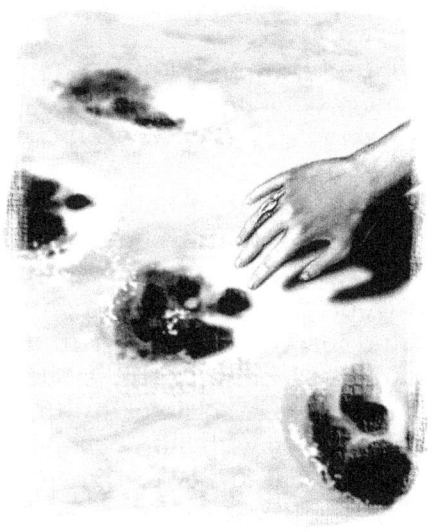

- 2 -

Barr kept his eyes on the right edge of the hill, where his father had gone off ahead. The forest grew more dense alongside the snowy outcropping of rock and frozen earth. On the hill itself, dead grass jutted up through the snow and swayed in time with a chill breeze. Long moments passed by, with nothing but the wind and bitter taste of black root to keep him company. Worrying the stem, Barr looked nervously about.

It's taking too long, he thought. He wanted to move closer, take a peek around the bend, but fear kept him rooted in place. *Something's not right. He should've called out by now.*

He tossed aside the black root and drew the hunting knife from his waist. Sunlight glinted off its keen edge. Though Barr was unused to handling a blade, its weight lent him a measure of comfort and gave him the courage to take a step forward.

A nice warm fire, Barr thought, trying to get a grip on his fear, *a steaming bowl of spiced stew, a snow-cold mug of milk with cinnamon and maybe even a plate of sugared apple and wild berry.*

The more Barr thought of being back at their cabin, the closer he drew round the bend. He came up short and cocked an ear, thought he had heard his father cry out. Unsure of where the sound had come from, he drew a deep breath and forced himself to run ahead. Listening intently, as he dodged between trees, he nearly choked on his heart at seeing a squirrel jump down and run away through the forest with all speed. Barr stood for a moment and tried to catch his breath, to hear anything beyond his frantic heartbeat.

The quiet around him was unsettling. Gone was the distant growl and any trace of his father's voice. Not a single bird broke the ominous silence. Barr thought he caught sight of a moving shadow at the corner of his eye. He saw nothing but trees when he turned. There was a trail nearby, footsteps in the snow, that could only have been made by his father. With a firm grip on the knife, Barr resolved to follow. By the time he heard the crunch of snow directly behind him, he could do little but gasp.

A gloved hand clamped over his mouth.

* * *

Tuvrin led the other Maurdon in chase of the wolf. Five in all, skilled trackers and hunters, they moved through the snow with no sign of their passing. They had been tracking the unusual creature since last nightfall, and Tuvrin was determined to see the beast dead. Forgoing rest and food, he pushed them on. What little trail the wolf left quickly grew old, as if the ground were too weak to hold its prints.

He gritted his teeth, as he followed the fading tracks, resolved to reach their end with all speed. For months the wolf had been plaguing their home, slaughtering any caught alone on the forest floor. The remains left behind were unlike any he had ever seen. Aside from the usual torn flesh and broken bones, each corpse was left with its final tormented cry frozen in place. Their voiceless screams haunted Tuvrin's sleep, left him weary and driven to grant them peace.

The wolf came into sight.

All five had bows drawn in an instant, sighting the wolf as it thrashed and cried out. Its foot had got caught in an iron trap.

"Hold," Tuvrin ordered.

He heard the snapping branch and footfalls in the snow just as scent of the human reached his nose. A brief moment passed before the man appeared. The wolf stood nearly as tall, could have crushed the man in a single bite, yet he didn't run away in fear or kill it from afar. Tuvrin watched on with disbelief, as the human tore a limb from a tree and proceeded to beat the wolf to death.

The others lowered their bows. Tuvrin gripped his all the harder, anger rising up in his throat. How long had he waited to catch the wolf in his sight? How many weeks were spent scouring the woods for a glimpse of its trail? No matter what others said, he knew the wolf was not a dumb animal. It moved with cunning, chose its victims with care. Had it been a man, they would have called it a murderer.

He should have felt relief at seeing the beast dead, but the anger inside him would not abate. Tuvrin wanted the wolf to die by his own hands, to send all his guilt and anger in a single shaft that would lay low the wolf and finally put his grief to rest. Any hope of vengeance died away in that moment, dashed out in a frenzied display. The human was covered in the wolf's blood, bathed in a kill that should not have been his.

The wolf growled and attacked.

Bows came up once more, leveled arrows toward the wolf, but Tuvrin ordered them down. They couldn't take the chance of being spotted. If word of their existence reached the human city, the wolf would be the least of their troubles. Hunters would descend on the forest by the hundreds, taking ears as trophy and leaving death in their wake. Though long-lived, not all of his people were old enough to remember those dark days. Tuvrin could recall them all too clearly.

When the trapper was dead, a pang of guilt struck Tuvrin, both for not helping when he could have and for the thrill that he felt at seeing the wolf alive. He had a respect for all life, did not want to see the man die, but he also had a duty to his people. It was too late anyway, the decision had been made and could not be undone.

Life is not fair, he reminded himself with a grim set to his jaw.

"Now," he told the others and let loose his arrow.

The wolf turned its head as Tuvrin fired, as if it sensed danger before knowing what posed it. Struck in the side, the wolf yelped and bolted for a deer path. It disappeared into the trees, as the Maurdon rose to give chase. While Tuvrin ran, he spotted a boy and stopped. The others came up short as well, their painted faces both anxious and looking in askance.

"There is a human boy," he said as explanation.

The Maurdon shared glances. One gave a curt nod and led the others running after the wolf, without so much as a look back. With thoughts of his own son

weighing heavy on his mind, Tuvrin fought down his remorse and turned toward the human child.
Am I no better than the wolf? he thought. *I killed this boy's father.*
Tuvrin worked his way around the trees, hoping to reach the child before the gruesome sight of remains came into view. There was a chance the wolf would turn back if it scented the boy, kill him and be gone in an instant.
It had happened before, Tuvrin reminded himself. *I will not let it happen again.*

* * *

Barr gave up looking over his shoulder in the hopes of seeing his father come running after. Whoever had taken him from behind had forced him to walk for nearly half a day. The telltale streamers of sunlight were fading softly out of the trees, casting the forest into an early nightfall. There was little chance of anyone finding him that day.
"Where's my father?" he demanded, concerned with little else since his abrupt departure. "Who are you, and where are we going?"
"You talk much for one so small," the tall stranger replied with an odd accent. He looked about the trees, as if he expected trouble. "It is better to be quiet."
"Better for who?" Barr asked under his breath.
He began to wonder if he was being taken by a slaver. His uncle Therol had often warned of it, how men stole children and beggars from the streets at night and brought them to work in the Psachlin Pits, far to the west.
I bet he is a slaver, Barr thought and studied the man closely.

He was taller than anyone Barr had ever seen, even taller than his father by two hands. The stranger was, however, unusually lean. Wearing leathers stained green and brown, the lanky bowman looked as if a piece of the forest had dislodged itself. His hair was dark, with a long tangled braid falling down to his waist. There were black pinions and dead leaves woven through the hair, as if he had been crawling through the forest for days. It was hard to distinguish his face, painted as it was with dark earthen hues, but the harsh emerald of his eyes stood out in glaring contrast, watching all around him with intent. There were two short swords at his waist, and over one shoulder was a quiver full of arrows, each one topped with a coal-black feather.

It was the bow, however, that caught and held Barr's attention. Slung across the man's back at an angle, so that it wouldn't get caught up in his steps, it looked as long as he was tall and made of a wood Barr had never before seen. The wood was dark like rich soil, and there were veins of jade running through its polished length, much like the marble statues and fountains in Alixhir's center square.

Yes, Barr thought, as he eyed what must have been an expensive weapon, *he is definitely a slaver. Who else could afford a bow like that and still look like a dirty tree?* None of it mattered, though, because his father would eventually find and rescue him. Barr was sure of it. *He wouldn't just leave me.*

"I'm hungry," Barr said.

Eating was the farthest thing from his mind, but he hoped he could slow them down by stopping for a rest. The man gave him a slice of dried meat from a pouch at his belt. It smelled like venison but went untouched.

"I'm thirsty," Barr said and was given a dark skin with a wooden spout. Its surface was slick in his small hands. He didn't drink.

"I'm tired!"

The stranger stopped and knelt before him with a serious cast to his eyes. Barr returned the look with defiance.

"Do you understand I am trying to help you?" the man asked. "There are dangerous creatures in this forest." He looked to the canopy of trees and fading light. "We have little time before night."

"I'm tired, though." Barr pursed his lips and stared at his boots. He was weary all over and he just wanted to go home.

"What are you called?"

Barr thought for a moment, cocking an eyebrow as he did, then answered, "I'm Barr. Who are you?"

"I am called Tuvrin. Let us get to safety, Barr, and then we can talk. For now," the man warned with a slender finger of his gloved hand, "we keep quiet and move swiftly."

Taking a deep breath, Barr nodded and let it out in a *whoosh*. In that moment, he caught sight of a tapered ear poking through the man's hair. Barr's eyes widened in awe, and his mouth fell open.

"You're an elf," he accused. "You are, aren't you?" Tuvrin's hand went up to his exposed ear. Barr went on without missing a beat. "My uncle used to tell stories, but I never believed him. You're real. Elves are real."

Tuvrin was quiet, his painted face more grave.

Brimming with questions, Barr could hardly find the breath to speak them all. It felt as if a fire tale had sprang up to life, and he was now caught in its middle. There were *elves* in the forest. But why was one taking him away? Why take him and not bring his father as well? He had never heard any stories of elves stealing away children, let alone still living in the forests. Every tale he had been told led Barr to believe that elves no longer existed. So why was one with him now? What was Tuvrin trying to protect him from?

With a nod, Tuvrin said, "I will tell you all you wish to know when we reach Geilon-Rai. We must hurry if we want to reach it by dawn."

"Shouldn't we rest for the night?" Barr felt safer in knowing Tuvrin was an elf, but he still wished his father would catch up.

"No one sleeps on the forest floor," Tuvrin replied. "Not since –" he paused, as if choking on the words – "not for some time now."

The two were then off through the trees again, with Barr taking three steps to the elf's one. It felt as if hours had gone by before he was simply too weary to walk. His eyes drooped low, as he listened to the drone of snow crunching underfoot, and his legs would carry him no farther. Gentle hands swooped him up, and cradled him as he slept.

"Rest now, little one," Barr thought he heard a voice say, but it came from off in the distance.

– 3 –

Barr woke with a start from a terrible dream, where a dark creature of clawing shadow drove him far away from home. A loneliness had crept over him while he slept, weighing him down. Starting as a dull ache in his middle, a feeling of emptiness grew outward and encompassed him fully. It was as if he were without any family or friend, no one to fend off the oppressive dark. In moments, the dream world dissipated, replaced with the contrast of memory. With each frosted breath Barr took, his dread slipped away until a calm settled the pounding in his chest.

Wiping sleep from his eyes, Barr pushed aside the coarse blanket that was scratching his cheek. He was in a tent, it seemed, a space large enough for two men, with a single bear skin rug. A stout pole ran through the center, where a circular piece of wood was both table and support. Atop its smooth surface was a wooden bowl of steaming broth and a mug of cold water.

Testing the tent with a push on its center pole, Barr realized the outer skins were stretched across two trees, their interwoven limbs lending an unshakable support. Nothing short of a fire or wild storm would endanger it. Placing a hand against the branches overhead, he was amazed to feel warmth spreading through them. With wonder in his eyes, he sat back down to eat.

The yellow broth was thick with spice that tingled his cheeks and warmed his middle. Barr drank the soup down and was still hungry. He looked about for some bread, when voices outside began to argue, two men he had never seen, speaking a language he had never heard. Sunlight filtered through the flaps of the tent. Though the wind had a cold bite to its touch, Barr decided to venture outside.

"What's going on out here?" he asked.

What met his gaze was not what he expected. The elves he knew of in storybooks lived in fantastical cities of polished marble walls, with grand towers and vibrant flags running from the ramparts. Here there was only another tent. Two elves in dirtied leathers stood outside, speaking in heated tones and waving their arms for emphasis. Though much alike, they looked different from Tuvrin in a way that was frightening. Their hair was dark and windblown, like a wild boar had run free through the brush. There was a feral cast to their eyes and a narrow set to their brows.

As one disappeared into the opposite tent, Barr tightened his borrowed cloak and stood waiting. Snow began to fall. An icy flake tickled his nose when he looked up at the slices of gray sky. He had never seen trees so tall. Their branches were so close together, like hands reaching out and taking hold, that Barr was surprised any snow made it through at all.

He began to wonder where Tuvrin had gone off to. Barr considered slipping away and trying to make it back to his father, but he had no idea how to find his way home. He looked to the other tent and supposed Tuvrin could be inside. Rather than run aimlessly through the snow toward a certain death, Barr decided to look for Tuvrin instead. He approached the tent and was met with the butt of a spear driven into the snow before him.

Barr looked up to see the elf regarding him with eyes that were black and full of hostility. In that rattling moment, pinned under a hateful gaze, Barr saw the elf's pointed ears as more frightening and foreign than majestic. A sneer crossed the elf's slender lips, and he spoke in halting common.

"Where think you to go?" he asked, holding the spear as if he might strike.

Barr pointed a small finger towards the tent. The elf looked more stern, if such a thing were possible, and without a word shook his head and looked away.

"I want to know where I am," Barr said and was ignored. He cleared his throat to get the elf's attention. "I want to get back to my father."

A wicked grin marred the elf's delicate features. "Go where you put, or I leave you with spear."

Barr stared up at him in puzzlement.

The butt end of the spear came snapping out with little sound or warning, caught Barr across the chest and sent him reeling to his back. As if nothing had happened, the elf casually returned to leaning on his spear and looked out at the falling snow.

Tears welled up in Barr's eyes, and his cheeks burned with the sting of betrayal. Aside from the pain in his chest and backside, he felt as if a dream of his had

been shattered, broken to pieces by the callous hands of the elf before him.
Elves are supposed to be nice! he yelled in his mind.
Getting up to his feet, Barr stood with both fists clenched and glared back at the uncaring elf. Helpless anger boiled up within him, a growing rage of frustration that could find no release.
The elf feigned another blow.
Barr quickly jumped back in fear and into the hands of a different elf. He looked up to see that this one had golden brown hair and looked more like Tuvrin than the first. His face was painted, and dried leaves were strewn through his single braid. With eyes a cornflower blue, he regarded the other elf with a steely gaze. Though Barr had already learned not to put much faith in how any of the elves looked, this one had a gentler touch.
"The council awaits your arrival," he said. His accented voice was subdued and respectful. He bowed and added, "I am called Galdein. Can you climb? Good. Follow carefully."
He led Barr a short distance away from the tents, to a tree of enormous girth. Galdein let out a whistle that cut through the chilly air, and a ladder of knotted leather fell from the darkened branches above. Barr tried to see the source of the rope, but the heavy limbs were so tightly interwoven that no light broke through their surface.
Galdein began to climb.
The ascent was difficult for Barr. He grew tired reading the History of Taellus, let alone pulling himself up an unwieldy rope. The knots allowed him footholds, but they weren't enough to make a difference. With his arms aching and lungs burning, only minutes had passed before Galdein reached down and pulled him up.

Barr took a firm hold around the elf's neck and adjusted his legs to avoid getting caught up in Galdein's bow.

"Hold on tight," the elf said.

Arms pumping vigorously and both feet finding holds without the aid of sight, Galdein had them up the ladder and through the slender opening at its top in no time at all. With his eyes closed toward the end, against the fast descending floor, Barr more felt than saw their breaking through to a solid platform.

"You may let go," Galdein said over his shoulder.

Barr slipped down the elf's back, truly surprised that someone so thin could possess such strength. Even his father, the strongest man he knew, would have had a hard time climbing that ladder. He looked down to where the leather rope was tied and saw it disappear through a wide circle closed over with leaves. Barr rubbed his nose and grinned at the foliage.

"We must go," Galdein said.

He nodded to the two elves standing guard in the shadowy alcoves of branch, two who until then had escaped Barr's notice. They returned the gesture, and Galdein led Barr down an opening to the right.

As he fought to keep up with an elven stride, Barr did his best to look around and not fall. It was the floor that astonished him most. Tree limbs, both thick and slender, were twined together like that of a haphazardly woven basket. Leaves and black soil filled what empty spaces remained, to make a solid and sturdy ground. The walls of the corridors and winding passageways were much the same, possessing a smooth surface of packed earth and branch. An occasional window offered a view out over the forest, where Barr glimpsed the green tops of elven homes stretched off to the distance. It was like an emerald sea of perpetual spring, beneath the snow-filled sky of winter.

Barr noticed as they passed openings that there were no doors in the tree city. Only a blanket of leaves, woven in the same fashion as the floor and walls, offered the privacy so cherished by humans. Barr recalled his uncle Therol once telling him how the elves were a peaceful nation and had little to hide from one another. His chest throbbed anew at the memory, and he began to think his uncle's stories might have been just tales after all. He certainly had never heard of them living inside trees.

"Magnificent, is it not?" Galdein's smile was warm and sincere.

Barr nodded, hoping to hear anything about where he was, but Galdein kept his eyes forward as they turned a final bend. Two guards stood watch before a large opening of leaves. They blocked the passage with immense wooden swords, crossed in the ground between them.

Barr eyed the two suspiciously, their long dark hair striking a not so distant memory. He rubbed his chest absently, as Galdein marched towards the doorway without so much as stopping to announce himself. The guards withdrew their weapons and kept their eyes straight ahead.

"Nyoln!" one said, loud enough to be heard within the chamber.

The low rumble of murmuring could be heard, as Barr was brought before a small gathering of elves. A total of fifteen were seated around the U-shaped table, with a graying elf in white robes at its head. All eyes were upon Barr, as he was seated against a wall.

He was stunned at the sheer size of the chamber, that such a place could even be possible. The whole room was carved from the bole of an enormous tree. Its walls were silky smooth to the touch and possessed a warmth he could feel through his clothes. Light shone over the large table from shimmering globes of colored glass, suspended as if by magic. He thought he could see little shapes flitting back and forth within the spheres.

Fairies? Barr wondered.

Astonished by the thought, lost in the flutter of tiny wings, he failed to notice the utter silence in the room. The entire council was staring at him, and he could see that more than one was unhappy. It reminded him of catching bugs in a clay jar when he was younger, poking at his prey with a stick. Barr grew uncomfortable under their scrutiny and squirmed on the stool.

One cleared his throat and caught Barr's attention. It was Tuvrin, the rugged hunter that had brought him to the tree city in the first place. The elf gave a nod of encouragement.

Three others had the same fierce eyes and dark hair as the guard who had struck Barr with a spear. They did little to hide their hatred but wore it plainly on their faces, the way some of the elves marked their cheeks with colored dyes. One other had cropped gray hair and unwavering granite eyes, his face a painted mask of the forest. Though that elf's visage was unreadable, Barr found it easier to meet his gaze.

There were two faces more pleasant to look on, smiles that eased his mind. The first was introduced as Roedric, Speaker of the Sun and head of the council. Though his dark hair was fading to silver, the only sign of age Barr could find among any of the elves, Roedric's arms looked well-muscled and used to hard work. Only a circlet of shining mithrinum gave note to his rank.

The second elf bowed his head with respect and presented himself as Seltruin, a Sage of the Illumin Valar. He was by far the oldest of them all, if his silver hair was any indication of age. He wore his in three braids, one that fell behind him and two that dropped on either side of his blue robes.

"Are you well?" the Speaker asked Barr.

The accent was thick and a bit difficult to make out, but Barr gave a hesitant nod in reply.

"Regardless of how he came to be in our care," Roedric said and glanced over at Tuvrin, "we are now responsible for the boy and his health. To cast him out could mean his death – or worse."

No one offered to elaborate.

"Suin est dispanitel! Limai tro vhest a sachraes donseh," one of the fierce warriors said firmly, banging a fist to the table.

"He is Ceiran," Seltruin said with a disapproving look to the rude elf and then to Barr, "First of the Narohk. You believe that?" Seltruin went on, asking Ceiran directly. "How can one 'small boy' bring about the destruction of an entire nation? He would be raised *among* us, not within the walled city of humans. No harm can come from his knowledge of our existence, if he never leaves here to reveal it."

Another motioned to speak, and Seltruin deferred with a nod.

Roedric leveled a stern gaze that other's way. "Speak in the boy's tongue or not at all," the Speaker warned. "He has every right to hear what is said, before we come to a decision."

Galdein came up beside Barr and put a hand on his shoulder. Too confused to understand just what was going on, Barr began to second guess his decision to stay. All he wanted at the moment was to go home. He couldn't imagine how worried his father must be, and the fact he had seen elves would mean nothing while trying to explain. Barr doubted his father would believe him anyway, thinking it one of his waking dreams.

"I am Westran," the other elf said slowly, as if each word tripped on his tongue, "First of the Gharak. More from the man-place will seek the child. When it is not found, they will not stop. They will search too closely the forest."

Tuvrin motioned to speak. "I do not believe that is so," he said firmly. "The unusual circumstance under which I found the boy left me no choice but to return here with him. As First of the Maurdon, I stand by that decision. I am confident he will be forgotten in time, and no threat shall come to the Sylvannis."

Forgotten in time? Barr fumed. A frown darkened his brow, as he opened his mouth. *Where's my father? What did you do to him?* he wanted to ask, but another elf started to speak.

"I am Uinar, First of the Ballar," the gray-haired elf said Barr's way, oblivious to any growing anger. "I see no threat in letting the boy stay." His voice was a ragged whisper, yet it carried throughout the chamber. "If one small human brings an end to the Sylvannis, then perhaps we are not strong enough to survive –"

"You miss the point," Ceiran interrupted. "It is not one boy that destroys us! He is but the beginning. Avoiding the humans has kept us alive for generations. Allowing one to live among us invites a return of the past. How long before they hunt us once more? How long before your ears adorn one of their mantles?"

Barr clenched a fist in frustration. No one was giving him a chance to speak, and all he could think about was his father.

Where is he? Barr wanted to scream. *What do you mean I'll be forgotten? You can't keep me here. I won't let you!*

"Young Ceiran speaks well," said another, "if not out of place." The elf sat with slender fingers steepled before him, wisdom etched in the calm of his voice. "We would do well to understand our past, to better see our future."

Roedric leaned forward. "I will not be responsible for his death. Letting the boy loose into the forest would be no less, and his blood would be upon all our heads." He paused, as if to gauge their reactions or daring any to speak before he finished. He sat back in his chair and continued. "It is said that young minds are most like to clay, easy to shape and mold. We could raise him to our ways. No threat could befall us from it."

"Assuming," yet another volunteered, "that *human* nature can be changed by teaching, if at all."

Barr grew suddenly cold, as if dark walls were growing around him and no one was there to help. He was alone in a room of strangers, people who had taken him from his father and the only life he had ever known. They spoke as if he had no home to go to, no place to call his own.

"Or at least restrained," a third added.

"I am Landrin, First of the Eneir and son to the Speaker," a fair-haired elf said with reluctance, as if it pained him to address Barr. To the council he added, "The fact remains that we are taking a gamble with our existence. Whether one boy can or will alter our way of life is not the point in question, but are we willing to take the responsibility of welcoming a human into our home? I, for one, say no. Too much is at risk, and I feel no sympathy for the son of a man who allowed himself to be killed, without any preparation for the boy's future. I will comply with this council's decision, but I say we leave this boy where he was found."

There were more than a few nods of approval.

Barr couldn't find the voice to speak, even if he were allowed. His chest and stomach pounded, as if one of the elves had just kicked him. Tears ran freely down his cheeks, left their bitter salt on his lips. He no longer heard what transpired but could think only of how alone he truly was.

What did you do to him! Barr accused in his mind, glaring at Tuvrin with a sudden rage that threatened to boil over. *Where's my father? Where is he?*

"And this from our future Speaker?" Seltruin shook his head, and Roedric looked shamed. "Have we grown so cold and distant that we no longer know compassion? This is a *life* we are discussing! If this is what our people have become, then we have no right to claim our peaceful defense of isolation. How can we let a young boy die, before he has ever had the chance to live? Are we no better than those you wish to avoid?"

"I will care for the boy." It was Tuvrin who spoke up. Ignoring the stares and astonished looks of some, he added, "It is well known that I have lost a son and mate, and never will I stop hunting the wolf who took them. But it was my decision to bring Barr to Geilon-Rai, and it is now my decision to raise him as my own. I invoke the right of House Shintae to adopt this human boy."

"Well said." Roedric nodded then leveled a frosty look at his son. "Our once enemy shall ever more be our kin. Let it be marked in the Eondin Scrolls. Barr of Alixhir will be known as Barr Shintae, son of Tuvrin Shintae."

Barr pulled away from Galdein and stood, his fists balled at either side and face red with an anger and frustration he couldn't hope to control. Tears burned his eyes and tightened his chest. His body trembled with rage, but he knew no way to vent it. Galdein placed restraining hands on Barr's shoulders and whispered consolation for his loss. Such a maelstrom of emotion swirled within Barr that the elf could not possibly calm him.

"He did not know?" Roedric asked, his voice filled with sorrow and pity.

Barr tried to scream, but his throat was constricted. The urge to run came upon him, a desire to find his father and prove them wrong.

He wouldn't leave me! Barr roared in his mind. *He wouldn't! You must have done something to him! You must have...*

Roedric nodded to Galdein, and Barr was taken to a corner of the room. Barr shirked away from the elf's touch and glowered at the council.

"How will your son contribute?" Roedric asked.

Tuvrin answered, "He will be a Maurdon. I will personally see to his training."

There were reluctant nods of acceptance, as well as the clear murmurings of unspoken displeasure. Seltruin placed a thumb-sized sapphire onto the table and slid it towards Tuvrin. Light from the globes above glimmered off its many facets, set the intricate detail of its golden stamp as a shadow lay sprawled on the table. The other elves become ominously quiet.

"That will not be necessary," Seltruin said with authority. "As the only living Sage of the Sylvannis, I call upon House Shintae to surrender one Barr, son of Tuvrin, to the Illumin Valar.

"The boy will be trained as a Sage."

– 4 –

It was past moonrise when Tuvrin returned to his chamber. From the doorway, he saw Barr asleep before the hearth, nestled in the amber fur of a bearskin rug. Galdein was seated in a rocking chair beside him. A warm glow from the fire outlined them both, casting shadows on the opposite wall. The room was filled with a peaceful quiet, with only the crackle of settling embers and the faint brush of wind against the shuttered window. A whiff of honeyed bread from the table touched against his nose. Tuvrin cleared his throat as a courtesy before coming fully into the room.

Galdein stood and moved toward the door, careful not to wake Barr. He greeted Tuvrin with a nod and spoke softly.

"I did my best to console him. I am afraid I know little of what comforts a grieving human."

Tuvrin looked past him to Barr, the boy curled up in ball with small hands clutching a blanket as he slept. He thought he had worked out all the details, how he would raise Barr as his own and give the boy a new life. It occurred to him then, he hadn't given much thought to what the next day would hold, their first day together as father and son. Though he still wrestled with his own grief, he would have to force it aside to help Barr through the loss.

"He is a child," Tuvrin said to his younger friend. "Human or otherwise, we are all much the same. It is only our perspective that differs. When your time here is short, every minute is like a drop of water slipping through your fingers. They are a strong and passionate people but grieve no more than you or I."

"You speak as if you admire them." Galdein glanced down at Barr, looking as if he tried to see the boy in a new light. "Aside from this child, I have never seen one. All I know of humans is what I have heard in stories."

"You cannot judge a forest by one tree," Tuvrin replied with patience. So few of the others had ever gone beyond the borders of Darleman that it often made him feel old to recall that dark time when humans brought war to their home. "There are admirable qualities in all of us. Unfortunately, few are without fault as a whole. Imagine how others might view the Sylvannis if, rather than the noble born Eneir, Ceiran and his Narohk were our emissaries."

Galdein looked as if he had tasted something sour.

"I would feel sorry for any *friends* we inflicted them on. To be fair, though, not all Narohk are unpleasant," Galdein said. "Ceiran is just louder than the others, so he is all anyone can hear."

Tuvrin took the young Maurdon by the shoulder. "That is precisely my point."

With a nod, Galdein said, "The boy is lucky to have you. I know your decision is an unpopular one, but you will always have my respect. Were it my son that died I–" Galdein cut himself short, as if realizing what a blunder he had made. "My apologies."

"No need. I know what you meant, and I appreciate the sentiment." Tuvrin glanced at the engraved pictures of his wife and son on the mantle, then turned back to Galdein. "Thank you for looking after him. Your own family must miss you by now."

"Most likely. Good eve, First Tuvrin." Galdein bowed his head. "I will see you at dawn."

"Sleep well, my friend."

Once Galdein had left, Tuvrin slipped into the chair as quietly as he could. He knew Barr would need a great deal of rest to fight through his grief and come to terms with the loss of his father. Months had passed, yet still Tuvrin struggled with his own sorrow, fought back the despair with fond memory and sheer will. It was thought among the Sylvannis that prolonged grief was an insult to the gods, an offense to the grand scheme and cycle of life.

They died too soon, Tuvrin argued in his mind, quarreling with a guilty conscience that would not relent. *It is not the same. Their lives were cut short by that murderous wolf. If anything is an affront to the gods, it is that vile creature.*

Barr stirred in his blanket but did not wake. Tuvrin made an effort to calm himself, unclenched his fist and took a deep breath. He reigned in his emotions, effecting a pose of calm that might later serve as an example for Barr. Tuvrin realized it was selfish to fume, that he only used anger to push back the grief. Though it went away for a time, it always came back – sometimes worse than before. He knew he had to be stronger than that. By his own decision, he was a father once more and could no longer let vengeance rule his thoughts.

Is that why I took him? Tuvrin wondered. *To save myself from grief? Or was it out of guilt for having let his father die?* He stared into the fire a short while, fraying the ends of a dark feather that hung down from his hair. *No,* he decided, *it was compassion. It may have been a mistake to let the man die, but I could not let the wolf take another. Too many others have fallen.*

Tuvrin watched Barr slumber, the steady rise and fall lending him a sense of calm. He felt himself growing tired before long. With hands clasped over his chest, he closed both eyes and let the fire's warmth lull him to sleep.

* * *

Seltruin made his way past children bearing baskets of fruit and vegetables from the gardens. Their laughter quieted as he passed, each one bidding him a good morning with solemn respect. A few turns down the hall, and he could once more hear them laughing. With a slight smile of his own, he made his way to the Speaker's chamber. Two Gharak stood guard outside the doorway, wearing green and black leathers, each of them bearing the feathered marks of seasoned warriors. They moved aside their spears, eyes transfixed ahead, and allowed him to pass through the door of woven leaves.

The chamber was warm and comfortable, despite the chill of winter outside the living tree. Lavishly decorated, the room was filled with shaped ironwood statues, bright tapestries that sprang from the vibrant hues of spring, and engraved furnishings that looked more art than fixture. Heat was provided by standing censers placed all throughout the room, their heady scent encompassing all. Lush furs of brown and gold, trophies from past hunts, were spread out across the floor of smoothed earth and branch.

More spectacular than any single decoration was a map carved into one polished wall, a combined work of Sylvannis craft, enchantment and ingenuity. Like a mold of the land, the known world was depicted in masterfully done etchings that shimmered and swayed as if alive. From the Psachlin Pits to Nuorn Haet, the Sey-Lambaern Mines to the Endless Sea, all were shaped with exacting detail. Mountains, hills and forests alike were formed in the malleable etching. As roads, highways or bridges were built, they magically appeared on the wall. Seltruin could think of nowhere on Taellus where a more precise map could be found, and gazing at its magnificence often left him with a touch of the divine.

The Speaker of the Sun was standing by the window, a short distance from the animated chart. He was looking down at the forest, as if lost in thought, but raised his eyes when Seltruin arrived. Roedric turned from the window and regarded his guest, before stepping away from the view. Clasping both hands behind his back, he gave a bow of his head but showed no sign of his thoughts.

"Sage Seltruin," Roedric said as greeting. "To what misfortune do I owe this pleasure?"

Returning the acknowledgement of respect, Seltruin bowed his silvered head ever so slightly. He could recall clearly the Speaker as a boy, a wild-haired scoundrel of a child that took what he pleased and acted on every whim his young mind could conjure. Though that child had undeniably grown older and more wise, stood before him now as Speaker of the Sun, Seltruin would forever think of Roedric as the boy who had stolen his herbs and leapt from the Great Tree in a misguided attempt to fly. If not for the numerous branches that slowed and stopped his inevitable fall, Roedric would have surely been killed. Seltruin suspected that was why the boy was allowed to live among them, considering all that the humans had done.

Of us all, he thought, *Roedric is most intimate with second chances. Perhaps he sees more than just a boy.*

"I wanted to speak in more detail about how matters concerning Barr are to be handled." Seltruin took the offered seat and settled into its cushions. Roedric took a seat across from him. "I believe I made it clear he will answer to no one but me."

"Yes, you have." Roedric's eyes held no contention on the point. "Go on."

"The boy will have no time for general studies," Seltruin said, letting the notion sink in. He wanted to be sure that Barr had time to adjust before being thrown to the wolves, as it were. For most elves, until now, the enemy in their stories had no face. Seltruin feared how Barr might be treated. "I think it would be unwise to have him joining activities with other children, while he is trying to cope with grief and adapt to these new surroundings."

"And is it wise that he should be trained as a Sage?"

Seltruin arched a brow. "Are you questioning your former mentor?"

"Merely curious," Roedric replied without betraying any other intent. "I do not doubt the boy has potential. I can see it as plainly as you. He is human, though."

"I did notice that, yes."

The Speaker paid no attention to the sarcasm. "With Vaelen slain, the future of the Illumin Valar is dubious. You will not live forever, my old friend." Roedric leaned forward in his chair, speaking so no others could hear. "What I am asking will be on the minds and tongues of many. Why should the fate of all Sylvannis be placed squarely on the shoulders of a human?"

Mention of Vaelen stung his heart. Barely a year had gone by since the young Sage had been slaughtered by the wolf. It mattered little how many times Seltruin had warned him not to go down to the falls alone, well out of range of Narohk patrols. No amount of berating or guilt would bring him back.

"Few, if any, show the aptitude or desire to be a Sage," Seltruin answered, as plainly as he could, "and I refuse to let our hopes die with my apprentice. I do not think it a coincidence that this child was placed in our care. He will weave, with or without our aid, and I have need of a successor." He let the Speaker consider his words before adding, "At worst, it will give us more time. It is unlikely Barr will live more than a century, but perhaps that will be long enough for the next generation of Sylvannis to produce a Sage, one that he will teach in turn.

"In the meantime," Seltruin added, getting to the point of his visit, "I think it would prove helpful if Barr had a companion from the Ballar. He will be spending much of his days alone, away from all but his father and myself. The added responsibility of raising a hound could occupy his free time and provide him with a much needed friendship."

"Agreed," Roedric said, getting to his feet. "He is welcome to one of Siltera's litter; she recently had six. There should still be sufficient time for one to bond with him." He looked as if a thought had struck him, then added, "Rutai and a few other Ballar brought back an interesting catch this past week. It was a hawk from the Ghaoylens, and I have yet to decide what to do with her.

With the proper supervision, she could grow to be an invaluable friend."

Seltruin considered for a moment. A Ghaoylens hawk was no trifling matter. At full size, one could easily carry a grown man in its claws. Of all the Ballar, only two that he knew of had a hawk as companion. Once bonded, the bird would answer to no one else.

"A most generous gift," Seltruin said. "I would have thought such a prize better suited to a Ballar. Why give it to the boy?"

Roedric replied, "As you say, we have need of a new Sage. Better that he should be a happy one."

* * *

Barr woke with a start and looked wearily about, thinking he had heard his father. The crackle of a fire and a gentle snore was all that greeted him. Sleep and dried tears had gummed his eyes, and he wiped them away with a sleeve. He pushed himself up on the rug and saw a pair of legs in the chair beside him. Still muddled from dreaming, he raised his eyes with a faint smile, unusually happy to have his father so close.

Memory came crashing down upon him, casting aside all trace of dream. With a sinking feeling, Barr realized it wasn't his father beside him and recalled with a painful clarity where he was.

Elves, Barr thought and looked about the room, wishing it was their cabin in the woods. *They said he was killed. That's why he brought me here.* Barr studied Tuvrin, watched the elf as he slept, all too aware just how different they were. *Why? Why bring me back with you? No one else seems to want me here.*

His eyes narrowed. *Unless... you killed him.* Barr quickly dismissed the thought. *No, it was the wolf. I could feel it. I didn't know what it was, but I knew it was there. I tried to warn you!* he cried in his mind, closing his eyes against the last memory of his father. *Why wouldn't you listen to me? Why? We could have left it there. Everything would have been fine.*

It's all my fault. Barr glared at the fire, his vision blurring as tears rimmed their edge. *If it wasn't for the dreams, you would have listened to me. You would have believed me.* He took a deep breath and let it out, let his anger fall away in a wave of remorse. *If I wasn't different, you would have listened.*

"He is gone," Galdein had told him the night before, "killed by a terrible wolf, a beast that has taken many. Tuvrin lost his wife and son. I have lost a brother. All of us have suffered." He had looked at Barr as an adult and not some weeping child. "You were brought here to live, because life must go on. We all must go on. There is a time for grief and time for living. You will know when one is done and the other has begun."

Barr watched the steady rise and fall of Tuvrin's chest, saw the weathered features of a woodsman like his father. If not for the tapered ears, the elf would have seemed very much like Daroth, a hardened man with a tender heart. If Tuvrin wanted to take care of him, Barr would let him. His only other choice was his uncle Therol and a city full of people that would throw him to the Guardians at first sign of the waking dreams. At least with the elves, he was safe.

The best way to honor your family, he remembered hearing, *is to live a long and happy life.*

Barr intended to do just that.

Abandoned as a small child, Barr was fortunate to have one such as Daroth take him in. He had no memory of his real parents but had learned early on that being with those who cared was all that truly mattered. He never questioned or rationalized what reason his natural parents might have had for leaving him. He only gave thanks for Daroth and loved him all the more.

Barr turned back to the fire, studied the wavering heat and fading glimmer of orange light reflecting off the veined wood of the hearth. Shadows flickered and played across the dancing flames, through a malleable scene of darkness within the glow. A spiraling myriad of lives grew upward and out, passed through the embers and into a gloomy recess, only to be replaced by a crackling spark...

...that once gleamed in her eyes. All that remained were the memories, pain that tightened his chest when he thought of home, joy that made the blood run warm when she smiled at him for the first time, again and again. Chareld felt as if he had buried part of himself...

...when the first clumps of dark earth fell over the open grave. How many had died in the fields that day? And for what? Their crops were gone, their homes burned and broken...

...beneath the weight of her grief. Other children cried out, wailing through the fires and clash of ringing steel. But not hers. Her baby no longer made a sound. Its arms hung limp at either side, swaying in time as she rocked back and forth, refusing to let go her hold...

...of his hand. Dorna looked up at her brother, tried pulling him away, but nothing would tear his eyes from their bodies. They had to get away, before someone found them, before the thunder of horses returned. With both hands, she took hold and frantically pulled, screaming...

...for help as he threw himself against the door. He could hear them inside, pleading for him to hurry, when the first terrible cry rang out. The smell of burning flesh reached his nose. Redoubling his effort, Ander crashed his

weight into the heavy wood and felt both bone and wood break apart...

Barr blinked away the startling visions and could once more see the hearth, where an overlapping image of his father took shape in the flames.

"Goodbye," Barr said quietly, ignoring the tears that fell from both cheeks. "I'll miss you."

The image faded in a swirling wisp of dark smoke. With a final sigh, Barr laid back down and went to sleep, his hands clinging to the soft folds of a heavy boot.

- 5 -

Tuvrin pulled aside the leather shutter and tied it off, letting in the morning sun as it rose over the emerald canopy of Geilon-Rai. As First of the Maurdon, he was afforded a home with a view that looked out over the interwoven branch and cover of leaves that marked other homes in the expansive tree city. A rolling sea of verdant growth, with snowy tops like froth, stretched off into the horizon. It looked as if the treetops themselves were a blanket above the forest floor, a leafy collection of hills and valleys, highlighted by billowy pockets of white. An occasional glimpse beneath the pseudo-grasslands gave sight to clear ribbons of icy blue water reflecting the light of morn. Birds flew in natural harmony over the whole, dipping and rising through the clefts, like a school of dolphin at play.

Barr was up as well, quietly eating a breakfast one of the Maurdon had delivered as a courtesy. Skilled hunters and gardeners, it was the Maurdon that provided for the Sylvannis. He was halfway through a bowl of steaming tubers and blueberries when Tuvrin took a seat beside him.

"I am sorry," he said slowly, searching for words. "At the time I took you, I believed I was saving your life."

Wiping his hand on a leg, Barr stopped eating but would not look up. "I don't want to talk about it."

"I think now that I was being selfish," Tuvrin went on, trying to explain the guilt in his heart. "When I lost my wife and son –" he swallowed hard, choking on the thought, despite the months that had passed – "it felt as if I had died with them. I could not bare the pain. I hunted the wolf without relent, hoping either to kill it or be lost as they were." He reached out to take hold of Barr's hand but thought it too soon and withdrew. "I was not able to save your father, but you I could keep from harm. I do not regret that. What bothers me and makes me feel a fool is that until now I never asked if you have other family, anyone you would rather be with... than me."

Barr looked up then, and it seemed there was fear in his eyes. "No," he said and shook his head nervously. "There is no one else."

"I will not lie to you, Barr. It will be difficult living here, and the council will not let you leave." Tuvrin saw the fear in Barr's eyes replaced with a silent resignation. "I would defy them for you. If for any reason you want to leave –"

"There's nowhere to go."

Seltruin cleared his throat before entering. "I hope I am not disturbing?"

"Not at all," Tuvrin replied and stood to greet the Sage. "We were just finishing our meal. Have you eaten?"

"I have." To Barr, he said, "Your lessons begin today. My study is down the corridor a bit. Go see if you can find which one it is."

A brief look to them both, Barr stood and left the room without a word.

"Is it wise to let him wander?" Tuvrin asked.

Seltruin frowned. "That is the second time someone has seen fit to question my judgment regarding this boy. Do you forget who I am?"

Though he tried not to, Tuvrin was forced to look away. He simply withered beneath the steely blue gaze, as if it stripped him bare and made him helpless against it.

"My apologies. I do not –"

"You care for him," Seltruin said more softly. "I can see that quite clearly. Honestly, Tuvrin, what do you think will happen to him if he gets lost? Barr *is* safe here in the city."

Tuvrin looked up sharply, thinking there was hidden meaning in those words. *In the city.* As if some accident might take Barr's life down on the forest floor. The protective nature of a father lent him the strength to return Seltruin's gaze, to see within those penetrating eyes and find no deceit looking back. No, it was the wolf Seltruin referred to, the one thing that threatened them all.

"He is my responsibility," Tuvrin said in way of an answer. "Barr is a strong boy, but he *is* just a boy. In a way, he reminds me of Dran." Tuvrin smiled in spite of the pain that memory brought. "I find it strange that I should care for him so quickly."

"Not so strange. You need each other." Seltruin put a hand to Tuvrin's shoulder in comfort. "There is only so much grieving one can take. Others may not see it, but I know that you do. Barr was not the one rescued that day."

Moisture rimmed Tuvrin's eyes, but he blinked away any semblance of tears. A nod was all he could manage. Seltruin added, "The Speaker has decided to bestow a gift upon Barr. I wanted to be the one to tell you."

"What sort of gift?" Tuvrin didn't want to appear ungrateful, but House Shintae had little need of gifts.

"A hound," Seltruin paused, as if gauging Tuvrin's reaction, "and a Ghaoylens hawk."

Eyes wide in disbelief, Tuvrin nearly stammered. "A hawk? By Celene's name, why? I – I can understand the benefit of a companion. I had a pet myself when I was a child." Tuvrin recalled fondly his time with Styrleof, a brown bear he had raised from a cub. A war hound was an *entirely* different matter. They grew larger than horses and could crush a man with one paw. As frightening as that may have been, the idea of bonding a child with a hawk was even more so. The slightest of emotional outbursts, and who knew what the bird might do. "But a hawk? A *Ghaoylens* hawk? Really..."

Holding up a hand, Seltruin looked as if he expected no less. "Roedric has assured me that a Ballar will be assigned to help Barr train them both. If it becomes too difficult, they will be weaned from each other."

"You cannot wean a companion once its bonded."

Tuvrin's voice was stern, perhaps more stern than he truly felt. He knew that a companion would be good for Barr, that it was an honor to be chosen for a hawk. Still, he didn't feel Barr was ready.

The old Sage gave a sigh. "It is within your right to refuse the gift, of course. I would ask only that you first consider Barr."

"He is *all* I am considering," Tuvrin said with a frown. "It is simply too dangerous."

"You may think that Barr will eventually be accepted into the Sylvannis, that others will view him as an equal, but I hold to no such delusion. He is ideally suited to be a Sage, both integral to society and apart from its people. Be aware that what lies ahead for this boy can be a dark and lonely future. He will have no equal among you." That steely gaze once more met his then softened to the understanding look of a parent. "I am not saying you will not be enough for the boy, only that he can and should have more. Give it some thought. The gift is a generous one, and I would not allow it if I thought the boy were in any harm. I care as much for his welfare as you."

"I will think on it," Tuvrin promised. "If I should accept this gift for my son, the Ballar who trains him will be of my choosing."

"Of course. That is all I ask."

Straightening his robe, the Sage turned to leave.

"Seltruin," Tuvrin said and stopped him. "Thank you. It helps me to know I am not alone."

Tuvrin had felt very much alone in his decision to raise Barr, regardless of the council's agreement. Hearing Seltruin speak of Barr's future, knowing that someone else cared enough to do so, set both his body and mind at ease. The relief was written plainly in his eyes.

Seltruin bowed his head and left.

* * *

Barr wandered the twisting corridor, noting the odd letters by each door of leaves. He assumed they were elvish, though the twisting scrawl was completely foreign to him. Knowing they would be of no use, he gave up on the markings and followed his nose instead. If there was

The Last Incarnation

a study nearby, it would most likely stink of vellum and ink. He recalled that smell of parchment on his uncle, and the thought only darkened his mood.

It's for his own good, Barr decided, rationalizing his decision to stay with the elves, rather than risk returning to Alixhir and live with the only relative he knew. *Sooner or later, I'd bring the Guardians on his head. Maybe if I manage to control the visions one day...*

He held onto that thought, the hope of at least appearing to be normal, when he could fit in without fear of drawing undue attention. It was a fleeting hope at best. Even if it were possible that he could one day keep the visions in check, Tuvrin's words hung over him like a cloud. *The council will not let you leave.* Barr gritted his teeth at the idea of being held against his will but reminded himself he could have left if he had wanted to. If he asked, Tuvrin would help.

He stopped and turned, caught the oddly mixed scent of many herbs and heavy dust. Stepping through, he found he was right. A small library greeted him, its walls lined with shelves of slanted tomes and stacks of scrolls. Two large rows jutted out from the right wall, numerous shelves filled to brimming with clay pots and glass phials, a vast collection of colorful liquids and powders. On the left-hand side of the room were tables with beakers and bowls, varying mortars and pestles, and a number of books held open with long silver page markers. A single desk and cushioned chair sat in the middle of the room, an island in a sea of musty lore.

Light shone in from two of the four windows spaced throughout the large chamber, no doubt responsible for the dust that filtered in and blanketed all. Barr thought to go close them, as he would if he were in his uncle Therol's scribery, but found the breeze from without to be pleasant. With the tree city itself giving off heat through its walls, the chill of winter was all but removed.

Barr walked over to one of the tables and dragged a wooden chair up to the center desk. He knew better than to sit in the cushioned seat. Glancing at the open books, unable to read a one, Barr fought and lost the urge to turn the pages, hoping to see some fanciful pictures.

When Seltruin finally arrived, he looked surprised, either at seeing Barr perusing his books or the fact he was there at all. Barr was gazing in wonder at the articulate drawings and diagrams done in colorful inks and coal, but he reluctantly put them aside.

"I did not expect to find you here," the old elf said. "I thought more to find you wandering the corridors with a bewildered expression. I am sure you noticed that *all* of the doorways are marked. They identify who resides within, as well as any appropriate titles of house and rank." He was quiet for a moment, perhaps waiting for a reply. "How did you know that this was my study?"

Barr shrugged. He didn't want to tell Seltruin that his study had an unmistakable odor. *Why tell me to look for it if you didn't expect me to find it?*

"I don't know. I just did."

"Does that happen often? Do you *just know* any other things?" Seltruin asked but only received a second shrug. "The knowledge of something without any real reason for having it is often a result of touching upon the higher self, most likely through dreams or meditation."

"I didn't dream about your study," Barr pointed out.

"Be that as it may," Seltruin said and moved on. "Do you see all the different books that are here?" He picked one up with an elaborately tooled leather binding, a spiraling gold and silver design. "Countless volumes of painstaking work, and all done in the hopes of capturing the essence of what we call magic."

"Magic?" Barr wanted nothing to do with it. "My father says –" he paused, and a frown darkened his brow – "said magic is dangerous, that the *furie* is a curse."

Seltruin nodded and took a seat. "He is right, magic can be very dangerous. So can a sword or a shovel, even a book as this one. All tools have the potential to cause harm. The outcome depends on how we employ them. The knowledge of magic that I possess, and hope to pass on to you, has an equal potential for good. I can teach you to use that knowledge so that no harm will come of it."

Barr shifted uneasily. "I don't want to be a turner."

"Hmm, yes, I suppose not." The Sage looked closely at Barr until their eyes met in an uncomfortable silence. After a few moments, he asked, "Do you know the origin of that word, where turners come from?"

"All I know is that turners are hunted. I would rather be alone than sought after by Guardians."

Seltruin gave a puzzled look. Opening the book in his hand, he turned to the beginning page and faced it toward Barr. Lifelike artwork consumed the aged paper, evoking a flood of memories Barr never knew in his own lifetime.

Hundreds were there, dressed in the finest clothes and glittering with a wealth of precious jewelry. They gathered in a circle upon a field of lush grass, while commoners stood farther out. Children danced to the wild tune of pipes and drum, their laughter sometimes heard above cheering parents. Colorful banners flew from long wooden poles all around the wide circle, and under each stood a small group dressed in robes of matching hue.

Seltruin said, "Not so long ago, magic among humans was a thing to be cherished. Tournaments were held at the beginning of each season or to mark grand occasions, and at these wondrous gatherings, weavers of magic would engage in a friendly competition to test their skills against one another."

Again the page turned, Seltruin's voice animating the scenes in lucid detail and emotion.

"Vivid illusions would fill the air above the crowd, brilliant colors that swarmed in tune to sudden music. Some would depict great battles long past, while others would shape mystical creatures that may have only existed in imagination. In pairs, the tourners would weave their spells above the crowd, and cries of 'yea' or 'nay' would decide who remained. This would go on until only one tourner stood the field, and the crowd would show their gratitude with tossed coins and a cheer."

When the page turned this time, the land grew dark and the people forlorn. There were no happy faces among them, and the only fine clothing lay on the backs of glaring tourners. The gathered people were covered in filth, tired and hungry beyond endurance. Children huddled by their mother's feet, with barely enough strength to stay awake. The faces of those who stood beneath the faded banners were twisted and cruel, their eyes glittering with a hatred and contempt for others.

Seltruin continued, "Tourners once shared their knowledge with one another, did what they could to help those in need, healed wounds or aided crops in growing. That time, however, had soon passed. The tournaments steadily grew into magical duels, most times resulting in death. This caused the tourners to become secretive, less willing to share their spells or expend the effort to help others. Their time, instead, was spent in preparation for each tournament, where the rewards became terribly greater."

The page flared with white light, and the scorched field darkened further, as ashen clouds spread their bulk across the skies. A heavy shadow settled over the crowd, a withered people now forced to show tribute to those with the *furie*. Two men in tattered robes squared off against each other, the air between them charged with their magic. Both of them had hair flying about in wild tendrils, as they eyed one another with disdain. Snarling, one threw his magic in a ball of swirling black. It pierced the other's defenses with a flash, brought the man down to his knees. The victor raised an arm in triumph and with the other clawed the air between them. The crowd looked away in unison, horror written plainly on their faces, as a blue nimbus began to envelop the fallen man.

"The victorious tourners would take the life force of those they vanquished," Seltruin said. "This gave great power to the survivors and reason enough to develop a deadlier magic. With each tournament, there were less weavers, though some did try to learn on their own or had a raw talent they hoped to improve. But a time soon came when the commoners would take no more."

He turned another page, and the smoke of burning villages engulfed the skies. Children cried out, as helpless parents watched them die. Men rose up to protect their families and were felled by the dozens, crushed by a rain of charred wood and burning stone. The ground rumbled and cracked, tearing away homes, as deafening winds rose up and smashed debris into those who tried to run. Through it all walked a single figure, a faceless tourner who had grown tired of waiting, who took the lives of common folk to quench her mounting thirst for power.

"In a rage of blind pride," Seltruin said, "the tourner thought herself invincible, and while taking the life force of a fallen mother, died at the hands of a child."

Barr saw in his mind the flash of a pitchfork, though the page before him remained still. His eyes were wide with disbelief, having never heard of such a story. The images he saw were as real as memory and could not be denied. The whole recounting left him feeling as if he had lived through it.

Seltruin closed the book. "The rest you should know. Tourners were hunted from all ends of Taellus, any trace of magic resulting in swift death at the hands of an angry mob. The name 'tourner' became twisted into turner, one who changes or transforms what was once good into evil, their touch darkening the world all around. Everything associated with magic became feared and hated. Some innocents were mistakenly killed by those who hunted turners, an order called the Guardians, but far more died who were truly touched with *furie*. Magic among your people has been driven to near extinction."

"My people," Barr echoed.

The tale was too fantastic, as if it had happened only in story and could not be a part of human history. Yet it was real enough to drive him away, fear of being caught by the Guardians forcing them into a life outside the city walls, a self-imposed exile from family and friends. Even now, living with the elves, Barr was a victim of that prejudice to magic.

The Guardians had no idea of Barr's existence, and he meant to do everything he could to keep it that way.

"There are other races who have magic," Seltruin explained, "elves among them. We are unwelcome in your land and have learned to stay away. Unfortunately, all of our magic has dwindled as well. Time has eroded our knowledge. What has not been recorded has died with those who kept it secret. Even the magic I possess is but a shadow of an erstwhile might, the last of an elven lore with few who are willing or able to learn."

Unsure what to think, Barr remained silent. His father had told him to repress the visions, to fight the *furie* within him. Magic was dangerous; his visions could be as well. Sometimes they gave birth to a magic that could hurt people or set fires with just a thought.

"It is that elven lore I would like to teach you," Seltruin said and leaned forward, "should you be willing to let me."

Things are different here, Barr thought. *Seltruin has magic, but no Guardians have taken him. Maybe it's safe here, hidden in the trees. I could tell him about the visions. What would he say? Would he still teach me?*

Barr asked, "How did the first weavers learn magic, if there was no one to teach them how it's done?"

A smile creased Seltruin's smooth features, and the old Sage nodded with what looked like relief.

"I can tell we are going to get along just fine," he said. "You have a sharp mind, my young friend, and your question is deserving of an answer. Unfortunately, there is only one person who can give it to you, and when you know who that is, you will be half way to finding the answer for yourself."

"Oh." Barr tried to sound enthusiastic but knew he fell short of the mark. He was thoughtful for a moment, absorbing all he had seen and heard, then wanted to see proof for himself. Not that he doubted Seltruin could weave, but Barr had never seen someone else conjure *furie.* "Can you make some magic? Or would that be too dangerous?"

"I do occasionally," Seltruin answered, "when the need arises. Geilon-Rai is far from many and guarded by powerful wards set long before my time. It is doubtful any beyond our boundary would hear what I weave." He reached into a small pocket within the confines of his robe, and drew out what looked to be dried crimson petals. "If you would like to see some, however..."

Seltruin waved his fingers in an intricate design while barely moving his hand. He spoke an almost musical incantation, no more than a few lilting words, and a brightness began to grow between he and Barr. From utter insubstantiality, motes of light in a myriad of color seemed to gather and swirl until they formed a distinct pattern.

The saurian head of a monstrous green wyrm loomed before Barr, its dagger-like teeth protruding from a dark maw that glistened with molten saliva. Its eyes were feral and glowed like lambent suns, threatening to burn the skin from his bones and char his hair into ash. Thick, black smoke escaped its flared nostrils, tendrils of coal that wisped up through the air, and a sense of horrible fear took shape in Barr's middle, as its head reared back to blow fire.

Barr screamed and shielded his face, blocking what he thought would be intense waves of heat. Rather than a stream of scalding flame washing over him, he was engulfed in a maelstrom of flowers. Wild roses, daisies, lilies, sunflowers and jasmine, the soft buds literally showered him in silken petals. He picked up one of the brighter purples and watched it blossom in his palm. Before his very eyes, it spread wide each petal, like the stretching of waking arms in early rise.

Then as quickly as each one had appeared, the illusions went away in a mist. No wyrm remained nor bed of soft flowers, but all were replaced with a sense of wonder and joy. Barr looked down at his hands, as if he could still see the soft petals and feel their silky touch on his skin. Somewhere during the fading excitement, Barr had opened his mouth and left it agape. He closed it finally and smiled, with a blush reddening his cheeks.

Seltruin returned the smile with a wink.

"Not bad for an old weaver, eh?"

The Last Incarnation

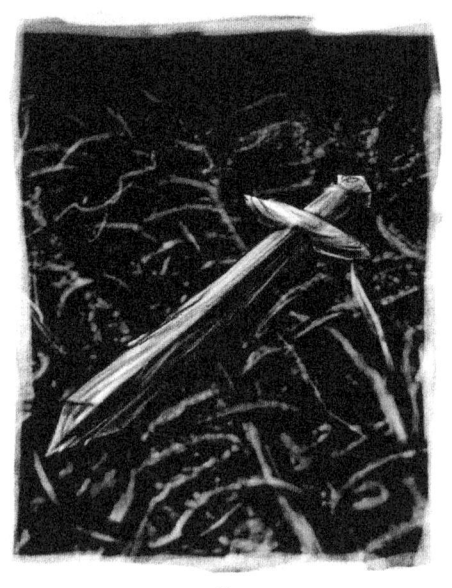

– 6 –

When Barr returned in late afternoon, he was tired from his first day of training. He had spent the initial few hours attempting to read along, as Seltruin relayed a brief history of the Sylvannis. In doing so, Barr was also introduced to the basics of elven language. There was only so much he could absorb in one sitting, however, so he spent the remainder of the day gaining an intimate knowledge of just how thick the dust could get in the study. Any notion of practicing magic had seemed to disperse with Seltruin's earlier illusion.

His whole body ached when he slumped down into a hard wooden chair by the table. Aside from the bearskin rug in front of the hearth, a tied up bedroll and one other chair, the small room looked bare. There were engraved pictures on the mantle, resting below a longbow pegged to the wall, but very few other adornments. It was a stark contrast to what Barr was used to seeing in someone's home. Even their rickety old cabin had bookshelves and a couple of oil paintings. The most elaborate thing Barr could see here was a pair of silver candleholders.

The sound of whistling came from nearby.

Looking over to one corner shrouded in darkness, Barr crinkled his brow and stepped closer. What he found was another door, its leaves rustling with the touch of a breeze. The whistling was coming from beyond, a lilting tune that sounded very much like birdsong. Barr pushed aside a strand of leaves for a peek and found Tuvrin tending a garden.

What struck him first, upon entering with a sense of dumbfounded awe, was how large the enclosed garden truly was. With the sleeping area behind hardly big enough to seat four, the adjoining garden stretched on for nearly twenty feet and was easily twice as wide. Barr could see no windows or other doors, but the entire ceiling was made up of open wooded slats, making clearly visible the sun and blue skies above. The ceiling was divided into different sections, each one able to be closed off – as two were now. Barr assumed the entire ceiling was angled to the east so that rain would simply run down the closed slats. He could see snow on top of the surrounding areas of the city, but none of it touched upon the garden. It was so warm that Barr imagined any snow falling over the slats would have melted fairly quick and fell over the side.

Barr slipped off his heavy tunic to avoid sweating and looked in wonder at the rows of bright vegetables, budding flowers and dark soil. Tuvrin was standing by a long table of potted plants, watering the fresh shoots of slender green, as he whistled and seemed absorbed in his task.

Clear water ran down a carved aqueduct on the eastern side of the room, traversing the half of a hollowed smooth branch and was carried off through the opposite wall. The western side of the garden had a similar branch pipe, leading out from a tiny room with a door, but that conduit was fully enclosed. It reminded Barr of an outhouse, and if it was, he could see why the pipe wasn't open.

"Back so soon?" Tuvrin asked and wiped both hands on his leggings. "I can have dinner prepared if you are hungry."

With a nod, Barr picked up his tunic and went back to sit down inside. Tuvrin put some meat on long pokers and hung them over the fire. While chopping vegetables on the table, he occasionally stopped to turn the metal prongs, then returned to making a salad of fresh lettuce, tomatoes, cucumber, radish and a few others Barr hadn't seen before.

"We should talk," Tuvrin said after a time in silence, still chopping with a short paring knife.

Barr didn't much like the sound of that, though the tone was pleasing enough. The last time he had heard similar words was the day before leaving Alixhir.

"What about?"

Tuvrin put aside the knife and finished placing the last of the diced vegetables in a bowl. He took a seat by the hearth and turned the pokers before speaking.

"We have a tradition," Tuvrin said. "When we lose someone close, we tie dark feathers in our braids. This signifies our desire for their spirits to be carried swiftly into the next life by a raven." He showed Barr his long braid of dark hair, interwoven with leaves and black pinions. "It is called the *feydra* of mourning. It would be little trouble to teach you."

I'm not one of you, Barr thought, looking on the braid and seeing nothing but dissimilarity between them. He could no more feel right about braiding his hair and sticking in feathers than he would about cutting his ears to tapered points. *Pretending won't make me belong.*

"No, thank you."

"I see. I just thought you might like to…" Tuvrin's words trailed off, as he glanced over at a picture on the mantle. "Tell me, do you know how to use a sword?"

Barr felt his cheeks burning. The fact he couldn't use a sword was a point of contention with his father. Daroth had often told him it was never too early to learn how to defend yourself, but Barr had no interest beyond the fun. To Daroth, a man who had spent most of his life as a mercenary, surviving by the edge of a blade, it was a serious matter and not to be taken lightly. For Barr it was just a game. His father may have finally realized that, which was why Daroth had given up trying and began to teach Barr how to trap instead.

Would he be alive, Barr wondered, *if I learned to use a sword and had no interest in trapping?* He quickly disregarded the notion, but there was still a guilt in his heart he could not easily shake.

"Not really," Barr replied. "I remember play fighting in the streets with a switch of hickory or a broomstick but nothing more than that. My father wanted to teach me, but learning to read came first. Besides," he said with a shrug, as if it mattered little, "a sword is far too expensive. What's the point of learning to use something I'd never own?"

"Nothing is without cost, Barr. Whether it is a sword, clothing, food –" Tuvrin held a hand to indicate the room all around them – "or life. Whatever we invest time and energy in, like my garden or your studies, comes at a grave cost."

"Why grave?" Barr asked.

Tuvrin appeared both sad and thoughtful. "Because nothing in this life is eternal. Each of us are given a certain amount of time, like a bag of precious gems. If you trade them wisely, you will feel no regret when your bag is empty."

Barr considered for a moment. He did understand the value of spending time wisely, but he couldn't see what that had to do with learning to use a sword.

Unless it's not about training at all, Barr thought. *Is Tuvrin just trying to spend time with me?* It seemed an odd thought, since they had only known each other a few days. *Is that why dad tried so hard?* It was possible. Each question seemed to lead him to another.

"How do you know when your bag is getting empty?"

"Ahh, yes, how do we?" Tuvrin took the meat off the fire, slid each piece down onto a plate and set the pokers off to the side. Finally, he replied, "If an answer exists, I do not know it. What I do know is that time is better spent living in happiness rather than in worry over where it has gone."

All at once, Barr thought he understood. *Enjoy the company of family and friends while you can. You never know when your bag will run out.*

With a knowing smile, Tuvrin filled a plate for Barr. "After we finish," he said, "I will teach you how to use a sword."

"Alright," Barr agreed. "I'll give it a try."

* * *

They entered the wide training room, where two younger elves were already practicing with staves. Barr noticed the two fought with bare feet and wore little more than leather breeches for protection. The way they lunged forward and back over the dark earthen floor, crying out like ferocious animals, before striking down as hard as they could, Barr thought it a wonder neither one became seriously injured. Much like other young elven males, the two were tall and lanky but had muscles that seemed carved of rigid flesh. Both afraid and admiring, Barr was glad he wasn't facing off against either one.

Taking two wooden practice swords from a rack on the far wall, Tuvrin handed one to Barr and began the lesson by showing him how to stretch his muscles. While he explained the dangers of fighting cold, the other elves wordlessly agreed to end their sparring. The looks they gave Barr as they left sent a chill down his back. He felt hatred in their stares, anger unlike anything he had ever experienced in Alixhir. Even when the visions had began, when his friends first took notice of the change, never did they look at him like that. Frightened and annoyed, he barely heard a word Tuvrin had said.

"We will begin slow," Tuvrin told him, unaware of what had transpired. He showed Barr the proper way to hold a sword and three basic blocks. "Do not worry so much about hitting me as defending yourself. Use what I have showed you, and keep your eyes on my sword."

He squared off against Barr, with a short wooden sword held in one hand. Tuvrin moved forward a step and brought the practice blade down, an overhead swing that smacked softly against Barr's. Once more to either side and another overhead, Tuvrin led Barr through a deliberate and consistent series of strikes that would teach him to block without thought.

"Your body has a memory," Tuvrin said, "much like the mind. If you train your muscles to do a simple task, over and over, they will react without the need of thought."

Minutes passed before Tuvrin began to alternate his attack, swinging twice to one side before switching to the other or feigning to the left while striking to the right. Each time Tuvrin swung, Barr raised his sword in both hands, blocking away the attempt with a resounding *crack*. The sound became a constant, a hypnotic drone, a thrum at the back of his thoughts. Its rhythm lulled and soothed with a growing murmur, a whisper raising its voice in the stifling dark.
    Before long, each block brought with it a flash, an empty spark in the far reaches of Barr's mind. It started small, like a dream, a distant glow on the horizon, but was soon forcing its way toward him. More and more, it grew out of control, until the glow was a blinding white that consumed all in its path, devouring his waking thoughts with a lightning voracity. The world vanished of all sight and sound, leaving naught but a void of muffled dark and groping fear. An instant of nothing, it waded through time, lengthening its stay, growing strong and alive.
    Each strike grew louder and brought with it a glimpse of an *other* place, a flickering scene that took shape all around, grew crisp in detail and then faded away. The incessant snap of wood on wood continued to increase, a melodic tune that sparked memory without thought. It lent vivid reality to the flashes of light, stretching time and place from vision to vision...
    Ludghar gave the order to charge, and thousands of men cried out in response, bellowing a call to Tempas. The clash of steel was a deafening roar, drowning out the dying screams of both man and horse. Waving his two-handed sword with one arm, Ludghar stalked through the field, killing indiscriminately, shattering steel and bone with each swing. Warriors, soldiers by birth or by deed, fell at his side with honor, a fitting end and all he could

hope for – when it was his time to go. For now, nothing could touch him. He was blessed by the gods, a living means to their ends, and justice...

...was all that mattered. Houra, a Shadow Guard with an eye as keen as her blade, faced off against the six brigands. Petty thieves, all of them, they had stolen from the impoverished people of this village, killed without mercy, and cruelly acted without fear of consequence. Until now. She had been sent to put a stop to it all, one sword against many, and not for the first time. With her blade in one hand and death in the other, she brought with her the means...

...to smite down the enemies of Tal, drive them to their knees, so they might grovel in obeisance before the war priest and his kin. The God of Steel and Vengeance demanded no less, wanted nothing more than the utter annihilation of his foes. Thaeryn Battlebrow led the field, brought his army to bear, to shed light on the unbelieving fools who would soon beg...

...to be freed. That decision could not be made by one knight. A holy warrior, devoted to peace, honor and the Noble Code, Derek sought only to bring them to justice. It would be left to the High King whether or not these men were murderers. Only he could pass judgment on their deeds. With the skill of a soldier and heart of a knight, he had spared their lives – for now. Riding back to the castle, with his prisoners in tow, Derek could only...

...rule his people to the best of his ability. The warring tribes of khorish were a passionate, strong-willed people. Broad trees of amber hue gave them temporary shelter and warmth, but the nomadic hunters would soon be driven out. Ariel Fareye sought to unite the tribes, give them hope and a promise of freedom. No more would they be victims of the outside world, slaves to a distant king. His people would know peace, though it cost them their lives. How *different things would have been if Farehn had lived, if that arrow...*

...hadn't caught Lauren in the chest and sent her reeling back against the pillar for support. Another struck her thigh with enough force to waver her stance, and yet one more entered her side. She was wracked with pain from a dozen wounds, but others were depending on her for their survival. With fierce determination, the Shielder stood strong, her sword in one hand and battered heater in the other. She stood ready to face them, the onslaught of orcs, and though they might crush her body beneath the weight of their arms, nothing would quell her spirit...

Barr swung out with blinding speed, knocking aside Tuvrin's guard, and sent the elf's wooden sword careening through the air and skittering across the floor. Barr's pommel caught Tuvrin on the backswing, forcing the air from his lungs in a terrible *whoosh!* Continuing the fluid motion, Barr dropped low and swept a leg out, hooked Tuvrin behind the heel and sent him sprawling to the floor.

As if clearing a haze that clouded his eyes, Tuvrin looked up and blinked furiously. Barr loomed over him, sword held ready to strike...

And the look in his eyes was terrifying.

* * *

"Barr!" Tuvrin yelled.

As if waking from a dream, Barr let out a breath he had been holding, and the tension fled from his arms. His furrowed brow then relaxed, and the edges of his mouth softened. Barr lowered his sword, and wondered why Tuvrin was laying on the floor with such a look of shock on his face.

"Chaendra's light," Tuvrin said with what might have been awe but sounded to Barr like recrimination.

Oh no. Barr dropped his sword and backed away. *It's happening again.* He looked around sharply but saw no signs of a fire. *No, no, not again.*

The walls were closing in with a palpable weight, crowded with the echo of memories – frightened, pained cries and shouts of bitter outrage. Barr's own fear rose up in his chest and made it difficult to breathe. The threat of being burned alive pounded in his ears, blotting out all but the rapid thumping of his heart. Eyes wide, he turned to run, but Tuvrin grabbed hold and pulled him down.

Barr fought against him, pounding the elf's chest in a frenzied effort to get away. Only when he realized that Tuvrin wasn't fighting back, was in fact holding him close, rocking and soothing, did Barr relent and cease in his struggle. He cried then, burying his face in the soft leather jerkin. The echo of raucous voices slipped off into the distance, carrying with them all the pent up grief and anguish in a flood of bitter tears. Barr could feel it all drain away, the burning at the pit of his stomach that came with the visions, the pain in his chest and fear in his heart.

"All will be well," Tuvrin promised, as he rocked slowly back and forth. "You need never run from me, Barr. You have nothing to fear from me."

Clutching the leather beneath his hands, Barr held on as if the world might tear him away. He looked up at Tuvrin, into his eyes, and saw more than the bright emerald and flecks of darker jade. He saw understanding behind the gaze, the acceptance of one who damns the world for family and friend. It was the look his father had when they moved away.

Barr laid his head back against Tuvrin's chest, his hold still strong, his eyes decidedly dryer.
No more running, he told himself. *No more.*

- 7 -

Even though Barr heard Tuvrin up and about, could smell the fresh bread that had been brought to their door, and saw the first rays of morning creeping up over the window, he closed his eyes tight against it all. The past few days had left him feeling drained, as if coming to grips with the loss of his father made him physically tired. Tuvrin may have only needed a few hours sleep, since he was always up before the sun, but Barr wanted nothing more than to drift back into dream.

"Tuvrin!" It was Galdein, his hair unbraided and voice pitched with urgency. "It has been seen again!"

Barr sat up with a start and turned toward the door. Though the Maurdon spoke in elvish, Barr was able to understand the few words, and their meaning was all too clear.

It's the wolf, Barr thought with a mix of fear and excitement. *They found it!*

Tuvrin dropped his food and headed for the door. He snatched up his bow from above the hearth and slipped his quiver over a shoulder. With a look to Barr, he turned and was out the door, racing down the corridor, with Galdein in his wake.

Barr was unsure what to make of that look, whether it was fear or concern or angry resolve that hardened Tuvrin's features. He must have seen that Barr wanted to go along. Barr wasn't sure why, but there was a part of him that needed to see the wolf, to prove to himself it was real. He had felt a malevolent presence in the forest that day, one that wasn't Tuvrin, but still...

How do I know dad's really dead? That was the single question lurking in the back of Barr's mind, raising suspicion at every turn. *I need to see that wolf.*

He threw aside his blanket and reached over for his boots. Checking them first for tree spiders, he slipped each one on and got to his feet. There was no need to get dressed, since he had slept in his clothes. It crossed his mind then to ask Tuvrin for some shirts and pants. Back in the cabin, Barr had at least three changes of clothes. Without a river nearby, it wouldn't be long before the smell became unbearable, and Barr doubted anyone would want him using the aqueduct as a laundry basin.

Barr was settled down at the table, eating a plate full of eggs and buttered tubers, when a voice called from the door.

"May I come in?"

The elf had sandy hair, thin eyebrows and a ready smile. He wore thicker leathers than others Barr had seen, and his shoulders were strewn with jangling bones that glistened white against the fire. From his tone, the elf seemed respectful. Either he hid his contempt well, or he didn't mind being near a human.

An odor struck Barr, as the elf came inside, a heavy scent of wet dog that threatened to crush his lungs or mar his face with involuntary crinkling.

A Ballar Niminwa, by the smell of him, Barr said to himself and was startled by the unbidden thought. *How would I know that –*

"I bring a gift from the Speaker of the Sun," the elf went on. He carried in a large wicker basket from just outside the door. "I had hoped to speak with –" a slight pause – "your father, but that must wait until he returns from hunting."

"It's the wolf, isn't it?" Barr asked, his earlier thought all but gone from his mind. A scratching noise came from inside the basket, soon followed by a pleading whimper. "What's in there?"

Lifting a coarse blanket from the basket, the elf showed Barr a raven-haired puppy the size of a full grown dog and a featherless bird equally as large. Both had yet to open their eyes, though Barr could see the dull blue beneath the hawk's fleshy lids. The hound went on scratching its paws against the edge of the basket, cocking its ears at the sound of voices, while the hawk bobbled its head on a neck too weak for support.

The elf put down the basket, which looked much heavier now that Barr could see inside, and rubbed behind the puppy's ear.

"This is Aren," he said, "and the other is Idelle. They are to be your companions." The hawk let out a frail screech, its mouth open for food. "Few among the Ballar have a Ghaoylens hawk as friend, let alone any from the other parties."

They're beautiful, Barr thought and reached out to pet the dog. Only vaguely did he hear what the elf had been saying. He was instantly captivated by the animals.

"I am here at the request of your father," the elf said, "and I will be teaching you to care for your new friends. These are not pets. They are companions and should be treated as such. In time, you will come to rely on them, in daily life and on the field, as much as they will depend on you."

"Thank you," Barr said after a moment. He looked up and asked, "What do I call you?"

"I am Jareid, Ballar Niminwa, of House Chopka." He stood and gave a stiff nod of salute. "I offer my arm, Barr, Illumin Valar, of House Shintae."

Getting to his feet, Barr wasn't sure if he should take hold of the proffered hand or grip it at the wrist. Jareid must have seen Barr's confusion and showed him to grip firmly at the forearm. The two shook for a moment in what felt like mutual respect, then turned their attention back to the basket.

Barr could tell the animals were both hungry and thirsty, as if he could feel it himself in his middle. It was faint at first, but the sensation began to grow the longer he watched them.

While Jareid gave instructions on what and how to feed them, Barr absently rubbed his forearm and was amazed at the belied strength of a people he thought looked like wiry trees. Like a determined root striking through unforgivable soil, or a length of supple eleru that bows but never breaks, elves were the forest incarnate. Their skin had the resilience of toughened bark, fighting off the cold with little or no clothing, the color of sunless groves or copper greaves after battle...

...*with blood standing out against the backdrop of blackened grasslands. They stepped from the trees as* shadows dislodged, orange-skinned and burning fury. Those frail bodies feigned weakness, their starving madness all iron sinew and grasping hands. With arrows drawn, bows and arms held taut, they slithered forward with the crunch of death beneath their feet. Through thin lips and jagged teeth, they called, 'Barr? Barr?'

"Barr?" Jareid shook him. "Out on mindwalk?"

"Sorry," Barr said and rubbed his eyes. The vision was gone from sight, yet something lingered at the edge of his thoughts. "You were saying something about milk."

Jareid said, "Speak with the steward at the pens. He will provide you with milk and meat in correct portions. It is very important that no one but you feed your companions, at least not until they have bonded." He hefted the large basket in one hand. "They will be twice this size in a week. You have only a few days with them here, before they must make their home in the pens."

"How will I know when they've bonded?" Barr asked.

"You will know," Jareid replied, "and when they do, it will seem to you as if it had always been so. I can no longer recall what my life was like before Rhake and I were joined." His smile seemed wistful. "I am sure it will be the same for you. We will begin training in a few weeks. Their eyes should open soon. For now," he said and walked to the door, "let them become used to you. Spend as much time with them as possible. Learn their scents, and let them learn yours."

I have a scent? Barr thought. "Wait. What about Tuvrin? He's gone after the wolf, right?"

"The Maurdon are hunting a wolf, yes."

"The one that killed my father?" Barr sounded almost hopeful, wanting Tuvrin to bring it back. He had to see that wolf, be it dead or alive. "Why didn't he tell me? I want to see it."

"This wolf has been troubling us for quite some time," Jareid said, halfway out the door. "You are not the only one who would like a chance to see it. He moved quickly, so as not to lose the trail. Mind your new friends, now. You can do more for them than you can for Tuvrin."

A frown darkened Barr's features, as Jareid left the room. He dropped down beside the basket, pulled Aren into his lap and began to brood. The pinkish hawk let out a watery cry, as if snubbed by the lack of attention.

"Sorry," Barr said and rubbed behind her neck. "I only have room in my lap for one of you. I can't imagine how big you two are going to be."

He picked up the hound and let it lick his ear, then laughed from the tickling bath. To Idelle, he cooed with a trill he never knew he possessed, and all three stayed together until Seltruin arrived.

The time for his next lesson had come.

* * *

Barr stacked the heavy earthenware pots as best he could, arranging some by size and others by the elven markings carved into their front. Holding different herbs and powders in both hands, their scents permeating the hardened clay, Barr could only guess that the containers were somehow important to Seltruin's work and needed to be kept in a passable order.

"The best way to learn each of these herbs," the Sage told him, "is to be responsible for them. It will be your duty each day to clean the pots and keep them properly arranged. To do that, you must know the name and use for each."

That was all Barr did for the remainder of the morning, study the elven script carved into each clay surface. He was grateful that none of the pots were bigger than his fist, though some required two hands to lift, and for the open windows that allowed fresh air to sweep through the dusty chamber. Running a finger along one of the heavy shelves, Barr considered once more closing off all the windows.

I'd rather have fresh air, he thought and rinsed his cleaning rag in a pail of brackish water. *The dust isn't why I'm here anyway. This is just something to do in the meantime.*

He was sure Seltruin intended for him to do more than dusting, and this was all some sort of test. His uncle had done the very same thing, except Therol's scribery had far more to clean.

"Careful with those," Seltruin said from his desk, reading from a leather-bound tome. His eyes scanned the page with intent, and not once did he look up at Barr. "Those marked with a nyae are quite poisonous."

Eyes wide, Barr put the pots down and backed away. He looked from Seltruin to the shelf then tried calmly to wash his hands in the filthy water.

Still the Sage read, his pointed nose leading the way across the page.

"You are in no danger of being poisoned," Seltruin said. "Perhaps tonight you might like to take the Bahram scroll with you, to acquaint yourself with the... stronger herbs."

"I can't read elven yet," Barr said. He picked up the tawny roll of vellum and opened it. "Do you have one written in common? I'm actually familiar with a few –"

"That one will do."

Seltruin waved his hand, as if swatting an insect away, and the scroll's waxen surface came alive in Barr's hands. The ink melted and squirmed like snakes on hot coals. Some broke away from their brethren to join with another, while others turned in upon themselves to form recognizable lettering.

It's Old Alixhiran! "How did you do that?"

A turn of the page. "I take it you can read that language?" Seltruin asked, his eyes still on the book in front of him. "Very good, Barr. Back to work then."

"Alright," Barr more sighed than said.

Patience is overrated, he thought and wondered if it was something he had heard or seen before. There was a sense of heat to the notion, the heat of a burning desert, where sunlight beat down on the parched earth and cracked its dry surface with an unrelenting fervor. It was a heat that bred odd trees, leafless and spiny, tall but shadeless...

Wind tore across the land without hindrance, picking up enough dust to wear away rocks and homes and people...

Suddenly, Barr felt eyes upon him and turned. Seltruin was looking at him, his gaze narrowed but unseeing. It was as if the Sage looked beyond and through Barr, into a different spectrum of light, eyes both focused and not.

"What is that you are thinking?" Seltruin asked. "Are you paying attention to your hands?"

One of the pots had spilled over, leaving a pile of reddish dust on the shelf that swirled in a faint eddy, as a breeze touched against Barr's cheek. He apologized and swept the seolin back into its tiny jar.

"Come sit down," Seltruin said and put his book aside. "Tell me what you were thinking. I could see it was something of import, so do not tell me otherwise."

"How can you see what I'm thinking?" Barr put the jar back in place and took a seat across from the Sage. He looked warily at the old elf, wondering if Seltruin could read his thoughts. "It wasn't important, either. It was just a daydream."

"Daydream?" Seltruin asked, puzzled.

What did Jareid call it? Barr thought and replied, "Mindwalk. Like a waking dream." Seltruin pressed him to continue, either forgetting or ignoring Barr's earlier question. *Why doesn't anyone ever answer me?* "I saw a desert with big dunes and red sand that sometimes made whirlwinds that stretched up –"

"You saw?" Seltruin leaned closer. "You mean you were thinking about this desert, not seeing it. Have you ever seen a desert before? Or even a drawing of one?"

"No. But I think I've read about them."

"Did you see it just now or did you imagine it?"

Barr shifted in his seat. "What's the difference? Don't you see things when you imagine?"

"Perhaps I am being too literal."

It was clear to Barr that Seltruin wanted to say more, maybe tell what it was that *he* saw or even how such a thing were possible. But he didn't. Seltruin was studying Barr the way his uncle Therol did, weighing something behind the blue mask of his eyes. It could have been yet another test, or a judgment of response, but Barr had no idea what to say or do.

Should I tell him about the visions? he wondered, ashamed that they plagued him. *What would he do if he knew? Would he still want to teach me?*

As it often happened when his visions were a problem, Barr pushed them down with the force of his will. He stifled them, locked them away behind a wall in his mind.

"I didn't see anything," Barr said firmly. Seltruin raised a brow in reply, whether out of surprise or sheer amusement, Barr couldn't say. "I should get back to work."

Without another word, he returned to the shelves.

* * *

"We were not able to catch it," Tuvrin said, as he took off his boots and placed them by the hearth to dry. "It is an uncommon creature, very fast, very strong."

Barr sat on the floor with Aren in his lap. "But it's the one that killed my father?"

Tuvrin was quiet as he checked his bow for flaws, running a thumb over its polished surface. He took a rolled up bowstring from a fold in his leather vest. After studying the twined linen by firelight, he rolled it back up and attached the small ring to a clasp on the bow's grip. The bow was then hung lengthwise over the hearth, held fast by four leather-wrapped pegs.

"It has killed many," Tuvrin answered and sat down across from Barr. "The Maurdon will hunt the wolf until it troubles us no more. Too many elves have fallen to its jaws."

"Humans, too."

Barr wanted to frown, to let anger overtake him, but the warmth of Aren's body in his lap was soothing, lulled him into a sense of happiness he felt guilty for allowing.

"Humans as well," Tuvrin agreed. "Tell me, are you upset because the wolf escaped or because you were not invited to hunt?"

Until that moment, Barr wasn't aware how upset he truly was or that others might have taken notice. Was it because the wolf still lived, and his chance to see it was gone? Was it because he wanted to hunt the wolf himself? He wasn't sure, but it made him feel better to have someone acknowledge it.

Tuvrin had nothing but genuine interest behind the smears of wild face paint, a solemnity that looked on

Barr as an equal. It sent a tingle of nervous pride through his stomach to know that an adult, any adult, could see how he felt without thinking of him as just a child.

"I don't know how to hunt," Barr began, his desire to learn written plainly in his manner. "I wouldn't want to get in the way."

"Neither did you know how to use a sword before besting me," Tuvrin said, a hand going to his middle, "and leaving me bruised, I might add."

Barr knew it was meant to make him laugh, but instead it brought an uneasy flush to his cheeks. He put Aren back in the wicker basket, covering him without disturbing Idelle.

"That was different," Barr said.

"Perhaps," Tuvrin said, "but it would have made you feel better if you were asked. It is not that you cannot hunt which is upsetting but the fact you were not included or told what was happening."

"I guess so. I just want to... to help. I feel *helpless*, like I'm too small to do anything but get in the way. I mean, no one really wants me here. They all look at me like I did something wrong, but I didn't do anything!" Tuvrin was quiet, allowed Barr to speak his mind. "What am I supposed to do? What do they want from me? It's hard enough to control my dreams or visions or whatever they are, and now I have everyone hating me! It's not my fault!"

"Not everyone dislikes you, Barr." Tuvrin put a hand to Barr's cheek, his touch cool against the burning of frustration. "I will show you, at early rise. You will join the Maurdon on our hunt, and you will see that many are pleased to have you – including myself."

Now Barr felt silly, but the icy glares of those two from the training room wouldn't leave him. He could feel their hatred, and it made him want to hurt them back, make them feel his pain twice over. He tried to let that anger go and focus instead on the wolf.

"I can help hunt it?" Barr asked, not really expecting to hear yes. It would be enough that he was allowed to go along and finally see the creature that had taken his father.

Tuvrin answered without hesitation. "You may. It is possible that you possess some hidden knowledge of hunting as well. Can you still fight with a sword, or was that an unconscious effort?"

"I haven't tried again. Jareid came by with Aren and Idelle, and then I had another lesson with Seltruin." Barr rubbed his eyes, repressing a yawn. "I'm a little afraid to try again."

"Have you spoken with Seltruin about this yet?"

"No," Barr said quickly. "I don't want to. Not yet. I don't want anyone to know. Maybe it'll go away, and then I won't have to worry about it."

"He can help you. The Sage is wise beyond any one person I have ever known." Tuvrin stood and moved the basket closer to the fire's half-circle of warmth. "Barr, you can trust him. Speak with him."

"I will," Barr said and yawned. *I just need more time.*

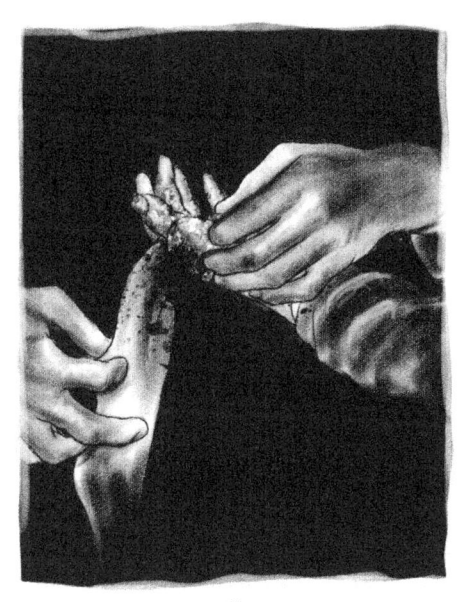

- 8 -

Time passed quickly for Barr in Geilon-Rai. He kept fairly busy under Seltruin's tutelage, mastering elven and its various dialects, the flora and fauna of each surrounding land and countless other bits of information he could only imagine were meant to help him become a Sage. Two years had gone by since the telling of deadly tournaments, yet still Seltruin had not broached the subject of *furie* or the weaving of magic.

"When will I learn magic?" Barr would ask from time to time, when the task of endless sorting and cleaning became too much to bear.

"Have you finished your work?" was all Seltruin would give as response.

The work was never finished.

After Barr had grown accustomed to organizing the earthenware jars of spices, herbs and oils, he was made to arrange the scrolls and books in an even filthier archive, in the room adjacent to the study. This small library was a nightmare, with its blanket of dust and moldy parchment. A single flickering globe, which Barr found was occupied with glowbugs, provided light for the entire room. To preserve the quality of each scroll, the library was kept tightly closed and without windows. The air smelled old and was stale in the lungs. What was worse, no matter how hard Barr worked to keep dust from the shelves, a heavy layer reappeared each night. He suspected Seltruin had something to do with that.

Before long, Barr could find any scroll by touch or by glancing at the symbols he had carved into each shelf. He spoke fluent elvish, including the dialects, and found writing to be almost second nature. His understanding of the language gave him an appreciation for the Sylvannis, for the intricacy of thought they placed in each chosen word. So much of their heartfelt meaning was lost in the translation, where the spiritual tense came across as a stiff and formal voice. He found the elves were actually a very passionate people, and more and more he grew proud to be among them.

The pots and books seemed steadily less in need of maintenance, both the library and study impossibly free of dust. This allowed Barr time to focus on a number of other things.

Most of what he had learned concerning flora was but an extension of the herb lore he already possessed. His study of wildlife, particularly of that in Darleman, was cause for enough excitement that Barr nearly forgot his impatience with learning magic. The mating habits and mannerisms of each creature not only helped him gain a keen understanding of how all life interacted and depended on one another, but it brought him closer to Aren and Idelle.

They spent hours together in the forest each day, where Barr observed all around them with admiration. He had a deep respect for the forest, of the creatures that made it their home and what simple beauty could be found at each turn. There was so much to see – from caves to streams, countless different trees, a waterfall or the ruins – that there hardly seemed time enough in the day.

Aren had grown tremendous, even larger than the next biggest hound by four hands. Neither Jareid nor any other Ballar could account for his unusual size. Aren stood taller than any elf and broader than three side by side. His coat was thick, soft hair of midnight hue, and was rippling with muscles beneath. He had the wide brow and short ears of any other hound, the stout tail and great paws, bulky chest and narrow middle; but what made Aren stand out, more so than his size, was the striking pale blue of his eyes.

Though Aren was large enough to ride, Barr had a difficult time climbing up and preferred to run on his own two feet. Both playful and oddly jealous, Aren never left Barr's side when they were out on the hunt, tracking for the mere challenge it offered, and the only other he would allow close was Idelle.

The hawk was a sliver of night, a winged shadow of feathers so black as to seem blue. A trim of white touched her ends, like a trailing of frost, and she looked down on the world with dark eyes. Idelle had a piercing cry that could set the forest alight and echo through the trees with an intensity that prickled the skin.

She too was a giant, standing taller than Aren, and had a wingspan the length of two wagons. Though not nearly as playful as her brother, the hound, Idelle was lighthearted and known to play tricks. Whether lifting Aren through the air in a mischievous prank, or landing to wrap Barr in her embrace, Idelle was a loving creature that put her family above all and was fiercely protective of her brothers.

In the two years since living with the Sylvannis, Barr hadn't once caught sight of the wolf. In the early months, all had been quiet, and some thought the wolf might have gone away. However, the deaths returned soon after and continued for a time. The Narohk suffered most for their inability to protect Geilon-Rai, though their pains were in standing only. Not a single archer among them was killed. The Maurdon did their best to track the lethal beast, on those rare occasions any prints could be found, but were largely unsuccessful in their attempts.

Thinking to use himself as bait, Barr had ventured into the forest alone – well, as alone as anyone could be, with a seven foot tall hound and a hawk like a small dragon. The empathic link all three shared allowed them to communicate simple thoughts. Having asked them to give him some distance, Barr did his best to look like easy prey and lure the wolf into attacking. Either the wolf was too smart to be fooled, Barr had finally decided before giving up, or he gave it far too much credit.

The attacks continued at an erratic pace, two or three in a month, then nothing at all for another six. All told, since Barr made his home in Geilon-Rai, the wolf had taken twenty-two lives. Though he always kept an eye out for the creature, Barr had decided more than a year ago not to devote all his time to the search.

Since then, he, Aren and Idelle had joined the Maurdon each morning and lent their skills to the hunt, helping to provide meat for the city. Whether it was with Tuvrin or Galdein or one of the other elven hunters, Barr and his companions were always welcomed to come along. Though still a young pup in the eyes of the Ballar, Aren was considered a boon to the Maurdon and valued for his keen sense of smell. Idelle was remarkable when it came to sighting prey, flitting through the trees as if daring the gnarled branches to stop her.

What made Barr such a valued hunter was not his mastery with a sword, which he found came with ease since that fateful day Tuvrin had decided to teach him, but his expert marksmanship with a longbow. Even the Narohk gave him grudging respect and thought he was born to the bow – no small compliment from the bowmen who hated him. Ceiran's party were the adept archers; that a human possessed skill surpassing any of their own was a sore point of wild contention.

Though there were four other parties, not including the Valar, Barr felt most at ease with the Maurdon. It was only the Narohk that showed an open dislike for him, while others seemed quietly tolerant. It never really dawned on Barr what his becoming a Sage had meant, both for him and the Sylvannis, until Seltruin explained the role of each person in Geilon-Rai.

The Narohk were the city's guardians from without, archers who could fell a man long before the arrow would be heard. If any hostile force managed to get past those deadly marksmen, they had the Ballar to contend with. In times past, when battle was common, it was the elven beastmasters that led the field, fighting with enormous war hounds and bears at their side, while screeching hawks took to the skies in aerial defense. Protecting the tree city from within were the Gharak, warriors adept at both sword and spear. Though they began as no more than royal guards, showpieces mostly, their role soon changed as conflict between the races arose. It was before such times, when peace ruled the lands, that the Eneir were called upon to act as representatives of the

Sylvannis. All born of nobility, the ambassadors of old had become no more than ceremonial figures.

Which left but one other: the Illumin Valar. Keepers of all elven knowledge, healers of both mind and body, spiritual guides and wielders of magic, the Sages who bore this cumbersome mantle lay at the very core of elven society. It was the Valar who were responsible for the welfare of all, including the tree city itself. While the other parties were versed enough in magic to enchant their own weapons and armor, their spells were but child's play in comparison. The Sages of the Valar used the power of life, from within themselves and the forest around, to fuel the wards protecting Geilon-Rai. They kept the Great Tree immersed in the ley lines below and hid the city from those who would do it harm. It was this, and more, that Barr had found himself a part of, and the stress of responsibility weighed heavily upon him.

As if in answer to the tension, the visions that plagued his mind intensified to the point of unbearable pain. There were times when he would fall into a lapse, his world blending from scene to scene, life to life, until he was awakened by the nervous shake of a hand. It was Tuvrin that had finally told Seltruin of the problem.

While the Sage was unable to say with any certainty what could cause such a thing, he had suspicions that led him to create an herbal mix. Intended to relax Barr's mind, until he could grow strong enough to control the visions on his own, the tincture was taken every morning with a warm glass of berry juice. It was only when Barr's emotions got out of hand that the visions overcame him.

"Each night," Seltruin had told him, "before you sleep, let the visions come, but keep firm control of how long they remain. Have Tuvrin by your side when you do, just to be safe. It will help you grow stronger, enable you to control them and possibly give insight as to why they

The Last Incarnation

occur. For all we know, they may only be waking dreams."

Seltruin might have been right, but Barr was certain of one thing; these were no ordinary dreams. Knowledge flowed through them, these visions of people and places both here and gone. They were the past brought to life, but only in his eyes. It was an odd sensation when he returned, after allowing the visions to come without struggle. If not for Tuvrin by his side, Barr would have thought his life just another vision, one easily replaced when some other fancy took hold.

The slightest phrase or insignificant object could send him off reeling through time and place. A scent of perfume, the feel of a rug, anything that brushed his senses could spark a new vision. Some would occur more than once, be it of a place or a person, but never exactly the same – like a story retold from memory. Not a day passed that Barr didn't picture his father, see him fixed in his mind with a recurring joy. That was memory, a picture or scene that played out with no change, forever imprinted by time and occurrence. The visions weren't so fixed, were more fluid in passing and crisp in detail than the blurry remembrance of what was past.

There was no merging of distant minds, no sharing of thoughts nor borrowed experience, no possession of body nor capture of soul, no collective intelligence nor theft of *furie*. Whatever the visions were, they came from within. Its internal nature was about all they could be sure of.

And yet the visions relayed understanding, emotion and all one extracts from living. Knowledge and skill laid dormant within, hidden beneath a thick and murky surface. With claws that momentarily broke through, rending the pliable cloud of unconscious, the visions let loose a thin strand of light that expanded and enfolded in a glittering panorama of sense and perception.

From an aged woman in the far reaches of Wensor came the art of culling flowers; from a gruff soldier in Grayledge, the craft of sapping; a smith in Emyr, a miller in Proscht, a speaker in Deorville, a wheelwright near Bedjwyck...

The names and places, knowledge and faces, went on in an endless sequence, with seams bound only by the mind of a child. At ten winters, Barr possessed the skills and abilities of a hundred lifetimes.

And still the visions came.

* * *

"When was the last time you asked?" Seltruin mused, speaking in elven. "It cannot have been more than a month."

Barr gave a knowing smile, answered in high old elven, "Two at most. I have been busy lately, what with reading and helping the Maurdon hunt."

"Your time can be passed more wisely, young Sage."

"I imagine so," Barr replied with a playful bow. "I eagerly await your instruction."

Ignoring the sarcasm, Seltruin sat in his cushioned chair by one of the worktables. Glass was a difficult and expensive material to produce, yet more than a handful of beakers adorned the Sage's table. Held over burning tallow by an ironwood collection of arms and tripods, liquids of various color bubbled and marred the inside of each glass.

"Perhaps waiting for my instruction," he said, "and not my guidance, is what has truly been holding you back." There was a significant pause, as he tended the mixtures. "I take it you meant *instruction* and not *invitation*?"

Waiting for a smile or any sign of jesting, Barr nearly stammered, "I – I would have no idea where to begin."
"No? Why is that? You study ancient texts..."
"I have read magics," Barr admitted, shrugging as if it were tantamount to reading a scroll on smithing before trying to forge a sword for the first time, "but how is that any kind of a start? Magic is more than reading, isn't it?"
"Of course it is," Seltruin replied and turned to give Barr his full attention. "But reading is the basis from which all known magic stems. I say *known*, because we practice what we are certain will work. What little knowledge has been passed down through generations of weavers is treasured and time-honored. We study the arcane sigils until they are forever burned in our minds, know their meaning as surely as we know that we live and breathe.
"You know these sigils," Seltruin went on, "and their meaning. I have seen it in your eyes, heard you speak them with an unshakable certitude. There remains only the linking of single parts, joining the two for a greater intent. What could follow but to voice the intention, channel your will through this vessel of words and bring about the desired end through the means of your own creation."
"I thought magic was memorizing incantations, like formulas for mixing herbs or blending oils." Barr wiggled his fingers in a child's mimicry of magic. "What about the hand gestures and ceremonies and patterns of dance?"
Seltruin gave the barest of smiles. "Magic can be and is all of those things, but they are merely tools to help us channel the *furie* we weave. After all, what is *furie* but a personal power? What then is a spell or incantation but a personal means of attaining a goal?"
"So it's possible to make magic without saying a word, lifting a finger or anything?" Barr looked shocked

and wondered why everyone didn't weave magic, if it was that simple.

"You make it sound much easier than it is, Barr."

"But it's possible."

"Yes," the Sage answered. "They are all helpful but ultimately unnecessary. The wards, chants and gestures all aid in focusing the mind, hone and direct the *furie* with greater precision and effect."

Barr still felt discouraged. "I could've been practicing this whole time. Why didn't you say something sooner?"

"You were not ready." Seltruin was emphatic on this point. "You may feel cheated or think what you have learned unimportant, but they are *very* important. You consider yourself an archer, do you not?"

"I don't see how –"

"Would you ever leave behind your bow? And why not? You could just as easily throw those arrows with all your strength. Just think of all the time you would save!" Seltruin leaned forward and poked Barr in the arm. "You could skip your bow practice, fletch more arrows instead. And why not? After all, the arrows are more important. That is, after all, the purpose of archery, to put the arrow in the target. What good is the bow then?"

"Alright, already!" Barr was embarrassed, upset and laughing. Though he still felt as if time had been lost, time he could have spent learning to weave magic, he couldn't help but be amused at Seltruin's explanation. "Why do you go to such lengths to make a point?"

Seltruin arched a brow but said nothing.

* * *

Barr took a seat on a wooden stool in front of Rinuor, a young Maurdon he had occasionally hunted with. There was a grievous cut across Rinuor's left hand, from the webbing between thumb and forefinger down to the middle of his forearm. Barr admired how the hunter sat firm and quiet, as Seltruin inspected the wound.

"You see," the old Sage said to Barr, "healing is but one of the many tasks you may be called on to perform. Be it sickness or a wound, it is your duty as a Sage to lend aid." The Maurdon flinched, as Seltruin prodded the broken skin and muscle. "This particular wound is not infected, but it is very deep. Your knife slipped while skinning a fox?"

Rinuor nodded, his eyes looking everywhere but on the wound. When they came to rest on Barr's, there was a shamed cast to his gaze, and an understanding passed between them.

I've warned you before, Barr wanted to tell him. *Keep your eyes on your knife, not on Aladai. What use would she have for a mate with no hand?*

Seltruin shook his head. "More likely your attention was not where it should have been. This will heal evenly, but you may not be so fortunate a second time. A finger's breadth to the right would have meant your bleeding to death. Barr," Seltruin said and stood back, "I want you to heal him."

"But how?" Barr held Rinuor by the arm, watched the blood trickling from the parted skin, and struggled to recall anything that could help. "I could bind the wound, make a poultice –"

"No," Seltruin said evenly, "you must heal him on your own. The body has the ability to heal many things but not always the strength to do so. You can lend your strength to Rinuor, help him to heal himself. Study the wound, see it in your mind. See it as your own. Open yourself to Rinuor, and let him draw upon your *furie*."

Barr closed his eyes and pictured the wound. In his mind, he saw the staunching of blood, muscles rejoin and knit together, and the flesh become whole without scar. He expected resistance, as he imposed his will on Rinuor, but the elf's body was eager to heal. It pulled at Barr with thin fingers that reached deep inside. He could feel the *furie* being drained from every part of his body and knew he would have to focus to control the flow. Rinuor's body would take care of the healing.

The strength of Barr's resolve was like the closing of a gate, slowly cutting off the outpour of *furie*. He could sense Rinuor unconsciously fight against him, wanting more and refusing to let go; but as the wound gradually closed, the need for *furie* subsided. Where the body continued to strive for balance, it was moments after the injury was fully healed that Barr could feel himself being pushed away. There was little enough left for him to give, so he broke their connection and breathed a sigh of relief.

The experience left him sore and in need of sleep. When Barr opened his eyes, he saw Rinuor flex his mended hand with a tentative ease. Seltruin wiped the blood away with a strip of cloth and nodded his approval. The cut was completely healed, with no trace of a scar on the pale skin, and all by Barr's doing.

"Thank you," Rinuor said warmly. "I owe you much."

Barr managed a weak smile. "You owe me nothing your friendship doesn't already give. Just be more careful with that knife. I don't think I'll be able to do this again for a while."

"Nonsense." Seltruin gave Barr a pat on the back but failed to notice the wince it evoked. "You will heal just as Rinuor has. All you require is a good night's rest. Now, you," he said to Rinuor, "have work to attend. Barr and I have a great deal to discuss."

Summarily dismissed, Rinuor gave a final bow of thanks before turning and walking out with the stiff pride of a young Maurdon.

Barr watched the hunter go with an unvoiced longing for bed. Seltruin cleared his throat, waking Barr from thoughts of sleep, and proceeded to explain all that could have been done better. Seltruin made it clear that he was proud of Barr as a Sage but reminded him also that there was still much to learn.

* * *

Later that night, Barr and Tuvrin prepared for the visions. Barr was even more tired after his discussion with Seltruin, but this nightly exercise was too important to skip. From head to foot, his body protested with each breath he took, but still he sought the calm that lay deep within every living thing.

"Ready?" Tuvrin asked, sitting opposite Barr on the rug.

Barr nodded, his eyes closed and breath still. He was wrapped in the warmth of serenity, the quiet in his mind like a blanket of dark. Across the black, he pictured a glistening silver void, its surface a play of rainbows...

...as the prow cut through the water. The sky was overcast, bringing early night with dark crawling clouds. A strong wind blew through the trees to either side of the river, set their hair to blowing in a wild mass of black. Muscled bronze and grizzled mien, each onahka stood ready to work or fight if need be. A long spear in one hand, a thick net of weighted hemp in the other, Kauntoch was ready for the beast. Rearing up from the depths of the water, like the God of Eat enraged, came a scaly maw and neck of silvery blue. Its saurian head took on darker hues of sapphire, as the water slipped away from its flaring

snout. Like a sliver of icy water, the creature bore teeth the gleaming white of frosted bone. Spears flew and struck against its arching neck. The obsidian tips only shattered or bounced off. Kauntoch let out a cry and led the others in swinging their nets. High over the boat they went, spinning wider as the weights forced them open. A cheer went up...

...from the crowd as the gladiator fell, ensnared by the net he himself hoped to use. Naked and weaponless, Graul used a sandal to kick dirt in a blinding arc. While the gladiator fought to clear his eyes and break free of the net, Graul used the only weapon at hand: the very chains that bound his wrists and made him a slave. After all, he was a captured soldier. He had killed scores of men, crushed the life from his enemies with a booted heel, burned homes to the ground and pillaged for no more than a few extra drinks. He wrapped the chain around the other man's thick neck and gave a pull. There was a watery gurgle before the snap and a final popping twist...

...of fate that brought Haelyn to the shore as the first boats arrived. She no more knew they meant to burn her village and enslave everyone she had ever known than they knew what a terrible mistake they were about to make. All became clear when the first arrows were loosed, and the swords came out with feral shouts. Their hateful eyes lost all sense of battle lust, as the rage drained away and fear took hold. A living pillar of fire, Haelyn let free the demon inside her, the burning wretch her heart longed to be. Sand rose up from the beach in an explosion of heat and became glass before striking the water. Shards of crystal pain tore through them, a precursor to the maelstrom of flame. Their boats were upended in boiling ocean, and those fortunate were quickly torn apart; the others were roasted alive in their armor. Haelyn fought to reign in the destruction, but she had let it go for too long.

The firecaller had warned her not to restrain her gift, and now it was out of her control...

"Enough!" a voice screamed, and the shaking began. Less harsh, "Enough. Come back."

Barr felt himself lifted up to a sitting position, and a hand took hold of his chin. When his vision cleared, he saw Tuvrin before him; he had the wide-eyed look of a soldier in a boat, with jagged glass and bright flames raining all around him.

Like tears, fire streamed down Barr's cheeks.

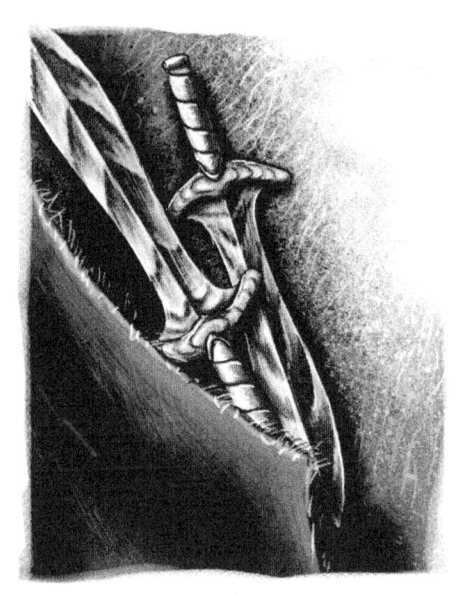

– 9 –

Tuvrin took a seat across from the Speaker, in a chair far too soft for his tastes. It had taken three days to schedule the meeting – yet one more sign that their friendship had been strained by his decision to take Barr into Geilon-Rai. Little more than five years had passed since then. Though he never once regretted saving Barr, Tuvrin did wish his son had not come at such a grave cost.

Many he once called friend had turned cold and cut off all relations. Others had been reduced to curt nods and stiff lips, a polite facade of bitter toleration. He didn't fault them for their reactions but fully shouldered the blame. Barely two centuries had gone by since humans had betrayed the Sylvannis, and those acts of treachery would not soon be forgotten. It occurred to him that he might have been gambling with their existence, courting doom – or at the very least, a war. If humans discovered the Sylvannis yet lived, they would probably burn the forest to the ground out of spite.

All his ruminations brought him back to the same thought; what was done could not be undone, and not a single consequence would make him wish otherwise.

Roedric sat with a patient silence.

"I wanted to speak with you about Barr," Tuvrin said. "This winter marks his thirteenth year."

"He has grown well."

Tuvrin was already judging Roedric's demeanor, saw the request denied in those eyes before he could even speak the words.

"It is tradition to celebrate their second rite at such a time." The eyes hardened. "A small gathering of family and friends is all that is needed to mark the occasion. I thought it best to speak with you first, knowing how strongly you feel –"

"Absolutely not," Roedric said. "Any reminder of his natural heritage should be avoided. It is in the boy's best interest to put such things behind him. He has been with us a very short time. Allow everyone a chance to adjust to his presence."

"Sage Barr is hardly a boy." Tuvrin gave a stony look of his own. "You know how short his life will be. How long before Ceiran and his Narohk *adjust*?"

Roedric scoffed. "It is not just the Narohk, Tuvrin. Open your eyes. Can you not see the general disdain before you?"

"I see it all too clearly."

Growing angry, Tuvrin exercised restraint and held his tongue before going too far. No matter that Barr had become a Sage in less than a handful of years, a span shorter than any that had come before him, he would forever be regarded as a mere human. Even their

Speaker of the Sun, voice of the Sylvannis, saw nothing in Barr but thick limbs and rounded ears.

"You misunderstand," Roedric said. "I genuinely like Barr. I would not have allowed him to stay if I did not see the spark of goodness inside him."

This is important, Tuvrin thought, berating himself. It was a human notion to value age so greatly, where its abundance was short and their lives mostly violent. He wanted to acknowledge Barr's passage into manhood by giving him this celebration. *Do not let pride get in the way. Anger will only make matters worse.*

"We both know those who have not yet accepted Barr," Tuvrin said with great calm, "most likely never will. He has exceeded all expectation, done all that was asked, and without complaint. This celebration would mean much to him, as much as the Awakening means to us."

He could see Roedric was losing patience.

"When Barr reaches his fiftieth winter, he is more than welcome to undergo the Awakening." Tuvrin tried to protest, but Roedric held up a hand and staved off all complaint. "You cannot change my mind. Barr will honor *Sylvannis* traditions – or none at all. There is no need to fan the sparks of a settling ember."

"Barr will be long dead before that ember grows cold." Tuvrin stood to leave. He didn't need the Speaker to tell him their discussion was over, though calling it such was a stretch. "I will do as you wish."

"Good." Roedric stood as well, offered his arm in farewell. When Tuvrin took hold, the Speaker kept a firm grip. "As much as I would like to accommodate the boy, I must do what is best for our people."

Our people.

The words echoed in Tuvrin's thoughts, turning his stomach with the realization that his son would never truly be accepted.

Tuvrin turned on his heel and left.

* * *

Sitting inside the rounded window edge, Barr looked down on the tree city. Imagining he could see through to the forest floor, he considered all he knew of the wolf.

A normal male matured by its third year, and rarely did one live beyond its eighth. Either due to poison in its blood from the food that it ate or wounds suffered from traps and a harsh life in the wild, odds were against its survival. Shy by nature, it was unheard of for a wolf to hunt for sport, and never would it have done so alone. A wolf was born with an instinctive need to fit within the hierarchal structure of a pack, and its very life depended on those others.

Barr was well versed in animal lore, but no matter how much he pored over what he knew, all he found were contrasts in the knowledge. When he was brought to live with the elves over five years ago, the wolf was already full grown. That it still lived was unusual, but no more so than its size. By all accounts, it was the largest wolf ever seen and stood but a foot shorter than an elf. It hunted alone, choosing its prey, and not once had it fed on a victim.

It was everything a wolf should not be.

As before, months had gone by without any sightings or deaths, but they would always return in due time. The elves seemed helpless to stop it, no matter the effort they put forth. The Narohk and Maurdon kept a vigilant eye, but none could capture or kill the beast. With all the time that had passed and whole weeks spent in search, Barr still never once saw the wolf.

Unable to guarantee safety, the elves had learned to adapt. No one wandered the forest alone, not even the Narohk that patrolled its borders. As if the Sylvannis were at war, the Ballar took it upon themselves to stray further from the city and attempt to fortify their home. The hounds would occasionally catch scent of a wolf, but rarely would it be the monstrous beast. The two times they did sight the lone wolf, it simply outran them and faded from view.

The Maurdon used numerous traps, from snares to pits, ironwood maws to weighted nets. Nothing they tried seemed to work. They hunted relentlessly, from one end of Darleman to the other, often away from the city for days. A dozen hunting parties were devoted to the task, but the Maurdon had little to show for their pains. On four different occasions, a group had spotted the wolf, even managed to shoot it more than once. Each time an arrow had struck, the beast yelped and ran off. Its tracks were impossible to follow. It was as if enchantment had caused the prints to grow cold, made the ground too weak to bear them.

The deaths were sporadic, as if the wolf hunted in cycles, leaving the forest for half a year at a time. It was suggested the beast traveled wide, perhaps came from a distant land where wolves grew as large as war hounds, though not an elf among them had ever heard of such a place. Another rumor blamed their woes on a shapeling, a diseased human that turned animal when the moon was full. There were stories of these cursed souls living far to the south, in a nightmarish land of everlasting ash and burnt trees called Lumintor.

It was Seltruin that discarded the notion, as the only one among them who had ever seen a shapeling. The disease that turned man into animal was fueled by magic and required *furie* to sustain it. Victims of a shapeling were drained of all life, with nothing left but a desiccated husk. Those killed by the wolf had been mauled, marred by tooth and claw but left otherwise whole. None of the bodies had shown signs of feeding; neither meat nor *furie* had been taken. It was highly unlikely the wolf was a shapeling.

But it was a killer and took innocent lives for sport.

Stop brooding, Aren said in his mind, though the hound was resting far below in the pens. Their empathic connection had grown well beyond the normal bonding of a companion. *We'll catch it, sooner or later. That or it'll die of old age.*

That creature will not allow itself to be caught, Idelle chimed in, and Barr could feel her in the air above the city. *It will kill or be killed, nothing less.*

Their training with the Ballar had been complete for a year, and both hound and hawk wore the enchanted collars of a companion as proof. Though the uncommon bond all three shared was often a topic of conjecture, it felt to Barr as natural as breathing. He could no more imagine himself without their voices in his mind, their feelings in his heart, than he could picture his life without magic. They were as much a part of him and who he had become as the incredible *furie* he wielded.

Two years had passed since Barr was deemed a full ranking Valar. Having mastered all that Seltruin had to teach, and in such a brief time as to appear nothing short of miraculous, Barr was given the white robes of a Sage. He only wore them on occasions that called for ceremony, preferring to wear his black leathers instead. With all the time that had passed, he still felt apart from the elves and felt guilty when wearing the robes. To an extent, it was from the cold stares and forced bows of respect, but deep down it was shame of the visions.

Though Barr would never say it aloud, in many ways he knew more than Seltruin. The memories of over a thousand lifetimes were housed in his mind, bubbling beneath the dark surface of conscious thought. Many of those lives possessed knowledge of magic, lore that had been lost from the world a long time. It was the power he could command that spurred on the guilt, both because it came without effort and it frightened Seltruin. The old Sage had never said so, but Barr saw it hiding behind the blue of his eyes.

Barr now practiced in secret, ashamed of all that he knew, and did his best not to use his full power in those times he was called on as a Sage. The last thing he wanted was to hurt Seltruin or embarrass his mentor by giving proof he had surpassed him. There was also the fear of being exiled. If any of the Narohk knew that Barr – a mere human – had grown more powerful than their *real* Sage, there was no telling what their petty jealousy would incite.

Thought of exile might have been wishful thinking.

You worry too much, Idelle said, her voice soothing in his mind, *and you give the Narohk far too much credit. Ceiran could never get you exiled.*

I wouldn't let him. Aren's rumbling growl echoed in their thoughts.

Barr sighed out his frustration. *I'd rather be exiled than insult Seltruin. Magic is so important to him, but I know he's afraid of what I might become. It's just easier to hide what I can do than to face his terrified look.*

You're overreacting, Idelle said. *Seltruin is proud of all you've accomplished. I can hear it in his voice when he speaks. Talk to him, Barr. You have nothing to lose by being honest.*

Don't I? What will happen if I tell him the truth, show him everything I can do? He would have to tell the council. Even if he didn't agree that I'm a threat, there's no doubt in my mind that's how they'd see me. I'd be thrown out of Geilon-Rai. Or worse.

Aren snorted. *No one would raise a hand to harm you. Not one of them.*

No, but they could send me away without both of you.

"Everything alright?" Tuvrin stood in the doorway, studying Barr. "You look worried."

He had a rolled up deerskin under one arm and laid the package on the table before taking a seat. Barr came over to join him.

"I'm fine. Just tired. I was up until late coaxing more ironwood from the Great Tree."

"I know." Tuvrin took a length of Barr's hair in one hand and let the strands fall away. "You should keep this tightly braided. How else would you keep from cutting it off with your kyan?"

Elven hair was thick and coarse, kept in tight braids both for adornment and practicality. Barr's was bright and lustrous, like silk of a chestnut hue. He refused to keep it braided for the same reason he didn't shave – to embrace the small differences between them. It wasn't his fault that elven cheeks were forever bare, and he saw no reason to forego his own whiskers. There was nothing he could do to make his appearance more pleasing to the elves, nor did he have the desire to do so anymore.

Barr pulled his hair back and tied it in place with a leather thong. "I like it this way. Besides, only Maurdon carry kyan."

Unrolling the deerskin, Tuvrin revealed two ironwood kyan. Jade veins stood out in the dark polished swords, both sheathed and bearing runes of protection.

"These are for you," he said.

Drawing one from its sheath, Barr admired the kyan. It was the length of his arm, from elbow to fingertips, and much lighter than he expected. He knew ironwood was stronger than steel, which made the enchanted wooden blade a fearsome weapon. Its edge was parchment thin and so sharp as to appear translucent. What struck Barr more than the beauty of its design was the unspoken message in receiving it.

No one outside the Maurdon wore kyan.

"I don't know what to say." Barr slid the blade back into its sheath. He nearly laughed and added, "This is the ironwood I gathered last night, isn't it? It's an honor but one I'm afraid I don't deserve. I can't imagine what others might say –"

"No one but I can order the crafting of kyan, and only I decide who wears them." Tuvrin gripped Barr by the shoulder with a look of fatherly pride. "I do not give this gift lightly. You have proven yourself countless times, to me and the other Maurdon. Though I cannot celebrate your second rite, I can make you the first honorary Maurdon. You are an adult now, Barr. Consider these a recognition of that. It is important to me that you know nothing in my life makes me more proud than the fact you are my son."

Emotion choked the words in Barr's throat. He felt as if he might cry for joy, overwhelmed with gratitude and a sense of accomplishment, but fought the tears down with a nod of thanks. He hugged his father close, smiling in the warmth of a returned embrace.

"I'm proud of you, too, dad." The word was no longer stilted on his tongue, the way it had been the first time he spoke it. "Looking back now, I'm glad that you found me that day."

There was a shadow behind the emerald of Tuvrin's eyes, and he briefly looked away. Though it was a terrible day to recall, Barr was happy with the way his life had turned out. He often wondered how things might have been if his father, Daroth, was still alive. Barr did still miss him but now loved Tuvrin as well.

We wouldn't be together, either, Aren pointed out.

"I like to think we were fated to cross paths," Tuvrin said. "Part of me died with Elahna and Dran, but finding you made me whole again."

"Thank you for these," Barr said, taking up the other kyan. He placed them both over the hearth with care, laying them beside the ironwood bow he had shaped and enchanted himself.

Tuvrin cleared his throat. "I meant for you to wear them, not hide them from sight. Let the Narohk balk, if they want. If any have words, they can speak directly to me."

"Oh, they won't. They'll just keep on glaring, like always." He had grown used to the stares but didn't want his father to feel the same sting. Barr slipped off his leather belt and took the kyan back down. "I'll wear them then."

"Good. You should go practice for a while. Using two swords is not as easy as it looks."

A wave of hunger swept over Barr, accompanied by a rumble in Aren's belly.

Barr rolled his eyes. "Maybe later tonight. Aren's hungry. Again."

It was good to hear Tuvrin's laugh. "I am infinitely fond of Aren, but he eats more than anyone I have ever known."

That was a compliment, right?

Barr chuckled. *As close as any you'll get, when it comes to food.*

"I'll go take him hunting."

Idelle added, *I already see a nice boar out by the eastern stream. You should hurry before it moves farther off.*

They could practically hear Aren drool.

"Be careful," Tuvrin said, "and be back before dusk. I had honeycakes made for dessert."

After fastening his belt, Barr straightened both kyan and snatched down the longbow as well. He waved and was off down the corridor, headed for the southern lift.

Hear that? he taunted Aren with a grin. *If you're especially good, I might bring you one.*

Silence was his only response.

– 10 –

With slow precision, Barr worked through a series of swings and thrusts, parries and blocks, practicing with wooden short swords that were weighted with three iron rings. He had been doing so for nearly an hour and was beginning to feel the strain in his trembling body. His muscles were thick and corded, yet another difference between he and the Sylvannis, and were being pushed to their limits by the endeavor. The routine helped develop and strengthen those muscles, and he hoped it would improve his overall speed with the kyan. He had to make up for the diminished shielding and shorter reach of the ironwood blades by being able to turn aside attacks and strike out with a fearsome alacrity.

Barr could have trained swords with the Maurdon, after returning from the hunt with Aren and Idelle, but he considered practice a way to unwind. Exercise was good for the body and mind, but he felt the solitude more conducive to the spirit. The training room was smaller than others and was typically avoided for its limited space. As such, it was perfect for Barr.

Will you be much longer? Aren asked.

Probably not, Barr answered without breaking stride. *I think I'm about done here. Why do you ask?*

Idelle replied, *Why else? The sooner you go eat your dinner, the sooner he gets a honeycake.*

That's not true, Aren said. *I was just curious, is all.*

Soon, Barr promised.

Others may have found the conversation troubling, for with it came the realization of never truly being alone. Barr felt the opposite, found comfort in their presence and had no need to be so alone that he was without them. Their voices in his mind felt as natural as his own. They were a part of each other, pieces of a whole, and together they were stronger than themselves.

Their support made the stares bearable, or at least easier to ignore. Barr could feel eyes upon him wherever he went, but the feeling was no longer as heavy as it once was. Only among the Maurdon was he at ease, where the sense of being watched subsided. The hunters afforded him the respect due a Sage, but more than that, they accepted him for what he was.

It was strange to Barr, having been human all his life, that his physical attributes would be so ingrained in who he was. Among the elves, he was not only a Sage; he was a *human* Sage. All that he accomplished, every goal that was reached, became qualified with that single marker. There was no escaping the unspoken contempt most of the elves had for his heritage, for the blood that coursed in his veins, the thick limbs and wide girth, rounded eyes and ears, lustrous hair and soft whiskers.

But even that was preferable to the open hostility of Ceiran and his Narohk.

His duties as Sage precluded any attempts to avoid them. They were the city's protectors, its guardians from without, and though they answered to Ceiran, they were as a whole accountable to the Illumin Valar. Any danger breaching the perimeter of Geilon-Rai was a direct result of some Narohk failing their task. It then fell to Seltruin or Barr to investigate and alert the council if the lapse was grave. A majority vote determined if any penalty was warranted, with the Speaker of the Sun having final say.

He suspected his responsibility of keeping watch over each party only served to worsen matters. Regardless of the reason for his stopping by the Narohk hall, each visit seemed to ruffle more feathers. Ceiran maintained the appearance of polite respect, but Barr could feel a burning hatred seething beneath that veneer. As much as he disliked the First Narohk, he was forced to admit the elf had a certain charisma about him, an air of confidence and persuasive design that had a visible affect. Unfortunately, Ceiran used that charm to sway others to his thinking, and his hold over the Narohk was absolute.

So Barr endured their muttered oaths and paid no heed to their glares. In the end, all he wanted was to do the task he was given and live out his days in peace, with both family and friends. There would always be those who saw in him nothing more than a human, an enemy from stories given flesh. There was little Barr could do in the face of such prejudice but do his best to put them out of his mind.

They're just different, Idelle said, *and not all feel that way. It's just the ones that do are more vocal.*

Barr stopped and returned both practice swords to the rack. He began stretching tired muscles to keep from getting sore and let his mind wander, as he worked out the tension in each limb.

She was right in that the elves were different. While he felt a great affinity with the Maurdon, there was no denying how unlike him they were. More than the bodily traits that set them apart, they varied their approach on many things. The Sylvannis wore little in way of armor or clothing, having a natural resistance to cold; Barr wore black leathers, lined with fur to keep warm, and still could not the keep the chill of winter at bay. They wore face paint and hues that easily blended with the forest; he refused to stain his skin and chose instead a black hooded cloak that merged him with the shadows. They stalked the knotted trails of the branches above and fired arrows from a safe and distant height, while he crawled the forest floor like a swift-moving wraith, inviting danger to come take its fill.

All these contrasts and more helped only to widen the chasm between them.

"Oh look," an elf said as he entered, "it's *Sage* Barr."

Though Barr didn't recognize the voice right away, he knew who it was as soon as he looked up. Harduen. Two others came in behind him, his slow-witted sidekick, Beiron, and a strikingly beautiful girl named Kiere. Both males were young, barely half a century, and wore the flaring paint designs around their eyes that marked them as Narohk.

Barr finished stretching his legs and stood, wiped his face with a towel and gave a nod of greeting to all three.

They think I don't know them. Barr chuckled inside. As of two weeks passed, there were three thousand, four hundred and eleven Sylvannis. He not only knew them all by name but had delivered the most recent addition. *Any bets one of them will insult me?*

None here, Aren said in a grumbling tone.

The Last Incarnation

Idelle said, *Ignore them and go have some dinner. Your hunger is almost as distracting as Aren's.*

The Narohk began to stretch. Kiere sat down near the back of the room and smiled while twirling a lock of sable hair. She was watching Barr closely, with obvious interest, though for what he couldn't be sure. It left him feeling like a bug in a jar.

Without a word, Barr walked toward the door, kept his eyes ahead and did his best to ignore their stares. He was used to the unwanted attention. He often wondered if an elf living among humans would have been treated the same way. They were nothing like the magical and light-hearted people he had heard of in fire tales. He was almost out the door when Harduen spoke.

"Unusual weapons for a Sage. I thought Maurdon were the only ones permitted to wield kyan."

Barr stopped and turned. "You are correct."

"Ahh, so you are a Maurdon now," Harduen said. He and Beiron were shirtless, most likely thinking it would impress Kiere, and both looked ready to spar. "Did Sage Seltruin finally come to his senses then? Commendable of your father to own up to his mistake and allow you to join his ranks."

Calm, Idelle warned.

"I'm a bit of everything, you could say. I wear the robes of a Sage and wield the kyan of a Maurdon. I have the companions of a Ballar and the noble patience of an Eneir. I'm charged with the ultimate protection of this city, as the Gharak," he simply couldn't resist the urge, "and I shoot far better than any Narohk."

Kiere laughed at that, like the tinkling of bells.

"Very amusing," Harduen said without the faintest hint of a smile and tossed a practice sword at Barr's feet. "Care to spar?"

"Just you or the of both you?"

"Both," Beiron quickly put in.
Don't hurt them, Idelle said. *Well, not too much. You can hit that Harduen a few times, though.*
If you don't, Aren said, *I will.*
"You should learn to play to your strengths. Narohk are archers for a reason." Barr tossed aside his towel and left the practice blade on the floor. He stood facing them, unarmed and waiting. "Let's see what you can do."

They came at him without hesitation, swinging wildly in their obvious attempt to cause harm. Barr sidestepped their attacks with fluid ease, twisting his body to avoid being struck. Ducking under a swing or turning it aside with a push, he let them both wear themselves out in the fray. When Beiron tried to punch him instead, Barr took hold of the elf's wrist and threw him into Harduen.

The two tumbled away into a corner.

"How is Chitters doing?" Barr asked Kiere. It had been nearly a month since he was called on to heal the poor cat – who, contrary to popular belief, don't always land on their feet. He stood casually talking to her, as the Narohk struggled to get up. "Still jumping about like always?"

"You remember that?" The surprised look in her pale eyes became friendly. "I never did thank you –"

They were back, thinking his attention was diverted while his back was turned. Barr dodged the attacks but returned them as well. Evading Harduen, he moved in close and tapped the elf over the heart with thumb and first two fingers pinched tightly together. He wasn't trying to hurt them, but he wanted Harduen to know that he could.

Beiron was swinging madly, his face red and lips flecked with spittle. Barr gave a hard slap across the Narohk's slender wrist, and moved in to touch the flat of his hand against Beiron's throat. The practice sword fell from numb fingers at the same time the elf crouched, gasping for air. Had Barr used any force at all, he would have crushed Beiron's windpipe; and the angry glare from the elf showed that he knew it.

"He is toying with us," Harduen fumed. Kiere was sitting behind him and laughed. He spun around in a rage and slapped her. "He insults you as well!"

Oh no, Idelle sighed.

Before Harduen could even lower his hand, Barr was upon him and kicking out behind his knee. Harduen fell over backward, as his leg crumbled beneath him, and Barr drove the elf further down with an elbow to the shoulder. Harduen collapsed to the floor with enough force to steal breath and laid still, groaning loudly, with his eyes tightly closed.

Narrowly avoiding a punch from Beiron, Barr ducked and came up with both hands. Palms flat, he struck the elf full on in the chest and sent him flying to the wall behind him. Beiron crashed against its hard surface and fell to all fours. Blood was running from his nose when he stood.

"Now you die," the Narohk said through gritted teeth and drew a long hunting knife from his belt.

Barr's eyes went wide with the force of a vision. It came without warning, flying up from his middle, and encompassed his presence with cold. Like a shroud of starry night, it blinded his view for what felt like the briefest of moments...

His eyes flashed with a yellowish light that extended out and lit up his face. In a voice that shook the ground with its depth, Barr faced his opponent and spoke, a chilling frost reaching out from his lips.

"Jaen ed li mindosh!" *I accept your challenge!*

"He is haunted!" Beiron gasped and let the knife fall. Stricken with terror, he edged toward the door. "Kiere, run!"

By the next cloud of frozen breath, Beiron was gone, and with him went a frantic Kiere.

Barr blinked and shrugged off the strange cold. With the darkness fully lifted, he looked about the room and saw he was alone with Harduen.

Where did you go? Aren asked. *I couldn't sense you.*

What do you mean? I – things got dark for a moment, but everything's fine now. Harduen was still groaning. *I wonder what happened to the other two? They must have ran off while I was dazed.*

Idelle pressed, *But what happened?*

I don't know. It was just a vision. Someplace very cold, with ghostly figures of blue light and yellow eyes. I think they were completely made of furie. Barr shrugged and picked up his towel. *I'm going to get some dinner. I'm suddenly very hungry.*

Harduen's groans followed Barr down the hall.

* * *

Ceiran wanted an open council, so that everyone would see the human menace that could potentially endanger all their lives. The Speaker of the Sun wouldn't hear of it and demanded that no word of the inquiry leave the council chamber. This was a grave accusation, and it needed to be handled quietly, without causing unrest.

For the second time in his short life, Barr was forced to sit by and watch the council in a heated discussion, as they decided his fate – as they had done just five years passed.

This is ridiculous, Barr thought. *I am not possessed by an evil spirit.*

Of course you're not, Idelle said, *but it won't be easy explaining that to them. They might see your visions as confirmation of being haunted.*

"There is no proof," Tuvrin proclaimed over the noise and called for quiet with the power of his voice. "You have only the word of those who openly show a dislike for Sage Barr."

Barr inwardly smiled at that. He had earned the right to be called by his title. He was glad for his father being there to support him.

"Since when," asked Westran, "do we question the word of *elves*?"

Roedric cleared his throat. "No one is calling into question *anyone's* word, but perhaps Beiron and Kiere were mistaken."

"The only mistake," Ceiran said firmly, "was in letting this human live among us. He should have been left in the woods to die with his father. For all we know, this *haunted* creature could be the very wolf that has been slaughtering our women and children."

Startled gasps ran through the chamber, their minds infected with the insidious thought. Barr jumped to his feet but was held back by two Gharak at his side.

"How *dare* you!" he roared. "My father was killed by that wolf!"

Barr needs our help! They could sense Aren smash down the gate to his pen and rush headlong for the lift.

Idelle was already hovering outside the window.

"Yes," Ceiran agreed with a calm demeanor, "he was. And *you* killed him. It is well known that the haunted possess strange powers," he said to the council, "and have no memory of their actions when the spirit takes them. I say this human *has* such a malevolent spirit controlling him, that he becomes the wolf and murders the innocent."

Tuvrin growled, "Enough of this! I saw the wolf kill his father. Barr could not have done it."

"But did you see them together when he died? Did you see Barr and his father together with the wolf? No. Because this human *is* the wolf."

At Tuvrin's uncertain lack of response, the council resumed its busied murmurs.

Barr glared at Ceiran with a burning hatred. "This isn't fair! He's making it all up to get rid of me." He shook off the hands that restrained him. "People were dying here long before I arrived. That's why you were hunting the damn wolf in the first place."

Ceiran dismissed that detail with a wave. "You would not recall your actions. The haunted never do."

"The purpose of this council," Seltruin reminded them, pointedly resting his eyes on Ceiran, "is to decide whether or not Sage Barr is in fact haunted. In the past, such an accusation was put to rest by undergoing the Denshyar. Would that satisfy this council?"

"As First of the Narohk," Ceiran said, "I would be satisfied."

The rest of the council soon agreed.

Denshyar, Barr thought as he glared about the room. *I shouldn't have to do anything! I didn't do anything! I blacked out* – and the memory frightened him. *I blacked out... Oh, no. What if it's true? What if I am* the wolf?

Don't be silly, Idelle said. *You said it yourself, you were just a small boy when you were brought here, and the wolf had already been killing people.*

But I've never seen it. In five years, I've never once seen the wolf. I black out sometimes, when the visions are too strong.

You blacked out for all of two seconds, Aren said. *That's not enough time to kill anyone. Don't worry, I'm almost there.*

The wolf should be dead. It's over eight years old, and I know it's been wounded more than once. What if the dark presence I felt in the woods the day my father died was actually me? What if the wolf has been dead all this time and I've –

Nonsense! Idelle was firm, like a chiding big sister. *If you were the wolf, we would know. That's all there is to it.*

"Have the Denshyar brought in," Roedric ordered, and a Gharak left to do his bidding. "We will have an end to this, one way or another."

Barr was familiar with the Denshyar, had read about it once while studying ancient rites. It was intended to reveal the true nature of any who wore it, and the results were often unstable. Wearing the mask exposed aspects of the spirit that most souls tried to hide, buried truths that laid deep within the unconscious. More than one elf had been forever changed by such terrible insight.

The guard returned with an ironwood box a foot wide and across. Its burnished surface reflected the light of a suspended globe, and the marble-like veins of emerald seemed to pulse under the glow. With steady hands, the Gharak left the box before Roedric and returned to his post at the door.

"Step forward," the Speaker told Barr and opened the box. Inside was a mask of pure mithrinum, enchanted metal of a frosted gold hue. Roedric carefully removed it with both hands and offered it to Barr. "You must wear the Denshyar to prove your innocence. No protests," he warned. "If you wish to stay here with us, you must honor our ways."

It was exactly what Barr had feared, hanging on the turn of those words. *If you wish to stay here.* Threat of exile loomed over his head, with the fear of being cast out from Geilon-Rai without his companions. He would never again see Tuvrin or Seltruin – or any of the dozens of other elves he had grown to care for as friends.

That will never happen, Aren rumbled.

Barr felt the blood drain from his face, stolen away by gripping fear. *What if?* The words echoed in his mind. He nodded weakly and took hold of the cold mask. It was solid mithrinum, yet it had the feel of soft skin. There were no straps to hold it in place, no holes at the mouth nor openings at the nose, for breathing. Barr would have to hold the mask up to keep it from falling.

The council was waiting. He could feel their heavy stares all upon him. With a hesitant last look about the table, Barr lifted the mask to his face.

The mithrinum flowed over him like quicksilver and adjusted to take the shape of his features. The mask rippled and molded to his flesh, a second skin of cold metal that reflected light from the hanging globes. His mouth opened in a voiceless cry, but nothing went in or out; no air nor words escaped. His eyes blinked furiously before closing tight, his pained expression touching on…

…thousands of them, men, women and children, all of a different size, shape and color. The clothes they wore were as diverse as their features, their hair and eyes, skin and muscle. Some were similar, but no two were exactly the same. All that drew them together was a thin cord of silver light that entered the back and passed through the stomach. The cord began off in the distance, where a small woman could barely be seen crouching in the dust. Barr wasn't sure if the light came from her or the dark soil, so low to the ground was she bent. And from her, the cord weaved in and out of the whispering crowd, their voices echoing in the growing mist.

Join us, he heard. Join us.

Barr could see that the cord touched him too, was firmly attached to his stomach and pulsed with new life. Looking behind, he could see no more cord. It ended with him.

Join us.

I'm already joined, he thought and laid hands on the cord. A massive vision rushed into his eyes with the force of a white blast of air. Thousands of visions, all at once, stormed his mind with worlds and lives that overlapped in chaos.

Join us! Join us!

The visions pounded his chest, tore through his gut with a howling wind. Like an ocean of living paintings, the colors swirling in a dangerous fury, Barr floated above it all, as hands shot out to claim him. They pulled him down into the bubbling mix, the colors bleeding into each other in a struggle to form a single vision.

Join!

His legs went under, melting his flesh.

Us!

He was disappearing into the paint, dissolving and spreading over the surface. He felt no pain as he melted like wax, his skin cooling and settling the vibrant turmoil. There was only the fear of fading away, the fear of death without making them whole..

Barr...

He cried out, and the mithrinum stretched, its silvery flesh crawling along each cheek. Light glinted off its wrinkled brow, spread a hazy glow about the mask and burst into a shower of silver-blue. Gasping for breath, Barr fell back to the floor, clutching his chest and fighting to get air in his lungs. Cries of outrage and fear shook the chamber.

"Barr!" Tuvrin shouted in alarm and rushed to his son. He pushed past a Gharak with enough force to send the guard sprawling.

Aren rushed into the room, shoving aside guards and anyone else foolish enough to be in his way.

"Great Celene!" one yelled in shock. "He destroyed the Denshyar!"

"What did he do?" shrieked another. "How could this happen!"

Standing over Barr protectively, Aren let a rumbling growl escape from his throat. In all of Sylvannis history, never had they faced one of their own war hounds. The silence that fell over the council accompanied startled looks of frozen panic.

Guards wisely sidled away from the dog.

"That will be enough from you," Roedric said to Aren with a steely gaze. "No one is going to harm Sage Barr." He looked down at the silvery puddles, all that remained of the Denshyar. "We must remain calm. There is an explanation for this, and we will find it."

"Yes, please," Seltruin said. "Let us stay calm. Barr has proven beyond any doubt that he is *not* haunted. The Denshyar is broken. His innocence is shown."

"But what does it mean?" an advisor asked, voicing the concern in all their minds.

"I will look into the matter," Seltruin replied.

"No one will speak of this," Roedric said evenly, his voice demanding attention. "No one. What has happened here must never leave this chamber. You will all swear to it now, by house and rank." His eyes met each of them and awaited their nod of assent. "There will be no more discussion of this, until Seltruin can tell us exactly what has happened."

The council faded away, drifting off to the distance in a haze of growing black, and in the comfort of numbing

sleep, the dream voices went on – peaceful but pleading, a whisper of hope.
Join us...

– 11 –

Two years had passed before Seltruin was absolutely certain of what had happened to the Denshyar. No mention of the shattered mask had been uttered in council during that time, but he could see memory of it in their eyes each time Barr's name was mentioned. The council members had been patiently awaiting a plausible explanation; the best Seltruin could offer them was a comfortable lie.

"What I tell you now," he said to Roedric, in the quiet of his study, "must never be revealed to the council. I will tell them that, after proving Barr's innocence, the elven enchantment could no longer account for human blood. The Denshyar was destroyed because the magic woven into it was intended for elves alone."

Seltruin glanced at the doorway, where he could see the blue outline of his wards protecting the room. It was doubtful anyone would be observing them through a scrying bowl, but too much was at stake to risk it.

"If that is untrue," the Speaker said, "then what *did* happen? Should I be concerned for the safety –"

"Of course not. We were perfectly justified in allowing Barr to become a Sage. In fact, I am convinced now more than ever that he was fated to be brought here." Roedric raised a brow but didn't comment. "At first, I believed the Denshyar was indeed damaged because Barr is human. After considerable research in the archive, I was able to discount that possibility. Though we now know very little of forging a Denshyar, we can be certain of its affect on *all* who wear it. I was able to gather the remains for study."

Seltruin placed a phial of silver liquid on the table.

"That is all that is left?" the Speaker asked, his tone incredulous. "The Denshyar was one of our most prized artifacts, and you are saying it is gone forever?"

"I am afraid so. Remaking the mask is beyond my knowledge. No record exists that explains how." Seltruin picked up the phial and shook it. The metal clung to its sides, turning the glass a silvery blue. "The mithrinum should have hardened moments after breaking apart. It retains no warmth and never really melted to begin with. As far as I can tell, the metal has been stripped of the magic that gives it shape. This liquid is the lifeless residue of mithrinum."

Roedric lifted the phial. "Barr did this? How? Is this why the council must never know?"

"There is a remote possibility," Seltruin replied, "that the Denshyar simply exhausted all its magic after all this time, or whatever vision Barr saw wholly consumed the mask's *furie*." He looked to Roedric in earnest. "There is one other explanation, one I feel is the most likely. Barr is Aneolae."

The Speaker's shock and disbelieving stare was on par with what Seltruin had expected. He could scarcely believe it himself. Being Aneolae, a soul living its final lifetime, on the brink of enlightenment, was an honor all elves – Sylvannis or otherwise – dreamed of one day achieving. Though debate raged over the details, elves firmly held to the belief of birth and rebirth, the cycle of learning called reincarnation. Some believed a soul could be reborn as insects or trees, while others more liberally thought one could be reborn as any of the numerous races that peopled Taellus; the majority, however, were adamant in their myopic view of life, that once born an elf, a soul was reborn an elf as well. Regardless, it was the dream they all shared that gave them a common ground, the hope and striving for the last incarnation.

"How can you be certain?"

"I have spoken with Barr at length," Seltruin replied, taking the phial back, "about what he believed to be just visions. Visions do not relay a lifetime of knowledge and skill, but what of memories? I have suspected for some time that Barr was an old soul, thus his intuitive grasp of weaving magic. It was the Denshyar, however, that convinced me he is Aneolae. The nature of the mask's enchantment is to interpret and reveal the purity of any who wear it. Barr's was too potent, and the attempt stripped away all *furie* from the metal, destroying the Denshyar completely."

Roedric was looking out one of the windows as he listened. When he turned his head and met Seltruin's gaze, there was worry in his eyes.

"If what you say is true..."

"No one must know," the Sage agreed, knowing what Roedric feared. If anyone learned that a human was close to enlightenment, the unrest might lead to Barr's death. "They would kill him for spite."

The Speaker sighed. "Has he at least been elven before? That would explain much, actually."

"He has, many times in fact, and not just Sylvannis." Seltruin leaned forward and took hold of his one-time student by the arm. "Barr must never be told, either. If I am correct, then what he has been reborn to learn will unlock his ascension. He must come to realize why he is here, on his own."

"The longer he stays here, the more danger he is in." The Speaker eyed the phial of silver liquid. "Someone will find out. If not by our actions, then by his."

Seltruin shook his head and knew it to be true.

"We must do all we can to protect him."

* * *

Barr crouched beside Aren in the snow, eyeing nine figures in the distance. The massive hound was down on his belly, hidden in the rippling waves of enchantment. Though Barr could see Aren through the haze of bending light, anyone more than a few feet away would have seen nothing but a strange imprint in the snow.

Orcs, Idelle told them.

Aren snorted out a billowy mist. *I can smell them from here. They have the scent of old blood.*

They wear blood, Barr explained, *like a badge. They believe it gives them the strength of those they conquer and intimidates others into making mistakes on the field.*

Barr had the memories of numerous orc lifetimes, both from tribes in the far northern mountain ranges and distant swamps to the south. He understood the rationale of why orcs acted as they did, could recall himself feeling justified and proud in wearing the blood and bones of those he had vanquished, but remembering it now made his stomach turn.

They're awfully close to the city, Idelle said.

I doubt they know it's there. His eyes narrowed, as he watched the orc soldiers clomp through the heavy snow and leafless brush. *Whatever they're doing here, it can't be good.*

They were a stocky race, a hand or two shorter than humans but much wider in girth. Their muscles were naturally dense, affording them strength well beyond that of a normal man. These few looked as though they came from the swamps, by their ruddy green color and sparse clothing beneath the chain armor. Orcs had thick skin and were resistant to the cold, but mountain orcs would have been covered in furs. With a crossbow strapped to each back and iron short swords at the waist, these orcs looked ready for a fight. As a warring people, they were always prepared, as if the lust for battle ran through their black veins, but these few were more alert than usual.

They're not hunting game, Barr noted. *It could be a search party, but for what? Do you see anything, Idelle?*

Nothing, for at least a day's walk. Odd that they should travel so far without mounts.

Just smell them, Aren said. *Can you imagine a horse that wouldn't buck them?*

He's right, Barr said. *Horses and orcs don't mix. They ride creepers when they can – reptilian monsters that have no sense of smell. Creepers need certain gases in the air to digest their food; they'd have a hard time surviving outside a swamp.*

How did they get past the Narohk? That blood smells stale and looks days old. Couldn't be from any elves.

I don't know. Barr slipped his bow down from his shoulder and drew an arrow. *I'm not waiting to find out, either.*

Barr gauged them at near three hundred and twenty yards. The wind was light, but there were a few trees in between he and the orcs. Timing would be crucial. He let his eyes relax, saw them up close by picturing them in his mind, like scrying but without the bowl of water. The longbow he used was enchanted for both distance and speed, but even an ironwood bow couldn't reach a target that far. Fortunately, Barr guided his arrow by focusing *furie* down its length. He could have simply held one in his hand and let it fly from there, but firing a bow felt more intimate.

He sighted the lead orc and fired.

Aren issued a guttural sound from his chest, a growl that rumbled the ground beneath him. A streak of black shot overhead, cutting through the air and sped toward the orcs like a shadow of doom. Four more arrows were in the air before the first hit its mark. Barr shouldered the bow, slipped his left hand beneath Aren's ironwood collar and threw his right leg up and over.

Aren bunched up his muscles and shot forward at an incredible speed. He was closing the distance with long strides that propelled them over snow and rock, dodging between heavy boles, slipping under a fallen tree that angled across yet another, until finally they broke out into the clearing and came close enough to the orcs to see the red of their eyes.

Idelle swooped down and snatched up an orc in each claw, causing the frantic soldiers to drop their crossbows without firing a shot. She loosed their flailing bodies into the trees. Their screams became gurgled thuds, as they crashed through branch and leafless bole, causing an explosion of splintering wood that burst out in a rain of deadly shards. They rolled over the snow and icy rocks, then slid to a stop and remained forever still.

The last two orcs were surrounded by the skewered bodies of five others, where arrows had cleanly pierced their necks. They both had their swords drawn, but were looking off in the wrong direction – where their comrades had been taken. When they finally saw Barr and Aren, what must have been startled gasps escaped their pinkish snouts, but the sounds came out more like wild snorts. Aren had let his enchantment fall away, allowing the orcs to see the source of their inevitable demise.

Barr brought his right leg back down and lifted both feet to Aren's side. As they drew close, he kicked outward and sprang through the air toward the left orc. Careful to avoid its already drawn sword, he grabbed hold of chain links with both hands and forced the orc down to its back. Foul breath blasted up passed its yellowed tusks. Barr flipped forward and twisted in the air, came down in a crouch and drew both kyan.

Aren had taken the right one up with a snarling bite and kept running, shaking the orc in his mouth. Closing down his jaws, he crushed dagger-like teeth through armor, bones and muscle. There was only the initial squeal of shock at being snatched up whole, and then nothing but the terrible crackle and pop of being broken.

He spit the orc out in disgust.

Barr and Idelle were glad they could only sense Aren's revulsion at whatever polluted miasma oozed from the orc and not share in the horrible taste.

Nearly gagging, Aren said, *That's the most awful, vile thing I've ever had in my mouth! What in the world do they eat?*

Barr had kicked away the orc's sword and drove both his kyan down over its throat like a pair of scissors. A ghostly blue fire enveloped the ironwood blades, and glittered in the crimson pools of the orc's horrified eyes. Thrusting both kyan downward, Barr cut cleanly through the orc's exposed neck and the frozen earth beneath, ending its miserable existence.

Anything they can get their hands on, Barr replied, *preferably alive. If they can't find an enemy to feed off, they'll turn on each other.*

Idelle landed next to Aren with a chuckle. *Maybe next time you won't try to sneak an extra meal.*

Oh, that's very funny. How was I supposed to know they tasted that bad? I didn't think anything *tasted that bad.* Pushing his nose through the snow to clean away the oily blood, he asked Barr, *Why didn't you just shoot them all anyway?*

Do you have any idea how long it takes to fletch an arrow? Barr was standing over the orc he had slain, studying its features. It was covered in dried blood, from the top of its boots – snow must have washed away the rest – to the ends of its coarse black hair. There were small bone talismans tied into its braids, shamanic blessings meant to aid in battle. *Besides, I took down enough that we weren't running the risk of being hurt. What bothers me is why they were here in the first place.*

Too late to ask, Idelle said, *even if you could speak the guttural snorts and barks that pass for their language.*

I can speak it. They wouldn't have answered, though. I can learn more from their corpses than I could from their lips. Barr pointed to the boots of one he had killed with an arrow. *Red clay means they passed near the western stream, by the Doughern caves. None of them have any food or supplies, and I don't see any wounds that we didn't cause.*

Narohk, Aren grunted. *I wouldn't be surprised if one of them let the orcs pass because they knew we were here.*

I hadn't thought of that, Barr said and frowned. *I think I'll just go have a talk with them.*

* * *

Barr left Aren at the pens before heading over to the Narohk hall. He strolled into the barracks, where at least a score of the painted archers were mending armor or fletching arrows.

"Who was assigned to the lower north area?" Barr asked in a loud voice. All eyes turned toward him with a mild disdain. "Who?"

Harduen stood with arms akimbo. "I was, until a short time ago. What concern is it of yours? Are you a Narohk now, too?" Other elves looked to each other with apprehension. Barr guessed it was one thing to insult him behind his back and quite another to disparage him openly. He was, after all, a Sage. "Did you lose your puppy?"

Puppy? Aren growled. *Pray he and I never meet.*

"You let a party of orcs get past you," Barr said, ignoring the remarks, and with a bit of satisfaction, watched the look of shock come over Harduen. There was momentary silence in the room, then a mad rush for weapons and armor. "Don't bother," Barr told them. "It's already taken care of. Next time, Harduen, I might not be there to do your duty. Try keeping your mind on the assigned task and not on Kiere. She's not interested in you. She never was."

The young Narohk fumed and would have charged forward to strike Barr, if another wasn't there to stop him.

"You do us further insult," he whispered harshly. "Say nothing. Let the Sage speak and be on his way."

Barr looked to each Narohk before turning to leave. He might have once feared – even gone out of his way to avoid – these rugged and hateful elves. He had become a man, though, and a man always faced his fears.

"Wait!" Harduen called, glaring at the one in his way. "I have something for your troubles, Barr Shintae."

A collective intake of break went through the room, some shaking their heads at such a grave insult while others anxiously awaited the confrontation. There was no doubt that Harduen would have to answer for the slight. The only question that remained was whether he would answer to Barr or to Ceiran.

"My proper title is Sage," Barr warned. "Speak with respect or not at all. I came here in the greater interest of the Sylvannis, in protection of Geilon-Rai. If you can't carry out your duty as a Narohk, or accept a rebuke when you fail to do so, then I will see to it personally that you are stripped of all rank and cast out of your party."

"You can do no such thing," one of the archers said, his voice uncertain.

"Please, please," Harduen said, his hands out wide in supplication as he approached. "I only wanted to give you a gift. To reward you for your pains and to repay an old debt."

Barr was waiting for it and sighed inwardly. *How could he be so plain?*

Idelle replied, *It would be better to let others punish his actions. Retaliation will only make you the villain.*

When the hand shot out to slap him, Barr caught it easily and gave a wrenching twist. Harduen's scream was almost enough to cover the sound of snapping bones. Others stood or jumped from their seats, unsure if they should pounce and looking ready to do so.

A single voice pierced the confusion.

"Hold!" Ceiran bellowed. "You," he ordered one, "take Harduen out of here, and have his wrist tended to. I take it your business here is done... Sage Barr."

It kills him to say it, Barr said, somewhat pleased at having caused Ceiran any discomfort. *It makes no sense why he hates me so much. I must have slighted him in a past life or something.*

Some people are just naturally hateful, Idelle said.

"Yes, thank you. I'm quite finished. Oh, Harduen," Barr called, "I guess you won't need to worry about your duties after all. I don't think you'll be using a bow for a while."

Ceiran nearly growled in Barr's ear. "There is no need for further insult. You have proven his better, now let it alone."

It was meant as a whisper, but others had heard. Ceiran was implying that Barr added insult to injury, but the First Narohk seemed to forget it was Harduen that had tried to strike Barr. What he really wanted to do was allow Harduen a chance to apologize and ask to have his wrist healed.

So little changes, Barr said. *Even though I've proven myself as a Sage, they still see only a human. I could heal his wrist, but they're all too proud to ask.*

"Save your advice for Narohk," Barr replied coolly. "I neither want nor need your counsel." To the others, he added, "Make sure all of the lower areas are checked once more. The party I discovered was in the northern section, and there could easily be more of them."

"I will see to it myself," Ceiran said and turned on his heel abruptly. He left out through another door to the back, where Harduen had been taken to be treated.

Harduen or Ceiran, Barr wondered as he left and headed back to his chamber. *He could've purposely let*

The Last Incarnation

those orcs past him, if he knew we would be there. Or Ceiran could have ordered him to.

I'm not so sure, Idelle said. *Harduen is fairly stupid. Such a scheme would be beyond him, and by the sound of his voice, he had no idea that orcs were nearby. As for Ceiran...*

Snake in the grass, that one. A wave of hunger from Aren came over them. *Shouldn't it be mealtime? I'm sure I missed a meal today.*

You're as likely to miss a meal as I am to fall from the sky. I could bring you something, if you asked nicely.

I'll get it for him, Barr said with a laugh. *If there's* —

He stopped and looked sharply at the hearth, as he entered the room. His quiver was delicately swinging on its peg, as if something had brushed against it. He looked around but saw no one else. With a shrug, he took a seat and changed his hunting boots for a pair of softer shoes. He was to meet Seltruin in the garden before dusk, when the lighting would be best for illusions. A smile broke across his lips, sending a nervous flutter of excitement through his stomach.

After I bring you some food, Barr said, *I'm heading over to Seltruin's garden. He and I are having our own little tournament tonight. I wonder what my dad would have said to that. 'Damn turners,' most likely.* Barr laughed, recalling how often he had heard that phrase while growing up. *I hope I'm not disappointing him. I know Tuvrin's proud, but sometimes it's hard to even remember what my other dad was like.*

If I had a son, Aren said, unusually somber, *I think I'd be proud of him no matter what he did. That could just be the hunger talking, though.*

Barr rolled his eyes and headed for the pens.

* * *

An orc hovered in the air above the garden, moisture glistening off its snout as it barked a fetid cloud of breath past blackened tusks. Its plate armor was pitted and edged with dark blood, much like the barbed short sword held ominously to fore.

A troll stomped out of nothing to stand before the stubby orc. Covering its muddied green skin was a bear pelt, stretching from shoulder to corpulent belly. The towering mass of sinew and flesh gave a toothless roar that shook both its wiry dark hair and leaves from the surrounding bushes and flowers in the garden.

The orc crouched and leapt, stretching as it sprang forward. A length of green scales slithered around the troll in a spiraling coil that ended with a maw full of teeth and flashing black eyes. The wyrm tightened its hold and reared back, a forked tongue jutting in and out of its saurian head. Its deafening roar echoed through the garden, followed by a venomous green cloud that encircled and choked the struggling troll.

Collapsing into a spray of blue water, the troll splashed to the ground and reformed as an elemental. Though shaped like an elf, both regal and handsome, it stood three times the size and rippled with the water that made up its parts. The liquid giant leveled a punch against the wyrm's jaw, splintering dagger-length teeth into jagged bones, and continued to pummel away without relent.

Barr was sweating from the exertion. It was growing more difficult to change and maintain his illusions. There were so many details, so many colors to keep track of. The sounds, the gritty surfaces, he made them all as real as his imagination could manage.

Black spines sprouted from the wyrm's flesh, its scales smoothing to a glinting silver. Then the entire image shrunk in on itself and emerged as a spiked club in the hands of titan. From beneath a jutting brow, eyes of a fiery orange glared at the elemental with a furious loathing. The club came crashing down on that watery head, beating away liquid chunks that splashed an argent rain over the garden.

It became painful to sustain the illusions. Barr was drawing on his own *furie* to fuel the complex scene, and the magic being sapped from his body was growing to an unbearable limit. Only once before had Barr completely exhausted himself by weaving a spell, and it had taken four days to get back on his feet. He knew how far he could push his body before needing rest, and he thought he reached that breaking point before an influx of power surged through his arms and legs. He could feel it center in his middle, filling him with new energy.

What is that? Idelle asked. *I feel dizzy.*

"Barr."

He could breathe easier now, lend more of himself to the illusion and its patterns of light. Color and texture were no longer a problem, and he added scent to the mix. The *furie* within him was bubbling over with a raw power that begged to be set free, and it felt good to let it loose, to channel it into the nearest magic. It felt good! Like gorging on food or quenching a thirst. Yes! Like a thirst! He was satisfying a need, a desire that overwhelmed his senses with an intense soothing that lent focus. He saw things clearer, saw *through* and *around* them, heard the thrumming of ordinary life in a way that was far from...

...the center ring. Heli stood over the charred remains of his opponent, yet another tourner quick to attack but slow with a shield. He literally glowed with the surge of new life, the stolen furie *of the dead fool at his feet. It was exhilarating...*

...to see the crowds of filthy commoners shy away in fear. Jhali Ab Fahr, the most feared weaver at this or any other tourn, was a woman. A woman! Her disdain for men left little room for mercy, but what few sparks of humanity remained were easily quelled by her maddening desire for furie. *It was no illusion...*
...that sent the crowd off running for their homes, away from the tournament. Wild eyes brimming with the life of those crumpled at either end of the field, hands clenched with furie *that begged to be released, Xeres strode across the bloodied grass and after the ragged commoners. Individually, they had little* furie *to take, but collectively...*

"Barr!" It was Seltruin, but he called from the end of a very long tunnel, an echo in a cavern that muffled its source. "Barr, stop it! You must stop this instant!"

The illusion faded to a mist that gently blew out and away. The sense of unbridled power left a dull aching in Barr's stomach, like hunger pangs from a thousand days without food. Still, he saw things differently. Seltruin was a golden body of light, firmly held to the ground by a length of silver incandescence.

"Look what you have done," the light said.

The sadness cut through his heart, enveloped his ears with emotion he neither wanted nor asked for. There was inexplicable sorrow in its tone, a pain that gripped his chest with accusation.

You did this, it said. *You alone. How could you? This waste is your doing.*

From one heartbeat to the next, Barr lost the intense clarity of sense that had taken hold. He was able to focus again with a mortal precision, one both lesser and greater for its limited perspective – for living with such a clarity would surely have killed him. There was unspeakable grief in Seltruin's eyes, a look of disbelief that left Barr wondering if he had done something horrible or fantastic.

A single glance around showed he had done both.

Nothing remained of the garden but a withered and lifeless brown.

– 12 –

Barr fell to his knees, looking agape at the ruin he had caused. Though his body ached from within, it pained him more to face what was left of the garden. All of the plants had withered and lost their vibrant sheen, their once emerald hue having faded to a sickly brown. They drooped, wilted and limp, over soil now barren. The center of each shrunken leaf was marred with black, as if it had been burned from the inside. Whatever colorful flowers had once brightened the garden, they were now nothing more than a memory. Their lustrous petals had shriveled and browned, their vitality all but consumed, until all that was left was a dull pile of ashen buds.

Kneeling beside him, Seltruin lifted what once was a tulip; both stem and brittle petals flaked away between his fingers. Debris fell about his robes, staining the pristine cloth with its touch.

"I didn't mean it," Barr said. "I – I'm sorry."

What did you do? For a brief moment, Barr wasn't sure if he was hearing Idelle or the accusing voice of the golden light. That blinding clarity had faded away, left an empty pain inside him, but memory of it echoed in his mind. All that remained here was death. *Barr, what happened? I've never felt you so sad.*

Look, he said and let them sense the garden through him. *I destroyed it all, stole its* furie *like a turner.*

"Make it right," Seltruin said, shaking his head in what looked like disbelief. Unfortunately, there was no denying the damage all around them. "You took life from the plants and soil. I – I do not know how, but you must give it back." His eyes were both frightened and pleading. "You can give it back. Tell me you can give it back!"

"I don't know! I can't feel it anymore. Whatever magic the garden gave me, I used on the illusion." Barr looked down at his hands, where the ashen stains might as well have been blood. "It just came to me, without any warning. I didn't try to take the life from these plants. I didn't *ask* for it. They just *gave* it to me."

"Then you took too much." Seltruin was calmer now. He seemed confident Barr could undue the harm he had wrought. "You must try to return the *furie*. Relax your mind, and think back. The knowledge of how must be there inside you."

"I'll try."

Be careful, Aren warned. *If there's anything I can do to help, just tell me.*

You're both a help just being here with me.

Reaching his hands into the brown ash, up to both wrists, Barr sought deep within himself for the *furie* to weave a spell. He was already tired and aching all over, but he found the strength to slowly leak magic into the soil and dried remains. It bubbled up from his middle, like the trickle of a soothing stream, reached up and flowed down his arms. Letting the *furie* shape itself, Barr allowed it to be drawn from his body. He could feel the garden respond to his touch, felt its fingers caress his, then seep up both arms. Further it spread, trembling the hairs on his skin, and encompassed him fully with its grasp.

In that startling moment, he found the soil could be as greedy as giving. It longed for his *furie* with unbridled voracity and sapped it in painful waves that wrenched at his middle. Barr fought to keep a steady release, a slow trickle that would revitalize the garden enough that it would regain strength on its own. The effort weakened him, sent cracks along the barrier of his resolve. He held out for as long as he could, but when he felt his spirit beginning to crumble, he severed the link with an abrupt force of will.

"Barr?" Seltruin was holding him up, supporting his bone-weary frame. "Are you alright?"

He looked down at the rich soil that was no longer a thick blanket of choking ash. The plants and flowers were not fully restored, but they lived again and would mend. More green than brown ran the length of each stem, and broad leaves had regained their emerald luster. Colorful petals were nowhere to be found, but their promise of return could be seen in the buds that sprouted atop heavy green stalks. Their beauty would once more spread throughout the garden.

"I did it," Barr replied, looking all around him to be sure it was real. "I really did it."

I don't feel so good, Aren said with an uneasy voice that mirrored Barr's queasy stomach.

Neither do I, Idelle said. *I'm going to rest at my perch.*

"You did indeed." Seltruin helped him to stand. "Well done. The garden is a little worse for wear, but it will replenish itself in time. With proper sunlight, water and a good deal of care," he fixed Barr with in arched look, "things should be as they once were in no time."

"What exactly happened?" Barr asked, walking from the garden at a slow pace, refusing the offered arm. He was headed for his chamber, with no need to explain why.

Seltruin walked beside him; his manner revealed that he knew what repairing the garden had cost. "I was hoping you could tell me."

"I'm not sure. I was getting weak and needed to stop. I couldn't keep up the illusion anymore, even though I wanted to. Just before I was about to end the spell, there was a surge of new strength. I could feel it seeping into my hands and feet, like drawing warmth from a fire." Barr winced at a sharp pain in his side, but continued to limp along. "It felt good, at first. I felt... powerful."

The old Sage nodded in understanding "Tourners once took *furie* from those too weak to resist. They were often drunk with the power, obsessed with attaining it." He gave a sidelong look. "But you say you did not wrest power from the garden. It offered it to you freely."

"And I took too much," Barr replied, recalling his lack of restraint with a sick feeling. "If it happens again, I'll try to fight it, push it away. I felt horrible when I saw what I'd done. I won't let that happen twice."

"The damage was terrible," Seltruin agreed, "but you were not aware of what was happening. This merits further study. If you could learn to control the flow of magic, taking no more than was needed or what would cause harm, the potential for good would be great. I must admit such a thing is beyond me." He stopped and gently turned Barr toward him. "If you mastered this magic, I would be honored if you could teach it to me."

Tired as he was, that still perked his ears. Weariness faded momentarily, as he studied the old Sage. The fear Barr had once seen behind those blue eyes was gone and replaced with an eager hope.

"You want me to teach you?"

"Knowledge is knowledge," Seltruin answered with a smile, "regardless of its source. I would consider myself blessed, that my student should surpass me, if only for the opportunity to learn."

Barr hesitated, gauging the risk of being honest. He wanted nothing more than to be completely truthful with Seltruin and tell him of all the wonderful things he had learned. There was more at stake than their friendship, however. If others knew of Barr's true power...

He was reminded of his encounter with the Narohk.

"If I'm able to master the technique," Barr said, "then I'd be more than happy to teach it to you."

Seltruin winked. "That is all I am asking."

* * *

Barr slept all through the next day and woke in early morn, rested and aching much less. Tuvrin was already gone but had left breakfast on the table, fresh bread and sliced apples with cinnamon. Barr took a mug off the snowy ledge outside their window and filled it with berry juice from a clay pitcher. While he ate, a thought struck him, and he fetched both his kyan from the hearth. He pulled one from its sheath and studied the runes along its burnished surface while finishing his meal.

He had been meaning to rework the enchantments for a while, but there never seemed to be enough time in the day. The runes carved into the ironwood blades formed powerful wards that strengthened the weapons, made them resistant to the elements and could set them alight with a ghostly blue fire. Barr's kyan could slice through stone, like a hot knife through tallow, but they were neither indestructible nor impervious to magic.

At least not before Barr set to work on them.

Though a kyan was shaped to have a wide blade, its runes were thick and took up the entire polished surface. Focusing his will, Barr caused the runes to waver, as if seen through a great heat. The lines of each symbol quivered and shrank, moved in on one another and ran along the dark marble like a blackened quicksilver. When Barr relaxed his magical grip, he had nearly twice the room to work with. He immediately began to scrawl new runes into the opened space. Once penned, he used his own *furie* to forever burn them into the blade, infusing the wards with his will.

The endeavor left him tired, though nothing like what he had felt in the garden. He thought a walk through the forest would do him some good, so he headed toward the lift and down to the pens.

It's about time, Aren said, his voice on the edge of sulking. *I haven't eaten since last night.*

Idelle said, *You do realize that's why it's called breakfast? Or is the whole notion of fasting lost on you?*

This from the hawk that can eat her weight in one meal. You are bringing food, right? he asked Barr. *I don't mind hunting today, but I'm starving!*

Do I ever come see you without food? Aren wisely chose not to answer. *Alright then.*

It wasn't long before Barr and Aren were walking through the forest, enjoying the fresh snow and chill air, with Idelle flying overhead and swooping down from time to time. Winter was Barr's favorite season, in Darleman or any other place. Though he didn't have the inherent tolerance for cold the Sylvannis possessed, he made due with a set of fur-lined black leathers. Aren seemed to be enjoying himself too, romping through the snow like a puppy at play. His thick coat of midnight fur was riddled with frost, but the hound didn't seem to mind. Barr laughed at the antics, afraid to tell his big friend that his days of being a puppy were long gone. Their fun was interrupted by a warning from Idelle.

Orcs! she cried but made no audible sound. *Only three this time. I'll scout ahead to see if there's more.*

We're barely an hour from the city, Aren said.

Barr was already moving toward the orcs. *We'll deal with the Narohk later. Let's take care of these first.*

He stopped and knelt when he could barely spot them in the distance and motioned Aren to his side. The hound was already invisible, his form rippling beneath the waves of bending light. They moved toward their prey, with Barr trailing his fingers over the snow. The faint whisper of magic tingled his ears, as he smoothed away their tracks and all trace of their passing.

The guttural rasps and sharp tones could be heard before the faint smell of coppery blood reached his nose. The three orcs clomped their way along a deer path, swords sheathed at their waists and looking nowhere but forward.

That's a patrol, Barr said, *and not a very good one. The way they're just casually walking through the forest, they must have no idea there's an elven city nearby. Have you found anything yet, Idelle?*

Yes, but you won't like it. There's an encampment to the east, another hour from where you are.

How many of them are there?

Hard to say, she replied vaguely. *I can't see the ones inside the tents. How many are in a tribe?*

Barr groaned.

He was about to move on the orcs when Aren warned him to hold. The hound lowered his head and gave a quiet snort in another direction. Barr narrowed his eyes and saw what had drawn Aren's attention. There was a single orc perched in a tree, crossbow held ready to fire. He was hidden beneath a canopy of snow and branch meant to blend his form with the tree.

A sentry? It appears they're planning to stay a while.

Aren asked, *Do we attack this patrol?*

I'm thinking.

Barr slipped his bow down and gauged the shot before taking aim on the sentry. He was only fifty yards off, and the path was clear. He nocked an arrow and took aim, then waited for the perfect moment when both orc and tree were aligned. Barr let loose the ironwood shaft, muffling its sound with the same *furie* that guided its course. Snowy feathers blended its passing, and where the arrow struck true, it held fast through knotted branch and thick muscle.

With the sentry unable to shout a warning, his prone form looking as vigilant as before, Barr was across the distance and fast closing on the other three. He pulled low his dark cowl and sped over the snow, the edges of his cloak billowing out in his wake. To the orcs, he must have looked like a wraith spawned from the dark of a nightmare. He moved towards them with an unearthly speed and silence born of magic, while Aren circled left and around them unseen. Drawing both kyan as he ran, Barr uttered a single word, and both swords flared to life with a transparent blue fire.

A final burst sent him ahead with enough speed to make it seem as if he had disappeared from sight. A trail of blue fire shot between two of the orcs, ending a few steps away, to where Barr stood enshrouded in his cloak. Startled gasps escaped their pinkish lips, as both looked down at the chain mail covering their middles; the metal rings had been severed, sliced clean through and passed both muscle and spine. The one on the left moved to speak but could find no voice; he collapsed in a wordless heap. The other dropped to his knees, shaking his head and blinking as if to clear away the waking dream. He fell forward and laid silent as well.

Barr kept his back to the last orc, watching him from the corner of his eye. With a grunt, then a roar that shot spittle from his tusks, the orc drew his sword and looked ready to charge.

He never had a chance to attack.

Aren took the orc in full stride, slamming into his body with enough force to send him flying. He struck a nearby tree in an eruption of splinters, sending a spray of dark blood in a steaming trail over the snow. The orc slipped down the trunk and laid still.

* * *

It was an hour on foot before the encampment came into sight, though their smoke could be seen from a fair distance. Hidden by a dense copse of trees, Barr and Aren studied the area from afar, while Idelle glided quietly overhead. The orcs must not have been there for very long; makeshift shelters were all that stood. There was a fire in the center of camp, where a number of warriors sat along freshly hewn logs and ate from a spitted boar. More tents were going up, and a few women carried supplies from a train of wagons off to the east, where the trail became wide. All of their horses were penned near the wagons. Barr guessed that's all they were used for.

At least twelve orcs guarded the perimeter, in pairs and fully armed with both crossbow and sword. Barr saw two more tree sentries from where he crouched, and Idelle spotted another three on the far side. Not including the women, who shuffled about on their errands, he counted at least sixty orcs in the tribe.

They mean to stay, Barr said. *Let's see if I can't change their minds.*

Barr gathered his will and surrounded himself with it like a cloak of light, shifting and changing each detail, until the illusion was complete. He appeared exactly as the third orc had looked – down to the scars on its hands and talismans in its hair. He then projected another image, a mirror of himself but as the orcs he had just fought must have seen him: wraithlike and hidden in shadow. No matter where sunlight struck, the illusion turned it away, remaining shrouded in cloying darkness. Pointing an illusory crossbow at the shadow's back, Barr grunted like an orc and winked at Aren.

I need you to stay here, he said. *Be ready to come save me, if this doesn't work.*

Aren snorted. *I have no idea what you're doing.*

Trust me.

Barr pushed the shadow ahead, into the camp, a prisoner he could shoot down at will. Towards the fire the two marched, as orcs came rushing from all sides with weapons drawn and food left cooling in the snow.

"I found this in the woods!" he grunted in orcish, loud enough so that all could hear. Then he let loose a throaty laugh that shook his armor. His raucous mirth soon spread through the bloodthirsty orcs with the infectious blaze of a fire.

The shadow turned its cowled head towards him. Crossbows came up in an instant, a circle of death that threatened to take the creature where it stood. Barr backed away, blending in with the crowd, as attention switched to his ghostly captive.

Warriors tried to grab hold of the shadowy figure, but their meaty hands passed through the illusion. They gasped with a shock that soon turned to fear, and frantic calls for the shaman went out. Barr nudged an orc with his mind, tightening the warrior's hold on his crossbow.

The bolt shot out and struck an orc on the opposite side of the illusion.

A volley of more bolts sped out towards the shadow, as nervous hands fired by instinct. Orcs crumpled to the snow in lifeless heaps. Many were backing away now, their fear of being shot taking precedent over the dark apparition among them.

"What goes on here?" a painted orc demanded with a voice used to authority. He wore furs and a feathered skullcap but no armor to speak of. "Why is this prisoner not chained?"

Their language grated on Barr's nerves; the fact he understood it only made it worse. He knew from personal experience that orcish life was harsh and cruel. The way they chewed and twisted each word was a moderate reflection of that anger, a mirror of the society that based rank on conquests and measured their own worth by the number of enemies they had slaughtered.

"I found this on patrol," Barr told the tribe's shaman, bowing his head with the proper respect.

"Chain it up with the others." The painted orc turned to leave, but the assembled warriors shuffled their feet in protest. "What do you mean it cannot be chained. Do as I say!"

Another, much larger, orc stepped out from the main tent, his body riddled with scars and smears of dried blood. He wore two double-bladed axes at his waist, and by the size of his arms, he was no stranger to wielding them.

"What goes on here?" the chieftain asked, pointedly looking at his shaman.

"A prisoner, my chieftain. They say it is a spirit and cannot be chained."

The crowd parted for the large orc, as he moved towards the shadow. He tried to take hold of the dark prisoner, but his hands grabbed nothing but air. He drew an axe from his belt and slashed at the shadow's chest. That, too, passed harmlessly through.

"This is magic!" the chieftain sagely proclaimed and turned an accusing stare on the shaman.

"Yes, it is," the shadow spoke in their own tongue. "I have come here to make you leave." It looked around at the gathered tribe, as if studying their number. "One way or another."

"You control magic," the chieftain told his shaman. "Destroy this spirit!"

The shaman nodded and came forward. His arms shot out toward the shadow, with fingers shaped like claws. He closed both eyes and began to chant. Light flared from his palms and quickly turned dark, a mist of blackness that danced outward and up. The vapor clung to his arms like a cloud of midnight, a growing storm of hungry gloom. The chanting continued to grow louder, echoed through the air and pulled a tendril of black from each orc.

He's drawing power from them, Barr realized.

"Enough," the shadow said and waved a cloaked arm toward the shaman. The painted orc began to choke, as Barr's will wrapped around his thick neck with a deathly cold grip. The shaman clawed at invisible hands, fighting for air, and his magic instantly vanished. "You will do as I say," the shadow warned, "or all of you will die."

Barr could have easily killed the shaman, let the orc gurgle and choke while the entire tribe looked on. Magic was a greatly feared and misunderstood force in orcish society. A shaman was held in the highest regard, since so few had the patience or ability to learn the mystical chants. A shaman kept the tribe healthy and their food free of disease. He gave protection in battle by placing totems that conjured spirits, and he gave strength to the warriors through the bone talismans he forged from the fallen. The death of a shaman was a terrible blow to any tribe, and one who was murdered would be avenged at all costs.

Kill the shaman, Barr thought, *and I'd have to kill them all.* He doubted he had the strength to do that, even if they were helpless to fight back.

Come in now? Aren asked.

Not yet. I think this will work after all.

A wheezing intake of breath from the shaman let them all know the shadow had released its hold. The orc coughed and fought to speak.

"I cannot kill this," the shaman said, his voice a ragged whisper. "It is stronger than I."

"Then we are helpless." The chieftain growled, grinding his teeth. "What are you?" he demanded of the shadow. "Why did you come here?"

"I died here," the shadow explained. "This domain is my burial ground. It stretches for two days in all directions. Only those who have passed on may stay here with me."

An icy wind blew through the gathered orcs, circling their necks and catching in their throats. It raced up along their armor, numbing fingers until none could hold a weapon. The shadow raised its arms as if to encompass them all in its eternal and cold embrace.

"Join me in death, or leave this place now."

The orcs practically knocked each other down in their haste to get away. If it weren't for the chieftain barking orders, they would have left behind the entire encampment. With all due speed, they took down the tents and placed everything inside the wagons. It was a matter of minutes before the camp was packed up and on its way south – for no less than a two day trip.

And all the while, the shadow watched on.

* * *

Barr watched the wagons pull away from the camp with a sense of pride and a growing smile. He had used magic to outsmart an enemy, tricked them into leaving the forest without ever raising a sword. He had protected Geilon-Rai from an entire tribe of orcs. His actions had saved lives; there was no telling how many elves might have died if the two forces had clashed. What he was most proud of, however, was that he had resolved the situation without ever letting the orcs know there was an elven city nearby.

He was so pleased with himself that he almost failed to see bars on the wooden door of the last wagon. There was a pair of hands gripping those bars, and they were not the hands of an orc.

Damn, Barr said, *they have prisoners. I can't be sure, but I think one is elven.*

The orcs may not have known about the city, but if the captive was an elf, it might have explained why they had planned to stay. Orcs loathed nothing more than elves and took every opportunity to kill them – or worse. Barr sped after the wagon, his illusion intact, with Aren running invisible beside him.

It took only a moment to catch up. Two orcs guarded either side of the wagon, looking forward and to the trees as they marched but never once looking back. There was a heavy padlock on the door, one Barr was sure he could cut through with a kyan.

I have the right side, Idelle said.

Aren said, *Left for me, then.*

A little silence, please?

Barr poked his head around the right corner of the wagon and waved a hand slowly outward at the guard. *Furie* left his palm in the form of a small bubble, its clear edges reflecting light from the sun as it grew. By the time it reached the orc, the sphere was large enough to fully encompass him. The guard looked around suddenly, as if catching sight of something odd, but Idelle was upon him before he could speak. She swooped in from the side and soundlessly took hold, carrying him off without so much as a jingle of chain armor.

The guard on the left met with the same fate, but in a far different manner. The orc's head simply vanished from sight, right down to both shoulders. He stood there on the trail for the briefest of seconds, unmoving but for the struggling arms, then went altogether limp. The top of his body was still invisible, until Aren tossed him to the side.

Yuck, Barr said and cringed.

It was quiet, wasn't it?

Barr climbed up to the door and looked inside. What greeted his eyes was by far the most beautiful elf he had ever seen. She was a little worse for wear, sporting a bruise on her cheek and a number of scrapes along her arms, but those eyes. Only in illusion had he seen so vibrant a green hue or a gaze so bright with life. She had honey-colored hair that spilled down over her shoulders and ended in a braid beyond her waist. So enraptured by the curves of her face, the slope of her nose, the delicate turn of her chin, that Barr nearly forgot what it was he was there to do.

The Last Incarnation

The wagon loped along as he gaped.

Of course he knew her, had seen her many times before and admired her from afar – though she wasn't aware of it. Sage or no, Barr had no misconceptions about a relationship with an elf. There was little to no chance one would happen. Had he been an elf, his station might have afforded him an arranged marriage with Lorelei. But he wasn't. He was human, and that's all there was to it. There were a few girls who had shown him attention, but Barr knew they were more interested in angering their fathers or engaging in a secret affair of forbidden love. He had no desire to be with any of them. Lorelei, however, was another matter entirely...

Shaking his head, Barr focused on the task at hand. He put the tip of his kyan to the iron lock and slipped the blade easily through, catching the heavy pad in his left hand as it fell away. Stepping to one side, he opened the door as quietly as he could. There were still more guards by the next wagon. His eyes were unused to the dark and saw little when he stepped into the cell.

Odd, I don't see her –

Lorelei crashed into him, driving her shoulder into his middle and forcing the air from his lungs. Her arms wrapped around his waist and took him backwards, off the wagon and down to the snow. Together, they landed with a heavy thud, though Barr took the brunt of the fall.

He opened his mouth to protest but didn't have the breath to speak. His instincts took over when she tried to drive a large wooden splinter into his neck. Barr held her by the wrist, pinned beneath her thin frame, and was wondering what in the world she thought she was doing by attacking him. Her other hand balled up into a fist and slammed down to his cheek with a hollow crack.

Aren and Idelle watched on, seemingly amused.

Barr had just about enough of that and kicked her off of him, sent her tumbling over and behind him to sprawl in the snow. He was up in a crouch, ready to strike, before she could even cry out in surprise.

"Just what in the blazes do you think you're doing?" Barr asked her in elven.

She looked up at him with a puzzled expression. He then realized he had forgotten to break the illusion. For all Lorelei knew, he was just another orc. He cancelled the spell with a thought, his form shimmered, and he was once again himself.

"Do you recognize me now?" he asked. She looked at him and began to cry. "Lorelei?"

He helped her up and was nearly crushed by her embrace. She held on so tightly, shaking and crying, that Barr had no idea what he should do. With his nose buried in her hair, lost in the scent, he hugged back and did his best to comfort her.

"Thank you," was all she said.

– 13 –

When Barr pulled the First Narohk aside to speak privately, it looked to him as if Ceiran was not at all surprised by the visit. He had a practiced air of confident resolve that seemed to show he fully expected it. Barr already had doubts that any Narohk would purposely allow a deadly enemy near the city, even felt guilty for giving such a betrayal consideration, but the First's demeanor was not bolstering faith nor was it helping to dispel the notion.

Ceiran closed the door and took a seat. "You look upset. What seems to be troubling the Valar that you require my assistance?"

"I wanted to give you the chance to explain," Barr said with as much calm as he could muster. He had just seen Lorelei back home, and what she had told him left his middle twisted with a mixture of anger and fearful doubts. "I know you're aware of the orcs in the forest. I find it hard to believe that you could possibly *not* know of an entire tribe but a two hour walk from Geilon-Rai."

"There are orcs nearby?" Ceiran raised a brow in mild disbelief but made no move to alert the Narohk. "You saw a tribe of them outside the city?"

Doesn't seem very concerned, does he? Aren asked.

"That's right," Barr replied, his cheeks and ears growing flush, as hold of his calm began to slip. "Over sixty orcs walked right passed your archers, breached the city's perimeter and attacked a Ballar." The elf sat with his arm propped up and was worrying his lip with a finger. The way he just sat there, unmoved by the news, caused Barr to ball up a fist. "Well? What do you have to say for yourself?"

"There is nothing to say," he replied. "I assume you would not be here questioning me, if any risk to the city remained. Nothing I say will undo the harm that has already been done." He stood and smoothed the front of his leathers, looked down on Barr and added, "I assure you, I will deal harshly with whoever is responsible. Is the Ballar alright?"

"Lorelei is fine. Her bear Myah, however, was slain and devoured."

Ceiran briefly crinkled his nose in what might have been a wince, but more likely was one of distaste – as if he was more disturbed by the idea of eating bear meat than the fact that a companion had been killed.

"Terrible news," he said with no sign of emotion, "but at least your woman is safe."

"Excuse me?" Barr wasn't sure if Ceiran was simply mistaken or insulting him with the implication of a bond that was commonly known could never be. "Lorelei is not my woman. I rescued her –"

"Oh, I see. By the way you are always admiring her, I just assumed you two were together." Before Barr could even frown at the comment, he added, "So upon sighting this tribe of orcs in the forest, so close to the city as you said, you took it upon yourself to rescue the woman with whom you are infatuated, rather than return with all speed and report to the council. Does that about sum up your actions, Sage Barr?"

He's goading you, Idelle warned. *Just leave it be and go straight to the council.*

No, Aren said firmly. *I want to hear his excuse for allowing Myah to be killed.*

He will never admit to that.

"My actions were in the best interest of Geilon-Rai," Barr replied. "We wouldn't be having this conversation if you and your Narohk were performing their duty. Lorelei told me the orcs knew exactly where to find her, that they couldn't have just happened upon her. She believes that someone allowed the orcs into the forest unchecked and told them where she would be."

Ceiran's eyes hardened at the blatant accusation. "I am sure she tells you a great many things. Regardless, there are any number of Ballar and Maurdon out in the woods. These orcs most likely slipped through unseen by my Narohk for whatever reason no one else saw them. Tell me," he added, before Barr could counter the flimsy rationale, "how exactly did you solve this little problem? Did you slay them all with your Maurdon blades, Sage Barr? Or did you magic them away with your powers?"

Just go, don't answer –

"I tricked them into leaving." Barr put his hands to the pommels of each kyan. "I pulled Lorelei from a prison wagon as the orcs were headed out of the forest."

"Impressive. I am sure she rewarded you," he paused as if considering the right word, "appropriately. So you *tricked* them. How wonderful. And you of course followed them to make sure they truly left Darleman. Not that I am questioning your obvious wisdom or the confidence in your bag of tricks, but it seems strange to me that you would just let an entire tribe leave without thinking they might come back. Unless you were too distracted by the Ballar to give it a second thought. Quite understandable, she is a very attractive young elf."

The First's meaning was not lost on Barr. "I was neither distracted nor worried the orcs would come back. My only concern is what brought me here to you."

"You took a great risk in dealing with them yourself," Ceiran said, and there was no misconstruing his words for praise. "What if your little trick had failed? Did you consider what would happen if they took you captive? They would have tortured you and found out where you came from. You endangered all of Geilon-Rai with your reckless gamble."

He just assumes I'd break under torture, Barr said, knowing he was being distracted from the reason for his visit. *If he knew the things I could do...*

Stop right there, Idelle said sharply. *You're letting him control this conversation. Why are you here in the first place? No amount of words will bring Myah back.*

They could feel Aren's hatred seething through his words. *Ceiran needs to pay for his actions.*

That's not helping.

Barr said, "I didn't come to discuss how I handled your blunder. I came to give you a chance to explain how such a thing could even happen." Shaking his head, he added, "I don't yet have any proof that this failure of duty was deliberate –"

"It would be wise," Ceiran cut off the accusation, as if preventing the words from being spoken would make it untrue, "if you let me handle this matter. You say the tribe will not be returning. I will take it on faith that you are correct and forego alerting the council to your acting without their direction."

"You can't just keep this quiet," Barr said, raising his voice. "Do you understand that Myah has been killed? She wasn't just some pet, to be mourned and replaced in a few days. She was the companion of a Ballar! Are you so out of touch with others beyond your own party that you can't understand what that means?"

"I am sure you feel the loss as keenly as Lorelei," the First answered, again insinuating a relationship that just wasn't there, "but it would be in our best interest if this lapse was handled with discretion. I will take care of the Ballar. What is important is that the council not discover what you have done. After all, I may be removed as First, but I would not be sent into exile. On the other hand, you may never again see your elven father, or Seltruin, the dog and hawk you are so fond of, or even Lorelei."

What does he mean, Aren asked, *by taking care of the Ballar?*

I don't know, Barr replied. *I'm beginning to think he had something to do with this after all. Why else would he be so eager to cover it up? If it was just a matter of some Narohk neglecting their duties, Ceiran would be held accountable, but his punishment wouldn't be that harsh.* As much as it pained Barr to think of Lorelei losing her companion, he knew Ceiran would not have been made to answer for it. *No, he wants the council in the dark about that tribe. What I don't understand is why. Why would any elf have dealings with an orc?*

The same could be said of the tribe, Idelle reasoned. *Why wouldn't they just kill Ceiran? Besides, if the two were working together, that would mean the orcs might know of Geilon-Rai. The orcs you faced made no mention of elves and were all too eager to leave. I don't think even*

your ghost would have turned them away, if they knew there was an elven city nearby.
 You're right. Barr kicked himself inwardly, berating himself for a fool. Even Ceiran had seen the flaw in his plan. *Unless the orcs didn't really leave. It doesn't matter, I'd rather be exiled than allow any elves be sent to the slaughter.*
 Barr had been studying Ceiran's features, trying to read the true intentions beneath the mask of unwrinkled skin and hard eyes. In the end, he was left with but one choice to make.
 "Be prepared to face the council for your actions," Barr told him. "The Sylvannis can no longer afford their safety in your hands. I intend to do everything I can to have you removed as First of the Narohk." He returned Ceiran's stony gaze with his own. "Exile or no."
 Barr left without waiting for a reply.

* * *

 After telling the Speaker all that had happened, Barr felt better for knowing that Ceiran would be dealt with, but his stomach churned with the fear that the orcs had feigned their hurried flight. He went straight to the pens for Aren, and the two met Idelle out by the first eastern city marker – tree runes that appeared as odd patterns in the bark and haphazard knots, to those who didn't know what to look for.
 Barr saw the tracks, as Aren caught its scent.
 It was the wolf, and the tracks were still fresh. By the depth of each print, he guessed they were just minutes old. At one time, he might have been excited to see any trace of the creature, but the hunt had been turned into a game. Though Barr had never once seen the wolf, its presence was an all too common occurrence. As if openly

The Last Incarnation

taunting him, its tracks would appear as evidence it was close, but the prints always faded with no sighting. The magic that caused the wolf's tracks to smooth over and die out also stole its scent from the air. Barr had little choice but to play the game of cat and mouse, knowing one day they would meet.

It had always seemed to him the wolf once chose its victims with care. Lone hunters, frail women, children of any size, all were taken swiftly and without remorse once the chance to do so was there. Though its tracks were long gone before Barr could arrive, each tale he heard was much the same: mothers that only looked away for a brief moment, one who slipped into the bushes for a call of nature, a hunter off alone to clear his thoughts...

The patterns lately, however, had begun to change. No one but Barr made the connection, but it was there all the same, clouding his thoughts like a shadow of guilt. As if bringing new depth to their game, the wolf was choosing its victims in a disturbing new way; all had some kind of contact with Barr.

That's simply not true, Idelle said, searching for the wolf. *It only seems that way, because you know so many.*

It's more than that, Barr argued. *Paella and I were becoming friends, though I only saw her for a little bit, when she dropped off breakfast. And Teryn was stopping by to see me a few times a week.*

Didn't he have a fungus on his heels? Aren asked.

At first, yes, but even after that was treated, he came back to talk with me. Barr was both following the tracks and keeping watch for an ambush. *Uella was coming to me for herbalism lessons; Rhin always seemed to want some trinket enchanted, but I knew it was just an excuse to talk about her father.*

I thought that's what being a Sage was all about.

It is, Idelle added. *Why don't you just say what's really bothering you.* After a moment of silence, she said, *You think Lorelei will be next, and you're trying to blame yourself for that too. When will you understand that bad things happen all the time. It doesn't mean they're your fault.*

Barr's eyes went wide and stared straight ahead. He seemed unable to think or move.

The giant wolf was standing in the distance, its beryl eyes turned toward them with a feral gleam. Not fifty paces away, it stood watching and waiting, as if it was time for the mouse to make its move.

Barr snatched an arrow from his quiver without drawing his bow and flung the ironwood shaft from his hand. It shot forward with terrible speed, rippling the air like heat rising from the ground in deep summer. The sound of its leaving pierced the forest calm, and it zipped toward the wolf in the span of a breath. The arrow glanced its hind end with enough force to knock the wolf sideways. The creature yelped, but the arrow failed to pierce its black hide. Sent off in some other direction, the arrow struck a tree and splintered its trunk.

The wolf fled as two more arrows were loosed.

Idelle tried to keep sight of the wolf from above, but the trees were dense in that area and riddled with dark branches. Barr slipped his hand beneath Aren's collar and held on while the war hound gave chase. He tried to keep his body as close to Aren's as possible; the trees in this part of the forest were only a few feet around and were crowded together in the small valley. Barr lost sight of the wolf in the midst of their dodging tall trees, but Aren still had a grasp on its scent. They slid over the icy rocks and snow in a sharp turn, then Aren ran them with jarring speed toward a grove.

I've completely lost it, Idelle said, her tone both disappointed and apologetic. *I'm following you, instead. If any of us can catch the wolf now, it's Aren.*

Aren said, *There's only one way into that clearing, and nothing's coming out without heading straight for us.*

They reached the grove and burst through, pushing past a thick cover of dried brush. Twisted branches hung low and snatched at Aren's fur, but nothing short of a stone wall would have stopped him. The scent turned to the right, and Aren followed suit, swinging his bulk in a half-circle. Barr leapt to the right from his friend's back, drawing both kyan. He tumbled once through the air, and came down ready to strike. He had expected to see the wolf cornered in the small clearing, but was met instead by a much different breed of foe.

Ceiran slipped through the trees and moved toward them. His bow was drawn, and he leveled it at Barr. "He is here!" the First shouted. More Narohk made their way into the grove. "Remain still, *Sage* Barr. I will fire on you, if you give me cause."

Aren growled and crouched low. *They don't have enough arrows to take me down.*

"If he attacks," Ceiran warned, "I will be forced to order his death." Idelle's cry pierced the air, a warning in itself. "Make any move to resist, either you or your companions, and we will be forced to kill you all."

Ten painted Narohk stood ready to fire.

"I followed the wolf in here." Barr looked about as best he could but saw no sign of the creature. He put away both kyan and calmed Aren. "What's this about? You have no authority to arrest me, regardless of what it is you think I've done."

"We have been sent by the council to bring you back. You are accused of slaughtering Narohk Harduen." The First lowered his bow. "Luckily, we found you before you could escape. Will you come peacefully, or do we need to bind your hands and drag you back to Geilon-Rai?"

Harduen? Idelle asked. *We haven't even seen that imbecile today.*

Aren said, *This is some kind of ruse.*

"Harduen's dead?" Barr tried to recall the last time he had seen him and had a hard time placing the day. "How? What happened?"

"I think you know," Ceiran replied.

"This is ridiculous, I haven't killed anyone. After I left you this morning, I went straight to the Speaker." Barr gave Ceiran a meaningful glance. "I've been out here ever since. Unless Harduen was slain in the past hour, you're looking to the wrong person, and you're wasting valuable time."

"The council seems to think otherwise."

Do you still have the scent, Aren?

No, it's gone. Seems it doesn't matter now. We're done hunting, either way.

Go with them, Idelle said. *It should be easy to prove your innocence. Then you can help find who really killed him.*

I shouldn't have to prove *my innocence.*

"Alright," Barr said. "I'll go with you to the council."

As they walked back to Geilon-Rai, away from the clearing and dense trees of the grove, a single thought gnawed at Barr, numbing his mind to Harduen's murder. It didn't bother him the way it should have, that an elf had been killed, or even that he was being blamed for the deed. The silent hatred of those around him, the smug grin on Ceiran's face, it all went by his conscious thoughts in light of one incessant question.

What happened to the wolf?

– 14 –

Standing in the center of a rounded chamber he had never seen before, Barr faced the council once more and awaited his fate. While the elves did have petty crimes, a child taking something they shouldn't have or a quarrel escalating to blows, there was little to no serious offenses. Aside from the wolf that had been plaguing them for years, the death of an elf was mostly unheard of. Barr imagined he had never seen this room before, because the Sylvannis rarely had need of its use.

The fading light of day shone through windows to the west, throwing shadows against the far wall and casting the room in a golden haze. With both hands behind his back and a Gharak at either side, Barr stood before the council in the middle of a circle marked out by colored sand. A ring within a ring, its outer edge was filled with elven runes that had no grounding in magic. From what he could surmise, they were merely a call to the gods, a plea for truth and innocence to prevail.

Ceiran arrived through the only entrance, stepping hurriedly into the room. Rather than take his seat among the council, he came to stand within the circle and faced them. Beiron was with him and took a seat against the eastern wall. At Ceiran's nod, a Gharak placed a leather bundle at one end of the table. The advisor seated there unrolled the skin and took from it a single arrow, which he then studied at length. When he was satisfied, he passed the ironwood shaft along.

Barr saw blood smeared across its length. Though he couldn't see the markings carved into the shaft, he knew with a cold certainty that the arrow was his. His mind jarred back to the day he had come home and thought he saw his quiver swaying over the hearth.

Oh no. He glanced over at Ceiran with narrowed eyes and saw the truth of the First's smug expression. *I can't believe it. He killed Harduen.*

That's a bit much, Idelle said, *even for Ceiran. There has to be a reasonable explanation.*

Harduen is dead, and I'm being accused of having murdered him. That has to be my arrow. Barr watched the grave looks of each council member, as they turned over the bloodied shaft and studied its every feature. *The only explanation I can see is that someone stole that arrow from my room and used it to killed Harduen.*

Any of the Narohk could have done that.

Aren said, *Yes, but Ceiran is the most likely. Even if he didn't kill Harduen himself, he could have ordered one of the others to do it. Or maybe this has something to do with the orcs.*

I have no doubt about that, Barr said. *The same day I tell Ceiran I plan to have him removed as First of the*

Narohk, and I'm suddenly being accused of murder? Either he's trying to discredit me, so the council ignores what I've told Roedric, or this is his revenge for coming forward.

"As you can see," Ceiran explained, "that arrow bears the mark of Sage Barr. The blood is Harduen's. I pulled it from his heart myself."

"I did not fire that arrow," Barr said evenly. "There must be some kind of mistake."

"Were you not hunting when we caught you?" Ceiran pressed. He motioned for one of the Gharak to bring the arrow over to Barr. "Is that your mark upon its shaft?"

"Yes, of course it is. But I did not kill Harduen."

"Barr," Roedric said, "this evidence speaks volumes. How do you explain this?" He held up his hand to quiet the muffled whispers. "You do realize what will happen if this council finds you guilty?"

"I do," Barr answered. As absurd as the accusation was, if he was found guilty, his life would be forfeit. *And Ceiran would have killed me with his scheming as well.* "That arrow cannot possibly be enough to convince you that I killed Harduen. Anyone could have fired it."

"It bears your mark," Ceiran reminded him, his voice losing its edge of calm. "This is *your* arrow. No one but you could have fired it. There are many witnesses to your quarrel with Harduen, how he openly insulted you and the struggle that ensued. You cannot deny that you did harm to Harduen, breaking his wrist and refusing to heal it.

"No," the First went on before Barr could speak, his arm sweeping the chamber, "we all know the hateful mien of humankind. It is not enough to cause injury, to return insult for insult. You would not be satisfied until blood was shed. *Harduen's* blood. So you followed him to his post, knowing he could not fire back at you with his bow. How could he? You broke his wrist! And when he was alone, unarmed and helpless, you nocked this arrow, took aim on his heart and let loose with a vengeance swift and cruel as *human* justice."

Waiting patiently for the elves to quiet, Barr met the eyes of every council member, hoping that just once they would see beyond his round ears and come to realize the obvious. He could see Tuvrin and Seltruin were unmoved by Ceiran's words, but others were being affected. A few seemed already convinced of his guilt.

"My mark on that arrow means nothing." Barr gave a sidelong look to Ceiran. "Whenever I'm not hunting, I leave the quiver by the hearth. Anyone could have stolen it from my room."

"It is not enough to murder one of our finest archers, but he now insults the Sylvannis as a people. By his own admission, he sees all of us as petty thieves." A few of the council grew stern at the insinuation, as Ceiran brought home his point once more. "Humans may have reason to suspect one another of thievery, but we elves do not."

I don't think this is going well, Idelle said.

Well, this is ridiculous. Even if that wasn't my arrow, they'd be accusing me of it simply because I'm human.

"There are no doors in Geilon-Rai," Barr needlessly pointed out. "I'm not suggesting that every Sylvannis is a thief, but to assume everyone *isn't* would be just as absurd. Anyone could have walked into my room, taken that arrow from my quiver and killed Harduen with it. You prove nothing to me, Ceiran."

"Unfortunately," Landrin said, "the First Narohk has no need to prove anything to you. He is your accuser and is here to convince this council of your treachery."

Barr felt his cheeks redden in frustration. His father quickly spoke, no doubt to prevent him from saying anything rash.

"Did anyone actually see Barr kill Harduen?"

There was no immediate response. It was Beiron that finally answered.

"No," he said and swallowed hard as he stood. The Narohk looked as if he might wilt beneath the gaze of so many elders. Barr also noticed that he looked anywhere but at Ceiran. "I found Harduen out near siydaer pass, with an arrow piercing his heart from behind. I alerted my second and whistled for help. When we removed the arrow and saw the Sage's mark, we all set out to locate him." Beiron swallowed again, looked down at his feet, and added, "We found Sage Barr close by. He had both of his swords drawn and faced off against First Ceiran. The Sage had a wild look in his eyes, and I thought he might kill the First, as well."

With a nervous glance to Ceiran, the only time he looked at him at all, Beiron bowed his head and sat back down.

He's frightened, Barr said, *and not of me*.

"Thank you." Ceiran bowed to the young Narohk. He then addressed the council. "Sage Barr is clearly guilty. He had both cause and opportunity, and his markings on the arrow that killed Harduen cannot be refuted. It is my recommendation, as First of the Narohk, that he be stripped of house and rank. His punishment should be dealt quickly, or at the very least with the same swiftness that he dealt with Harduen."

"Without a witness to the act," Roedric said, "we have but one way to resolve this matter."

Barr groaned. "Not the Denshyar again."

Members of the council looked warily to one another, as if they feared even mentioning the previous incident. Seltruin cleared his throat and broke the uncomfortable silence.

"You may face your accuser," he said, "in a trial by combat. The gods watch over this circle and judge all who stand within. He who has their blessing will be found innocent and set free."

I don't like the sound of that, Idelle said.

Barr was afraid to ask. "And the one who doesn't?"

"Must die at the hands of the victor," Seltruin replied evenly, his eyes relaying concern to Barr.

He knows I'll win.

Seltruin? Aren asked. *He's no fool. And only a fool would think Ceiran stands a chance against you. Gods or no, there isn't an elf among them that can defeat you.*

Ceiran knows it, too. Barr shook his head, grasping what the First had planned all along. *Seltruin is worried I won't kill Ceiran.*

Idelle said, *You'll be exiled. That's what this is really about? He killed Harduen to get you exiled, so your word would mean nothing against his. The only proof that the orcs were here –*

Is Lorelei. Barr was suddenly worried for her safety.

"We will neither tolerate the taking of life," Roedric said in a grave tone, "*nor* the laying of false accusation."

"Don't you see how irrational it is, what you're asking me to do? In order to prove myself innocent of murder, I have to take the life of my accuser?"

The Speaker leveled a steely gaze at Barr. "Trial by combat has nothing to do with skill and everything to do with faith. You cannot kill your accuser; you can only be judged by the gods and enact their decree."

Tuvrin said, "Barr, you will be exiled if you go against the council and refuse to participate." His voice seemed to be pleading. "I know it may seem wrong to you that one of you must die, but you must put that aside and trust in faith. This is a very serious charge, and I cannot help you. If First Ceiran is incorrect, he will pay for the insult with his life." Tuvrin gave a look to Ceiran that seemed to say, *One way or another.*

"I will face him in combat," Ceiran said, all too pleased with himself, "sword to sword, and I will prove once and for all that this recreant human should never have been allowed to live among us."

The Gharak cleared the floor, and Ceiran moved to the west end of the room, where the light streaming in from the windows behind him would be to his advantage. A guard slid one of Barr's kyan across the floor. Ceiran drew an ironwood long sword and patiently waited for the trial to begin.

You have no choice, Aren said. *Think how much better off the Sylvannis will be once he's gone. Exile is not an option.*

He's right, Idelle said. *There is only one reasonable way out of this mess. Don't forget that Ceiran is the one who killed Harduen. He must pay for his crime.* Barr could hear the fear in her voice, as well as Aren's. If he refused to kill Ceiran, he would be exiled without them. *There really is no other choice.*

Barr looked to his father, as if for the last time. *There is always a choice.* He picked up the kyan and stood ready. *Even if we don't like either one.*

"As Speaker of the Sun," Roedric called out in a voice of authority, "I call upon Celene and her kin to bless us with your presence. Let the truth of this matter prevail."

Wasting no time, Ceiran charged forward, swinging his blade with unusual skill and speed for a Narohk.

"For Harduen," he said and growled with each swing. "You *will* answer for his death."

Their swords clashed in a quick succession of strikes that rang through the chamber, each swing a test of the other's ability. Ceiran had the benefit of a greater reach, but Barr was the faster and clearly better trained. He easily dodged and parried each attack, giving himself more time to think. His defensive posture only served to frustrate the Narohk.

With neither hate in his heart nor the presence of the gods, Barr could not bring himself to exact justice for a crime he wasn't absolutely sure Ceiran had committed. It was possible that someone else stole his arrow and killed Harduen, for any number of reasons, and found Barr to be the perfect scapegoat. Ceiran could be no more than a hateful elf that blamed humans for all his woes. That didn't necessarily make him a murderer.

Even though Barr tried no more than to keep Ceiran at bay, his reflexes acted out without thought. There were a number of cuts to the elf's wrist and forearms where Barr couldn't help but take the openings. There was no doubt that Ceiran was a practiced swordsman, but many of his moves were reckless. It was apparent to Barr that the First was purposely trying to lose.

Barr stepped to the side of an overextended jab at his shoulder and sliced Ceiran across the ribs; it was a much more grievous wound than he had intended.

Damn it.

"Alright, that's it." Barr sheathed his sword. "I will not take his life."

Ceiran's eyes went wide at seeing his opponent unarmed, and he stabbed with all his strength at Barr's middle. Barr turned and avoided the attack, spun about and grabbed hold of Ceiran's wrist with his left hand and broke the slender bones with a swift strike of his right. The elf cried out and dropped his sword, then fell to both knees and clutched his shattered wrist in disbelief.

"I'm not going to let you kill me, either." Barr looked to the council and saw the disappointment both Tuvrin and Seltruin shared. To Roedric, he said, "Do what you think is right, but I will not kill him. I was sworn to protect the Sylvannis at any cost, giving up my life if need be. I mean to keep that vow."

A Gharak took Ceiran from the room, and four others approached Barr from all sides. He handed the kyan back to one of them, a bright-haired elf named Intari. Barr had delivered the guard's daughter just five months ago. The child had tried coming into the world feet first, and Barr was forced to turn her about in the womb. There was a sadness in Intari's eyes, what Barr thought was a mixture of eternal gratitude and impending grief.

The Gharak's premature mourning did not bode well for Barr. *It's alright. I knew this would happen.*

"You were warned," the Speaker of the Sun said in an ominous tone. To the council he added, "Sage Barr of House Shintae has refused to abide by our customs. If he cannot honor our ways, he can no longer remain among us."

"Wait!" Tuvrin demanded, getting to his feet. "I will not stand by and let you cast my son out of the city. He is still just a boy!"

With a gentle hand, Seltruin urged Tuvrin to sit. "The Speaker might also consider that the Sylvannis will be left with no Sage in the future, if Barr is removed from the Valar. Though he has failed to prove his innocence, neither has Ceiran proven his guilt."

"You should know better than any that the trial is about neither." Roedric gritted his teeth and refused to give more thought to his decision. "Sage Barr, of House Shintae, of the Illumin Valar, you are forever stripped of house and rank, stricken from the Eondin Scrolls and exiled from Geilon-Rai. You will be sent from the city with nothing but the clothes on your back. You will not be allowed to take your companions with you. Go where you will, but never return here, on penalty of death."

No! The anger in Aren's voice was a palpable force, bordering on promised destruction. *They can't separate us. I won't let them!*

The Gharak moved to restrain him, but Barr held up a hand to stop them.

"Please," he said, more to Intari than the others, "Don't make me hurt you."

Fear and uncertainty took root in the their eyes. The four Gharak looked to the Speaker for orders.

Go to the western city marker, Idelle told Aren. *Meet us there, Barr. They can't keep us apart if we don't let them.*

"You go too far," Tuvrin said to Roedric. "Even if I allowed this to happen," there was no doubting the unspoken point, that the Maurdon answered to him first and the council second, "under no circumstance will you send Barr away without Aren and Idelle."

"That would endanger us," Landrin said. "If he tells others of where he has been, they will not likely believe him. Companions will only add credence to his story."

"Just so," Roedric said. "It is too dangerous for us to allow companions to go with him."

"You don't have a choice," Barr said with great calm, hoping the council would see to reason on this one point. "I will honor your wishes and leave Geilon-Rai, but I do so on my own terms. You can test my powers, if you feel the need, but I imagine Seltruin would advise against it." He let his gaze fall upon each council member, though more gently on Seltruin and his father. "I would like to keep my vow and do no harm to the Sylvannis, but if you force me to act, I will hold you all responsible for the consequences."

The Speaker looked dubious. "Seize him."

"I am sorry," Intari said to Barr and took hold of him by the arm. The other three grabbed hold as well.

"So am I."

The Gharak were thrown by some unseen force and crashed into the walls far behind them. They each slid to the ground and were still.

"Barr," Seltruin said, rising slowly from his seat. Barr could feel his fear from across the room, like a tangible scent in the ether. "You have proven your point, there is no need –"

A stream of fire rose up from Barr's feet and circled his body like a coiled snake. The crimson trailers of flame danced about like salamanders at play, as they reached up toward the ceiling in a column of flickering light. The council recoiled from the waves of intense heat, some shielding their eyes from the burning air on their skin, while others forced themselves to look on.

"Do I have your attention, Speaker of the Sun?" Barr asked, his eyes ablaze with the fiery magic, his hair billowing out in the searing tumult. "Will you risk your city here, at this very moment, or later when I leave with my friends?"

Embers began to flash all about Roedric, as if the very air that surrounded him were catching fire.

"Go then!" he yelled, his eyes tightly closed. "Take your damned companions and your infernal magic with you!"

The severe heat died away to a whisper of warmth, but its touch was forever imbedded in their minds. The helix of fire ceased its ascent and faded, leaving wisps of telltale light around Barr. He held a hand out and fed the tree *furie*, healing the scorch marks on the floor and ceiling.

"Just remember," Barr told the council, his eyes on Speaker Roedric, "it didn't have to be this way."

He turned and quietly walked from the room.

* * *

Arianaolis stood within the darkness of the mists, a place of starry sky and forever water that lapped against her. She knelt in its warm embrace and watched Barr before the assembled Sylvannis. Though her fingertips caressed the image of her grandson, the scene within the blackness did not ripple.

"The Seers warned you not to interfere," came a voice from out of the great distance, across the inky stretch of cloying haze. It was her daughter, of course. As Matron of the Guiding Mists, Daesidaoli saw all within her realm. "Why do you toy with our future?"

"He is your son," Ariana said. "I can feel our blood run through his veins. I have waited so long just to see him, and now that I know where he is –"

"I want him to be with us as much as you do. He is my son," the voice echoed, reverberating its sorrow. "The Seers were clear. He will come back to Faeron in his own time. Any sooner or later may cause the prophecy to fail."

And endanger the future of all worlds, came the not so distant memory of her conversation with the Grand Seeress.

"I will not tell him who I am," Ariana explained, at last giving voice to the plan she had been formulating for days – ever since she first discovered her grandson yet lived. "The bracer has been in our family for generations. It has the heart of Faeronthalsos within it."

"Mother, you cannot." Daesi's voice was softer then, lacking in conviction. "Any contact at all, whether he knows you or not, could alter the path he walks."

"The bracer will protect him. He is being driven from his home with the elves," Ariana said, unable to hold back her tears any longer. The pain of being within reach but not able to touch him was simply too much to bear.

"It will take care of him. After all this time, Aislin may even lead him back home."

"What of the warning? The prophecy may or may not come true, but the Seeress said giving him Aislin would put his life at risk."

Ariana watched Barr walk away from the council. "If you saw what he can do, you would not believe the warning either. When you return from Danarriden, you will have time to see for yourself."

"Fezuul sends his love."

"Of course he does." Ariana waved off the image in the water, ending her scry, and touched the tips of her fingers to the mithrinum bracer at her wrist. Aislin was warm to the touch, and thrumming a melodic tune in her ears. "Arch Demon or no, he is a fool all the same."

"True," Daesi agreed, "but he is your fool, not mine."

– 15 –

Barr went back to his room to pack what few things he wanted to take with him. There were some shirts, his summer leathers, an engraved portrait of he and Tuvrin, and his herb kit that was a gift from Seltruin. His Sage's robe hung from a peg by the hearth. Aside from his kyan and bow, there was little else left he called his own. All of the books and scrolls along the shelves belonged to the Sylvannis.

Barr left those behind with the robes.

We're waiting for you, Aren said, *and we're alone.*

I'll be there soon. You don't have to worry. No one will be following us.

We'll see about that.

Tuvrin cleared his throat before entering, a moment Barr had been dreading since his performance before the council.

"I'm sorry," Barr said right away.

"No, no apology is needed." There was sadness in his eyes, but pride as well. "I had no idea you could... that you had become so powerful."

"I didn't want to make anyone uncomfortable." What he feared all along had come to pass, the nervousness in their eyes, the cautious manner in which they dealt with him. He saw it in Seltruin at the trial. Even Tuvrin didn't seem to know what to make of Barr now. "I hid my new powers, from you and everyone else, because I knew how others would react. It was bad enough just being human, where most people only hated me. Now everyone's afraid of me too."

There was no hesitation when Tuvrin hugged him, putting to use that elven strength in a warm embrace. Barr held his father just as tight, knowing this was their goodbye. When they parted, Tuvrin gripped him by both shoulders.

"I was never afraid of you," he said. "Only for you."

"The way Seltruin looked at me." The leather pack felt heavier in his hand, as if he were hefting an added burden. *It's probably just as well that we're leaving.* "He was so frightened."

He still cares for you, Idelle said. *Maybe you can pen him a note later and explain. I'll bring it to him after all this has settled down.*

"You most likely took him by surprise. Or perhaps he was just afraid for the others. The Speaker is known to be stubborn. I for one am glad you left him no choice." Tuvrin went to the drawer he kept his clothes in and brought out a leather pouch the size of his palm. Coins jingled from within as he passed it to Barr. "This is for you. It should be more than enough for a comfortable life in Alixhir."

Pulling open the drawstring, Barr was amazed to see mithrinum, platinum and gold coins from a number of different realms. It was by no means a small fortune, by any standard. He imagined it must have taken Tuvrin quite a while to amass such a treasure.

"I can't take this," Barr said and tried to give it back. "I don't deserve it. I've disgraced our family name today. All because I wouldn't kill Ceiran. How strange is that? Here I am, being accused of murder, and when I don't kill my accuser, I get exiled."

"You did the right thing, Barr. Any other outcome would have made matters worse. There is no doubt in my mind that your arrow was stolen. What troubles me is why Harduen was killed."

"We both know why," Seltruin said from the door. "To dishonor Sage Barr before the council. It was the only way to ensure they would disbelieve his charge against Ceiran. Unfortunately, it worked."

With a respectful bow, Barr said, "Sage Seltruin, I –"

"There is nothing to say," Seltruin interrupted and waved off any attempt at apology. "I came only to see off my fellow Sage and to tell you it has been my honor to both teach and learn from you. I will admit, you took me by surprise in the council chamber." The old elf looked sheepish when he smiled. "I realize now that if anyone should hold such power, it is you. I am proud to call you friend, Barr, now and always."

"I was lucky to have you as a mentor. I just wish we could have had more time together. I don't want to leave Geilon-Rai." Barr was more worried for them than he was for himself. "What of Ceiran? And the orcs?"

"Both will be dealt with," Tuvrin promised. "The best we can hope for is that Ceiran will be replaced as First of the Narohk. As far as the orcs, Ballar and Maurdon have been sent to secure the forest. I was sorry to hear about Myah; she was a magnificent bear."

She was the strongest of her litter, Aren said with some pride. *Of the bears, I think I liked her most.*

"I can't imagine how Lorelei must feel." Barr hated to think what his life would be like without Aren or Idelle. It made him wish he could somehow comfort Lorelei and ease the pain of her loss. "If there's anything I can do to help with the orcs, I'd be happy to lend a hand."

Seltruin gave a reproving look. "As much as your aid would be appreciated, you know it cannot be accepted. Your exile means more than simply leaving Geilon-Rai. Once gone from the city, you must never again have contact with the Sylvannis."

Just hearing it out loud caused a pang in his heart. For seven years, every aspect of his life revolved around the elves and their city in the trees, learning to care for the health of both, to keep them safe, to put their lives above his own. He did so gladly. Barr had a love for the forest and of the Sylvannis as a people that he knew would never be returned. That didn't make his being a Sage mean any less, however, and at times made it more fulfilling in those moments when he saw others truly appreciate his work.

Tuvrin said, "I will miss you, Barr, but it is for your own good that you put Geilon-Rai behind you now. You cannot give in to the temptation to return." He gave Barr one last hug. "You will always be my son; no scroll can tell me otherwise."

"You may no longer wear the white robe of a Valar," Seltruin said with a friendly pat to the back, "but you will forever remain a Sage. No decree can take back what you have learned here."

"Thank you," Barr said to both of them. There was so much more he wanted to say, to thank them for all the time and effort they put forth on his behalf, but he had difficulty finding words that would suffice. And time was growing short. He knew the longer he stayed, the harder it would be to leave. "I'm going to miss you both."

With that said, he slipped the pouch of coins into his pack and headed out the door.

At least I'll have you two with me. Barr stepped onto the western lift for the last time and was lowered to the forest floor by two solemn Gharak. *If I can't stay here in Geilon-Rai, the next best thing would be to take a part of it with me.*

The word *home* played through his mind, but it no longer held the same meaning. Home was a tangible something that others had and took for granted, a place that offered them comfort and refuge. To Barr, home was not just a place but a notion. It had become more than a hole carved out of the ground, more than a collection of stones or piled wood. It was an impression that gripped his heart and filled his spirit with a sense of belonging, a warmth that lent him hope and the assurance all would be well. It was the very same feeling Barr had when he was with Aren and Idelle.

Home would follow him wherever they went.

* * *

When Barr stepped off the lift, he could see Ballar in the pens picking up debris left behind from Aren's hasty departure. He chuckled at the thought of any war hound being thwarted by wood and rope. It was only rigorous training that kept a companion from leaving his stall whenever the mood struck.

What exactly are you implying?

Nothing, Aren. Barr chuckled again. *You're just too big for this world, is all.*

"Be on your way," Ceiran said from behind, "and be sure never to come back. It would be a shame to have to kill you after having spared your life."

Barr raised a brow. He noticed the elf's wrist had been healed and guessed Seltruin must have done it. He had an irresistible urge to break it again.

"You spared nothing. If memory serves, it's I that did the sparing."

"I think Harduen would beg to differ."

"Speaking of begging," Barr said without missing a beat, "did he beg for his life before you shot him, or did you sneak up behind him and take his life without a sound?" He moved closer to the arrogant elf, taking small pleasure in the stifled fear he sensed. "Isn't it strange that you sent a Narohk on patrol, with a broken wrist, all by himself? If you hadn't killed Harduen, the wolf surely would have."

"There were worse things out that day than the wolf."

Already bored with the game, Barr jumped right to the question that was plaguing his mind.

"What do the orcs really have to do with all of this? Either you're working together with them and told them where Lorelei would be, or you're truly incompetent and killed Harduen to cover up the mistake." Barr saw the glitter of machination behind his eyes but had no way of knowing for certain, one way or the other. "You knew I'd go to Roedric and tell him how you let a damn army slip past your patrols. The only way to make the council doubt my word was to convince them I'm a liar. Well, there are Maurdon and Ballar out looking for that tribe right now, and when they find them, your days as First Narohk will be numbered."

Seemingly amused, Ceiran said, "A lively tale. Does it help you sleep to deceive yourself so?" Without giving Barr the chance to retort, he went on with a wave of his hand. "No more words, human. I can only stomach so much. I came to give you a final warning. If you come within the boundaries of Geilon-Rai, the Narohk will not rest until arrows fill your corpse. Make no mistake, I hate you and your kind with a passion you cannot begin to conceive. Nothing you do or say can account for the blood you humans have shed."

"Noble words from the mouth of a killer." Barr turned to leave, but stopped and said over a shoulder, "Here's a warning for you, elf. If we ever cross swords again, I'll do much worse than break your wrist."

Ceiran gave a wicked grin. "Where strength and skill fail, there is always guile. Pray to your gods that our paths do not cross. You will not like the outcome."

Idelle said, *I'd love to dump him in an icy river.*

Is that all? Aren asked. *Why give him something so soft to land on?*

Barr laughed and walked away, with the fiery gaze of a frustrated elf burning a hole in his back.

"By the way, Aren and Idelle send their love."

* * *

Lorelei caught up with Barr as he was leaving. He moved at his own pace, ignoring the four Narohk that were following him along the path. Though they kept a fair distance, he knew why they were there. Barr could still see the sadness in Lorelei. Her eyes were red and a bit swollen from crying; her hair had slipped loose from its braids.

"I hope I never looked like that," Lorelei said, noting the unbridled hatred each archer had for Barr. "I never did understand the Narohk, but then again, I am sure they say the same of the Ballar."

"I've gotten used to it. Tell me, how are you doing?" He couldn't bring himself to say the words.

"Without Myah?"

Barr looked as if he were the one that had lost a dear friend. Lorelei was right, though. Few understood the tie between the Ballar and their companions, but Barr was intimately familiar with the bond.

"I wish I could have found you sooner."

"Without you," she said, "I would not be here. I fear to think what the orcs might have done, considering how they –" She swallowed the words. Barr agreed they were better off left unsaid. "Now I have a chance to avenge her. The Ballar have been sending groups out to look for the tribe. I will be joining one later this evening. Will you be returning to Alixhir?"

"I'm still debating." He glanced back at the Narohk and wondered how far they planned to follow. "Honestly, I was thinking of looking for the tribe myself. Hmm, how's your cheek? That bruise has gotten noticeably blue. Let me have a look."

In a brief moment, all her scrapes and bruises were healed, and the sigh of relief she exhaled caused Barr's heart to skip a beat. All too aware of his hand against her cheek, he let her go with a nervous smile. Lorelei absently touched where the bruise once colored her fair skin.

"I came looking for you, because I wanted to thank you again before you left. I have heard some awful things about you, but I know they are untrue."

When their eyes met, Barr saw in her look something more than just gratitude. A part of him wished that what he saw was attraction, while the more vocal remains put that thought from his mind. Discovering she had feelings for him, on the day he had no choice but to leave, would be nothing short of torturous. Yet that foolish other part couldn't help but grasp at the hope.

Ask her to come with us, Aren said.

Shush!

"Of course it's untrue," Barr said. "I'll admit that I didn't particularly like Harduen, but I didn't wish him any harm. No matter what others might say, I know I didn't kill Harduen; and that means someone else did." He paused to consider the best way to warn her. "Lorelei, I want you to be careful of Ceiran. I don't want to make accusations without proof, but I have a strong suspicion that the tribe of orcs so close to the city and Harduen being killed are in some way linked." He reached out for her hand and hesitated. When she slipped her fingers in his, relief flushed his cheeks with warmth. "I wish I could stay, if only for the chance to get to know you better."

"I would have liked that very much. No one has ever cared enough to risk their life for me, like you did." She squeezed his hand in what felt like goodbye. "You are a good man, Sage Barr. I am only sorry it took this long for me to realize it."

Barr looked up to gauge the time and reluctantly met her gaze. "I should get moving. I think I'm agitating our archer friends."

"Where will you go?"

"I thought about visiting my uncle in Alixhir, but I'm not sure it's a very good idea. It might be best to leave some things in the past."

"You should go see him," Lorelei said, moving closer. "Family is very important. As are friends."

His body leaned in of its own volition, craving more of her touch. *I could easily fall in love with her.*

Idelle mused, *What makes you think you haven't already?*

The Last Incarnation

After what seemed like an awkward eternity, Lorelei put both arms around him in a warm and delightfully tight embrace. Barr's stomach danced to the flutter of a thousand tiny wings. With both arms about her waist, he pressed his face to her neck, and his nose became awash in her scent. His eyes closed, bare skin against hers, the feel of silken hair, Barr was soon lost to the moment he hoped would never end.

When they parted, she kissed him on the forehead, a lingering touch that burned him with yearning. He could still feel the memory of her lips pressed against him when the Narohk called out from behind.

"That is enough!"

Barr turned sharply, his hand to the hilt of a kyan by reflex. The four painted archers stood with bows drawn, and two of them were trained on Lorelei.

"You were ordered to leave," another said. "And yet here you are, contaminating one of our women."

The first scoffed and added, "Are you so foolish as to think she could ever desire you?"

Lorelei blushed, betraying her true feelings.

"What I do," Barr told them, "is no concern of yours. I suggest you leave now, or –"

"You will kill us?" the Narohk finished for him. "Yes, we know only too well how you handle your problems, Barr of Alixhir." The others laughed at his insult. "Would you like to see how we handle ours?"

Barr swung his arm out towards them in an arc, his palm outstretched and will brought to bear. Their bows, arrows and all, flared to life with an intense flash of light. The magic burned through leather gloves and the pale skin beneath. All four Narohk cried out in pain and would have dropped their weapons, had the ironwood not simply fallen away in the span of a breath. The ashen remains were carried off on the wind, in a shower of gray mist and drifting flakes.

The elves scampered back up the trail, frightened eyes glancing back, as they ran with hands clutched to their chests in an attempt to quell the pain.

Barr's anger died away with a sigh. "I'm sorry you had to see that. I was afraid they might hurt you."

"I have never seen anything like that," Lorelei said, and when she turned to face him, her smile brightened with the wonder of a child. "That was like a story book come to life. Have you had such magic this whole time?"

"More or less."

You'll regret it, if you don't ask her, Aren said.

"The council is foolish." She looked upset, though not at Barr. "My father included. To think a devoted Sage with your power would kill anyone, let alone with an arrow, is absurd. Is there any way I could change their minds?"

His laugh came unbidden. "Sorry, no. What I did in the council chamber... Let's just say that bridge is burned." He gathered the courage to ask, "Would you like to come with me?"

The silence was painfully long.

"Yes," Lorelei said at last, "but I cannot. Everything I have ever known, my family, my friends, are all here in Geilon-Rai. To leave them behind is too much. Not to mention the danger of an elf in human lands."

"I hadn't thought of that. It's alright, though. I was just being selfish."

I'm sorry, Barr, Aren said. *I really thought she would come with us if you just asked.*

"Not selfish, I would –"

"I have to go," Barr said abruptly and turned to go.

"Wait!"

Lorelei turned him about and kissed him softly. Their lips touched for only a brief time, breath commingled in a moment of shared desire, a taste of bitter yearning in one another. There were tears in her eyes when she finally pulled away...

And walked out of his life forever.

– 16 –

Barr met up with Aren and Idelle a few moments later. They were patiently waiting beside the city marker, where its runic pattern in the bark stood out more than usual beneath the fading light of day. Though saddened by the enormity of what he was leaving behind, his family and friends, the only home he had known for many years, the Sylvannis and their enchanted city in the trees, the sudden prospect of love from where he had never hoped to find it, seeing Aren and Idelle lessened that burden of sorrow he brought with him. He could still feel Lorelei on his lips, but the pain of seeing her go was beginning to diminish.

At least we have each other, Idelle said and nuzzled Barr with her head.

Running fingers through her downy feathers, he gave her a hug and endured Aren's wet nose pushing in for attention. With a chuckle, Barr let Idelle go and hugged the big hound as well.
We'll always have each other, he said. *Wherever we decide to go, we can at least be certain of that.*
Alixhir? Aren asked. *I've never seen a human city.*
Not yet. I think we should make camp for the night, before it gets much colder, then go see if that tribe really left.
I haven't eaten since morning.
And you still have the strength to stand? Barr ruffled Aren's hair behind an ear. *Let's get some more distance between us and the city before you go off hunting. Then I'll gather wood for a fire and see if I can't coax a temporary shelter from the trees.*
Idelle said, *I'll go scout ahead and find us a good spot. It would probably be best to stay away from any of the sentry points.*
It was getting dark by the time Idelle found them a place to rest for the night, a half-circle of dense trees that would make them difficult to spot from the east. She also caught sight of a lone boar rooting for food a few minutes away. Aren left to get dinner, while Barr started picking up any dead branches he could find and stacked them into a pile for the night.
Once he had a small fire going, he approached the trees they intended to sleep by. Individually, they were not very wide; Barr could slip his arms around one and nearly touch the tips of his fingers together. Densely grown side by side, however, the collection of trees would make a perfect shelter for the night.
Barr slipped off his leather gloves and placed a hand on two different trees. Through them, he could feel all of Darleman, from the depths of every gnarled root to the

heights of each knotted branch. They were all connected, made one by the touch of a single enormous tree. Called the Niyaen by the Sylvannis, the Pillar of Life, it was also known as the Great Tree. It was the center of Geilon-Rai, a sentient tree with a root system that stretched far and wide throughout the forest. Like a multitude of fingers, those roots were interspersed with every other tree; it lent strength to their limbs and the vitality to keep sickness at bay. It provided warmth for the elves and life to the forest, but more than that, it gave the means to mold trees into any shape.

Insinuating his will through touch, Barr was able to speak with the Niyaen, though neither of them ever used words. It whispered in his mind like the breath of a wind, a lilting sway of leaf on the breeze. He let it fill him from within, reach into every wide chasm and dark crevice of his spirit. It washed over the silver water of his will, read desire on its surface and saw to his needs.

Acting on his wishes, the trees began to change.

The leafless branches overhead arched forward and down, providing cover from any snow that might fall. A gentle warmth rose up and stretched out from the trees, melting ice from their trunks and clearing the blanket of snow from the ground. Moisture seeped into the soil and was gone, leaving the earth dry and inviting. When a cold wind blew through and set the fire to dancing with a wild flicker of complaint, branches twisted their fingers into a timber weave that shielded all trace of the bitter gust.

Thought of Tuvrin came to mind in a flash of brief wondering, and an image of him hunting came to bear. Barr could see his father with a group of Maurdon, felt them in the woods far to the south and on an easterly course through aeryn grove. He knew they were looking for the orcs. Barr let the image expand and sensed a number of search parties, Maurdon that kept watch for sign of the orcs and Ballar that strode through the forest with a brazen air. War bears and hounds moved in step beside them, ready to pounce at any moment. Even further out were the Narohk, patrolling the woods from its branches, their eyes scouring the snowy floor for any danger.

Though he only glimpsed the shadow in passing, he felt something amiss in the forest. Tracing back toward the unsettling darkness, Barr realized what he sensed in that miasma of hatred was the tribe the Sylvannis were hunting. The orcs were hidden in a sanctuary, just a day from the city. It was a haven for Narohk, a place to go for supplies or rest when needed, so they could replenish strength without returning to Geilon-Rai. A waterfall ran through the center of the hidden grove, and the only way in was the cave tunnel behind that fall. Barr doubted the tribe had stumbled in there by mistake. Whoever they were working with must have told them how to find it, and the orcs were now biding their time.

The Niyaen sensed a more pressing danger and made Barr aware, sent the image reeling through the trees to rest just outside his small camp. Five Narohk were there, skulking through the branches overhead and came to perch in the quiet dark. They each nocked an arrow and took sight on Barr, no doubt hoping to catch him off guard.

Narohk! Aren yelled out in warning, as he returned from his meal. *I can smell them in the trees!*

I see them now, Idelle said and took flight.

Barr said, *Leave them to me.*

Gnarled boughs became wiry and alive, from the tips of their branches to the end of every limb. They moved with purpose, like the grasping fingers of a hand, and swiftly took hold of each elf. Wrapping around both ankles and wrists, legs and arms, waist and neck, the limber branches were more like living vines and soon had a firm grip on the Narohk. Their bows fell from numb hands and tumbled downward, with not a single arrow being fired. Crying out in shock, horrified that the forest would turn on them, the elves fought to break free but to no avail. They were helplessly trapped, unable to move, captured by the very trees they made their home in.

"Do you understand now?" Barr asked with a calm and patience beyond his years. "Being called Sage means more than just bearing the title. The council can take the name from me, but the power is still mine." A wispy end of branch by each elf whipped out and struck a cheek in quick succession, marking their pale flesh with the elven symbol for traitor. "I'm going to let you go, so you can return to Ceiran and show him how useful his guile is. Tell the First that he can come face me himself, and let your brother Narohk know that the next time I see one of them, I will not be so gentle."

The branches tightened their hold, eliciting choked screams, then let the elves fall unceremoniously to the ground. They picked themselves up and ran east with all speed, back home to Geilon-Rai, with failure etched in their skin.

Barr severed his connection with the Niyaen.

I don't know why I'm surprised, he said and put his gloves back on. *I should've known Ceiran wouldn't leave well enough alone. This just proves he's behind Harduen's death.*

What about the Narohk? Aren asked in a rumbling tone. *There were five of them, and they were all willing to follow Ceiran's orders to murder a Sage!*

They might've thought they were exacting revenge. Not that I condone their actions, but it'd at least explain why they'd want to kill me. I'm still convinced that Ceiran shot Harduen himself, though.

You know, Idelle said, *this could have all been just a ruse. Ceiran had to know they would fail. He's hoping you'll return to Geilon-Rai and accuse him of trying to kill you, maybe use it as proof to clear your name.*

And the penalty for returning is death. Barr shook his head at the devious scheme. *Ceiran always was a tricky one. Speaking of which, his orcs are still in the forest. They're holed up in deila falls.*

That's a Narohk sanctuary.

Aren snorted his disgust at the treachery. *Do we go now or wait until sunrise?*

We wait, Barr replied, *but we're not going to attack. I want to find out exactly what it is they're doing and make sure it's Ceiran they're working with.*

I should fly back and tell Seltruin, Idelle said. *No matter what we find out, the council needs to know that the orcs are still here, and the Narohk have done nothing about it.*

Alright. But not until I speak with their chieftain.

* * *

Barr woke early the next morning, hours before light broke through the trees. A nearly full moon covered the forest in its silvery haze. He put out the dying embers of the fire with snow and began packing away his bedroll. Aren opened his eyes at the faint hiss and cloying smoke. His sigh was either one of longing for more sleep or regret over the loss of whatever dream he had left behind.

About breakfast, no doubt.

Be nice, Aren said. *I'm still not completely awake.* He rose and stretched with a mighty yawn then looked about the camp, as if something were missing. *Did you say something about breakfast?*

Yes, I said we'd be skipping it. I want to get to deila before dawn.

Idelle was already in the air. *Be careful of patrols. I'll let you know if you come close to any Narohk.*

Stay far above the tree line, Barr warned. *If they spot you, they'll know we're nearby.*

While Aren could use his collar to become invisible, if only for a short time, the enchantment woven for Idelle was much different. It enabled her to fly faster than her size would normally allow and at heights where the air grew thin. Though her vision was keen, it was even more so with the collar. She could soar from a vantage unseen by those on the ground and still see the color of their eyes as they looked up.

Don't worry, they won't see me. You just make sure they don't see you.

With his fingers trailing *furie* behind, Barr smoothed his tracks from the snow, as they made their way to the northeast. The stealthy precaution slowed their pace, but he thought it better to move without notice than deal with being spotted. With eyes to the branches above as they went, they both watched for Narohk that might slip past Idelle, unlikely as that might have been.

Sentry coming up on your left in five minutes.

Aren faded from view, a wavering of dispersed light, like heat rising off a fire. Continuing their cautious pace, using the trees as cover, they approached the tree sentry rather than avoid him. When the Narohk became visible as a distant shadow in the tree, Barr stopped and took off his gloves.

Hold on, he told Aren.

With one palm pressed flat to the tree on his left and the other hand outstretched, he drew *furie* from the soil and roots beneath. Snow began to melt from the warmth, as a haze of magic rose up from the ground and set the hairs on his arm to standing on end. He only took what was needed, a whisper from a storm, and channeled it through the trees with his will. Scrying the Narohk for an unobstructed view, Barr watched the painted elf yawn and fight vainly against the sudden burden of heavy lids.

Alright, he's asleep. Let's go.

There were four more sentries on the way that either similarly took a brief nap or were distracted by noises in another direction. They only came across one patrol, and the two Narohk went chasing after an illusion of the wolf. It took three hours to reach the valley, where a cave hidden by dense trees led into deila falls. The sanctuary was not enclosed, just difficult to reach without passing through the tunnel. Idelle was able to keep watch from above, noting the orcs had made camp but had no fire to speak of.

They're definitely hiding, she said, *either waiting for the elves to give up or word from whoever it is they're working with. I didn't see any of them in the forest, so they're not bothering to check on the search parties.*

My guess, Aren added, *is they're waiting for Ceiran, or at least one of his Narohk to deliver a message.*

Or possibly a sign, some kind of signal like smoke or a marked arrow.

That would be more likely, Barr agreed. *I still can't imagine any of the elves, Narohk or not, having direct contact with orcs. In any case, we'll soon find out what's going on.*

There was no sign of a guard inside the entrance, so Barr headed into the tunnel and left Aren standing watch just a few paces within. The light from behind Barr soon faded and was gone. Using the wall to guide him along, he stepped through the darkness, over mud and uneven ground littered with puddles, and followed his ears to the waterfall. By the time he reached the water, rushing past on its way to crash over rocks below, Barr had changed his appearance with illusion.

He stepped out onto the ledge, inches from the fall, and startled two orcs who were meant to keep guard. Not a word was said when they saw who he was. Their eyes were fearful, which was odd in itself, but they made no move to draw weapons and attack. Both warriors had many scars, a sign they were proven in battle, so why be afraid of an elf?

Though Barr was puzzled by their reaction, his image of Ceiran revealed nothing to the orcs. He paused briefly, realizing his suspicions were true, then strode down the path to their camp within the grove. The air of confidence he wore like a shroud of armor did exactly as he had intended; it let those who looked on him know he was in charge, and their worried glances seemed to agree.

They recognize Ceiran. They've all seen him before.

I can be there in seconds, Aren said. *If anything goes wrong, just hold them off 'til I get there.*

Everything will be fine, Barr reassured him. *This is just what I was hoping would happen.*

The chieftain was waiting in the center of camp, with his colorful shaman lurking close behind. Barr gave the orc credit. Whatever it was that made the others shirk away, their leader stood with both beefy arms crossed in a silent defiance. Perhaps being the largest of them all was only in part why the orc was their chieftain. His eyes were hardened crimson, like two little rubies, and they met where Ceiran's would have been – three hands above Barr's own. The chieftain said nothing, a grudging mark of respect, and waited for Ceiran to speak first.

"They still hunt for you," Barr said in fluent orcish, enduring the grating sound on his ears. He looked about at the frightened warriors eating raw meat and noted the distinct lack of any horses. With a steely gaze, he asked, "I assume no one will find your wagons?"

"Destroyed and buried, as you instructed." A nervous cough from the shaman caused the big orc to turn a baleful eye his way. He looked back to Ceiran and asked, "When will you return our elder?"

Elder? Barr looked to the shaman and understood. *I guess that's why this one was so weak when we first met. He's still learning from another.*

"When you have kept your end of our bargain."

"I have kept my end and more!" The chieftain lowered his arms but made no threatening move. "Has she been turned?"

Aren asked, *She? I thought females were practically slaves among the orcs.*

They are. This one must have real power. Barr shook his head and considered, though Ceiran remained calmly still. *Why would Ceiran kidnap an orc shaman, and how exactly would he turn her against them?*

Where would he even keep her?

Barr was afraid he already knew the answer to that. "It is no longer safe for your tribe in these woods. If you stay here, you will eventually be found. Consider our arrangement ended. Make your way out of the forest late tonight, and never again return. I will send your elder to the ruins far south and outside Darleman."

"Unharmed?"

"She will be with you by dawn tomorrow."

Barr turned and headed back up the path. He could feel the eyes of every orc upon him, their burning hatred but undeniable fear. Under any other circumstance, he would have expected one of them to attack from behind, but not even the angry frustration he saw in their hearts was enough to give rise to action.

There's nothing a tribe wouldn't do for their shaman, Barr said, *but why are they afraid of Ceiran? Even if I told them the truth, that the woman was dead, I don't think a single one of them would attack.*

Well, they don't seem to be afraid of the elves, Idelle said. *They're holed up just a day from the city.*

No, not the elves, Barr agreed. *Just Ceiran.*

– 17 –

Sitting before a small fire, in their new camp for the evening, Barr added more snow to the ironwood pot. He had a collection of tubers waiting to be boiled. Propped up by two Y-shaped branches on either side and a stick running through its loops, the emerald-veined pot not only didn't burn, but it added a smoky flavor to the food. Though the flames were low, Barr had made the cooking fire wide to spit three hares beside the stew. He was ready to slip in the pared tubers when Idelle landed a few paces off.

Did he understand you? Barr asked.

I think so. Idelle ruffled her feathers, shaking off the melting frost. *I believe our Seltruin is better suited to his library than the trees. His avian is sorely underused.*

As long as he knows what Ceiran has been up to, you can forgive his poor clucks and whistles.
What did he say? Aren asked. His eyes never strayed from the meat on the fire. *Will something finally be done?*
He didn't say anything but repeat back part of what I told him. By the grave look and sudden departure, I can only assume he went to inform the council.
Good, Barr said. *One less thing to worry about.*

There were other things troubling him beside alerting the council, like what the tribe would do when their elder shaman didn't appear the next morning. They were so frightened of Ceiran that it was possible they might not do anything, as doubtful as that would be for orcs. The loss of a shaman should have driven them into a bloodstarved frenzy. But it didn't. The orcs were cowed, even their chieftain – despite his weak show of defiance. While Barr struggled with the notion that an entire tribe of orcs should fear a single elf, the First Narohk or otherwise, a more disturbing thought pushed its way forward.

Barr didn't know Ceiran at all.

For most of his time among the Sylvannis, Barr was convinced the First Narohk was but a petty and spiteful elf, driven by a hatred for humans and the desire to be isolated from the rest of the world. Prior to recent events, Barr would never have thought Ceiran was capable of murder, let alone dealing with orcs for some unknown purpose. He began to wonder how many of the elves who had gone missing were victims of the wolf or were taken as payment to the orcs. Lorelei would have been one of them, the few who had vanished without a trace. It was always assumed that the wolf had carried them off.

No matter how hard Barr tried to piece together the logical strands to make a whole, there was still too much that made little sense. Why or how would Ceiran capture a powerful shaman? Other Narohk could have helped, but that seemed just as unlikely. If he did take her, what did he do with her? Was it fear that truly kept the orcs in check, or was it dread over what he might do to their shaman? What use could Ceiran possibly have for orcs, that he would allow them so near to Geilon-Rai?

Stop it, Aren said. He left off staring at the hares and rested his gaze on Barr. *They don't want us anymore. Why should we care what happens to them?*

I care. I didn't want to leave.

We weren't given a choice. We did more than our part by telling Seltruin. He looked back to fire. *Beyond that, they don't want our help. Time to start looking forward.*

Idelle said, *As much as it pains me to say, Aren is right. Luckily I don't have to say it often.*

I can't, Barr said. *I can't just leave behind my life like that. Not again.*

He was reminded once more of what he had lost the first time he traversed this path, when his father Daroth had been taken and Tuvrin entered his life. All the pain and sorrow came back from those days, opening the old wound to a fresh flood of salty regret. *What might have been* was a heavy burden, and it weighed on him, body and mind. Though Tuvrin was far from dead, he was just as lost to Barr as Daroth. As if coping with the loss of all his family and friends again weren't enough, he felt even more terrible about his desire for Lorelei. Barr would never again see his father or Seltruin, and all he could think of was her.

Barr felt the tingle of magic at the nape of his neck, heard its whisper in his ear as he turned.

"He is magnificent," a woman said, as if she had been seated there all along, and indicated Aren with a fond smile.

She looked almost elven, with her tapered ears and delicate features, but she was far smaller than any Barr had ever seen. Sitting upon a warmed stone beside the fire, pale skin glittering by its light, her gaze fell upon Barr and startled him with its color. It was not so much the deep azure cast of her eyes that stood out in stark contrast to the norm, but where there should have been clear white encircling the blue pools, both orbs were as black as pitch. Barr imagined he could see the sparkle of starlight against their glassy surface, then noticed she was studying him with equal interest.

He tried to look away, to note instead how her waist-length raven hair fell in curls down her silken wrap, or that she went barefoot and sparsely clothed in the bitter peak of winter. There were strands of woven silver in her hair, along both wrists and ankles, and the glowing circlet of tiny runes about her neck had the appearance of living jewelry. No matter how many little details he caught sight of, his efforts were to no avail. Drawn to that impish smile and the odd pairing of color in her eyes, Barr had no choice but to stare into their depths.

He pushed aside the uneasiness in his middle and found his voice once more.

"Who are you?" he asked, echoing the thoughts of both Aren and Idelle. There were no tracks in the snow leading up to where she sat, and the magic he had heard before noticing her arrival left him thinking she appeared from thin air. "How did you get here?"

She's beautiful, Aren said. *So small and pretty.*

Shush. Don't assume beauty means she's harmless.

"You may call me Ariana," she replied. "I am a spirit of the forest, a friend to the trees. The one that connects them all allows me to travel where I will."

Idelle said, *She doesn't seem dangerous.*

Somewhat relaxed at hearing her mention the Great Tree, Barr introduced himself and both friends. Ariana gave a respectful nod in greeting to each of them, then turned back her attention to Barr. Without asking, she stood and moved closer, knelt inches away. He would have normally felt uncomfortable at being so close to an attractive woman, but there was a familiarity about her, a soothing ease to her manner. It was as if he had known her before, the lingering memory of a past that could not yet be recalled, a partial glimpse into what might have been a vision and not just the hazy edges of faded time. From within the folds of her ivory wrap, she took out a smooth bracer of solid mithrinum.

It brought images of the Denshyar to his mind, the smooth and featureless mask that had sparked the most troubling vision he had ever had. Barr instantly recoiled but grew more assured when Ariana simply held it in hand. Covered with runes he had never before seen, the bracer was artfully decorated. The patterns, however, did more than look pleasing to the eye. Their aesthetics belied a terrible power, one that prickled the hair on his skin and set his spine to tingling.

"This is for you," Ariana said, offering him the bracer, "for all you have done for the forest. Consider it a token of our friendship, a parting gift to keep you safe."

With some reluctance, Barr reached out a cautious hand and touched his fingers to the metal. He traced the runes along its surface, surprised by their inner warmth and the power they exuded. Ariana was watching his reaction with a curious expression. She didn't seem to be offended by his hesitation, but it was clear that she neither understood it. When Barr finally decided he saw nothing wrong with the bracer, he took a firm hold and snatched his hand back as if bitten. The look in his eyes was one of betrayal.

Though it only lasted the briefest of moments, all his senses were assaulted in that short span of time. Images flashed before his eyes, too quickly to comprehend, and it felt as if a flurry of whispers had washed over him in a gust that shook his soul. The wind smelled of fresh rain and left the taste of dried honey in his mouth. A dozen voices in all, sounding as if they had spoken from a great distance, not one could be heard clearly over the tumult they caused.

What happened? Idelle asked.

Aren sounded frantic. *For a moment, I couldn't sense you anymore. Even though you're standing right here, I – I couldn't hear you.*

"That bracer is alive," Barr accused, upset that she hadn't warned him.

Even more unnerving was her calm insistence of the gift. Her hand was still outstretched.

"It is. Items of great magic often develop sentience over time." Ariana offered the bracer once again. "It will not harm you in any way."

"Why didn't you tell me?"

"I do not understand. What is the matter? Is the gift not pleasing to you? I could find another, if you prefer."

"That's not it. I just wasn't prepared –" Barr let out a sigh. "Suffice it to say that I've had my fill of mithrinum artifacts. Thank you for the offer, but the gift isn't necessary. Your friendship is reward enough."

"I see," Ariana said and lowered her hand. "And you will not reconsider? Aislin was excited at the prospect of knowing you."

It has a name? Aren asked. *I say leave it be. I don't like whatever it is it just did.*

"You can speak with it?"

"Aislin. Yes, though not the way you and I converse." She looked thoughtful for a moment, as if searching for words. Though she spoke in elven, Barr knew by her accent that it was not her native tongue. "I can hear it strongest in dreams. While awake, it is barely a whisper."

"I heard more than one voice, at least a dozen, and the sound of them drowned out... other things."

"That is unusual. Perhaps it was the excitement. If you would not mind trying again, I am sure Aislin is far calmer now."

Alien as they were, all ringed in jet black, Ariana's eyes were still soft. The gentle pleading he saw in them melted his resolve.

"Honestly, I –"

"Please? It would mean a great deal to us." At Barr's slight frown, she added, "I speak of the Niyaen and the other nymphs. You underestimate our appreciation. This is not a gift we give lightly, and I assure you that it is necessary."

Idelle said, *If it means that much, maybe it wouldn't hurt to try.*

Maybe. I guess I can always just stick it in my pack.

I still don't like it, Aren said. *How can anything stop us from hearing each other like that?*

"Alright, I'll try."

Ariana handed him Aislin.

Holding the bracer in his palm, Barr expected to hear the same tirade from before. Only the barest of whispers reached his mind. It sounded as if someone were talking at the end of a long corridor, a breath of a voice that went on without pause. An image then flashed in his mind, a memory from another life, a fraction of a vision. He was a child named Branyc, barely ten summers old, and stood before the master wheelwright he was to be apprenticed to.

"Hello, young sir! So good to finally meet you!"

As that vision disappeared, another came to take its place. He was a very young girl then, with not a tooth to speak of. An elderly woman knelt before him and helped him to stand. The playful smile she gave made him giggle to no end.

"Oh, I've waited a long time to see you," the woman said. "Do you know who I am?"

The image faded, and all became quiet.

That wasn't so bad, Idelle said. *I could still hear you, but you seemed very distracted.*

I still don't like it.

Barr inwardly laughed. *Aside from frequent meals, what do you like?*

Speaking of which...

"It does seem better," Barr said. He pulled up his left sleeve and locked the bracer in place. "Thank you, again. I'll wear it with pride, as a reminder of the forest."

Unexpectedly, Ariana kissed him on the cheek.

"I am glad that it pleases you. I must be going now." She straightened his leather sleeve, hiding Aislin from sight. "Do not let others know you possess such a magic. The world outside the forest is not so forgiving of our ways."

"Of that, I'm well aware."

"Be careful as you travel west. There is a danger in the woods that is better left alone." Ariana backed away, looking as if she were trying to etch his every feature into memory. She turned and walked toward the trees. Before completely vanishing into a cloud of billowy white mist, her voice carried back, "We will meet again, Sage Barr. Until then, stay safe."

Barr thought long on the strange woman and the even stranger gift she had given him – a living bracer named Aislin. He wondered if the Denshyar had also been alive, before it burst into a shower of liquid pieces. And what of those eyes? Never before had he seen or heard of such a thing. Though Ariana looked no older than twenty years, her wondrous eyes had an ageless quality of wisdom.

All this and more Barr thought on before sleep, unlike others who shared the fire. Aren's grumbles could be felt as well as heard. The hound seemed consumed by a single, unrelenting thought and spent most of the night in a foul mood.

All three hares were terribly overcooked.

* * *

Deryn woke with a start, pain tearing through his middle like the claws of a specter. Sweat trickled down his face in icy rivulets, as the brush of a winter wind fell over him. Though the cold nipped with a bitter fervor, it was not what caused the awful tingling at the nape of his neck or set his fingers to raking gouges in the earth. He could sense them nearby, hear the beat of their hearts in his mind, and felt the blood coursing in their veins from afar. It was their presence that caused him such pain, doubled him over and drove him to action. There were demons in the forest, and nothing short of their untimely demise would ease his suffering and put an end to his torment.

The geas demanded no less.

He was up and off into the snowy wood with a speed that belied his form, leaving behind both mount and gear. He sought only to dull the curse's hold on his body, to find any relief that he could. Snow and brush bent to his will and were pushed aside by an unseen force. In a frenzied desire to reach his prey with all haste, Deryn moved at an inhuman pace. Furie *engulfed his body in a nimbus of pale light, as if a star had fallen from the sky and made its way through the forest.*

Though he could see their trail as a thick crimson smoke in the air, his other senses cried out from the assault. The demon scent was like a physical blow, a rancid odor that smacked of rotting eggs. The stench was so strong, Deryn could have tracked them by nose alone. The wrenching magic that pulled at his gut, twisted his insides and led him painfully on, was but a distraction compared to the smell.

    The forest was eerily quiet, with only the sound of his mount keeping pace. The whirring in his ears, however, went on without relent. It was the flutter of their hearts, rapid thumps that strove to drown out all else. What other creatures were stirring in the dark of early morn made no noise to speak of – but one. The piercing cry of a hawk rang out in the distance, growing louder as it drew near and soon flew overhead.

    Deryn soared through the trees with incredible speed, using magic to run at a tireless pace and propel himself forward in great leaps. Dodging outstretched branches, slipping under fallen trunks and over icy crags, he more flew than ran to his prey.

    His mind was consumed by the geas.

    A trail of steam left tell of his passing, as snow melted at the touch of his magic. Into a clearing where four stone pillars lay rooted to the icy ground, Deryn came to a jarring halt and surveyed his foes. All tooth and scale, fire and claw, three lumbering demons howled their rage at the defiant stones before them. The power of his blessed curse then overwhelmed him, engulfing his body in the holy fires of the god Curoch. The three demons turned in unison, their narrowed yellow eyes like tiny suns in a crimson sky.

    Deryn drew both swords and attacked.

* * *

    They had been working the pillars for the better part of a night, clawing away at the enchantment that held fast the ley stones. The lunar ring was a portal to the lands of Faeronthalsos, both a gateway and means of destruction. Kharo slavered at the thought of finally breaking through and the unbridled carnage that would soon follow their success. Tirelessly, all three demons fought against the portal, wearing away its protective wards by smashing their wills against barriers both stone and magic.

The ring was weakening, too.

Kharo could feel it, sense the glyphs crumbling with each strike. It drove him on, gave him renewed strength and encouraged him to redouble his efforts. His terrible claws marred their stony surface, leaving behind long gashes in the coarse pillars. Tendrils of fire erupted from his fists and sent tongues of flame licking outward over the stones. Try as he might, though, the sigils still stood. It was as if the magic of Faeron mocked them, dared to be broken, but would not give way to their strength.

Kharo became lost in the chaotic glee of destruction, much like his kin, and failed to notice the human until the whisper of magic scraped across his spine. He felt the paltry creature call forth spells of protection and began to wonder if its meat would taste as sweet as it smelled. Though Kharo had seen few humans in his time, this one looked delightfully insane. With eyes wide and teeth bared, it stood boldly before them and seemed ready to enter a frenzy.

"Jhu re ne tok," *It is a hunter*, his brother Chel said and licked his lips with a warty tongue.

He had never before seen one, but stories about them passed from den to den. From the time of his first transformation, Kharo had been told of the god-cursed humans compelled to slay demons. Though he felt no alarm at facing the marked creature, he looked on with a newfound respect.

Jhont laughed at the challenge and flew off to greet the hunter with fang and claw to fore. His demise was a blur of scaly flesh and blackened bone that showered the forest floor with his steaming remains. Flecks of crimson skin and dark murky blood were then splattered across the human's face in a semblance of grisly war paint. The small creature's wild-eyed gaze gave rise to a grin, a parting of lips and gnashing teeth as feral as any demon.

"Barok!" *Attack!* Chel roared.

They both flared their wings and shot to either side of the clearing with unnatural speed. Their talons bit into the earth as they went, igniting a wall of red flame as tall as the trees. Chel drew a sword of midnight crystal, its icy edge bearing the complex runic patterns of demon magic. Kharo drew his whip and loosed its barbed ends, the entire length suddenly alight in dark fire.

Surprisingly enough, the hunter rushed in to meet them, its tiny blades flashing out with a barely contained rage. Though Kharo and his brother towered over the small human, it seemed all too eager to face them. Sword brought to bear, cackling with glee, Chel swung time and again at the impudent creature. It dodged his poorly aimed attacks and returned each slice with an accuracy born of magic.

The sheer delight that Kharo felt, blood rising to a boil, overcame his senses with the sheer prospect of taking life. His whip circling overhead, a sinewy length of inky flame, Kharo drew back in preparation to strike. He never saw the immense hound that crashed into his side, breaking his body in stride.

Its growl in his ears was the last thing he heard.

* * *

When Barr woke before dawn, he sat up to find Aren and Idelle silently watching him. He felt the concern that was mirrored in their eyes and looked about their camp for something amiss. The wan silver light of early morn revealed nothing.

What is it?

You had a very strong vision, Idelle replied with some caution, as if she were unsure just how much to say.

Aren said, *Ariana just left. She... cleaned you up.*

I don't understand. What do you mean –

There was a commotion in the distance, shouts that echoed about the trees and were followed by the buzzing of arrows. Barr couldn't make out what was being yelled, but he imagined the Narohk had given up all pretense of stealth and were charging the camp to kill him.

The fire still burned, fed by someone else. Idelle was up into the air without another word, and Aren turned sharply about. Barr got to his feet and drew both kyan, thinking it strange the elves would attack from the west.

Why did they bother to sneak around the camp, if they planned to make so much noise?

They aren't Narohk! Idelle warned.

He saw the arrow come at him, slicing through the air, before any sound of its passing reached his ears. Deftly turning aside, Barr narrowly avoided being taken in the shoulder. Aren bounded off to the side, slipping through the trees with all speed, as another arrow came flying by.

Barr crouched low and waited for whoever they were. With a swipe of his boot, he sent enough earth in an arc to put out the small fire, blanketing the camp in sudden darkness. His eyes adjusted to what moonlight sifted through the branches above, as the sound of running boots came from up the trail.

A single figure came dashing toward him, looking over a shoulder in panic and paying little attention to where he was going. More arrows flew past, as he stumbled into the camp. When the man came within a few feet, Barr leapt out and gripped him by the waist with one arm, taking him down to his back in a smooth twisting motion meant to knock the air from his lungs. With his left kyan to the man's throat and the other ready to plunge, Barr could hear the archers that gave chase fast approaching.

"Why are they chasing you?" he asked quietly, in unforgiving tones. With a glance down, he saw a black cotton doublet with violet pantaloons. "What are you, a thief? What crime did you commit?"

The man looked terrified, shaking his head in frantic confusion, but made no attempt to answer. It was then Barr realized that he had been speaking in elven. Three men and a woman came into sight, bows drawn and arrows ready to fire. They stopped and focused their attention on Barr, training arrows on his back. Each of them wore a swatch of crimson cloth that wrapped about the forehead and fell behind in a sweeping tail.

"Who in the blazes are you?" the oldest looking of the three men demanded, with authority in his voice.

Barr let his prisoner go and turned on the others. *Crimson Order?* Even as a small boy in Alixhir, he had heard many stories about them. *Why would the Thieves Guild be out in the forest?*

Probably chasing one of their own, Aren surmised. Barr could see light reflected off the hound's eyes, behind the unsuspecting thieves. *I don't think they plan to leave quietly.*

"Why do you chase this man?" Barr asked. "He is unarmed and clearly no threat."

"I have a clean shot," the female said to the first. She was taller than Barr and might have been attractive if not for the dirt smearing her cheeks. "Let's end this and go home."

"What is he?" another asked. "I've never heard an accent like that before."

"He might fetch a good price," the third added.

The thought of using magic crossed his mind, but Barr knew he couldn't let any of them leave the forest if they saw him weave *furie*. The last thing the elves needed were Guardians scouring the trees for any sign of a turner. No, if he was going to subdue them, he would have to do so by hand.

"Go back the way you came," he told them. "I don't want to hurt any of you, but I will if you leave me no choice."

Barr heard the tensing of bowstrings and knew they would fire, before the lead thief gave voice to the order. He rolled away and threw both kyan, as Aren pounced on one from behind. The woman fell, clutching the ironwood sword in her chest, and dropped her bow without firing a shot. The other kyan sliced through arrow and bow, then lodged itself in the lead thief's shoulder. He cried out and dropped to his knees, then was knocked aside by Aren's bulk and the wriggling body in the hound's jaws. Idelle swooped in and took hold of the dazed thief, her claws biting deep into both shoulders and carrying him off.

He crashed soundly against a tree in the distance.

The remaining archer had already loosed his arrow and was hurriedly reaching for another. Barr had rolled out and away, barely avoiding the barbed end, and got to his feet in one motion. He gritted his teeth, and with a deliberate calm, walked towards the thief unarmed. Barr leveled a kick that splintered the bow, then spun quickly about and struck the thief across the jaw with his other boot.

While the thief was still sprawling in the air, upended by Barr's powerful kick, a dagger took him in the chest and sliced through his heart. He fell backward to the ground and lay still. Barr turned to see his previous captive, and the frantic look that once haunted the thief's eyes was all but gone, replaced by a grim determination. Another throwing knife slipped down from a sleeve and into his palm.

"Do I need one for you, too?" he asked Barr.

Aren was behind him and padded up without a sound. His snort was a warning that set the man's hair billowing forward.

Barr raised a brow. "I'd reconsider if I were you."

– 18 –

The thief gave a disarming smile, and his throwing knife disappeared back up a puffy sleeve. He eyed Aren curiously over a shoulder, glanced at Idelle as she came to land beside the doused fire and finally rested his gaze upon Barr.

"I was jesting, of course. You have my gratitude for rescuing me."

There was no denying the stranger was a handsome man. He had sandy colored hair, neatly tied in back, and gray eyes that brightened with his smile. Barr had never felt that he himself was unattractive, but even a cursory glance at the thief made him uncomfortably self aware of his own shortcomings. It was a fleeting thought that he gave no more time to, just another detail listed off in the attempt to gauge the thief's intent.

Though dirtied from the chase, the man seemed no worse for wear. His leather boots were free of mud, his silken pants without a tear, and his doublet was still tucked neatly in. There were traces of brush scattered about his dark overcoat, but it seemed to Barr that the chase could not have gone on for very long.

He doesn't seem nearly as winded or frightened as he was before.

Idelle said, *I wonder why he was running. The way he threw that knife, I imagine he could have killed his pursuers without much trouble.*

"I didn't rescue you," Barr said. He kept a wary eye on the man while retrieving both kyan and wiped the blades clean on the clothes of the fallen. It had been so long since he spoke the human language that it felt stilted on his tongue. "I defended myself."

"Regardless, I am in your debt." He bowed his head without taking his eyes off Barr, still flashing that toothy smile. "I am Ealdan Ap Wynshir, a simple player with the Noble Troupe. We hail originally from Garand, but we do travel a great deal. Perhaps you have heard of us?"

Barr began gathering their things in preparation to leave. With the fire out, their breakfast would have to be a cold one.

This one can't be trusted, Aren warned, looming over the thief and ready to strike. *He has a scent about him I've never smelled before. It makes my skin crawl.*

He's been looking over the camp, too, noting how the tree is bent and the snow is melted, but he hasn't said a word about it. Barr gritted his teeth, inwardly berating himself. *I'm going to have to be more careful about using magic.*

"There was nothing simple about that knife you just threw. What exactly did you do before... performing?"

The Last Incarnation

Ealdan pulled a frilly kerchief from his coat pocket and covered his nose with a casual look to the bodies. A wave of flowery musk soon overpowered any scent of the forest, taking with it the coppery stench of spilled blood.

"Oh this and that. You keep rather strange company, my friend. Are you a turner?" It wasn't so much the question that took Barr by surprise, but the way in which it was casually asked. Ealdan went on without waiting for an answer. "Not that it would matter to me, seeing as how you rescued me and all, but it would be nice to know if I should be worried more about Guardians than the Order. Dangerous, are they? Your friends, I mean. They look quite fierce, especially this one. He must be the largest dog I have ever seen."

He is a slippery one, isn't he? Idelle left to search the area for any more guests. *He's not at all what I would have expected humans to behave like.*

He's not like any I've ever met, Barr replied, *from his clothes to his demeanor. People from Alixhir are much simpler and too afraid of Guardians to talk openly about them.*

"Shouldn't you be getting back to wherever it is you were running from?"

Barr looked down at the bodies, considering if he should bury them out of respect for the dead. Predators would feed on them, otherwise. The morning sun was finally breaking through the trees, and though he was in no hurry to reach Alixhir, Barr felt inclined to let the forest deal with the remains.

"That really is the oddest accent," Ealdan said and tapped his chin with a glossy nail. "It sounds familiar, sort of rolling like the Steoric of Adarrin but with a chop here and there like the Ynisz of Ramora. You have the smell of a woodsman," he added, studying Barr with a critical eye. "One with little use for water, I might add.

You dress like a thief but have the look of a hunter. Maybe –"

Barr rested both hands on his kyan. "Did you just call me a thief?"

Why doesn't he just leave? Aren began snorting with impatience. *That odor is giving me a headache.*

Ealdan paused with a look that seemed calculating, as if he were carefully choosing his reply. Barr imagined he might have had that same look whenever Aren or Idelle spoke, a brief moment of distraction that appeared as concentration. This thief, however, had no such excuse, and the delay only served to add further insult.

"No, of course not. I meant only that you could pass for one. Believe me, as an actor, that is a commendable trait. The ability to believably portray another profession is a highly valued skill." It didn't seem to occur to him that only another actor, or a thief, would prize that particular talent. "I noticed your weaponry is as strange as your company. Are they made of wood? I admit they had a certain level of effectiveness, but really, a wooden sword is about as absurd as another I have seen. It was a blade of solid mithrinum. Have you ever heard of such a thing? Granted, the metal is enchanted and has some desirable properties, especially for molding jewelry, but as a weapon? I think not."

"You talk much," Barr noted.

Much? Aren asked, incredulous. *It's a wonder he stops to breathe. He's said more in the past minute than I ever heard from Jareid in a day.*

All seems well from up here. Not a person in sight. Idelle gave a girlish chuckle, as if delighting in Aren's discomfort. *It's very quiet and peaceful.*

Next time, take me with you.

Now that would be a sight.

"Perhaps. It could be that you are simply not used to two-legged company. I imagine they are not much for conversation." Ealdan dabbed at his nose with a glance Aren's way, showing disapproval for more than just the lack of witty banter. "Believe me, as much as I seem out of place to you, here in the thick of the woods, you sir would stand out in a city street like a wagon with no wheels."

"I guess it's just as well we're not in a city. So, why exactly were your friends here trying to kill you?" Barr took a piece of dried meat from his bag, sat down and began to chew. "And me."

"Do you think you could move the bodies first? They smell dreadful."

"You look like a capable man. Besides, I'm so overcome with my own odor that I hardly noticed them."

The sarcasm did not seem lost on Ealdan. He looked from Barr to the bodies and frowned at his dilemma. Aren moved to sit beside Barr and take a handful of meat, sparking hope in the actor's eyes that the large hound might drag the corpses away.

Aren sat quietly and chewed his breakfast.

"Oh, very well." Ealdan untied one of their red cloths and used it to cover his hands. He pulled each of the bodies a fair distance away, complaining all the while. "I would not have thought it possible for them to smell any worse!"

He's killed before, Barr said. A distant memory of a past life flashed in his mind and was gone. *The first time I saw a body, my stomach churned. Look how easily he handles them.*

Aren said, *He seems more disturbed by dirtying his hands than the fact he helped kill one of them.*

While the actor wasn't looking, Barr removed Aislin from his wrist and pushed it to the bottom of his pack.

He then sealed the knot with a ward. Nothing short of magic would undue it.

Just in case.

When Ealdan was finished, he returned and dabbed at his forehead. He caught sight of them eating and looked as if he might choke in revulsion. Barr assumed the actor was used to a more delicate morning fare. They had precious little left, so Barr didn't bother to offer him any. Instead, he cleared his throat and reminded Ealdan to explain.

"I'm waiting," Barr said.

When Aren finished his share, he turned toward the actor with a hungry gleam in his eye. Ealdan must have mistook it for pleading.

"Sorry," he told the hound, with both hands open. "I did not have the presence of mind to bring along food. My departure was a bit... hasty." To Barr, he said, "Once more, I would like to express my gratitude for having saved my life. There is, of course, no need to apologize for ruining my cravat with your display of acrobatics. It is quite unnecessary, so please do not bother. I absolutely will not hear of it." Ealdan was quiet for a moment, while Barr slowly chewed and continued to wait. "Well, now that that is behind us, I can get on with my tale. I *do* love to tell a good story! Unfortunately, this one lacks the appropriate drama for one such as myself.

"I am afraid it is all just a misunderstanding, you see. As I said earlier, I am an actor, and as such, I must practice my parts with utter devotion and perseverance. It was on such an occasion, just this past night, that I was trying my hand at picking pockets. Yes, I know, a criminal and lowly act, but I had no intention of keeping what items I procured. No sir, I would have returned them with my usual enigmatic smile and offered a most gracious apology for having practiced –"

"You stole," Barr cut in, summing up the lengthy tale. He was unused to interrupting, but this actor could seemingly go on without breath.

I knew he was a thief, Aren said. *We should just go. Why do we care why he was being chased?*

Ealdan gasped. "Please, sir, I... I... I am sorry, but in all the excitement, I failed to ask your name. Barr is it? Hmm, as in Barranthalos. Quite popular name in Astor, I am told, though I do not suggest the trek. Awful place, if you despise the cold. What? Oh, yes, my apologies. The story. Well, my *friends*, as you so quaintly put it, are members of the Crimson Order. It is of no small credit to myself that my skills as an actor so far exceeded my own expectations that I was actually thought to be a *real* thief! If you can believe such a thing," he said with disbelief, then quickly added, "that they thought me a thief, not that I can act. Well, to shorten the tale –"

Aren lowered his head to both paws and snorted a sigh. Ashes from the doused fire billowed up in a cloud towards Ealdan, evincing a series of sneezes that quite ruined his kerchief.

You did that on purpose, Idelle accused with a laugh.

Maybe.

"Augh!" Ealdan coughed and sputtered but tried to continue with his story. "I was then chased," he sniffled, "for not paying my dues. The Crimson Order is a sort of Thieves Guild. Augh!" He blew his nose with a honking snort that resounded through the forest. "The rest you know."

"What will you do now?" Barr asked and gathered up his pack. He planned to head for Alixhir, without the actor in tow. "Will this Crimson Order keep hunting you? Perhaps you should stay here until things have settled down."

Another pause for thought. "They will most likely try to find me again. I could just pay them the tribute they feel I owe them, with a small recompense for any loss," he added with a nod to the trees and bodies behind. "You know, I could learn a great deal from studying one such as yourself. One can never have too many characters in one's repertoire. Would you be interested in hiring on as a personal guard?"

The idea of becoming a mercenary reminded Barr of his father. He often wondered what it must have been like for Daroth to be a sellsword. Of course, it would was out of the question for Barr. Few enough places would accept he and his companions without question, and the life of a mercenary was riddled with travel. He threw his pack over a shoulder and began heading west.

"No thanks. I'm not for hire."

Without waiting for an invitation, Ealdan fell in step beside him.

"It appears we are headed in the same direction. No sense in traveling alone when there is company to be had."

Whether he meant Barr or himself was unclear.

He's going to prattle on for the rest of the day, Aren fairly groaned. *Can't you just put him to sleep? He'll wake up none the wiser.*

Convinced I'm a turner, no doubt. We're not far from Alixhir. Once we get there, we can go our separate ways.

"If you insist on coming along, keep the conversation to a minimum."

Ealdan nodded at the sage advice and promptly ignored it.

"You would not happen to have an extra cloak or fur, would you? No, hmm? Ah, just as well. Perhaps this strenuous exercise will get the blood flowing. Say," he said with a start, "did you suggest I stay quiet because of some danger that might be about? Odd how I had not really given it any thought before I came traipsing into these woods. Imagine that! I ran to the forest without the slightest thought to the danger. Well, other than what danger lay behind, eh?" He tittered, and the color of his cheeks brightened with his mirth. "In any case, was there any particular reason to keep our voices low?"

Barr only sighed and quickened his pace.

* * *

They made good time. Even though Barr had no need to hurry, Ealdan's chatter spurred him on. By the time the sun reached its zenith, they were only hours away from Alixhir. Barr was already giving thought to how he would go about finding his uncle, hoping the scribery was still there, when Idelle warned of danger ahead.

There's something large in the trees, not far off to your left. I can see it moving about, but it's not going anywhere. It looks wounded.

Careful what you say, Aren added. *You don't want this Ealdan knowing you can hear our thoughts.*

Idelle saved him the trouble and let out a cry.

"What is it?" Ealdan asked, startled by her call.

"I'm not sure," Barr answered. "Idelle may have spotted something. I'll go have a look. If it's something dangerous, it's best to deal with it now, rather than let it sneak up on us."

The perfumed actor blanched. "If it is dangerous, should we not avoid it? I thought I hired you to protect me, not *drive* me into danger!"

"You didn't hire me," Barr reminded him and made a show of leading Aren about the trail. "Stay here. You're making it difficult for Aren to smell anything. We'll be back when it's safe."

"Well, how do you know here is any safer?"

You know, Aren said, *this would be the perfect time to just leave him. You didn't plan on staying in Alixhir anyway.*

He is the strangest person I have ever met. Barr led them through the dense trees and underbrush, careful not to let the sound of his boots in the snow give sign of his approach. *With all his pomp and complaining, it's easy to forget that Ealdan is neither helpless nor harmless. He's plenty skilled with those knives he has secreted away.*

You're too used to caring for everyone you know, Idelle said. *Even with all your misgivings, you're worried he's still in danger.*

Aren snorted. *That's why you won't leave him? He's not an elf, and even if he was –*

I know. It just seems... rude. It's not that I feel the need to protect him, I just don't want to cause any undue trouble before we even reach Alixhir. He's a vocal person, Barr added with a bit of sarcasm. *I don't doubt for a moment he would talk about us, to whoever would listen, if we just left him out here to fend for himself.*

He made it in just fine, Aren said. *He can make it back out again as well.*

A pained cry came from ahead. Moving carefully between the slim trunks and numerous low-hanging branches, Barr saw the trail of upturned snow and greenish black blood before spotting the fallen troll. Its tuft of brown hair was frosted with white from the top of its head to the wispy end at its lower back.

Though he possessed the memories of more than one troll, Barr was still astonished at the creature's size. Seltruin's illusion had done little justice to the long-legged race. Barr assumed they looked much smaller in his mind because, in his memories, he was one of them. While others may not have been able to tell at a glance, he could see that the troll was female. She had a leaner frame and a more delicate build to her shoulders, but he knew all too well the belied strength of those slender muscles. Female or no, this troll could crush a man with one hand.

There was a yellowish cast to the warts on her skin, like flecks of sunflower over an olive sea. Her nails, coarse and brown, were splintered from her attempts to dig her way forward over snow and icy ground. Dressed in sparse leathers and marked with painted swirls, her appearance reminded Barr of a shamanistic ritual that involved dancing about a large fire, in the confines of a massive cave. He could see by her wrist totem that she was claimed by the pack's alpha. He had no idea where she was trying to go but imagined she was desperately fighting to reach shelter.

With Aren close, Barr moved ahead of her and knelt with both hands open and empty, showing he meant no harm. The troll issued a weak growl and tried to speak. Blood flecked her thin lips, and the clouded blue of her deep-set eyes were bleary with pain. Rolling onto her back, exposing garish claw marks across the abdomen and breasts, she breathed heavily and looked as if she were waiting for death.

The wounds were all too familiar.

It's the wolf! Barr looked around sharply, waiting for it to attack. *Aren, keep sharp. Do you see any sign of it, Idelle?*

Nothing. You don't think it followed us...

Focusing his attention back to the troll's wounds, he quickly surveyed the damage. By the deep gashes and continued bleeding, it looked as if her middle was left in complete ruin. Her chest bone was exposed, and the jutting ribs were broken.

"Can you understand me?" Barr asked in his best approximation of trollish. It felt too guttural and biting on his ears, but she looked up when he spoke. There was a sense of recognition in her eyes.

"You... are troll," she said, swallowing blood. "I can... see it... in your spirit."

"I'm going to help you. Don't fight it, alright? Just try to relax, and let the warmth flow through you."

"No. Not safe... here. You must go!"

Barr ignored her plea and put his hands to either side of her middle. *Furie* bubbled up from within him and ran down the length of both arms in a ghostly mist that surrounded the troll in a pearly nimbus. Her body shook and trembled with the power of Barr's magic. Steam began to rise from the melting snow all around her, revealing damp earth and tangled roots beneath. Her jagged wounds then started to heal. Puss and soiled blood faded away, leaving behind muscles that joined together over mended bone and thick, leathery skin that lost its uneven edge before slowly closing.

Once more, her body was whole.

Barr let go his hold and sat back in the snow, trying to catch his breath. Aren was there beside him, licking his face while he regained strength. Weaving always left him drained, and he knew there was nothing to do for it but wait.

The troll had her eyes shut against the sharp pains of mending but opened them then, as if waking from a wonderful dream. She turned her gaze to Barr and sat up, testing her renewed skin with disbelief and wonder.

"You, too, are shaman."

"Somewhat," Barr agreed. "I help others, when I can."

She got up to her knees, towering over him, and leaned in close to take a long breath of his scent. There was a sensual aspect to the action that startled Barr.

When she slowly withdrew, her eyes on his, she gave a nod of satisfaction and pulled a flat stone from a pouch at her waist. Though she marked it with a finger, nothing could be seen on its polished surface.

"My blood oath," she said and handed him the stone. "Keep it with you. If you are ever in danger, I will know of it. I am called Chamal. Let the spirits bear witness to this oath."

Small bones and stone beads jangled in her hair, as she bowed her head in respect. Barr wanted to reach out and lift her face, to tell her there was no need of a debt, but he knew better than to touch her. She belonged to another. Blood oath or no, custom would have demanded his death. Instead, he bowed as well and put the stone in a pocket close to his heart. She recognized it as a sign of esteem and smiled.

Without another word, she jumped up and leapt away, sprinting through the trees with incredible speed. How the wolf had ever caught her in the first place, Barr couldn't imagine.

With any luck, Aren said, *the wolf is eating Ealdan right now.*

Barr stood suddenly, alarmed by the thought. He was ready to go racing back down the trail, when Ealdan stepped into view.

"You should have killed it," he said, as if he were discussing the fate of some insect at his foot.

That neither the troll nor Aren had sensed the actor's presence was of lesser consequence than his possibly having seen Barr weave. He waited for the accusations, expected the irrational anger and hatred that fear often inspired. He wondered if he would now see one of those hidden knives, and his hands slipped down to both kyan of their own will.

Ealdan frowned ever so slightly.

"You would think you did not know me," he said. "Is your memory so short? Oh, I see, I have offended your honorable sensibilities by suggesting the troll should have been killed." He dabbed at his nose with the perfumed kerchief. With a shrug, "You cannot blame me, really. It was a filthy creature that smelled dreadful, and it might have eaten any one of us, had the circumstance been different. Sometimes it is better to rid the world of such things. They may just come back to haunt you."

There was no mention of weaving magic or speaking with the troll. Barr relaxed somewhat and began walking back towards the trail, with the intent of reaching Alixhir before night. He called back over a shoulder to Ealdan as he went.

"It's not our place to take a life because it may one day pose a threat. All life is precious."

"Yes," the actor agreed smoothly, "but some are more precious than others."

– 19 –

On the way back to the trail, Barr studied the forest for any sign of the wolf, making sure not to alert Ealdan. The last thing he needed were more questions, especially those he had no desire to answer. The wolf was known to hunt most of the forest, roaming through the trees in a pattern no Maurdon could discern. Still, Barr could not shake the feeling that the wounded troll in their path was more than coincidence.

Why didn't it kill the troll? Why attack the troll in the first place, if it didn't plan on eating or killing it outright?

Idelle said, *Not all of the animals think as we do. Some attack for the pleasure of doing so. I don't think you can attribute reason to the wolf's actions. Unless, of course, you're still convinced that it's stalking you.*

"I will certainly be glad," Ealdan said to no one in particular, "to be gone from these trees and back to the warmth of a fire. A little wine, some companionship, and all will be well! Hmm, I believe Lord Adroc's gathering is tonight." He raised one brow and gave a half-smile, his eyes lost in some distant musing. "I imagine Camille will be there as well."

Ealdan went on, mostly ignored.

If it's nearby, Aren said, *I can't scent it. There was no trace of it in that clearing, either.*

Well, keep a sharp eye. I'd rather be looking over my shoulder until we reach Alixhir than be caught unaware from behind.

We're very close, Idelle said.

Barr had already caught sight of the smoke in the distance, rising above the trees in a gray haze. Though he couldn't hear it, he imagined the bustle in the streets, the echoing clang of a smith's hammer, and the laughter of children at play. It was as if one happy moment from his past was forever etched in his mind as the daily goings on of city life. He knew it to be otherwise but allowed himself that brief time of reverie, wanting very much to be happy about seeing his uncle, to push aside the dread of having to explain where he had been all these years and why he had chosen not to return until now.

"Of course you would want a white wine for that, but there is no telling what some people will consider to be..."

You'll both have to stay outside the city walls. I'm taking us to where I think my old home was. I have no idea if it's still standing, or if someone else has taken it for their own, but it would be nice to see it once more.

I can stay close by without going with you, Idelle said and flew past. *I'll be high enough that no one will notice me.*

I won't be in any danger.
Aren said, *You haven't been there in a long time now. There's no telling how much has changed. Just look at this one. Imagine if they all acted that way.*

"...not to mention the final overture. Ah, but what is to be done but to sit back and enjoy. Why, I can recall..."

Like I said, this won't be a long visit. I just want to see my uncle again before we go looking for our new home.

Have you given any thought to where that might be? Idelle asked.

Aren said, *Someplace with lots of game, I hope.*

I was thinking the further we go, the less trouble we'll have with fitting in.

Fitting in doesn't concern me half as much as filling my stomach from day to day.

Idelle gave a short laugh. *You make it sound as if you only eat once a day. For myself, I just prefer some open space to stretch my wings.*

We'll find something, Barr promised. *A place we can all be happy. A quiet place. With no actors.*

"...and he had the nerve to tell me that vests went out of style the last season. The day I take advice from an understudy is the day I leave the stage, but for good." Ealdan turned to Barr and said, "I want you to know that I appreciate your hiring on with me after all."

"You didn't hire me."

"I promise, you will be well compensated. Just as soon as I collect on a debt, that is." Ealdan took in a deep breath and let out with a broad smile. "I can smell the morning bread already. Well, not really, but I recall what it smells like, and let me tell you, it is wonderful! Gods, what is that? What an awful looking place."

To say the least, the cabin had fallen into disrepair. Its shutters hung limply from hinges long broken, rusted and swinging in time to a breeze. The roof drooped over the porch on one end, where the support beam had given way but not quite fallen over. There were telltale traces of numerous storms, mud stains on the weathered planks, holes in the thatch where strong winds had simply torn it away, branches of a fallen tree poking over the back and scratching against the creaking roof.

"It has seen better days," Barr admitted. "It looked much better the last time I was here."

"When might that have been? You cannot be more than two decades old. This place is simply ancient."

Barr took a leather cord from his pack and used it to loosely tie Aren to the porch. He meant it as more of a show for Ealdan.

"Wise decision," the actor said. "They would not have let you into the city with him anyway. Good luck tying down your feathered friend. You never did say, you know. Where did you find them? I could think of any number of ways to make a show –"

"You could go on by yourself," Barr prompted, hoping for the best.

"Nonsense. We have come this far together, no point in going our separate ways just yet. Besides, I need to find that Jontry fellow that owes me a wager, so that I can pay you. Do you have any interest in hiring on as a personal guard? You know, on a more permanent basis." Ealdan scratched a cheek with a mischievous grin. "You never know who might seek to do an actor harm. Why, this one time, by the shine on my boots I swear, this countess from Darcy approached me after a show –"

With a look that seemed to say Barr wished he were staying and Aren going in his stead, he gave a farewell and began walking toward the city. Ealdan fell in step, continuing his tale without missing a beat, and went on with his story until they had left the forest behind and the walls of Alixhir loomed high before them.

The stone blocks that made up the protective outer wall looked carved by hand and set with an exacting precision. Long banners fell from the parapets in blue and yellow, depicting a gauntleted first against a back of rugged mountain. Guards patrolled the top, no doubt watching either side of the wall for trouble, while archers were stationed above the portcullis. The entrance to the city was massive, with heavy iron gates on both sides of a T-section. Wagons were entering full on one side and leaving empty on the other. Barr guessed they were farmers or traveling merchants, delivering their goods to market.

A river ran through the city from west to east, both a source of fresh water and a means of carrying away the vast refuse thousands of people made daily. Barr had never studied the aqueduct system in Alixhir, but he found himself interested as they came closer to the main gate. He never noticed, as a child, just how impregnable the city seemed.

Standing at the gate left him humbled.

"State your business," an uninterested guard said, his eyes on the daughter of a farmer that had just passed.

"Morning, Herol," Ealdan said. "My friend and I are just returning from Tapping Manor. Tell me, how is your wife? Is she over her illness?"

"Aye, sir. Thank you for asking." The man's smile seemed genuine, which surprised Barr a bit. "You two have a good day. The wife and I hope to catch your show later this week."

"I will see to it tickets await you at the door."

They passed beneath yet another iron gate, where the push of a lever would send it crashing down with all speed. There were murder holes on either side, fist-sized openings that allowed archers to shoot without fear of reprisal. It was a good twenty paces of darkness before they entered the city, where a final iron gate stood ready to thwart any invading army. When they stepped into the light of a bustling city, Barr could see two wooden doors flat against the wall to either side. Thick as three men standing shoulder to shoulder, those doors hung on hinges as big as his forearm and would be near impossible to breach once locked into place. A heavy iron beam was secured by pulleys and chains, so that it could be raised and lowered by horse.

I don't recall the main gate being so heavily guarded.

Aren replied, *It doesn't look so bad from here.*

You stay out of sight. The last thing we need is more trouble. Barr frowned as Ealdan led the way through the crowd. *Why is everyone looking at me? You'd think my ears were pointed or something.*

It must be your natural charm.

Well, you are dressed a bit differently, Idelle noted from above, *and few are openly wearing their weapons.*

Looking to the homespun tunics and simple linen breeches most people were wearing, Barr understood why his leathers would stand out. They were designed for practicality, to keep him warm and protected, but they were also masterfully crafted and ornate in their own way. Living among the elves for so long a time, he had grown accustomed to the needs of all being met without question, where not a one was left wanting. The notion of an elf coveting another's belongings would never have entered his mind. He was reminded just how different things were among humans. The more desirous eyes that turned his way, the more he realized how much he had taken for granted his life with the elves.

Barr felt a tugging at his sleeve.

He looked down to see a young girl, her flaxen hair grimy and pasted to her head. She wore a burlap top much too large for her thin frame, tied around her waist by a rope. Mud trailed up her legs, from bare feet to scraped knees, and her outstretched hand was raw from the cold. Though her eyes were rimmed with the dark of weary hunger, they held a glimmer of hope in their hazel pleading. That a child could be treated so badly both saddened and angered him. Barr was reaching for his bag when Ealdan turned around.

"Go on," he told the girl in a stern tone. "This one's mine."

The weak innocence faded and was replaced by a narrowed look of contempt. Ealdan's frown darkened as well. He moved as if to take a step toward her, and the child bolted away into the crowd. Try as he might, Barr could see no trace of her passing.

"What was that all about?"

"Beggars," Ealdan replied, looking as if he had tasted something rancid. He turned about and continued on, calling back as he spoke. "They are the eyes and ears of the Order. You may think you fit in here, but I assure you others have taken notice of your arrival. Weaponry tends to stand out, expensive ones more so. Word of an unusual stranger will reach the guild before long, and soon one will be given your mark."

"My mark?" Barr quickened his pace to keep up. "What exactly does that mean?"

"It is a sort of contract, permission from the Order. An agreed upon percentage of whatever is stolen will be given to the guild as tax."

"Thieves collect taxes?"

"They pay them as well, and that money has to come from somewhere." Ealdan waved at two young ladies passing by in a carriage. They returned the gesture with obvious interest, giving the actor cause to grin. "So long as the guild refrains from working certain quarters and pay their tithe, they are allowed to ply their trade without interference."

"Are you saying the king *allows* them to steal for a share of what's taken? That's ridiculous! What in the world has happened here –"

"Look at it this way. No matter what measures are taken, there will always be thieves. Rather than devote a vast amount of resources to stopping them, why not work with them and control them instead? The Crimson Order is then responsible for policing their own. If any get out of line, they deal with it themselves. The king's coffers grow, allowing him to further build up the city, and the restricted areas stay safe with far fewer guards."

Barr stopped and fumed. It didn't matter that he no longer lived in Alixhir, that he was no more a part of that city than he was Geilon-Rai. Still, he was furious that the king would so blatantly abuse both power and station, leaving the poor and defenseless to fend for themselves. What good was a monarch that stole from his people?

Ealdan must have noticed he was walking by himself. He turned and faced Barr's outrage.

"I know what you are thinking," he said, staving off any ensuing tirades with both hands, "but such is the way of things here."

"You seem to know quite a bit about thieves."

"And you seem to care an awful lot about strangers. Look, I know what I do from researching my part. I have spent a great deal of time among members of the Order. There is nothing more to it than that."

Satisfied with his explanation, Ealdan went back to leading the way. Barr took in a deep breath and calmed himself with a sigh.

You can't make right every wrong in the world, Idelle said from her vantage in the skies.

That doesn't stop me from wanting to try.

"Here we are," Ealdan said and stopped before an inn. "This should be safe enough for you."

The cobbled road here was less traveled, being a good distance from the main square. The inn looked clean, from the outside at least, and it seemed as good a place as any to start looking for his uncle. Barr didn't trust his memory to find the scribery on his own, and he certainly didn't want Ealdan to know any more than was needed. Barr looked up at the painted wooden sign, a depiction of a fellow whose rotund middle spun in the wind.

"What makes this one any safer than others?"

"The Portly Inn? Well, for a start, the barmaids will not drug you and take all you own." Ealdan winked. "You know, a promise of pleasure turned into headache and empty pockets."

Barr raised a brow. "That wouldn't be a problem."

"No, of course not. I meant no offense. Still, you can never be too careful. The innkeeper is a friend of mine. Just let him know I sent you, and he will discount your fare. The rooms are modest, but the food really is exceptional. Once I have collected my debt, I shall come looking for you here. Try not to wander off and get lost." Ealdan gave a wink. "We are no longer in the forest, you know, and I dare say the city is a fair bit more dangerous than your trees and trolls."

"I'll keep that in mind."

Barr walked up the handful of steps and pushed his way through the double doors of the inn. From behind, he could still hear Ealdan saying farewell. All trace of the actor's voice faded away, replaced by a multitude of conversations and the din of a busy kitchen.

The main room had two large fireplaces on either side, and the numerous wooden tables between them were full with guests enjoying a meal. Some spoke in hushed tones, immediately noticing Barr, while others went on laughing and drinking, without a care but for the mug in hand. Artful tapestries helped brighten the room but not nearly as much as the noonday light shining through each colored glass window. A barmaid stepped from the kitchen door to the right, hefting a large tray of steaming food and an earthenware pitcher.

Beyond the kitchen door, a bar stretched the length of the inn. Behind that stood the man for which the inn must have been named, a bearded fellow of unusual girth. If the food at the Portly Inn was half as good as Ealdan claimed, the innkeeper was a living testament to its quality – assuming he ate what was served. His head was bald and shone with sweat. He was busily cleaning a row of mugs, with the same rag he had just used to wipe down the bar.

"You're just in time!" the innkeeper said with a great smile, catching sight of Barr at the door. "Meals come with the room, and we're just now serving."

Barr walked over and sat upon a stool. "The food is good, I take it?"

"My daughters do all the cooking. Let's just say I didn't get this way from drinking." The man gave a chuckle at his own joke, shaking the fleshy folds beneath his chin. "Trevor's the name, though most folks here call me sir." He paused, as if waiting for a reply. "That's a joke, son."

"Ahh. What do you have available? Most likely, I'll only be here for one night."

"A mat in the common room is a silver. The private rooms are two and a half. Additional occupants cost another silver." Trevor rinsed the rag in a bucket of water and set about cleaning a second tray of mugs. "The meals come with both lodgings, three a day and no more. If you don't mind my asking, what sort of accent is that?

I've worked here thirty-odd years and never once heard anything like it."

"That's a long time," Barr said and fished out a coin from the bag in his pack. "You must know quite a bit about the city. As you guessed, I'm newly arrived. I'm looking for someone, a scribe named Therol."

Barr slid the coin across the bar.

"That's platinum," Trevor said calmly and placed both mug and rag to the side. He eyed the coin with a practiced eye but didn't reach out to touch it. "Dwarven stamp, from Quereg... How in the world did you come across it?"

"I travel here and there and do a fair bit of trading. If you could exchange that for me, I'd much appreciate it."

He's going to try to cheat you, Idelle said. *I can hear it in his voice.*

I know. If he can save me any time in finding my uncle, then it'll be worth it.

"May I?" Trevor asked, hesitantly reaching out a meaty hand. At Barr's nod, he picked up the coin and turned it over in his palm, running a finger along the edge and embossed depiction of a forge. "It's wonderful. I'm a collector, you see. This might just be another coin to you, but to me... I'll give you five gold marks, and you can stay here as long as you like."

Barr studied the man's face. "You can do better than that," he said. "I may not know the true value of this coin, but people I know very well. And you, my friend –" he leaned closer, studying the man's features – "are trying to cheat me."

"What? That's absurd. I've never cheated anyone in my life!"

"There you go again," Barr said casually. "When you lie, your left eyebrow quivers. I'm pretty good at noticing that sort of thing. Now, this coin is worth twenty gold, isn't it?"

"Bah!" the barkeep sputtered, sweat rolling off his nose. "It's not worth more than twelve." His brow didn't quiver. "Well?"

"My mistake. I'll take ten and that information I wanted."

"What about a room?"

With a nod, "Alright, and a private room."

Trevor pulled out a lockbox and secreted away the platinum coin within. He then began counting out a small pile of silver. Barr cleared his throat and gave a meaningful look.

"Oh, old man Therol. Good sort of fellow, though a bit senile if you ask me. His shop is down on Quill Street, with the other scriveners. I think working with all that ink has had an ill effect on him." Trevor looked up from his coins and added quietly, "He hasn't aged well at all."

Old man? What's that supposed to mean? He was my father's senior by a few years only. How can he be old?

Maybe he's as bored as I am, Aren offered.

Shouldn't you be off hunting for food? I won't be back any time soon, you know.

Trevor scooped up the silver coins and slipped them into a small leather purse. He tied the strings and handed it to Barr.

"Sorry I don't have any gold. The least I can do is give you something to keep them all in."

"I appreciate that," Barr said and secured it in his pack. "I'll be back soon. If someone named Ealdan comes looking for me, tell him he can leave the package with you. I trust you won't open it."

"Of course not. You're a friend of Ealdan then? You should have said something! I would have offered a better price for the room."

"So he told me."

Barr turned and headed for the entrance.

"I lock the front doors at midnight," Trevor called after. "Be sure you're back before then. You don't want to be caught out in the streets at night."

With a wave behind, Barr was out the doors. He had a general idea of where Quill Street was and headed east toward the Makers quarter. Provided he didn't get lost, he would be face to face with his uncle before long.

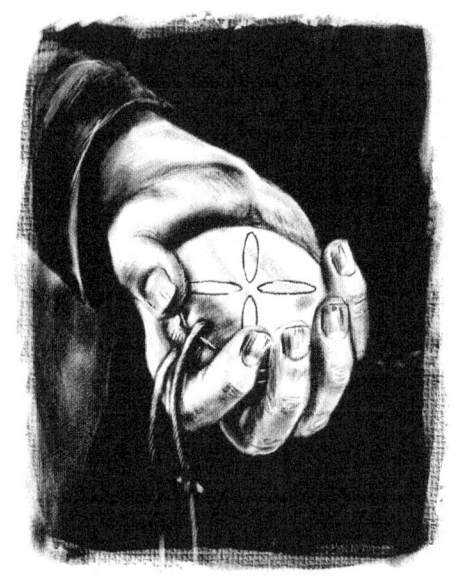

– 20 –

udging from what light shone through the growing clouds, Barr guessed night would be fast approaching. He hoped to find his uncle before dark. Being lost in the streets, with only lamplight to see by, was not a cheery thought. A heavy droplet touched his cheek, as he made his way through Tailors Row. Others felt the rain as well and hurried to bring inside their rolls of garment and colorful thread.

Take the next right, Idelle said.

Barr quickened his pace, ignoring the chill each new drop brought. The cobbled street became slick, causing his deerskin boots to slip more than once. Though he never lost his footing, it was a challenge to wend his way through the others running for cover. A resounding crackle of thunder echoed all about, promise of an even greater downfall to come.

Left. Go left. I can see it now, though the sign is more weathered than the others.

I hope he has a fire going, Barr said and turned left. *I think I remember which one it is now.*

It was a three-story building of wood and stone, much like the others, but its whitewash and blue trim were faded and showing marks of age. The sign hung from one chain, twisting lopsided in the wind, and a single brass bell was fastened beside the double-doors. Barr rang for service, which drew a curious look from the proprietor next door, but no one came to answer. With a polite nod and a smile to the nosy fellow, Barr began to feel around his pockets, as if looking for a key. He leaned in and covered the lock with one hand, blocking all sight of what he was doing, then manipulated the tumblers with a flicker of *furie*. In just a matter of moments, he had the lock picked and was inside.

From end to end, the walls were covered in shelves. Each one was laden with rolls of vellum, stacks of yellow parchment or clay vials stained with black ink. The only light to be seen came in from behind. A blue-white flash of lightning sent his shadow across the room and revealed a staircase hidden by the dark. It was behind a long counter and led up to the second floor.

"Hello? Is anyone here? Uncle Therol?"

Closing the door behind him, Barr carefully headed for the stairs. The wooden steps creaked beneath his feet with each step, as if protesting the weight of a stranger. There was a room off the stairway, much like what was below, where light from a single glass window showed a collection of various papers and inks. Two writing desks sat at either end of the room, though no work could be seen fastened across their tops.

This place seemed so different when I was a boy. It's strange to see these rooms without the light of a dozen candles. Barr could see a thick layer of dust on the door. *He must have given up his work a long time ago. I'm not sure he's even here.*

Maybe he's at home, Aren said.

No. Barr looked up at the darkness of the third floor. *This is his home. His room is up top. If he was here, he would have answered by now.*

Well you won't find him by standing there.

Barr turned from the dusty room and climbed the last stairs. When he reached the top, he was met by a closed door, with a flicker of light shining through the opening at his feet. He heard the crackle of a fire and an undeniable snore, both which made him smile like a child come home.

He's here. He was just asleep.

He knocked quietly. "Uncle, can you hear me? It's Barr. Hello?"

The door was unlocked.

The warmth and gentle light was a stark contrast to the dust and disuse seen below. Two large windows were covered with white drapes, but still they let in streamers of fading day. Most of the room's brightness came from a large hearth and standing bronze candleholders. A framed painting of the countryside rested above the hearth, and a rug of forest-green encompassed most of the wooden floor. A few chairs and a table were off to one side of the fire, but before it was a long couch, occupied by an old man. His snowy head rested upon a feather pillow, and he was tucked in beneath a fur blanket. The peaceful sight of his uncle made him smile all the more, though the ragged sound of the man's snore nearly caused Barr to chuckle.

The wrinkled skin and frail hands, sunken eyes and thin frame, all were wrought by time that simply couldn't have passed.

I don't understand. I haven't been gone that long.

Perhaps, Idelle offered, *grief has aged him beyond his time.*

Wake him, already, Aren said. *I've heard bears sleep more quietly.*

Barr tried to gently shake him. "Uncle. Uncle Therol, wake up."

The old man gave a snort that put thunder to shame, then opened a bleary eye. He smacked his lips, as if he had been dreaming of food, then frowned as he caught sight of Barr. He reached into a shirt pocked for wire-rimmed glasses, which Barr noted had no lenses to speak of.

"Yes, yes, I'm awake," he said through the tangles of a long scruffy beard. "Who the blazes are you? Don't you knock before coming into a man's home and place of business?"

"My apologies. It's just been so long, and no one was answering the door."

"We're very busy here. You can't just come barging in because you were made to wait!" Therol looked down at his rug, where rainwater was staining it a darker green. "My rug! You could at least wipe your feet off before breaking into my chamber!"

"What is going on in here?" a robed figure asked from a second doorway. He wore leather gloves and was all but completely hidden beneath the shadows of a linen cowl. "You should not be in here."

Therol got to his feet, refusing Barr's help. "I thought I told you to lock up," he scolded the younger man. "And you. Get off my rug!"

"Look, I'm sorry about the rug –"

"I *did* lock the front doors," the other said and came to Therol's side. "He must have broken in."

"Hooligan, that's what he is. Fetch my cane! I'll show him what's what."

"Uncle," Barr said patiently, stepping away from the rug, "don't you recognize me? I'm your nephew, Barr. I'm Daroth's son."

Therol looked as if he had been slapped, so quiet and shocked did he become. His venerable eyes misted over, and his hands began to tremble. After a moment, he shook his head, as if dismissing a memory.

"Impossible," he said at last. "Both Barr and Daroth were killed years ago, out in the forest. They were torn to pieces by a –" Therol caught himself and gave a shrewd look – "wolf. A very large wolf. They're dead. I don't know what game you're playing at, but you're wasting my time here. Please leave, or I'll have my apprentice show you the door."

While the threat was not lost on Barr, he wondered how the frail younger man could throw anyone out. His shoulders were slender and drooped beneath the robe, and his gloved hands had the delicate frailty of a woman. He couldn't help but wonder what the apprentice was trying to hide beneath the cowl and gloves, or the long robes and soft boots. It was as if he were trying to conceal every inch of his body.

The apprentice came forward, intent on fulfilling his master's promise. Barr held out an arm to keep the frail man at bay and was taken aback by the belied strength that met his hand. Barr's hand was pushed aside with the casual ease of a fly being shooed away.

"You have been asked to leave," he said politely, but a threat of violence ran the edge of his tone.

The Last Incarnation

"I *am* your nephew," Barr insisted. "Will you just take a closer look at me? It's been a long time, and I've changed almost..." *as much as you.* "Just look."

Therol reluctantly agreed and stepped closer. He took a hold of Barr's chin and studied each feature. Moving Barr's face from side to side, as if looking for something in particular, he finally rested his gaze on those amber eyes. Therol's scraggly beard then parted in recognition, as breath escaped his thin lips.

"Oh," he gasped, his eyes clouding with tears, "Barr, it *is* you! Gods above, how can this be? I saw the bloodied snow, the torn trap and pieces... Oh, Barr, it's you! You're alive!"

Barr smiled with relief and hugged his uncle close. They held each other for a while, all sense of lost time no longer between them. Barr found himself happy to have family once again. All his frustration with the elves, his uncertain future, his guilt over abandoning his uncle, it all slipped away in the single embrace.

"I'll make some tea," the apprentice said and left.

Therol held him back for a moment. "Wait. Barr, this is Dar-Paj, my apprentice. He's been with me a long time now."

"Pleased to meet you," Barr said and took the offered hand. He had the sense this Dar-Paj could have crushed every bone in his hand had he wanted to. The apprentice nodded and went to the hearth to brew a pot of tea. "Why don't we sit down and talk?"

I've never met anyone so strong.

"Yes, please!" his uncle said happily. "I want to hear everything! Barr, Barr, where in the world have you *been*? By the sound of your accent, I'd say you were very far away. You could've come to me sooner than this, you know. I would've have taken care of you."

Even stronger than the elves? Idelle asked. *That is unusual. Perhaps he is like them, in that his muscles are denser than yours.*

It's more than that. There's something about him, a subterfuge I can't quite put my finger on.

Barr pulled up a chair from the desk and sat across from his uncle. Careful in what words he chose, he explained everything that had happened that day in the forest, when Daroth had left him alone to go deal with the wolf. He made no mention of Tuvrin or the elves.

"But where have you been? Why didn't you come home?" Therol seemed angry at first, but his ire faded away in a shake of his head. "I've missed you terribly. If only you knew what I've gone through."

"It's complicated," Barr said weakly. "But what of you and these white hairs, the beard and wrinkles? Uncle, what in the world happened to you?"

It was Therol's turn to evade. "Well, I – uh, that's... also a bit complicated."

Dar-Paj cleared his throat with a meaningful cough, his cowl turned Therol's way, before leaving for the kitchen.

"Your apprentice seems complicated, as well." Barr leaned forward, genuinely concerned. "Is it wise to share your home with such an odd person?"

"I know it seems that way, but it's only because he doesn't know you. He only hides himself, because he is ashamed. That boy is like a son to me, and I trust him implicitly."

"Enough to tell him why you've aged unnaturally?"

"Those swords," Therol said, studying them close. "I have never seen anything like them. Is that some sort of marble? Tell me, are you a soldier? Did you become a mercenary, like your father?"

"They're wood, actually, and no, I'm not a soldier. I'm more of a healer, really."

"What sort of healer wears swords?"

Dar-Paj returned with a tray full of pottery cups and jellied bread squares.

I can't tell him about the elves.

Then don't, Aren said. *Then again, he's not likely to tell you why he's aged if he thinks you're keeping secrets.*

Idelle said, *He's right. You don't have to mention the Sylvannis, but you're going to have to tell him something.*

"About where I've been," Barr began, taking the cup of hot tea Dar-Paj offered. He was surprised to see the apprentice take a cup for himself and pull up a chair between them. "I can't tell you much, because I took an oath not to speak of it. Lives would be in danger. What I can tell you is that I was treated well, and my father was not killed by an ordinary wolf. That same wolf has been alive all these years, hunting the people I called friend. I saw sign of it in the forest just yesterday."

Therol's hand shook so badly that he had to put his cup down for fear of spilling. "It's here, in Alixhir? You're sure of that?"

"What? No, it's out in the forest. Even a wolf as odd as that one isn't foolish enough to enter a city. It stalks lone prey, women and children." Barr clenched a fist to hold back his frustration. "I've been hunting it for years, but only once did I come close to killing it."

"That explains much," Therol said, smoothing the wrinkles of his face with a speckled hand, "but sadly, you only know half of the story. Tell me, are you still troubled by visions?"

"They're not like they used to be," Barr answered guardedly.

"But you still have them? Good, good. Then maybe it'll be easier for you to understand. In all your time away, did you encounter any magic? I know how fear of the Guardians might keep you from speaking, but I assure you, you can speak freely about it here." Barr nodded slowly, and his uncle continued. "Well, quite some time ago, I realized that we all have it in some way. Your visions, for example, are a sort of magic. Oh, don't be so surprised."

Barr's eyes widened at the thought. "Sorry, I just never thought of them that way. My visions are more like dreams than anything else. What does this have to do with the wolf?"

Therol shook his head sadly. "Sometimes I wish I didn't know. What I'm talking about isn't the great magic you hear about in stories by the fire, but it's a magic all the same. Dar-Paj, would you bring me the wooden box from my desk? Thank you. He's a good student," Therol told Barr, stroking the length of his beard. "I found him some time after you and your father were lost. He lives here with me and helps out with what work comes my way – oh, thank you, son. Here," he said and opened the box, pulling out an iron medallion, a broken chain that once held it and a folded sheet of parchment. "This is what I wanted to show you."

Has he been scrying? That can't be why he's aged. He would have had to have exhausted his own furie... Barr left the thought unfinished.

"Uncle," Barr said with caution, "why aren't you worried about the Guardians? When I was last in Alixhir, the mere mention of magic sent people off into hysterics." He leaned forward in his chair. "I mean, that's why father and I left in the first place."

"The Guardians are still feared, and rightly so. Their reach goes far beyond what many believe. I am, however, an old and tired man, little threat to anyone. As far as the world is concerned, I'm a scholar and scribe, nothing more. Never would I speak of magic outside my own walls, and what little of it I do wouldn't draw the notice of a Guardian right outside my door." Therol scratched at his pointed nose with a grin. "I occasionally do some translating and scribe work for the local Justiciar, and in exchange, she leaves me be. Our agreement is tentative at best, but I'm safe from harm so long as I'm of use to her. In any case, tell me what you think of this."

Barr took the medallion in hand, then dropped it as if he had been bitten. The metal was cold enough to leave his fingers numb, and he frowned at his uncle while shaking some feeling back into his fingers.

"You *are* touched," Therol said, a wry crinkling to his left brow. "I thought as much. I'm sorry about that. I didn't think the medallion would affect you so strongly. But," he said with a pointed finger, picking up the piece, "this is what I found near your father's... remains. This is what Daroth's attacker was wearing."

"Father was killed by a wolf," Barr said, wondering if his uncle was a bit senile. "I've seen the creature myself. It's unusually large, very old and very smart, but it's just a wolf."

"Open that parchment," Therol said. There was a charcoal drawing of a man's face, with the medallion suspended from his hand. "That is the man who killed your father, a priest of Revyn. If you doubt me, just take the medallion again. Hold it, this time. Don't let it fall from your grasp, and tell me what you see."

He held the round metal out to Barr.

With some trepidation, Barr readied himself and took the medallion. A cold beyond the ice of winter gripped him, coiled around his hand and ran the length of his arm. It spread with the slowness of thickening blood, sending frost through his veins in a tingling numbness. And with the cold came the darkness of a vision, the black nothing that shrouds the mind before a brilliant flash overwhelms the senses with a time and place that was or will be.

This vision, however, was different from the others, seen from the hazy perspective of one both there and not. Barr didn't see through the eyes of one who stood by the priest in green flowing robes or watch the scene from the vantage of those who prayed in line before the altar. He floated above and around the huddled figures, flitting past the white robes of initiates without stirring their folds, hovering above candles, leaving no trace at all of his presence.

It was the man on the parchment, his aquiline nose and zealous eyes, the cheeks flushed with pride and arms extended in worship. In his hand was a medallion, the iron chain a polished gray-blue that glinted in the candlelight. Hooded men approached the altar one at a time, bowed low their heads in homage or fear. His arms came down on quivering shoulders, taking firm hold with an unshakable faith.

It was the eyes that convinced him, their reflective feral glow. They were the eyes of a predator, and locked away behind them was the bestial spirit of killer.

It was him. Barr could see the maniacal gaze of triumph and glory, twisting the sharp features of a once handsome face. The medallion was in his hand, mocking, reminding, a cold emblem of death. *He's the wolf. I can see it within him.* He was a shapeling, a cursed man with the heart of a beast, one who changes form to slake a thirst for warm blood. *He hunted and killed all those people. All that pain and suffering, families ruined, all at the hands of one man...*

The man who killed my father.

The thought sent Barr reeling with rage, flying up and back, through marble and stone and darkness and sky. Higher and higher, he screamed at the night, clawed at the temple that fell away from his vision. A collection of straight lines in a blackened land of snaking hills and rotting trees, the building was no more than a spot of detail on a map that encompassed the world. The lights of Alixhir loomed in the distance, but it was the temple in Lumintor that called to him, a beacon that summoned, a landmark that cried.

It was his own voice echoing through the clouds. *He can't be allowed to kill again. If no one else can stop him, then I will.*

Barr gave the medallion back and stood.

"You saw him," Therol said, nodding as if to himself. "Now you have your answer. I look as I do from endless nights of searching out that monster of a man. But using magic has its price. Without a care for my health, I persisted, continued to watch though it ate away at my *furie*. With each sleepless night, my power waned. I was consumed with avenging you and your father's death, obsessed over the face on that parchment. But now," he dismally shook his head, "I have almost nothing left. There's nothing for me to do now but pass on what I've learned of magic."

Dar-Paj bowed, the point of his hood drooping low.

Are you alright? Idelle asked. *I've never felt you this angry. What did you see?*

"I saw," Barr said through gritted teeth, biting back the emotion that threatened to choke him. He wasn't prepared to relive his grief like that. "I know now what I have to do."

The wolf. It's a shapeling, a man that becomes a wolf and feeds on others. And I know where he is.

I'm ready to leave when you are, Aren said, his voice edged with the growing rage that Barr felt.

"No, Barr." Therol laid a gentle hand on his nephew's shoulder. "Don't torture yourself the way I did. It cost me nearly all my *furie* before I accepted it. Whoever he is, that priest is too well guarded by another magic to find him. It's only his intimate link with that medallion, his faith, that allows us to see him at all."

Try to be calm, Idelle said. *You need to think things through before making any rash decisions.*

"You don't understand. I *saw* him, in a temple at the center of Lumintor." He fixed his uncle with a determined look. "I'm going there. I'm going to find him and finish what he started."

"You'll do no such thing!" Therol stood as well. "You're brash and untrained. Please, see to reason, Barr. Granted, you have innate talent, a strong magic within, but you don't know how to *use* it! And I'll not lose you, not now. You've only just come back, and already you're looking to go."

Aren said, *We have no choice. If you know where to find it, we have to go after. Think how many more will die if we don't.*

"I don't expect you to understand, uncle, but I do know how to use my magic. I *have* been trained."

He drew a kyan and spoke the name of a sigil carved in its blade. "Pakrah!" The ironwood edge flared with blue light, then Barr plunged it into the wall by the hearth, to the hilt, through solid stone. He moved the hilt enough to prove he could cut the building in two with no more effort than parting a warm block of tallow. He sheathed the kyan and faced his uncle once more.

"Don't think I'm expecting to just ride into Lumintor without any quarrel, or storm into this priest's temple to casually talk over father's death." Barr noticed Dar-Paj stand beside him, closely following the conversation but not saying a word. "I will make plans once I'm there. Try to understand, uncle. I have to do this."

"You're young and foolish," his uncle scolded. "I'm only afraid you'll learn too late that you're *not* invincible. I can't come with you," he added mournfully. "I'm too old and weak, my magic all but gone."

We should return to Geilon-Rai, Idelle said. *Tell them what we've learned. The Maurdon would come with us to finish the wolf.*

More likely, Aren said, *the Narohk standing guard would shoot us on sight. We've been exiled. They won't welcome us back, no matter what news we bring.*

Dar-Paj pulled down his cowl, revealing skin the metallic hue of frosted gold. He looked little more than Barr's age, with gaunt cheeks and a square chin. His eyes reminded Barr of the woman in the forest, but the apprentice's were gold where there should have been white, with his irises the rich and vibrant brown of freshly turned soil. There was something about his gaze, an air of confidence or resolve, that made Dar appear wise beyond his seeming years.

"I would go with you," he said, shaking out the white length of hair that trailed down the back of his robe. When he spoke, rows of pointed teeth could be seen gnashing with each word. To Therol he added, "You have been more than a mere friend or mentor to me. These past years, you have been like a father. But I must know where it is that I come from, why I look the way I do, and why I cannot remember who I am. I will not find those answers here among the books and scrolls." He turned to Barr. "I have been waiting for an opportunity to leave this city behind, to search for others like myself. You know the world outside these walls. You could show me. In return, I would keep you safe. I am far stronger than I appear."

"I'm sorry, but I'm better off by myself. I'll be headed into danger, and no offense, but strength or no, you'd be more of a hindrance than a help."

Barr, wait. Shouldn't you give this more thought? He could sense Idelle land on the roof. *If what you say is true, that this wolf is a man, wouldn't there be others just like him there? In all our years, we haven't been able to kill the wolf. How will we face an entire pack?*

Aren said, *That's only because it always runs away. If we know where it lives, we can sneak in and catch it off guard. There won't be anywhere left to run.*

We don't know if there are others, Barr said. *Even if there are, how can we let them go on killing?*

"I may not have any memory of who I am," Dar-Paj said, "but of one thing I am certain. I am anything but a hindrance. Do not assume I have no skill with weapons or that I am merely stronger than a normal man. I could tear this building down around us, stone by stone, and not break a sweat. I can hear your winged friend on our roof. I can look out that window and tell you what the guard at the front gate is wearing." He took a deep breath and let it out with a sigh. "If anything, you should see that I am sincere in my words. I have no other motive but to find others like me, to find the home that I lost, the friends and family I must have. My memory will never be restored, so long as I stay within these walls. And perhaps, by accompanying you, I can repay your uncle's kindness by keeping his nephew from harm."

"You can hear Idelle on the roof, but you didn't hear me calling out downstairs?"

Dar looked sheepish. "I was asleep."

"Why come with me?" Barr asked. "The likelihood of encountering someone like yourself... I've never seen anyone like you, apart from the eyes."

"I don't believe what I'm hearing," Therol said, falling back to his seat. "You're both daft! Barr, you can't just walk into Lumintor! As far as anyone else is concerned, it's just a barren land with dark stories of monsters. No one actually believes that shapelings are real. But you and I know the truth. They *are* real. And if even half the stories have a glimmer of truth, there are hundreds of them living in those ruins."

Dar-Paj said firmly, "All the more reason to take me."

He's persistent, Aren said. *I like him. Take him along, and let's go.*

Aren! Idelle fumed. *Stop encouraging him!*

"Alright. Gather up whatever you can carry in one satchel. I'll see to our supplies." Dar-Paj left quickly, and Barr pulled up his uncle for a farewell embrace. "Truth be told, uncle, I never planned to stay in Alixhir. I just don't belong here anymore. I had no intention of stealing your apprentice, but it seems he's been waiting to go. I only meant to see you again before I found a new home, somewhere."

"I knew Dar was unhappy, but this. This is madness. You'll both end up dead, and I'm too old to grieve again. Not like that."

"I'll return when I'm done," Barr promised, "just to show you I'm safe. Then I'll see what I can do about helping Dar find his people."

"I still say you're a damned fool, but that doesn't change the fact that I love you. I just wish I could talk you out of this nonsense. Fancy swords or no, I don't think you fully realize what you're heading into."

"I know there's a man out there murdering innocent people, that he has been for years. How can I do nothing when it's within my power to stop him?"

"Just because something can be made right doesn't mean you're the one to do it." Therol worried his lower lip. "Tell the Guardians, Barr. They'll scour that fetid land until nothing remains."

"Tell them what, exactly? That I caught sight of a shapeling in my scrying bowl? You know as well as I do that they'd lock me away, or worse, and that killer would still be free. Whether the stories are true or not, there's at least one shapeling out there, and I mean to bring it down."

"I am ready," Dar-Paj said and put a single leather bag by the door. He approached with some measure of reticence, like a child searching for approval, then gave the old scribe a gentle hug. "I shall miss you a great deal, Master Therol. Once I discover the truth about myself and where it is that I come from, I will return to thank you properly for all you have done for me."

"You don't owe me a thing." Therol blinked back the tears that threatened his vision. "You're the son I always wanted. Never forget that. You always have a family here with me. Now, both of you go, before I call the Guardians myself."

"Be well, uncle," Barr said. "We'll both see you again soon."

"You better. I won't live for much longer, and if you die, I'll find you."

We should bring him, too, Aren said. *He's got fire.*

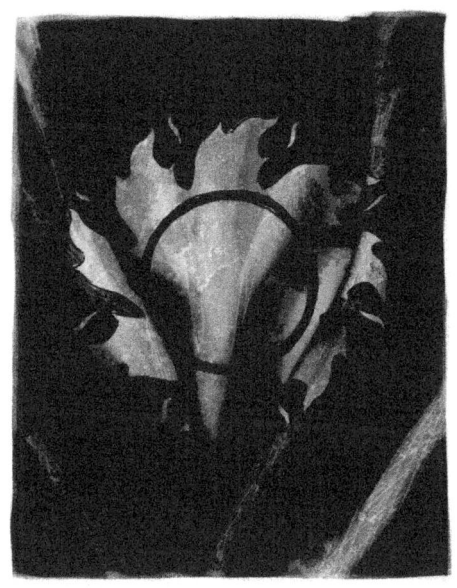

– 21 –

The heavy rain had somewhat let up and settled into a fine mist that embraced all with its chill. Barr pulled the fur of his leathers tight about his neck and rubbed the outer side of both arms for warmth. Dar-Paj walked beside him, hidden once more within the dark of his cowl and thick robes. He seemed unaffected by the bitter cold but was more concerned for the few others caught out in the rain and the sidelong glances they cast toward him.

It just occurred to me, Idelle said, gliding far above. *What if Ealdan wants to come?*

He thinks he owes me money, so he's probably long gone by now. Barr considered. *What made you suddenly wonder about that?*

After a brief pause, she replied, *Oh, nothing.*

"I should probably warn you," Barr said, and stopped short when he realized it was too late.

"Barr!" Ealdan said happily, standing beneath an awning in front of the Portly Inn. "I have been waiting out in this cold for quite some time."

"You could have gone inside. Dar-Paj, this is Ealdan. We met outside the city, and he's been... around ever since."

"Pleasure to meet you," the apprentice said, his cowl dipping low in a bow of his head. "Any friend –"

Barr cleared his throat. "Are you just dropping off something for me or...?"

Ealdan found sudden interest in his shoes. "About that. I could find no trace of Jontry, so I am a bit light on coin at the moment. I came looking for you to explain and offer dinner as recompense. An acquaintance of mine is throwing a banquet this evening."

"That's very generous," Barr said, trying to remain polite, "but unnecessary. We won't have time. Both of us are leaving early in the morning."

Aren said, *Speaking of which, should I stay here or meet you outside the gates tomorrow?*

Meet us, but be careful you're not seen.

"What a coincidence! I was just thinking of visiting my cousin in Eternoll. Assuming you are heading west, I could join you on the road for a short time."

"We'll be going south."

"South," Ealdan said, puzzled. "There is nothing south, not for days, and even then only Lumintor. And no one goes *there* willingly." The actor looked as if he read something of Barr's intent in his expression. "You should reconsider, if that truly is your destination. Lumintor is an ashen forest of burned trees, blinding fog and utter devastation. The soil itself is dead, nothing can grow there. My troupe and I spent weeks lost in that land and never once saw an animal or bird."

"You have been to Lumintor?" Dar-Paj asked with great interest.

Oh no, Aren said, knowing where this would lead.

Ealdan nodded gravely. "It was horrible. We became lost in a storm on our way back from Systeria. There is a perpetual haze over Lumintor, like a thick cloud of gray smoke, and it is filled with the stench of rotted eggs. Believe me when I say there is no food or water to be had. If you plan on passing through, bring twice as many supplies." The actor tried to peek beneath Dar-Paj's cowl. "Just curious, but is there a reason you hide your face like that? It is wonderfully distracting."

Don't even think it, Aren warned. *Just don't.*

Barr sighed. "Just how well do you know the land? There's a temple in its center that we need to get to. Did you see anything like that while you were there?"

"A temple?" Ealdan chuckled. "What, like the stories of shapelings and dark shadowy monsters? I think not. I saw no sign of anyone anywhere in that wasteland. The path we were on was barely passable. I cannot imagine anyone building a temple without some sort of decent road to wagon in materials." He saw that Barr was not jesting and cleared his throat before adding, "Yes, I am all too familiar with the land. I could easily find my way out again. Say, are you thinking of asking me along as a guide? It would be dreadfully frightening," he teased and mimed the claws of a monster, "but perhaps in exchange my debt would be paid?"

Idelle offered no comment but a long wind of muffled chuckling.

Barr looked around to be sure that no one could hear. Quietly, he asked, "What if I told you the stories were not far from truth? There's at least one shapeling.

We saw sign of it yesterday, and I mean to track it down and kill it."

"You are serious. Well, then, that changes things a bit." Ealdan looked down, as he ticked off numbers on each finger. "People would pay a great deal to see a play about such an adventure, you know." More counting. "I would be rich." He met Barr's gaze with a wild-eyed grin. "Alright then, I will do it! Lucky you came across me. I doubt you would find a single person in all of Alixhir that has stepped foot in that cursed land."

"Yes, that's just what I was thinking... how lucky I am."

"Absolutely! Just think, there will be no shortage of good conversation."

Aren's groan echoed in Barr's ears.

"And here I thought we'd be forced to endure miles of peace and quiet."

"Ha! Not while I am around!"

* * *

Normally, it would have cost Barr an additional two silver to share his room, but it turned out that Trevor really was a friend of Ealdan's. The rotund innkeeper was all too happy to wave the fee and had some leftover stew and bread brought up to them, though dinner was already passed. Dar-Paj settled against a wall as he ate, while Ealdan made himself comfortable in a wooden chair by the shuttered window. Barr was finishing his meal when Aren asked what had already been troubling him.

How do you plan to kill the wolf without magic?

Bringing Ealdan along meant openly weaving *furie* was out of the question. Barr knew he could trust Dar-Paj to not go running for the Guardians, considering the many years he had spent with Therol learning to scry, but Ealdan was another matter. There was no telling what the actor might do when faced with a weaver, when forced to see that magic was just as real as the shapeling they meant to kill. Would he take it in stride and see that Barr was not one of the crazed turners that stole *furie* from the helpless? Or would he react with the mindless fear and misdirected anger like so many others had done?

If we catch him off guard in his temple, Barr replied, *he won't be in wolf form.*

"So tell me," Ealdan said. "How can you be sure this wolf is a shapeling?"

We know almost nothing of what a shapeling can do, Idelle said. *What's to stop him from changing into a wolf inside the temple? He wouldn't need to hide it from any others there, because they're probably shapelings too. A more important question would be, how are you going to handle more than one wolf?*

"A wolf that large," Dar-Paj offered, "must surely be one of them. Those stories might be told to frighten young children or caution the unwary from entering such a barren land, but that does not mean there have never been creatures both man and beast."

We may just have to trust Ealdan and hope for the best. If we catch the wolf alone, arrows will suffice. If not...

"Personally, I do not believe any of it." Ealdan put his bowl down and stretched back in his chair. "The whole notion that a society of shapelings exists, so close to a major city like Alixhir or even a town like Systeria, is completely absurd. Someone, somewhere, would have noticed."

"Shapeling or not," Barr said, "there's an extremely large wolf out there that's been killing innocent people for years."

"And you expect to find it in a temple among the ruins of Lumintor? I understand you are not telling me everything. I am merely curious as to why you would use a children's story to enlist my aid."

Dar-Paj asked, "If you do not believe what we have told you, then why agree to come at all?"

Aren said, *Because he has no one else to torture with his endless conversation.*

"I have taken a liking to our friend Barr here. I know firsthand how dangerous Lumintor can be. Without my help, I do not think either of you would return."

"The wolf is real," Barr insisted.

"I am sure it is. But have you ever seen it transform into a man? Or vice versa? It could very well be a large wolf and nothing more. All that aside, regardless of why you are going to Lumintor, I shall respect your privacy and reserve judgment for another time. I am only glad that I can repay you for your assistance in the forest."

It's getting late, Idelle said. *You still need to gather supplies and horses in the morning.*

Aren asked, *You know how to ride a horse? I'm not even sure I know what one looks like.*

Not far off from a certain war hound I know, and yes, I know how to ride.

"We should get some rest," Barr said and blew out the lantern beside the bed. "We can talk more once we're underway."

"Sleep well," Dar-Paj said and wrapped his traveling cloak tightly about him.

Ealdan went to sleep without a word.

* * *

It was well into night when Barr woke to see Ealdan standing by the window, peering anxiously down at the street through a barely opened shutter. He looked as if he were afraid the sliver of moonlight that shone through might betray him to whoever it was that he saw. Barr got out of bed quietly and came up beside him.

"What is it?" he asked, careful not to wake Dar. "More friends of yours from the Crimson Order?"

"It looks like a command from the Justiciar."

"Guardians?"

Ealdan stepped aside so that Barr could see. "Two pair have been passing by this window for the better part of an hour. That might not be so uncommon, but those three across the way. They have not moved for as long as I have been watching."

If not for the silver insignia on each man's breast, Barr might have mistaken them for mercenaries. They wore heavy chain mail coats, stained black as the robes that hid them from lamplight, and each was equipped with a heavy broadsword and armguard. Only moonlight shone off the cobbled street at either end, where it looked as if the lamps on each corner had been forgotten or doused.

"We should leave," Ealdan suggested, his voice tinged with fear.

There was a patrol, Idelle said, *but I can't see them anymore.*

Barr closed the shutters. "Guardians only concern themselves with weavers. If they're here, it's for someone else."

Could they be here for me? Or Dar-Paj? Barr put the thought from his mind. *I haven't used any magic at all, with the exception of unlocking Therol's door.*

Your uncle said your visions were a sort of magic. Did you have any tonight?

No, just a dream that I was back in Geilon-Rai.

"What about this one?" Ealdan nodded towards Dar-Paj. "Why does he keep himself hidden, even here in the dark?"

"I am no more a weaver," the apprentice said and looked toward them, "than you are."

"Yet you can hear whispers from across the room?"

"This room is not so big, and I was already awake. If you have done nothing wrong, you have little to fear from the Guardians."

Ealdan blinked. "Have you been living in a cave your whole life? The Guardians can and often do arrest totally innocent people. Right or wrong has no part in what they do." The actor held up a hand for silence. "Did you hear that?"

Barr listened. "I don't hear anything."

"That is my point. I could hear their boots against the cobbles before, but now I do not hear a thing." He opened the shutter and looked down. "They are gone. All of them. Quick," he said and headed for the door, "let us be gone from this place. They could be coming for us at this very moment!"

Aren grumbled, as if he were pulled from sleep. *What is he jabbering on about now? You'd think his jaw would eventually get tired.*

"You're not making any sense," Barr said. "Why should we run from Guardians that haven't –"

A knock at the door cut his words short. Dar-Paj was up in an instant, with a stool in hand and ready to strike. Barr narrowed his gaze in unspoken agreement. Guardians or no, someone knocking on their door this late at night did not bode well. He drew both kyan and nodded for Ealdan to open the door. The response was not quite what he expected.

"Absolutely not!" the actor mouthed. "I told you!"

Barr pushed him aside and called out, "Who is it?"

"It's Trevor, the innkeeper," a voice quavered. "Please open the door. I have somewhat to speak with you about."

"I see." Barr unlatched the door with an outstretched kyan and stepped aside, allowing room for the door to open without striking him. "Come on in then."

As expected, the door opened and crashed against the wall. The obese innkeeper was clearly thrust into the room, nearly falling over his own legs as he fought to regain balance. When nothing happened to his corpulent person, two men burst in with swords drawn. There was a flash of red cloth about their foreheads.

They're not Guardians, Barr thought quickly. *They're thieves from the Order.*

The first one turned immediately to face Barr and struck out with a short sword that was meant to kill, not wound or disarm. It took only a breath to surmise the deadly intent. Barr pushed aside the attack with his left kyan, driving the other's blade into the wall by his side. A quick thump across the jaw with the pommel of his right kyan, and another to the forehead for good measure, sent the thief to the ground in a heap.

The second was through the door as the first began falling. He was taller and much broader across the chest than his partner, but he moved with the same deadly purpose. His gaze fell upon Dar-Paj, and his blade followed suit. Wielding the stool like a weapon, Dar caught the incoming sword between its legs and gave a twist that tightened its hold. A snap of his wrist then pulled the sword free, sending it skittering across the floor and under the bed. The look of surprise on the thief's face did not last long, because the stool then splintered across his head. Dar-Paj caught the man before he could fall over and easily lifted him off the ground with one hand. Held firmly against the wall, his feet dangling in air, the beefy rogue tried furiously to blink sense into what he was seeing.

"Are you sure you have the right room?" Dar-Paj asked politely.

Do you need me? Aren asked. *I can be there in –*

No, Barr said, disarming the unconscious thief. *We dealt with them already. Stay outside of the city until we leave.*

"Perhaps he'd like to sit down and talk about it." Barr tossed the short sword and various knives onto the bed. "His partner is otherwise indisposed. I suggest you leave out no details, or you'll both be exiting through the window."

Though the man stood a hand taller than Dar-Paj and weighed easily three stone more, the frail apprentice handled him as if he were a child's rag doll. He forced the thief to sit against the wall, where both Barr's kyan and the glimpse of an alien golden stare bore down on him from above. Ealdan kept to the other side of the room, but his hand was never far from a silk cuff.

The innkeeper swallowed, as if fearing any movement would draw undue attention.

"My apologies," Barr said. "Were you at all hurt?"

"No, I'm fine." Trevor slipped a handkerchief from his pocket and dabbed at his bald pate. "Thank you for not killing me, and all that. I know I'm no small target. I'll leave you to talk with your new friends."

A *tsk!* toward the conscious thief, and the chubby innkeeper was gone.

"Talk," Barr said evenly.

"He knows why we're here," the man answered back, nodding to Ealdan. "He owes us, and he's planning to leave. Lady Errymes might've overlooked the money, but he, err, broke off relations with her, if you get what I mean."

Aren said, *He's going to be more trouble than he's worth. These thieves will follow and keep attacking until he's dead.*

Or until he pays them.

"Exactly how much does he owe?" Barr turned a withering gaze toward Ealdan. "Maybe he can pay you right now and call things even."

"Afraid not," the big thief said and shrugged. "The Lady gave orders. She wants his head. I could, however, be persuaded to believe that he disappeared... in any direction you like. If you know what I mean."

"Can he be trusted," Barr asked Ealdan, "to do what he says he will?"

"Of course not. He would take whatever coin we give him and then make another attempt when the advantage is his." Ealdan stepped closer. "They will follow, no matter how horrible the destination. I am truly sorry. I had hoped this mess was behind me. I can make things right with Errymes when we get back, but paying this thief will not help us."

We can't leave without supplies, Idelle said. *Maybe Trevor can help keep the thieves out of sight until we put some distance between us and the city.*

That's a good idea, Aren agreed. *An even better idea is to tie Ealdan up with them. Then they won't have any reason to chase us.*

We still need a guide, Barr reminded him. *We could end up lost in the fog for weeks.*

What about scrying?

I could try, but I don't know how reliable that would be. So long as that priest stays at the temple, I can find him with the medallion. That won't help us get through Lumintor though.

"Barr?" Dar-Paj waited expectantly. "What do we do with them?"

"You can trust me," the thief promised with a smile. "Haven't you ever heard of honor among thieves?"

Barr replied, "Only that there is none. Ealdan, go ask Trevor if he has anything to tie them up."

"You don't have to do that –"

"And gags."

Ealdan nodded and was out the door. He returned within moments, rope in hand. With a toss of one to Dar-Paj, he knelt and began tying up the unconscious thief.

"I have an idea what to do with them," the actor said and finished. "A little brandy on their clothes and another thump to the head, we can leave them outside for the constable to lock up."

"Hey now!" the thief protested.

Dar-Paj knocked him out with a short jab to the temple. "This idea has merit. The constable will keep them locked up for a day. That should give us plenty of time to get moving."

"Again," Ealdan began and stood, "It was not my intention to make your journey more difficult. If you wish to reconsider and have me stay behind, I will of course understand."

"Once we've dealt with these two," Barr said, "I think we should try to get some more sleep. Tomorrow is going to be a long day, and we're all going to need as much rest as we can get."

With a nod of thanks, Ealdan gave a hand carrying the two thieves out.

* * *

The others went back up to the room, while Ealdan was to look for a constable. Instead, he untied the two thieves and woke them with the whiff of a foul-smelling vial that he pulled from a pocket. The largest of the two,

Oloff, rubbed his forehead with a palm and got shakily to his feet. The other merely grumbled and left off to keep watch.

"Everything go as you planned?" Oloff asked.

"Well enough. The rest of your payment is being kept at Highcross safehouse."

"Pleasure doing business."

Oloff turned on his heal and left, tapping his partner on the shoulder as he went. The two of them disappeared into the dark of an alley, with no sound of their passing left behind. The shadows in that alley grew darker still, more solid and lustrous, like thick panes of black glass. Though the night was chill enough to frost breath and ache bones, the cold from this darkness sent ice across the cobbles.

"Come," Ealdan commanded, and from the darkness stepped two figures in long cloaks and blackened mail. "Time is short. The plan remains unchanged, as do your orders." He eyed their garb and the fiery insignia. "Will there be any problem with missing Guardians, or are these guises fabricated?"

The tallest one answered, its face hidden within the dark of a masked helm and low cowl. Its voice echoed all about them but reached only their ears. Like the whisper of death's shroud spreading over bodies still warm, it coiled over their bodies and hid them from sight.

"Illusion only, my lord Markus." His figure wavered beneath the pale moonlight and coalesced into a perfect likeness of Ealdan, though with eyes that glowed the faintest glimmer of emerald. "You know well what powers we command."

"Yes," Ealdan said coolly, as he faced his illusory double, "and I require no demonstration. Remember, Feraesk, just where it is your powers come from." The double bowed its head and was once more a hooded

Guardian. "Enough of this, I must return. Stay behind and out of sight, especially from the hawk, but be ready when I call. When the sword is revealed, we will strike... but not a moment before. Now, away with you."

The two bowed their heads as they backed into the darkness and disappeared. The other ten revenants would be nearby as well, hidden within the dark or shrouded in disguise. Though fifteen long years had passed since they all had awoken from enchanted slumber, the time they had been waiting for was finally at hand. If Barr did not possess one of the Emblems at this very moment, it would only be a matter of time before he did.

And Markus only needed one to find the others.

Much like his Brood wore disguises to conceal their true nature, he wore Ealdan like a cloak that kept at bay the mistrust. It was far from the perfect ruse, but it did serve its purpose well.

Your ruse, as you call it, does not work half as well as you think.

No matter how many times the god spoke in his head, Markus never got used to the vibrations. They ran the length of his spine and shook his middle with each word. Though he would never say it aloud, there was a tiny fear in his heart that an angry yell might have killed him.

It works well enough. I am accompanying them to Lumintor, am I not?

Watch your tone, Revyn warned. *It is by my will alone that he sees in you anything resembling good faith. Heed my words when the time comes, and the Emblem will be yours.*

If he had it with him, he would have used it just now in the attack. He heads toward certain death at the hands of your children. How will he survive the temple?

Sacrifice is a part of any change for the better.

You could warn them we are coming, leave the temple abandoned so we find nothing –

No. The God of Change was quiet for a moment, then added, *They are part of a much larger endeavor, and their numbers are easily replenished.*

Markus gave a curt nod, wondering if he was held with an equal regard.

I must return, he said and headed for the door. *They will grow suspicious if I take any longer.*

Nothing but silence followed after.

– 22 –

They were up before dawn and assaulted by a drop in temperature that no fur or heavy cloak could stave off. The cobbled streets, once slick with rain, were now iced and more dangerous than ever. It was quiet in the dark of a new snow, where not even the sound of stray dogs could be heard. Only the wind accompanied the crunch of each step, when they parted ways outside of the inn.

Little more than an hour had passed before they met once more, near the southern gate and under scrutiny of the guard. Since it was Dar-Paj that did most of the shopping for Therol, he knew of a merchant that would overlook being woken before morn. A few extra coins, and the sleepy-eyed man was more than happy to do business in his night robe. From a small burlap sack of tubers to a large roll of dried meat, extra skins for water to blankets and tinder, they purchased enough supplies for a ten day journey. Even in the worst of weather, Barr was confident they could reach Lumintor in four.

While they were off gathering supplies, Ealdan went for a fresh change of clothes and horses from an acquaintance. Though he had traded his cravat and silken shirt for a more practical linen doublet, his polished black shoes for riding boots, a perfumed kerchief still found its way into the ensemble. At their timely arrival, he bowed with a flourish and presented their mounts.

"This is Jax," he said to Barr, presenting a chestnut mare, "and this is Tarem."

Dar-Paj approached the dark gelding, as if studying its every curve. The horse seemed skittish and whinnied in protest at the man shrouded in cloth. From one of his pockets, Dar pulled out an apple and held it out for the horse to eat while whispering in its ear. In just moments, the two were fast friends.

"What did you say to him" Ealdan asked, amused by the display. "I have never seen Tarem eat from out of hand."

"Only that I am a friend and will keep him from harm. He dislikes your aroma, by the way. It irritates his nose."

Ealdan gave a *hmph* and put away his kerchief.

"We are being watched," Barr said, arranging some supplies into Jax's saddlebags. "Is permission required to leave the city before dawn?"

"No, they just have nothing else to put their eyes on at the moment." Ealdan tightened the saddle on his blue roan and added, "Speaking of being watched, I have seen no further sign of the Order. Hopefully, the two I sent off with the constable will be keeping his company for some time."

Looking about from the confines of his cowl, Dar-Paj said, "I shall miss this place, though not every memory of it is pleasant. Until I find others, I am afraid this is the only home I will ever know."

"Others?"

"We should get going." Barr fastened one last strap and led Jax toward the gate. "There's a storm headed this way, and it's only going to get colder."

"I have been thinking of the best route. There are roads we could take that lead nearly to the outskirts of the forest surrounding Lumintor, but if time was of the essence –"

"It is," Barr said. "I have no idea how long he'll be there, so we need to move as fast as we can."

"In that case, it would be best if we travel along the road to Laurenthos for a day and then head directly south. It will not be the easiest journey, but it will most certainly be the fastest."

He almost sounds useful, Aren said. *Next thing you know, he'll be cooking meals for us too.*

Be nice. We'll be there in no time.

One of the four guards nodded in greeting, as they passed beneath the portcullis. It was even colder in the tunnel, if such a thing were possible, and Barr was tempted to weave a spell just for warmth. Only memory of the Guardians outside his window stayed his hand. Once they were riding south, the promise of vengeance would keep him warm.

Is it vengeance or justice? he wondered. *I can't let him kill again, but I won't say that avenging my father wouldn't make me feel better.*

It's both, Aren said. *I know you, Barr. Even if the wolf didn't kill your father, you'd still be going after it.*

Idelle said, *Someone needs to. I still think you're going about this the wrong way, but that doesn't mean I don't agree that something must be done. The murders must stop, one way or another.*

They passed through the outer portcullis, and each mounted up. Barr looked back over a shoulder, as he left Alixhir for the second time. He took the lead with a gentle nudge, easing Jax into a trot. Aren was up the road, just a few minutes away, and Idelle was already overhead.

"Have you given any thought," Ealdan began, "to what we will do when we find this wolf?"

"Honestly, I won't know until we get there."

A silence followed, as if the actor expected more. "So, we are still with the shapeling story then? Fair enough. Did I ever tell you of the time I was in Noria, preparing for a role as a viscount, when this –"

Aren stepped from behind a large brush beside the road, startling the horses and interrupting Ealdan.

"Good lord!" the actor yelled, struggling to keep his horse from bucking him to the stones. "Easy, now! Easy, Smoke. Good, good fellow."

Barr rolled his eyes at the chuckling in his head. "Was that really necessary?"

Aren licked his chops.

"I take it," Dar-Paj said and dismounted, "that you are familiar with this creature? I have never seen a dog so large."

"He is... unusual. Aren is a war hound, bred for size and strength, courage and apparently poor humor."

The apprentice walked straight up to him and put a hand behind one ear. Scratching in a soothing manner, Dar-Paj admired Aren's healthy coat. He then removed a glove, as if in a gesture of respect, and allowed his bare hand to be sniffed.

"Aren, is it? I am Dar-Paj, and it is my honor to make your acquaintance."

I like him. Aren closed both eyes and bowed his head. *He knows I understand him, but he isn't saying anything about it. His scent feels... very old. And sad.* They could feel emotion welling up within the hound. *How can anyone be that sad.*

Are you alright? Idelle asked.

Fine, just a bit... no, I'm fine.

"He seems taken with you," Barr said and smiled. "If you look up, you'll see my other companion, Idelle. You heard her on the roof at my uncle's. She'll be keeping an eye out from above and let us know of any trouble."

"Are you expecting some?" Ealdan asked.

"I'd rather go in expecting trouble and be pleasantly surprised when there is none than to go unprepared on the hunt."

Dar-Paj put his glove back on and mounted up once more. "You keep interesting company," he said to Barr.

"True," Ealdan agreed. "There are not many that can claim friendship to a renowned actor *and* a man of such extraordinary hue."

"I was referring to Aren and Idelle."

"Ah, yes, I suppose they are unusual as well. Then again, neither one of them can fill a theater at a silver per chair, and I daresay your particular affliction –"

Barr cleared his throat and rode on.

"My affliction," Dar-Paj said, kneeing Tarem forward, "is only uncommon in these lands. If I were with my own people, I would have no need for disguise."

"How strange you should be convinced that you are any different –"

Dar-Paj took down his cowl.

Ealdan looked surprised at the sight, at the frosted gold skin and long snowy hair, at the small jagged teeth and strange earthen eyes rimmed with an even brighter gold, the sunken cheeks and proud chin, or the youthful

visage that belied such a confident air. Though Ealdan moved his mouth several times in the attempt to reply, no pithy remark was forthcoming.
That silence endured for the better part of an hour.

* * *

Daesi knelt in the dark waters, trailing fingers across the stillness and causing ripples through the reflection of stars overhead. Once more she looked down on her son, at the silvery brightness of his spirit. It was subtle at times, a shimmering glow about his body, and then for brief moments it would flare with the blinding radiance of a sun. It made her smile just to see him, to caress his image in the waters, but her happiness was now shaken with fear and a motherly concern.

"They are very old," she said across the waters, to her Queen on Faeronthalsos. "It is no coincidence they are with him while he has Aislin in his care."

From her throne, Ariana replied across the distance, "I fear I may have made a terrible mistake."

"Of that much we agree."

"I meant for Aislin to protect him, not draw danger like a lodestone." Daesi could feel her mother's pain with each word, the fear much like her own but intertwined with gnawing guilt. "We could take him away, bring him here to live with us. The prophecy does not say how he comes –"

"Mother, no. You cannot shape prophecy to your own ends. You may cause more harm than you already have." Frowning down at the image of her son riding south, she added, "If I could just find some way to speak with him. They are heading for Lumintor at this very moment. If that cursed land does not kill them, then the shapelings surely will."

"You cannot remedy one mistake with another," the Queen cautioned. "If we cannot interfere ourselves, then we can only hope that Aislin will keep him safe."

"He does not wear the bracer, which may be for the best. So long as it remains hidden, the other two will not desire to wrest it from him."

"You would have him enter Lumintor unprotected?"

"There is little I can do for that now," Daesi replied bitterly. "All I can do is observe and hope for the best. I will keep you informed, if things should change."

"Please do."

It was quiet once more in the mists, where the only sound to be heard were the faint ripples of fingertips through the water.

"The Matron of the Mists cannot interfere," Daesi said over the image, "but perhaps someone else can."

* * *

It was later that night, while Markus took his turn at watch, that he began to speculate over the fate of each Emblem since his awakening. A fire crackled behind him, its flickering warmth on his back a stark contrast to the biting wind across his face. Sitting upon a rock, enjoying the heat it sapped from the flames, he looked out into the dark and mused.

The Emblems were first given shape as wreaths, he said to himself, long since content with the notion that Revyn might be listening, *and then changed themselves into swords when the need arose. What if they have taken new shape yet again?* He glanced over at Barr, watching the child sleep and mulling the thought over. *He could have one with him, and I would be none the wiser. For all I know, it could be hidden as a necklace or a bracelet.*

Have you seen him wear any mithrinum at all?

No. But I see many places in which to hide one, should he have it. He toed the snow with a boot, as a thought took shape. *When you and yours forged them, you imbued all twelve with a piece of yourselves. Why can you not sense where they are?*

Revyn, it seemed, was in a charitable mood. He gave an answer without mocking or posing a question of his own.

When father gathered the Emblems and hid them away, his touch lingered within and gave them new life. Not even we can sense where they are now.

Markus pulled his cloak tighter. He could have asked Revyn for warmth, but the noise would have woken Barr. The wonderful irony of having to hide his power from a child, one who so desperately hid away his own magic, did little to liven his mood or keep at bay the cold.

What of your children, could you not send them out to scour the realm in search of each sword?

I grow tired of questions you ask time and again.

Yes, I know, the urge to feed could overwhelm them and renew the old wars, but it would be worth it if they could find but one.

Only wind across the snow answered back, a hollow voice of winter that gave promise of more cold. Markus shrugged inwardly, used to the wild moods and fits of brooding the elusive god could fall into. Still, as far as conversations with the divine go, things could have been much worse. He had no headache or bloodied nose, no ringing in the ears or fractures along the jaw.

All things considered, it was an amiable exchange.

* * *

Most of the next day went by uneventfully, with a seeming library of stories from Ealdan and the occasional break for rest and a quick meal. They did their best not to push the horses too hard and kept them well fed with grain they brought along. Dar-Paj had no more apples to win over his new friend, but he managed to find a carrot now and then from somewhere in his satchel. Aren went off in the early morning for a hunt and came back with a renewed vigor for the journey. Whatever it was that he fed on seemed to have a lingering odor that offended a certain nose, and they were treated to the all too familiar scent of a perfumed kerchief for the rest of the day.

They were due west of Laurenthos, where the land turned to sweeping hills and sparse trees, when Dar-Paj caught sight of the wagons. Thin stalks of brown grass sprouted up through the snow, a difficult meal for any horse, and no road could be seen for miles.

"Slavers," Dar-Paj said to the others, slowing Tarem down to a casual gait. "This far from the road, they must be attempting to hide their cargo."

I don't see anything, Idelle said with disbelief. *Unless he means... Oh, I see them now. They're at least an hour off.*

"Slavery has been legal for quite some time," Ealdan said, dismissing the apprentice's concern with a wave of his kerchief. "So long as we have criminals and debtors, there will always be slaves."

Barr frowned at that, recalling stories as a child of men who stole away the unsuspecting to work in the mines. Countless children disappeared from the streets, beggars and urchins, never to be seen again.

"Not all slavers limit themselves," Barr said, "to what our kings deem lawful."

"What, stories of drunkards and orphans stolen away during the cover of night? It may make for good theater, but Garrick would never stand for it." The actor gave a long sniff to show his indifference. "Besides, our friend is letting his imagination run away with him. I see nothing but trees and snow."

Nearly half an hour passed when Barr reigned them in, all four wagons finally in sight. Covered with burlap, they were cages on wheels. Though it was slow-going, the caravan moved due west, a good distance from the road and any merchants or travelers that might be upon it. Not quite the behavior of legitimate slavers.

I know what you're thinking, Idelle said. *You can't be the hero every time. That's not Lorelei in those wagons, and those men have already seen you. Two of their scouts are heading back right now.*

"How in the world?" Ealdan narrowed his eyes at the apprentice. "You mean to tell me you saw those wagons, from way back there? Not a weaver, eh. I suppose all gold-skinned men can hear whispers from afar and see beyond the means of any hawk."

"My remarkable vision does not change the fact that those are slavers, and they would not be so far from the road if all they carried were criminals and debtors."

Aren let loose a rumble in his chest. *I'm with you, if it's what you want. I know we're short on time, but that priest hasn't moved since we left. When you scried in the ice last night, you said he was still inside the temple. We could rescue these people and be on our way tomorrow morning. The wolf will still be there.*

It's too dangerous, Idelle warned.

"Forget what you are thinking," Ealdan told Barr. "The sort of men that guard slave trains are not to be trifled with. If you attack, they will see you as a criminal. Do you understand what I am saying?"

Barr replied, "The Psachlin Pits are a few days from here, just northwest of Eternoll. They're headed in that direction. If we just ignore them, those innocent people will spend the rest of their short lives digging in a mine. Could you live with yourself if that happened?"

Ealdan was quiet as he considered.

"What of the people who will die when your wolf goes free? How will you save them when you yourself are a slave?"

"How many are there, Dar?"

"Four drivers, eight guards and three scouts. Two of those scouts have already returned." Dar-Paj seemed to look closer. "Every one of them is armed with a sword. The scouts carry bows, and two of the guards are hefting heavy crossbows." He shook his head. "It would not be wise to attack them openly. Even if I could dodge bolts or arrows, I doubt I could take down more than three."

"Alright," Barr relented. "We'll let them be. For now. We'll continue south until we reach that large hill. We'll make camp on the other side, and once it's dark, I'll go after them myself."

"That is entirely –" Ealdan began and was cut short by a withering look.

As they rode on, pointedly ignoring the slavers, a cry for help rang out and was followed by guttural shouts. The woman called out once more, and then all became quiet.

Dar-Paj halted Tarem. "They killed her."

"What!" Barr wheeled about, angry at himself. "How can you be sure?"

"I heard the crossbow fire and strike. She... there were startled gasps from others, crying. I –"

"Both of you listen closely. I want you to continue south without me. I'll catch up when I'm done." Barr leveled a gaze at Ealdan. "I mean it, don't follow me. Get over that hill as fast as you can."

Barr was already riding toward the caravan, when Ealdan called after, "Why, so you can go join whoever it is that just died?"

Go with them, he told Aren. *Make sure they can't see what I'm about to do.*

And what of the prisoners? Idelle asked. *What will you do when every one of them sees you weave? Even if they don't run in fear, screaming for the Guardians, you could never return to your uncle.*

I won't let any more of them die.

Barr could hear Aren's growl from behind, a warning for the others to do what they were told. The guards ahead had noticed him coming and stood with weapons drawn, ready and waiting. Barr stopped and got down from Jax, sent the horse off with a slap to the backside and carried on by foot. He didn't want Jax getting hurt when the fighting started. With both hands outstretched to either side, he began drawing *furie* from the land. The snow beside him dissipated into steam, as grass beneath it browned further and died away. Like heat rising off the flat of a rock in full summer, the *furie* covered his body in a wavering shimmer.

Barr! Aren warned. *They're running around me and heading your way! I can't stop them!*

Damn it. Barr was nearly to the wagons, where the wide-eyed guards were frantic with the desire to flee, and their prisoners turned away in their cages, cowering with a greater fear for the man that approached. *It's too late then. They've already seen.*

Drawing both kyan, just feet away from the guards and engulfed in a tumult of blistering heat, Barr dropped to one knee and drove his fists to the ground. The *furie* found its release in an explosion of visible sound. Men were picked up by the shockwave and thrown full force against the wagons, bending iron beneath their bodies and knocking over two cages. Other guards merely flew through the air, arms and legs flailing wildly for control, then landed hard and remained still.

Throwing knives sprouted from the chest of a slaver, toppling him out of a wagon. Ealdan jumped from his horse at full gallop, rolled once and slid to a stop on both feet. Two more knives were let loose in one fluid motion and struck with enough force to lift the two scouts in the air. They both dropped to the ground, as their bows and arrows flared into ash.

Dar-Paj rode Tarem straight into a guard, breaking the man's body along with his crossbow. A bolt was fired, but it struck harmlessly into a wheel. One of the drivers jumped down and rushed forward, no doubt hoping to unseat the robed figure. Dar kicked out with a boot that crushed bones and pierced lungs with their fragments. The driver fell, clutching his broken chest and gasping for air that wouldn't come.

I guess they're not totally useless, Aren admitted with the rush of battle in his veins. He leapt past Barr and bit into one driver, while pulling him down from a wagon with another. Their screams drowned out the relentless growls and tearing.

Barr moved towards the last driver, both kyan ready to counter the terrified man's feeble sword. Before the two of them clashed, the other disappeared in a swoop of great wings and sharp talons. His cries followed him past and faded quickly away into the distance.

"Look out!" Ealdan shouted and leapt at Barr.

They both went down, as the arrow struck home. The last scout stood between two wagons, bow drawn and reaching for another arrow. With a swipe of his hand, Barr set the bow and shaft ablaze with fire and turned them to ash in an instant. Aren was upon him then, catching the archer in his jaws and crashing into a wagon with the full bulk of his body, twisting iron bars with the force of momentum. The hound continued to wrench and tear through the man, long after the body stopped moving.

"Ealdan?" Barr turned the actor on his side and felt the slick warmth of blood. His hand came away a bright red. "Can you hear me?"

There was no answer. The arrow was lodged between two ribs in the back and looked dangerously close to the heart. Looking closer, Barr could see the pronged steel tip poking out the other side of Ealdan's chest. Pulling it through would be out of the question. The actor's breath was already fading and could barely be heard, with its watery rasp.

Dar-Paj slid through the snow and was beside him. "Is he alright? What can I do?"

"We don't have much time. Can you break off that tip without moving the arrow inside him?" It easily snapped off in Dar's fingers. "Good, now hold him steady while I pull out the arrow."

Blood pooled beneath Ealdan and escaped even more quickly, as the arrow was pulled from his body. His skin now pale as snow, the actor's breath grew shallower still. Barr placed a palm over Ealdan's heart and could feel the life slipping away with each slowing beat.

"He has lost too much blood," Dar-Paj said. "Even if we could staunch the wound with fire, he looks to have taken damage inside. He will continue to bleed within. I am sorry, but he is lost."

"I told you two to stay back," Barr said, gritting his teeth against the weight of impending guilt. He looked over his shoulder at the silent men and women that watched on from behind bars, their eyes bearing down with both judgment and expectation. Turning away from them he said, "He's not lost just yet."

His right hand still over Ealdan's heart, Barr put the other to the ground and drew *furie* with all the will he could muster. Snow burned away in a flash of steam that stretched across all four wagons in a rising circle of gray fog, then disappeared on the wind as smoky wisps. What stalks of grass there were flashed like embers and were consumed, curling in on themselves and blowing away.

The ground then flared for a brief moment in a webwork of light. Like glowing veins, life pulsed through them and passed into Barr. Across his body and down to his hand, it entered Ealdan and surrounded the actor in a glow of shimmering white that shrank in on itself and entered the wound. Flashes of light escaped his open mouth, as if the magic healed him from within.

When Barr could no longer maintain the connection, he collapsed in a heap on one side.

− 23 −

Dar-Paj rushed to one side and turned Barr onto his back. He could see the steady rise and fall of rhythmic breathing and was relieved that his new friend was but asleep. It wasn't the first time he had seen a weaver pass out after exhausting their own energy, where sleep was all that could replenish the loss. Aren laid down beside Barr, looking up calmly, as if he was used to the display. Dar-Paj absently brushed a gloved hand over the ashen debris, where once stalks of grass awaited the spring. Though he had seen master Therol weave magic in the past and managed a bit of scrying himself, what Barr had done was well beyond anything either one of them could ever hope to accomplish. It twisted his stomach with a thrill of both excitement and terror.

"Let us out of here," a gruff voice demanded from behind. The man cleared his throat and added, "If you please."

An unconscious reflex had Dar checking his cowl and robe, making sure both were tight and his features unseen. He let out a sigh and stood, wiping the ash from his robes, as Ealdan began to stir. Slowly, as if waking from a prolonged sleep, the actor opened his eyes and sat up. The fading sun was low on the horizon, and the cold of night would soon be upon them. Dar-Paj had no need of a fire himself, but Barr would need one to keep warm while he slept.

What will they do? he wondered, distrust gnawing at his every thought. He turned toward the cages and looked them over, the women and children huddled for warmth, the men clenching the bars of their cages in anticipation of release. *Will they be too grateful for their freedom to worry over what they saw?* There was a frightened desperation in more than one pair of eyes. *Or will they turn on their rescuers? I could leave them there until Barr awakes.*

"That one," the man said, misconstruing the delay. He pointed to one of the fallen drivers. "He has the keys."

"What happened?" Ealdan asked, getting up to his feet. His eyes widened when he caught sight of Barr. "Is he alright? I tried to pull him out of the way –"

"He is fine," Dar-Paj answered, curious at the actor's sudden concern for others. Could it be that Ealdan was not as shallow as he first appeared? "You took the arrow in his stead and nearly died. He healed you and now rests."

"There may be more of them," a second man warned. "Hurry and let us out!"

"Please," a woman begged. "We haven't eaten all day, and the children need blankets."

"You think they will turn on us," Ealdan said in low tones, so the others couldn't hear, "because of what they saw."

"What you saw," Dar returned, "pales in comparison to what occurred after you fell." The actor looked around at the ring of scarred earth, its char darkening with the coming of night. "I am all too familiar with how your kind treats what they do not understand."

"What do you suggest? Keep them locked up until Barr wakes? That will only serve to anger them. We must let them go immediately, to gain their trust. Freeing them will go a long way."

There were mutters and grumblings passed between the prisoners, worried talk over having traded one captor for another. Dar walked over to the driver and fetched a ring of iron keys. He unlocked the first cage while talking over a shoulder.

"We will need to make a fire straight away. All light will be gone soon. We can use these wagons to block the wind, by moving them into a circle."

A woman thanked him as she stepped down from the wagon. She then helped two children, a young boy and a girl, get down from the cage and hurried them off to one side. Casting fearful glances at Barr's prone form, none of the captives would go near him. When the second cage was opened, a rugged man jumped down. He stormed past Dar-Paj and headed right for a slain guard. The man snatched up a sword and turned toward Barr with a grim determination.

Aren was there to meet him head on.

"We'll have to kill it," the man said to two others, who also hurried for swords of their own. "Grab a bow, and keep an eye out for that bird too."

Amazed that the warning growls and sheer size of the hound did nothing to deter these men, Dar assumed they must be soldiers or mercenaries. With no weapon of his own, he would be hard-pressed to subdue them, unusual strength or no. Before he could give much thought to what he should do, a man was trying to wrest away the keys from his grasp.

"I think not." Dar easily snatched the ring away and then bent each key. He tossed the useless iron and took hold of the man by the throat. "Drop your weapons, or I will kill him." Dar lifted him off the ground and shook his body in midair. "Believe me when I say that I can break him in two."

"Do it," the one seemingly in charge said, not once taking his eyes off of Aren. "No idea who he is, and I'm not dropping my sword 'til that turner is dead."

A knife sprouted from his wrist, and the sword fell away. Ealdan drew another and narrowed his gaze, ready to take down the other two.

"Drop them," the actor said evenly, "or I drop you."

An elderly woman came forward. "Stop this, all of you! This is no way to treat those who risked their lives to free us. You, let that man go, and you," she said with a withering look to the hound four times her size, "stop that growling this instant!"

It looked as if the poor dog actually pouted, but he did what he was told. No one came any closer to Barr, and Aren somewhat relaxed.

"We should leave them here," Ealdan said, pointedly ignoring the old woman, "gather Barr and head for that hill before any more of them decide to attack."

"No, please," a woman begged from one of the locked cages. "Don't punish us for what they did."

Why are they all looking to me for answers? "There are still innocent people here," Dar said. "We can tie up these four and let them go in the morning."

"There is no such thing as an innocent person."

"Your friend is ill," the older woman said. "I can tend to him, if you stay. Help free the others. Let them get a fire started, a meal cooked and the children taken care of. Your friend will be safe in my care."

Ealdan raised a brow. "The day any one of us is safe in your care is the day I eat my cravat. Fine, we can stay. But the next one of you who raises a hand against us will be feeding the crows with these others."

From the depths of his cowl, Dar-Paj saw Ealdan in a new light. The actor was just that, a man of many faces, and Dar wasn't sure if he liked what he saw. While he did risk his own life to save Barr, Ealdan was more than willing to let these others fend for themselves and die in their cages. Was it that he cared only for those he considered a friend? Which was his true face, the long-winded story teller that cared more for clothes and coin than anything else in life? Or was it the dark killer that rode into battle without a second thought, throwing knives as fast as he could draw them?

Ealdan noticed the look and studied Dar-Paj in turn.

"Fine," Dar said and broke open the remaining two cages, twisting off their iron padlocks as if they were made of dried reeds. "We will need volunteers to begin gathering wood. Two of you can help me rearrange these wagons, and two more can start passing out whatever food, water and blankets can be found."

Though none of them had been captive for more than three days, there were already a number of wounded and signs of starvation. Apparently, delivering healthy slaves was not required for payment. The woman who was shot with a crossbow had died instantly, and her husband was still in the throes of grief. He rocked back and forth, muttering over her still body, and refused to leave the cage where she was killed. Blankets were brought to keep him warm, but he used them to cover his wife.

The elder woman cradled Barr in her lap, caressing his forehead and running fingers through his hair, while others continued to work around them. Dar-Paj could hear every beat of Idelle's wings as she kept watch from above, heard the labored breathing of those out cutting wood for the fire, listened to mothers feed their children with a calm sense of relief, yet he could hear nothing of the whispers that passed from her lips. Whatever the old woman was saying, her words were like eddies stretching out over dark water, beyond reach of all but those caught in their path.

And in the grip of slumber, Barr stirred.

* * *

The forest was in the crest of spring, full of color and life, with the warbling of birdsong all about. Wind played through trees enraptured by the light, and betwixt their branches came a vibrant sunfall of gold. Motes drifted on the air, catching hold of that light and spun it about like children at play.

Across the way was a wholly different scene, where the forest was draped in the growing slumber of fall. It was nighttime there, in the midst of shedding trees, and a silver glow encompassed all with its cooling touch. The ground was littered with the remnants of play, a bed of orange and brown that patiently awaited the snow.

Between them both was an endless stream of ebon water, a flowing warmth that split the seasons and showed nothing of itself. Walking through the eddies, his bare feet immersed, Barr saw naught but the shimmer of stars overhead reflected in its glassy surface.

He was then within a grove, traversing all distance in the span of a thought. Surrounded by trees, thick grass underfoot, he saw daylight fade away in a single breath. A fire sprang up in the center of the grove, a pyre that stood nearly three times his height. About it danced a troll, her body writhing to unseen drums. Small bones and stone beads jangled in her hair, keeping time with the stomp of each foot. Barr looked down at his hand, as if noticing the marked stone for the first time.

"Chamal?" he asked, and she was suddenly before him, her blue eyes close to his, her breath on his skin. "I know you."

"My blood oath calls to me and tells me of a danger." It felt to Barr as if she were looking through his flesh, to the spirit behind his eyes. "Many lives will be lost."

"The slavers? It's alright, we took care of it."

"The danger is not passed," Chamal warned. "I talk of a dark spirit, an ancient spirit, one of the first to be blessed with eternal life. He travels with you, waiting to strike. If he is not stopped, he will undo the world."

"Who is it? Ealdan?"

"I know not what name he calls himself, only that he is not human like you." She put a hand to his cheek, as if a mother caressing her child. "You cannot take him with you into darkness, for only one of you will survive. He is not how he appears. Trust only yourself."

She was gone from him then, but the warmth of her touch lingered, as if part of her were still with him. He couldn't bring himself to believe, to see anything of the dark intent she so strongly cautioned against. Yet what of his past, the convenience of lost memories, or the strange appearance and old scent that Aren spoke of? Was it coincidence that Therol found him, or was it the other way around?

As if mirroring doubt, the forest gave way.

* * *

Barr opened his eyes and felt rested, with little to no aching in his bones. He had no idea how long he had been out, but it was much shorter than he was normally used to. Weaving to the point of exhaustion was usually precursor to a full day of sleep, but he could hear voices all around. The fire beside him had yet to grow embers and was still being fed with freshly cut wood. He looked up into a shimmer of lustrous blue eyes, his head still cradled in the elder woman's lap, and was startled by the act of rare kindness.

Are you alright? Idelle asked, her voice betraying concern.

He looks fine, Aren said, lifting his head long enough to cast a glance Barr's way and then letting it droop back down to his paws. *I wasn't worried.*

"Your color has returned," the woman said, helping Barr to sit up on the blanket. "Something hot to eat and a bit of drink?"

At his nod, she went to fetch him a meal. Looking over to one side, he caught sight of Ealdan. The actor gave a nod, as if welcoming him back from an uncertain fate. Barr could see unspoken relief in those gray eyes and wondered at the change, at the goodness overlooked. Had he misjudged Ealdan? Without any hesitation, the actor had risked his own life to save Barr.

Why would he do that?

Stupidity is my guess. Aren yawned but turned an interested eye, as the elderly woman brought over a bowl of stew. *That doesn't look half bad.*

Somehow I'm sure you've already eaten. "Thank you very much," Barr said to her. "I'm Barr, by the way. Is anyone injured?"

"Some, yes. Eat first, and get your strength up. I am afraid few will be accepting of your aid just yet."

With that, she left to tend others.

They all saw me weave, Barr said, his appetite all but disappearing. *Has there been any trouble?*
Aren moved closer and sniffed at the bowl. *Nothing we couldn't handle. The four tied up, over by that wagon, thought you'd look better with a sword in your chest. We convinced them otherwise.*
It's been quiet since then, Idelle said, *with everyone working at making a decent camp for the night. If those storm clouds to the east turn our way, some of them won't make it to see morning.*
I'll do what I can for the wounded.
If they let you.
"So," Ealdan began, no doubt longing for the sound of his own voice. "You are a turner."
"I guess I am. Does that bother you?"
"Well, to be fair, you are not like any turner I have ever heard of. From all accounts, it seems I should be thanking you for saving my life." Ealdan absently rubbed at his chest, where the arrow had struck, though the only sign of its passing was a bloodied hole in his shirt. "I would have liked to have seen it. From the look of this clearing, it was quite a sight to behold."
Barr took a drink from the skin she had left him. "I don't know, I wasn't looking. And you don't have to thank me. If anything, I owe you my gratitude."
You didn't need him to stop that arrow, Aren said, risking a taste of stew. *All he did was get in the way.*
"I would have done the same for any of my friends. You better act quickly, if you have any desire to eat that."
"Stop that," Barr said and pushed Aren away. "Go find your own meal, if you're that hungry." He moved a bit closer to Ealdan and asked, "How did these people react? I can see they're still afraid, but do I need to worry about any of them doing more than ignore me?"

"I believe we adequately dissuaded any thought of dissent. They know they are free to leave come morning and return to their lives, which is a far sight better than what lay ahead for them at the mines." Ealdan cast a glance at those nearby. "Grateful but wary is how I would describe them."

"Alright. Try to get some rest."

Determined to help, Barr got to his feet and walked straight toward the four bound men. Fear passed across the eyes of one, who quickly turned away, while two others only sighed and looked as if they expected the worst. Only one of them met his gaze, with an angry defiance, placing blame for some wrong – imagined or otherwise – squarely on Barr.

"You won't be able to keep warm this way," Barr said and began untying them. "I'm fairly sure there are no more slavers nearby, but that doesn't make this camp any safer. You have the look of soldiers, all of you, and the others will need help getting back to their homes in the morning. I won't be going with you."

"Why should we trust you?" the one man said, his hatred of turners apparent. He had a knife wound at the wrist, most likely from Ealdan.

"I'm not asking you to trust me. I'm asking you to take care of these people." Barr sighed. "Look, I'm sorry for whatever pain it is you've suffered at the hands of magic, but I can no more be held responsible for that than you could take blame for my father's death because he was killed with a sword. Magic is just a tool, and I try to use it the best I can to help others. I came here and risked my life to free you. If you feel the need to judge, then judge my actions."

Barr got up and left them, hoping his words had at least some effect. He knew better than to offer to heal the man's wound. Dar-Paj was standing nearby, waiting from the dark of his cowl and long robes. Seeing him struck a not so distant memory, of a warning in dream and the doubts they had conjured. As much as he wanted to believe in Dar, there were too many questions about him that had no answers.

"Is that wise?" the apprentice asked.

"I've made worse decisions in the past. Will you see they're armed and take turns at a watch? I think the others will sleep easier, if they feel that they're safe."

Walking about the camp, Barr could see little more than bumps and scrapes on the people that ignored him, or at least nothing that would warrant a confrontation. Aside from the dead woman in the wagon and her inconsolable husband, the others seemed no worse for wear. Given time, they would all be well and back to the lives they had come from.

A large group had gathered around the fire, where the elderly woman was beginning a tale. Not wanting to disturb them with his presence, Barr stayed back in the shadows and took a seat by a wagon. Aren walked up and laid down beside him, resting his head on Barr's leg. The two of them relaxed and listened to her story.

"In a time not so long ago, there lived a man by the name of Nedryn, and it was his wont to take long walks in the forest by his home. He was friend to all creatures and had an eye for beauty that often led him astray. As such, it was not so passing strange that when he came across a young maiden taking drink by a brook that he fell instantly in love with her, so captured by her beauty was he. Never had he seen such a delicate face or hair so dark and soft that the sun would mistake it for the canvas of night. Her name was Daesidaoli, and she too fell deeply in love with Nedryn, for never had she met a purer heart or clearer love of nature.

"By the next new moon, the two were joined in the eyes of Hearn and the Mother Goddess. They exchanged tokens of love, he a silver ring passed down from his mother's mother, she a seashell locket that forever housed the ocean song. Their shared happiness seemed complete. But it was not to remain so, for soon they were joyous beyond any measure. The love that bound them brought with it a child, a son they called Aoleontril, in honor of her father. It was then that Daesidaoli could no longer stay. She was expected to return and present her son to the Queen Arianaolis, for, you see, Daesidaoli was a fairy.

"When Nedryn was told the truth, he agreed to cross over to Faeronthalsos, and through the mushroom portal they went. In his heart, however, Nedryn felt betrayed, and he silently plotted to take his son away. He would allow no one but humans to raise his child. Late one night, when all were asleep, he took Aoleontril back through the portal and left his son with a gentle old widow. He knew Daesidaoli would follow him to the ends of Taellus, and out of love for his son went as far away as his feet would take him.

"Nedryn still wore the seashell locket of his love, and Daesidaoli used her fairy magic to seek it out. When she found the gift, she also found Nedryn, tired and alone, still running and frightened. Her heart was broken that he should treat her so, that her son was forever lost, and with all her *furie*, she laid a curse on her husband to equal her pain. Nedryn became a monster, a winged creature that could soar through the clouds, but she also took his eyes for his blinding distrust of all that was not human. By night, he became as stone, a living statue frozen in time. By day, he lived as the hideous beast, could feel the warmth of the sun on his face but never again know the beauty of its sight. Only his son's forgiveness could break the spell that would evermore leave Nedryn alone and in darkness."

The group was captivated by her story, lost in the world and images she wove. Left suddenly without words to hang upon, they sat together in a silence broken only by the crackling of wood on the fire. As Barr expected, it was Ealdan that spoke first, all too eager to take the stage and entertain a gathered crowd.

"Lovely story," the actor said, "though not much for a point. It has the proper conflict, but there is little to no resolution. How about something a bit cheery? I know one of a barmaid that had –"

"Actually," the old woman answered, "I am rather tired. It has been a long day and one I would sooner see done than prolong. If you would all excuse me, I shall find some spot to bed down."

Others agreed with the sentiment and begged off for sleep. The fire was large enough that its heat reflected back off the wagons, making most of the camp a warm enough place to slumber. Soon, a number of bedrolls and blankets laid sprawled about the ashen ground, and the only sounds to be heard were those few keeping watch. The mood seemingly spoiled, Ealdan got to his feet and left for a walk, claiming the brisk air was good for his lungs. One of the soldiers nudged another and chuckled, sharing in an unspoken joke.

Barr shook his head and settled against a wagon for some rest.

* * *

By the tingling chill in the pit of his stomach, Markus knew that Feraesk was near. All of the revenants gave him a similar sensation, but Feraesk was something different, stronger and wild. Once immortal, now undead, only his spirit still animated his rotted shapeling corpse.

Without magic, he would not be able to mask the horrific odor that would fill the air with death and decay. Magic was his greatest strength, his single means of existing in a state of unlife.

It was that core of magic that fueled the revenant's corpse and gave Markus a sense of who he once was. As first lord of his people, feared ruler of the luminarron, he all but glowed with the overwhelming strength of his own *furie*. But as Ealdan, a lowly thief and performer, he stole or borrowed what magic he could. The bond he shared with his twelve revenants, the Brood, was forged in their creation by the God of Change. It's all that had sustained him these past fifteen years. Bereft of any *furie* of his own, no longer immortal, the newly awakened Markus had only his servants to keep him alive.

"You called, my lord." Feraesk's voice was a hollow dissonance of spirit and flesh. "I have come to serve."

"Where are the others?"

"Not far, lord. We have followed, as you instructed."

Markus looked back over a shoulder. The camp was quite a distance off, marked by the faint glow of its fire. Anyone out walking this far would have to be looking for him.

"Let no one see you," he told the revenant, "even in the robes of a Guardian. Do as you have been, stay far behind and out of sight of that hawk."

Feraesk's eyes grew alight with a shimmering green. "There are ways to mask our appearance. We could travel beside you, and none would know. Even now, we are hidden from sight."

"Do not be so sure of that. This Barr is a keen one, and we both know the prophecy. He has the power and knowledge of many lives." The revenant's eyes remained unwavering. "If I could only control him. Nothing would stand in my way. The Emblems would be yours, but this world, *all* of Taellus, would be mine to command! Have you any idea of the power?"

"Yes, my lord. You have often spoke of it." Feraesk looked off into the distance. "A life approaches, beyond that tree."

It was back from the direction of camp. Straining his eyes, Markus could see the bobbing light of a torch and cursed his mortal vision. *It won't be long now. I will have my immortality back.* The torch continued towards them.

"Shall I deal with it?" the revenant asked.

"Have the others bring whoever it is here to me. If, however, it is Barr or Dar-Paj, let them be."

Disguised as Guardians, the others descended upon the poor man like a living plague of fluttering dark robe and bony appendage. Not so much as a yelp escaped the man's lips, as the torch fell away from his hands. Only the hiss of fire on snow could be heard, as the night grew skeletal fingers that dragged him away with a merciless speed. Falling in a heap before Markus, the red-faced mercenary cried out a silent plea. His eyes wide with recognition, throat strained with magical fear, he could do little more than whimper the terrible screams he must have imagined.

Markus stood over the sellsword with arms crossed. "What, no more voice for laughter? Have you changed your mind about hearing my tale? Well, let me tell you about the ignorant whelp of a human who meddled into the wrong one's affairs. I have to warn you, it does little to warm the heart, but there *is* a lesson to be learned. Listen closely."

A nod of his head, and the revenants attacked.

No screams, no cries nor a single groan of pain could be heard above the tearing of cloth and flesh. Through muscle and bone, their fingers clawed without mercy, leaving behind a bloodied pile of snow and muck. The few embers of *furie* the dead man once possessed were absorbed by the Brood in a mist of silvery blue.

"Not much of a moral," Markus admitted over the remains, "but it *is* one you never forget." He looked up at the half circle of death. "Go, all of you. Continue to follow, but stay out of sight. If the hawk becomes a problem, I will let you know when and how to deal with it."

Feraesk bowed his head and led the others off in a bounding mass of shadow. Markus straightened his shirt and turned about, then began the long walk back to camp. The fluttering in his stomach faded the closer he got, and by the time he could feel the fire's warmth, his sense of the Brood had all but disappeared. Still, he knew they were close by and would answer his call. Gazing out of over the collection of sleeping bodies, Markus amused himself with a single thought...

How easy it would be to have them all killed.

* * *

Dar-Paj tossed in his sleep, lost in that shadow realm both real and imagined. Pictures turned in his mind's eye, as if the paint on a canvas had yet to dry. The past mingled with fantasy, unconscious desire guiding and molding some painful truths into tolerable memory. Only the brightest moments ever stayed for long, but like staring into the splendor of dawn, the pain could be great and lasting.

"*Why look you so sad?*" *Eorana asked.*

When Dhar'paogi looked on her, he saw her mother. Beautiful as any sunfall, her hair and eyes the same golden hue, Eorana was a constant reminder of the love he bore his mate. Dhar'paogi turned his eyes aside, regarded the mountains that stretched out before him. Better to take in their majesty than suffer the moment surely to come.

It's at the point where the dreamer grows aware, that the dream becomes fickle and stubborn. Shaping desire no longer holds sway but molds with the hands of an angry child. What pictures don't fit get jammed into place in a vain attempt to take control, but nothing can tame the flights of fancy, as sure as no man can hide from himself.

One instant she's falling, crying out for help, and the next she's beside him with a hand on his heart. Each blade of grass on the peak where they sit becomes distinct in all its greenish hues and glossy texture. The rocks take on a life of their own, from the stones at their feet to the sharp boulders so far below. All around, life is teeming in every crack and crevice his eyes can lay hold of, but the shadow looming over them is by far a darker shade than any brightness he could glean. Even Eorana's smile pales under its weight.

"Why so sad?" she had asked, but how could he explain? How could he tell her when he could barely face it himself? Shame burned his cheeks, but it could not compare to the fire in his breast. Eorana called to him, over and over. Her gaze was just too much to bear...

"Hard time sleeping?" Ealdan asked, sitting nearby. "I saw you tossing but did not want to disturb you. Sometimes, even a restless sleep is one sorely needed."

Dar-Paj rolled to one side and looked into the flames. Something danced on the edge of his thoughts, a flicker of golden hair, like the twist and turn of the fire... but then it was gone, replaced only by a sense of longing and loss.

"From the time Therol found me, nightmares have haunted my sleep. What is most peculiar about them is that I can never remember what it was that I dreamt – just as I cannot recall who I am."

"That is peculiar. Have you ever tried meditation? That sort of waking dream often sparks a great deal of imagery. Of course it all has to be sorted out in the end, but you just may find the source of your problem."

"I have done some meditating as part of my studies." Dar-Paj looked over at Barr, asleep beside Aren. "But I have never tried exploring my dreams. I have always just contented myself to restless nights and tried to adjust as best I could."

Ealdan shrugged. "Well, something to think about, at the least. You could always try naga root. It might be a little difficult waking up in a split, but it would definitely help you sleep."

"Yes," the apprentice said with less than relish, "that is something to consider."

When Dar-Paj finally laid back down on his double layer of blankets, he found more comfort in the cold ground at his back than in the wide expanse of vast stars overhead. The very spaciousness of it, the unlimited depth, reminded him of another time, of another place...

...A mountain range, where the peaks touched off the edge of heaven itself and billowing clouds rippled down their rugged bulk. Trees wrestled among the rocks, shedding their seeds and skins in a struggle to the top, and in their wake came the life of stubborn brush and wild flowers. With desire and a little sunlight, they too sought to spread their roots, fanning out in waves of emerald dotted azure and gold. Upon such a feast rose the sure-legged animals, leaping from ledge to root and eating their way to the top.

The top.

They all strove for that yet unattainable height, the unknowable hidden above jealous clouds. The rocks and dark soil were for legs alone. Let the clouds then have their skies, they would say, and the mountain peaks as well. Only one among all had the gift of both worlds, the winged who soared about the lush valleys and burrows before stretching their eyes and bodies overhead. Their piercing cry was a keen of delight that left envy trailing a wingspan behind.

And there was Eorana, her hand reaching out as she slipped down the moss-covered rocks. She cried for his help, her voice strained with fear, but went inevitably down with all speed and no hope. Without her wings, she would crash helplessly off the mountain side and crumple against the valley floor. It did no good to look or leap.

Dhar'paogi was just as helpless to act.

– 24 –

There was a dull pain that gripped his chest before he realized the darkness was fighting against him, refusing the touch of light on his skin. It was more than just a heaviness that weighed on his eyes or a weariness in his middle that kept him from rising. Dark waters caressed him, from head to toe, like delicate fingers that soothed and restrained. The sound of it lapping up against him drowned out all else. Even the rapid thump of his heart slipped beneath the nighttime shroud that covered his eyes in star-strewn black. It turned his breath cold, as a healing warmth spread from the hand of another to the depth of his heart.

It was more than disconcerting, the helplessness he felt. Though his cheeks burned at the thought, he felt no real shame. There was something familiar about the place, a sense of welcome and belonging. He was sure he had seen it before, as if it stood at the edge of a vision once forgotten, or a memory confused with dream.

The darkness receded, breaking all thought, and took with it any notion of remembrance. The silver reflection of moonlight cut across the water, but nothing of the stars could be seen. He sat up and looked about, alone but for the multitude of whispering voices that softly called to one another across the wake of each ripple, there one moment and gone in the next. Worlds touched against his skin and were carried off, faded to shadow and returned anew.

Memory came back to him then, the flash of a blade turning end over end, the single cry of pain that ended in stillness. He hurried to find her but had nowhere to turn. All was open before him, one direction as far and hopeless as another. That beam of moonlight followed his vision, no matter which way he turned, lighting a way into the black of unknown.

The pain in his chest was gone, no longer a concern, as he raced through waters that splashed up his legs. Shadowy creatures shuffled along to either side, but he gave them no notice, as the light led him on. Black shapes flitted to and fro, descending with a keen, but only the silver glow held his attention.

Fog rose up like a storm all about, accompanied by the limbs of a forest long dead. Dark sign of its passing went by underfoot, a blanket of cloying ash that spiraled with each step. It clung to his legs, slowing him down, trying vainly to steer him away. In the hollow of a muddied field, he found her quiet and alone.

She no longer screeched or twitched from the wound in her side. Earthen feathers were torn and broken away, her eyes clouded to all but the hereafter. He reached out a hand to catch hold of her spirit, but the life had already died out. There was nothing he could do to save her, no magic to call on, no furie to weave. The touch of a breeze passed through his open hand, as if her final breath had escaped and took hold in parting.

It touched his cheek then, brushed back his hair, and settled into a calm all around him. Before the tears could well and the loss take root, he uttered a farewell of his own.

* * *

Barr woke with a start, the breath of an imagined wind still fresh on his skin.

Idelle?

I'm awake, she said. *What's wrong? You sound near frantic.*

Sorry. Just a bad dream. I thought you... He sighed and rubbed the sleep from his face. *Earlier, when I was out, I think the troll shamaness paid me a visit in dream. She warned me we were in danger, that we –*

"Sir?" It was one of the four men who were tied up at one point. "Name's Farn. Don't mean to bother you and all, but since you're already awake. I think Wilem's gone missing."

"Missing?" Barr got up to his feet and fastened his cloak back on. "Everyone's asleep. Was he on watch with you?"

"Aye. He went off in that direction, to relieve himself. That was a good hour ago, by my reckoning." He was older than Barr but not by much. He glanced nervously in the distance, to where Wilem disappeared. "I thought it best to tell someone, before I go off and look."

"You were right to wait." *Aren, wake up. We have a problem. Idelle, do you see anyone walking about outside the camp?* "Why don't you stay here and keep watch. I have experience in tracking, so it might be best if I go."

Farn looked relieved. "Alright. Just give a shout if you need me."

There's tracks to the west, but I don't see anyone. The trail just ends.

Aren came walking up as Barr said, "If you hear me shout, wake everyone and start running to Laurenthos."

He waited for Farn's nod before turning away. If something did happen to this Wilem, it was best to be prepared for the worst. Careful not to wake anyone, Barr secured his kyan and threw his bow over a shoulder. He walked to Ealdan and toed the actor with a boot.

"Not now, Tara," the actor said groggily. "Let me sleep a bit longer." Barr toed him again, with more force. "Hmm, what? What is it?"

"Keep your voice down. One of the men on watch has gone missing."

"I see." Ealdan got to his feet and brushed the dirt from his clothes. "Any others, or just the one?"

Barr looked about more closely. "I'm not sure, really. I didn't pay all that much attention to them... Wait, the old woman. The one who told the story. She's gone, too."

"Well, I doubt they ran off together."

Why are you telling him? Aren asked. *Forget him, and get Dar-Paj.*

I'm not sure that's a good idea anymore. I was trying to tell Idelle earlier –

"Is something amiss?" Dar-Paj asked quietly, putting aside his blanket and coming over to join them. "I could not sleep anyway. What is the matter?"

"It's nothing," Barr replied. "Stay here with Farn and keep watch. Two of the others are missing, but there's only one set of tracks."

"Perhaps one carried the other. I should go with you, just in case."

"It makes more sense for you to stay here," Ealdan said. "If Wilem carried one of them, he may come back for more."

"You make it sound like he's a slaver himself," Barr said. "Either way, we need someone to stay here, and I'd like to get going before the trail gets old."

Dar-Paj nodded and joined Farn beside the fire.

They followed a set of tracks out of camp, those of a heavyset man with plain shoes. If Wilem was a soldier, his gear would have been stripped when the slavers took him captive. Barr had no idea what the man could have been thinking, going off on his own into the cold, in the dead of night, let alone carrying the extra weight of a woman through snow. Were they related? Did they get impatient for home and simply up and leave? The tracks went on into the dark for some time, without changing course, and just one set the whole way.

"You seem cross with our golden friend. Did I sleep through a quarrel?"

I was wondering that myself, Aren said.

Idelle prodded, *You mentioned a dream and the troll from the forest.*

Her name is Chamal. She told me we were traveling with a very old and dark spirit, one that isn't human. Barr looked back at the camp disappearing from sight and wondered why Wilem would have come so far. What if it was more than that? What if he saw something and went to look? *She also said if we continued on with this person...* He couldn't finish the thought, still haunted by the memory of his most recent dream. *Let's just say her warning unsettled me, and I think it's worth being more careful, considering where we're going.*

Aren sniffed along behind them. *That doesn't mean it's Dar-Paj. For all you know, it's this one right here.*

You're the one that said Dar had an old scent. "Just curious, but how did you know it was Wilem that left?"

"Sorry?"

Barr knelt where the tracks ended and studied an odd impression beside them. It looked as if a torch had fallen in the snow and left behind faint traces of ash. The footsteps hadn't faded nor were they trampled about in a mass of tracks. They just stopped, as if Wilem vanished into thin air... or was snatched up and carried off.

Can you see any other creature from up there? Barr looked out over the snow and saw no other tracks. "How did you know it was Wilem?"

"Because he was on watch with Farn. You said one of the men on watch was missing. I could see Farn as well as I saw you, so..."

Nothing. Aside from that camp, there isn't a living thing in sight.

That's odd, Aren added. *I can't smell anything from here. Not even us.*

"Something's wrong." Barr felt the tingle of magic, but it was faded, distant, like words lost in the wind. "Whatever happened here, it wasn't natural. Something took Wilem and probably the old woman."

"Wonderful. I can smell the execution fires already." When Barr looked up curiously, Ealdan elaborated. "You can be sure the blame for their disappearance will fall squarely on us. When the others wake and see some are missing, few questions will be asked before they start pointing fingers."

I hate it when he's right. Leaves a taste in my throat like sour meat.

"We were all asleep. Farn saw us asleep."

Ealdan shook his head. "None of that will matter. Unless you want another fight on your hands, I suggest we leave at once. We can be miles from here before any of them know."

"Whatever did this is still out here," Barr said firmly and stood. "We can't just leave these people to be picked off one at a time. That's not who I am."

"And I commend you for that, truly I do. But that will mean nothing to these people when they tie you to a stake and cheer as you burn." Ealdan looked away, as if reliving a painful memory. "I have seen others burn for much less."

He may have a point, Idelle said. *Look at how some of them reacted after you rescued them, calling you a turner despite saving their lives. They would have killed you, if Aren didn't stop them.*

"Alright. We'll head back and gather our things."

"What of Dar-Paj?"

"He's still coming with us," Barr answered, "for now. If we all need to go our separate ways at some point, I won't take the time to discuss it with either of you."

It took a few minutes returning, and not another word passed between them. Ealdan stopped to gather their things and walk their horses out of camp, while Barr waved Farn over to one side, where they could talk quietly and not wake the others.

"Wilem's gone," he explained, "and so is the elder woman, from the look of it. To be honest, I don't have a clue where they are. All I do know is, there's only one set of tracks leading out of this camp, and they end a good distance that way. They just stop."

"He was attacked? I'll wake the others. We can –"

"No, you don't understand. There's no blood. There's no other tracks at all. I can't explain it."

Farn narrowed his gaze. "Maybe your bird friend got hungry. I saw her snatch a man right off his feet and carry him off."

"Which is why we're leaving. I promise that Idelle had nothing to do this, but we don't have time for your fear and accusations." Barr eyed the camp one last time, the people he had saved and was now abandoning. "As soon as the sun comes up, gather everyone and leave. Don't go separate ways, unless you absolutely have to, and keep your eyes open for anything."

Reaching out, Farn stopped Barr from leaving.

"If I had magic like you, I would use it to help people when they needed it. Not just when it suited me." It was clear he was afraid, that pride kept him from asking Barr to stay. Anger was his only recourse. "You turners are all alike."

"Take care of them, Farn."

With that said, Barr turned and walked away, toward the horses and friends that were waiting. While it was possible that Dar-Paj was all Chamal had described, there was little to be done for it just then. After all, it was only a dream, and as vivid as his dreams had been of late, it was hard to give one more credence than another.

All he could do was hope for the best and trust that his instinct had not steered him wrong.

* * *

They rode on for some time in relative quiet, with Ealdan speculating as to what could have happened to Wilem and then correlating the conjecture with a number of plays he had either seen or performed in – mostly the latter. From mythical dragons to ice dwelling worms, rocs and gryphons to mean-spirited dwarves that burrowed up through rock and snow, Wilem was subjected to all manner of horrible fates. There were, of course, even more fantastical suppositions, where the mercenary was truly a great turner himself and walked from camp so that others wouldn't see him use magic.

"That's not possible," Barr said. "I would've heard it."

"You can hear magic? I mean aside from all the fire and explosions. He could have magicked himself away without blowing up the area, you know. Probably took the old woman with him."

"Magic itself makes noise. You'd hear it, if you knew what to listen for."

Once they were away from the others, Dar-Paj took down his cowl. He gave Barr a sidelong glance at what must have seemed like a lesson in weaving.

"I have been meaning to ask since... since our clash with the slavers. When this is over, when we have helped you defeat this shapeling priest, would you be willing to teach me?"

Morning crested the horizon, like a fiery blanket seeping across the hills and glittering off the snow.

The road isn't far off, Idelle said. *As far as I can see, there is no one upon it.*

"Let's stop here for a bit," Barr said and dismounted. He let Jax roam free, while he spied a good place to kneel in the snow. Aren came up and laid down beside him. "What of my uncle? Won't he expect you to remain his student?"

"Most likely," Dar-Paj replied and let Tarem roam as well. He watched Barr waving a hand over the snow in a circle, where its edges turned hard with ice and its center filled as that snow melted away. "This is what I mean. Such a thing is beyond Master Therol, and as much as I care for him, I truly wish to learn more."

Ealdan let Smoke go and came over to observe. "Who in their right mind would not want to learn magic? Well, apart from the trouble with Guardians and the whole world mistrusting or even hating you, that is."

You still think Dar-Paj is the one she warned about? Aren asked.

I'm not sure what to think. Barr took the medallion from a pocket and thumbed its insignia. Focusing on the water, he called up an image of the priest. *If it was Ealdan, why would he have saved my life?* The image slowly fell away, revealing a study with a soft bed and numerous bookshelves. *Dar doesn't remember who he is, or so he claims. What happens if he suddenly recalls, and we find he's not the man we thought he was?*

"Amazing," Dar-Paj said. "Your uncle was never able to move the image about like that."

"Can you leave that room? You know, go walk about and see what we see?"

"No," Barr said and ended the scry, "not really. When I first saw the temple from above, I was pretty angry. I'm not sure I could do it again. Normally, I need a center of focus, a person or an object. The only way to scout the inside of that temple would be to follow him around. If I maintain the scry too long, he'll become aware, feel like someone's watching him. Right now, the only advantage we have is surprise."

"Hardly," Ealdan scoffed. "I watched you best more than a handful of armed men in one strike. I can easily take down three or more. Even our golden friend here managed a thump here and there. Short of having an army, this priest fellow does not stand a chance."

Aren got up and shook the snow from his coat. *I have to say, he's still annoying, but he's beginning to grow on me.*

"We'll find out soon enough," Barr said and took hold of Jax's reins. "Another day or two, and we should reach the forest surrounding Lumintor. After that, how soon we find that temple is up to you."

Ealdan gave a toothy smile. "I can hardly wait."

* * *

They were an hour passed the road from Laurenthos when daylight began to fade. The Gaebridon range had been in sight for some time, but they were just now able to make out the dark line of a forest through the fog ahead. Rather than press on and risk getting lost, Barr decided to make camp in the field just outside the ashen woods. Aside from the forest, there were no trees nearby to provide them a fire, so instead they gathered large rocks into a circle. Drawing *furie* from the land, Barr melted away the snow in a small area, drying the ground, and used what he had taken to heat the ring of stones.

"Interesting way to keep warm," Ealdan said. "Any chance of a magical fire to heat up some food?"

There's a boar three minutes east of here, Idelle said from above, *if anyone is interested.*

I'll be back when I'm done, Aren said and walked off.

"Just use one of the rocks," Barr replied. "It should provide enough heat to boil water. While you make us a stew, I'm going to place a ward over this area. That way we can all sleep tonight, instead of taking turns keeping watch. If anything comes near, I'll know."

"I see. You will have to show me how that is done sometime."

Dar-Paj finished brushing down Tarem and joined Ealdan at the ring's center. He took out some carrots, celery and packages of salted meat from a satchel.

"I believe the herbs and spices are in your pack."

"Herbs, eh?" Ealdan chuckled. "Did you manage to pack a flask of wine while you were at it?"

The apprentice went back to his horse and pulled a silver canteen from another satchel. He returned and handed it to Ealdan, then began cutting vegetables into a small kettle.

"I thought it would help keep us warm," he said in way of explanation. "There is only so much a blanket can do."

Walking from one end of their circle to another, Barr began tracing sigils in the air. A faint trail of blue light followed the tip of his finger and disappeared, as if too weak to hold its shape in the dark. He drew five different symbols before tying them all together with a last sigil over the center stone, where their dinner was cooking. It began to snow when Barr finally sat down.

"How do you know it will work?" Ealdan asked. His only answer was a knowing smile and a nod toward the drifting snow falling outside their little camp. "How did you do that?"

What flakes touched upon the ward simply fell down an unseen half-shell all around them and began to pile up in a growing ring of snow. Ealdan got up and walked out of the circle, then laughed when the snow touched his face. Retaking his seat, he toasted Barr with a drink.

Adding meat to the stew, Dar-Paj said, "Clearly, there are uses for magic I would never have dreamed of."

"It's just a matter of channeling will and *furie* toward the same goal." Barr refused the offered wine and chose water instead. "I used to think all magic was spells and incantations, but those are really no more than tools. A blacksmith can forge shoes without a hammer. He just needs something else to shape the iron with."

"Now that would be a sight," Ealdan mused. "You know, all this talk of magic has me thinking. Before we ran into those slavers, you were careful to hide what you can do from the two of us. Now that we know, there is no need to feel threatened of us running to the Guardians."

"What's your point?"

"Just that you can feel free to use whatever magic you might have at your disposal. If you have some mystic trinket or doodad secreted away, for fear of its discovery outing you, so to speak, you can use it now to defeat these shapelings."

Dar-Paj cleared his throat. "There is only one we can be sure of."

You still have the bracer, Idelle said. *Maybe Aislin can be of help once you get inside the temple.*

The bracer? I almost forgot. He looked over at his pack, where the mithrinum piece was hidden. *I'm not sure it would be of much use. Ariana only said that it was enchanted. She never said what it could do.*

Ealdan followed Barr's gaze but said nothing.

"There could be others," Barr admitted. "I've only seen a dozen or so men and women around him at any given time, but I know the temple isn't a small place. It could easily house four times that many."

Dar-Paj seemed incredulous. "Four times? How can we possibly face that many and survive? Barr, I came along in the hope of keeping you safe, but there is little I can do against so many."

"I'd understand if you wanted to go back."

"Hmm." Ealdan considered the thought. "That might be for the best, really. With only the two of us, we could sneak into the temple and go after this fellow without worrying about his friends."

"Why would he need you?"

"I have some experience skulking about, after all. Not to mention, I could pass myself off as one of them, if we managed to procure some of their garments. I am an actor, you know."

Barr's eyes opened wide at the idea. "That's brilliant."

"Of course it is. Wait, what is?"

"We'll disguise ourselves and sneak in." Barr used a bowl to scoop out some stew and began eating. "I already know what some of them look like and what they wear. I'll just weave an illusion around us, make us appear like people he knows."

"You can do that?" Ealdan looked impressed. "That would save me a fortune in costumes and makeup."

"Alright," Dar-Paj said between spoonfuls of stew. "I feel much better knowing we have a plan. I will go with you into the temple."

What about Aren? Idelle asked. *I don't mind keeping watch from outside, but nothing short of a meal will stop him from going.*

Count on it.

That's fine, Barr said. *The illusion will cover him too. I can make him appear however I want.*

"I appreciate your help. Both of you. I expected to be facing this shapeling alone, but I'm truly glad that now I don't have to."

Ealdan lifted the silver canteen. "To friends."

* * *

Stirring fingers through the dark water, Daesi kept a close vigil on her son. Her guise as an elderly human had brought them together for a short time, but she couldn't risk staying longer than she had. With Aislin still hidden and the elder spirits traveling beside him, the danger Barr was in grew more dire with each step he directed toward Lumintor.

"The Queen told me what was done," a voice echoed through the waters, stirring ripples with each word. "You both were warned what could happen."

"I am aware, Grand Seeress. Even now, I keep watch over Aislin. If anything should happen to my son, the artifact will be returned to Faeronthalsos"

"See that it is." Elaedraoni was quiet for a moment, then asked, "How is my future son faring? Is he still determined to avenge his human parent?"

"He is." Daesi caressed his image and wished she could do more. She sighed and asked, "Is your daughter well? I hear the visions have not been kind of late."

"I do worry for her," Elae replied in a gentler tone, "but she has her father's strength."

"And her mother's strong will."

"That too. I am sorry for what is happening, Daesi. If there is anything I can do, that does not interfere, please know that you can ask."

"Thank you, dear. I just long for happier times."

"What could be happier than a joining?" Elae's voice grew more firm, the Grand Seeress once more. "I must tend to other matters. You know what is at stake, what can and cannot be done."

"Be well, Elaedraoni. Give my regards to Fluora."

With that said, Daesi was left alone within the mists, alone but for the image of her son.

* * *

By morning, their camp was encircled with snow, and beyond the warmth of their rocks was the full brunt of a winter frost. It chilled their breath into billowing mist and stiffened muscles with every step. Once into the dark forest that surrounded Lumintor, they walked into a wall of dense fog that stretched off into the distance and took with it all trace of a landscape.

The horses had to be led through the trees, which grew at odd angles and jutted up like the fingers of a gnarled hand. Stranger still, despite the fresh fall, there was no trace of the storm to be found. The ground before them was cracked and frosted over with cold, but not a flake could be seen on its blackened surface. It looked as if a fire had raged across the land for such a long time that the snow simply turned into steam, sending out the heavy fog that left them frozen and blinded beyond the length of a horse.

What sickly trees were wedged between the cracked earth bore nothing but charred limbs and exposed roots. The air was stale and had the stench of rotted eggs, a biting scent nearly as sickening as the diseased growth that must have once been a verdant forest. No hills rose up underfoot, no creature stirred nor made a noise above the foggy silence. There was nothing but barren death and the choking remains of a blowing ash that clung to all it touched.

Markus dulled the smell with a kerchief and led the others on, following Revyn's direction.

"This could be a problem," Barr said, a hand over his nose and mouth. "Well, at least we don't have to worry about sneaking towards the temple. We should be fairly well hidden in this fog."

"Then again," Markus said without cheer, "so is the temple."

How far are we?

It will be some time, Revyn answered. *Half a day, at this pace.*

Your children live in such an inviting domain. No wonder they wander off and kill woodsmen.

Save the charm for your new friends. I am far from amused. The god said nothing for a time, as they passed through the fog. *Besides, what makes you think that his death was by chance?*

Markus knew better than to answer. Revyn often gloated about his wit and the elaborate schemes that he devised, but rarely did the god share in details.

"Aren can't smell a thing in this fog," Barr said, "and Idelle can barely keep track of where we are."

A few hours had gone by, and still they saw no sign of anyone nor heard anything but their own breathing and the clapping of hooves on the frozen ground. What little sunlight managed to break through the gray clouds overhead settled over the fog as a dull haze. Moisture covered their clothes with a fine mist, bringing with it a chill that the wind carried home. Ash swirled in eddies on a noiseless breeze and clung to the dampness, leaving them covered in a filmy black that turned their hair grimy and gummed their skin with an uncomfortable grit. They took to wearing torn strips of cloth as masks, to keep the soot from their mouths, but the occasional gust set their eyes to stinging with little to do for it but endure the tears.

A patrol is nearby, Revyn said with indifference. *If he does have an Emblem, perhaps an encounter with two of my children will draw it out.*

You led us to two shapelings?

"I hear something," Dar-Paj warned, turning an ear ahead. "It sounds like armor... and voices, but I cannot tell what they are saying. The words are too guttural, as if the fog is drowning them out."

"They're coming this way?" Barr asked. At Dar-Paj's nod, "Then let's sit here and wait. Don't make a sound."

Barr drew both kyan, and the massive creature he called a hound readied to leap with raised hackles. Two knives of his own in hand, Markus listened at the fog for a mark. The gold apprentice had no weapon to speak of and no doubt waited for someone to pummel.

Did I mention my children make horses skittish?

They could all hear it then, the deep voices and chain armor. Smoke was the first to grow anxious, before the other two followed suit and neighed their discontent. Too late to do anything but get out of their way, Markus stepped aside and let the horses run back the way they came.

Regardless, the patrol was alerted.

They came bursting through the fog and sliding to a halt, a soldier in full plate and chain armor astride a massive wolf. The steel that covered the man's chest and shoulders was so black as to gleam with a bluish cast, and the helm that both hid and protected his face bore the grimace of a snarling ebon wolf. He was a beefy fellow, with muscles bulging underneath the mail shirt and leather leggings, and his booted feet came near to dragging along the ground as he rode. The wolf itself had a wide chest and looked heavy across the shoulders, with eyes gleaming an emerald rage and dark hair up on end.

Barr leapt forward and attacked, taking the soldier off his mount and rolling to one side. Aren took the wolf full on, knocked its head down with a paw and bit into its neck. The hound thrashed about but couldn't seem to break through its thick hide. Dar-Paj moved in, waiting for a chance to strike, and managed to level a kick to the wolf's side that crushed ribs and evinced a pitiful yelp.

Markus threw a knife, but it bounced harmlessly off the soldier's helm. *I cannot get a clean throw! If he kills Barr, all this work is for naught!*

Then stop him!

Easily deflecting his opponent's attacks, Barr pushed aside the steel blade and slashed out with his kyan. It was clear that the man was somewhat skilled with a sword, but he stood little chance against Barr. What he lacked in ability, however, he made up in brute strength and a stubborn will to fight on, despite his wounds. He was already bleeding from half a dozen cuts, but that did little to waver his resolve.

Two more knives struck against him, with no result, before the third slashed him along the jaw and drew his attention away. Barr knocked the man's sword upward and plunged a kyan through his middle. The hawk must have been waiting for a chance to assist, for she swooped down and snatched the weapon right out of his hands. When the soldier refused to die and grabbed a hold of Barr, the second kyan was thrust through his heart.

The growling and yelping went on without relent. The hound twisted and thrashed, never once letting go, while Dar-Paj shattered bones with every kick he could land. Gritting his teeth, Markus strode up to the wolf and took a handful of its mane. He yanked back its head as hard as he could and drove a knife, to the hilt, across its neck. Through sinew and bone, he near sawed the wolf's head from its body.

In disgust, he let the bloody mess fall away.

"Is anyone hurt?" Barr asked, standing over the dead soldier. "Are you alright, Ealdan? You look pale."

"I am fine." Markus tried to calm himself and gather his knives. "They are just harder to kill than I expected."

The wolf returned to its natural form, a naked and broken man. Around his neck was a medallion, much like the one Barr carried. The soldier had one beneath his mail as well.

"I didn't expect that," Barr said, pulling out the iron necklace. "They must all wear one, or these two are also priests."

"They ride each other?" Dar-Paj asked.

Markus looked down at the naked man with disdain. "Well, they would have no shortage of mounts, I imagine. I somehow doubt these two are priests, from what we saw of that man in your puddle. This one is in full plate, like a footman. And if they have soldiers –"

"Then there's a lot more of them than we thought." Barr looked about, through the fog. "Still, they wouldn't patrol far from their temple. We must be close by."

Shutting his eyes, Barr pulled *furie* from the land. The fog about them shimmered, like shifting waves of heat, then returned once more to its billowy state. Dar-Paj seemed perplexed, as if he noticed no change, but Markus could see the haze that blurred their every feature. Colors looked brighter, but the lines that defined them were less sharp, as if they blended with the rolling gray that engulfed them on all sides. Though the gold one might not have seen it, Markus was sure.

Barr had woven an illusion all around them.

– 25 –

Rather than try to break through the frozen ground, in an attempt to bury the two men, Barr decided it would be best to hide the bodies off a fair distance, away from the patrol route. He and Ealdan did their best to cover over the bodies, while Dar-Paj and Aren rounded up the three horses. It was clear they could no longer ride their way to the temple. There was no telling how many more shapeling patrols were ahead, and an unreliable mount would be nothing but a hindrance. Instead, Barr marked the area with a sigil, so he could find it later on, and left all three horses tied off.

"Hopefully, we won't be gone that long anyway." Barr held out a hand, as if to invite Dar-Paj ahead. "I think you should lead us for now. With all this fog and patrols roaming about, your ears and nose are our best bet."

"Alright. Any chance we can backtrack whatever path those two left?"

"Not likely. If they're anything like the wolf I know, their tracks will already be gone."

As Barr predicted, there was no sign of the patrol or which way they had come. Even the site where they had died bore no mark of the scuffle, aside from those tracks Barr and the others had left. That was when he realized they had been careless. It was well within his ability to mask their tracks, having done so on numerous hunts, but he was so focused on reaching the temple, that all thoughts but revenge were put aside. He did his best to go back and cover their trail, despite the time lost in doing so. It did, however, give him an opportunity to be alone and secure Aislin beneath a leather sleeve.

It was midday before Dar-Paj began to lead.

With Barr walking behind them, erasing their trail with the faintest whisper of *furie*, the apprentice strained his senses to make out a path through the fog. No birds but Idelle took wing on the fetid air, nor creatures but Aren could be found. That left every sound and scent drawing his attention, slowing their pace to a near crawl. Hours went by, with them passing near two patrols in all, before Idelle finally caught sight of the temple.

I see it! she cried. *Veer to your left and follow that ravine. Be careful, though. There's quite a few of them about.*

"Wait," Barr told them. "Idelle can see the temple. It's over this way."

"How do you and she communicate?" Ealdan asked, following his lead. "Do you and the hound talk to each other in much the same way?"

"Now isn't the time. Stay close, and remember we're soldiers on patrol. Don't look at the others, keep your eyes straight ahead, and let me do all the talking."

"Others?"

Aren growled, and the actor went silent.

Breaking through the fog, like a hazy dream prior to waking, the temple came into view before them. Its ivory steps and bleached stone led up to a building of rounded curves and windowless design, where dark alcoves gave home to massive statues all around. From gilded soldiers to frightening beasts, each figure looked alive. Scrawled across the entirety of the temple's upper section, each man-sized block was covered with rows of vast sigils and wards filled with iron. Even from this distance, the aura of enchantment about the building rang out in Barr's mind, threatening to shatter his concentration and the illusion he fought to maintain.

A number of soldiers and priests walked about the grounds just outside, where four elliptical fountains were joined at the center by a sundial. Armed guards in black livery stood at either end of the pillared steps, vigilant as their statue counterparts, and equally unmoving. With great calm and determination, Barr led the others on, past disinterested eyes that cared for naught but their own agenda. Only one soldier went by and offered a salute. Barr returned the gesture, fist to chest and then down, but never turned his gaze toward the man.

I'll keep watch from outside, Idelle said.

If things go awry, I want you to go back to Geilon-Rai and tell Seltruin. Don't try to help, Barr warned. *Just let others know of this place.*

Beneath a raised iron gate, they passed through the main entrance and drew no more attention to themselves than those robed men and women that bustled from one end of the great hall to the other. Two massive wooden doors were open to either side, stretching up from the dark tiles to the vaulted ivory ceiling overhead. Hundreds of thick candles in brass holders ran the length of the

The Last Incarnation

hall and gave light to colorful frescoes trimmed in gold. Polished to a mirror sheen, each tile had the glassy appearance of water. Stretching off into the distance, in either direction, the hall echoed with the clap of many feet. It seemed all were heading the same way, so Barr simply followed suit and was surprised at the enormity of the chamber they soon entered.

Divided into four sections of tiered seats, stone rows covered in red cloth, the room tapered like a wedge that culminated in a platform. Steps on either side rose up to the open dais, where all that could be seen was a great altar of ashen black. It had elaborate carvings along the bottom, angry grimaces both man and beast, and across the top was a single row of iron runes. Draped along the walls were vast tapestries done in crimson, stirred by the many bodies of those entering the room. They wavered in the air, like waterfalls of fresh blood, and each one held a visage in ebon of four distinct creatures: a wolf, a bear, a boar and a demon.

More were joining the throng of robed priests and armored soldiers, carefully choosing their seats. It looked like all of the guards were relegated to the back, while the others seemed arranged within their sect by the color of their vestments. First went pure white, then red edged with gold, and the final few were in black with silver trim. The soldiers, both men and women, wore masked helms that depicted their sect.

Barr directed his friends to stand with those of the wolf and did his best to take stock of their numbers. Two score in each section, a rough estimate at best, was far more than he had planned on facing. Each soldier bore arms, either axes or swords, though many among the demons wore claws. Some had half-shields strapped to one arm, while others were adorned with a myriad of spikes. Barr could only assume that the unarmored had weapons of their own, be they magic or martial, but was more troubled by one pervading thought.

Every one of them was most likely a shapeling.

From a passage at the back of the platform, stepped the man Barr had scried, the one whose medallion he carried, the wolf that had taken his father. Following after him came eight others, black robes with red masks, that seemed strange for their varying height. One of them stood two hands taller than a normal man, while three were very short by any standard. Odder still, the one least of height was twice as wide at the shoulder than any of the others.

The gathered crowd immediately cheered, pushing away all thought, and set the nape of Barr's neck on end. They were a pack of wild animals, crying out with feral spirit, and the focus of their zeal was the man Barr had come to face. He stood at the dark altar, arms raised over the clamoring mass and eyes alight with a beryl glow. The roaring din seemed to feed him, made him appear larger than just a man, and the faithful chanting that soon followed set the chamber to rumbling with every word.

"Khulfa! Khulfa!" they cried out, and their collective voices inspired him to howl.

* * *

Markus followed behind Barr, eyes darting in every direction to gauge distance and targets. There were robed shapelings passing by, without so much as a word, and a guard stood to either side of them with every three steps up toward the temple they took.

How is this possible? he marveled. *Even if two of us wear the guise of those we killed, what is he making the*

other two look like? Are your children so many that they cannot recognize strangers among them?
They are not so many as I would like.
Once inside the temple, Barr led them down a large corridor and into some kind of ceremonial chamber. So many shapelings surrounded them, that Markus began to worry – not only for his own safety, but that he could do nothing to save the boy from the bloodshed sure to come. Feraesk had already searched all their belongings left with the horses, and the revenant found nothing in Barr's satchel. If the boy was hiding an Emblem, it was either somewhere else or on his person right now.

All around him, the shapelings began to roar and howl, like the filthy animals they were inside. Still, not one of them made a move to attack.

He is more powerful than I thought, to fool them like this.

Revyn chuckled, like a plague of scarabs across the spine. *The illusion is child's play. Without my assistance, you would have been discovered long ago.*

And when the fighting begins?

Markus could hear no response above the clamor of zealous chanting.

* * *

The realization fell over him, like the grip of a cold shadow, stirred the fears at the pit of his stomach into a hardened knot of determination. Barr could no more let these other shapelings survive, to hunt innocent people whenever they chose, than he could allow this Khulfa to go free. In the same instant of suddenly knowing what it was he had to do, he also felt regret for the fate of his new friends. Barr had no misconceptions. He could bring this temple to the ground, destroy every last one of them, but his friends and his own life would be forfeit as well.

Gritting his teeth, his mind set on what must be done, Barr stepped out from the other wolves and began walking toward the platform.

Aren was by his side. *What should I do?*

Just follow my lead. When the time comes, stay at my side and keep them away.

Strange, Idelle said. *There's some kind of commotion going on outside. Quite a few are leaving the temple, and the guards are abandoning their posts.*

The illusion dissipated, like mist through a fire, as Barr reached the platform steps. He could sense Ealdan and Dar-Paj behind him, but his attention was wholly focused on the priest – on the wolf shaped like a man.

Shapelings took notice of strangers in their temple, and the eight upon the dais rushed forward to stop them. Bestial red masks completely hid their faces from sight, but no colored ceramic could hope to conceal the terrible loathing that they bore.

Khulfa waved them off. "It's alright. Let's hear what our brave neighbors have to say."

By the smell of them, Aren said, *they can probably tell you're not a shapeling, because you don't stink like rotted meat.*

With a restraining hand on Barr's shoulder, Ealdan whispered in his ear, "Take care what you say. All our lives are at stake here."

Barr pulled the medallion from his pocket and held it up for the priest to see. Some in the crowd breathed a sigh of relief, as if they gathered these few had come to join the shapeling ranks.

"Is this yours?" Barr stepped closer and held it out. "Does this belong to you?"

"It looks like one of mine. Ah child, have you come to join us then?" The eight atop the platform raised a fist into the air, signaling the throng to cry out a cheer. "Do you hear?" Khulfa said to them all, his voice carrying throughout the chamber with a force of will brought down to bear. "This one has come to join us!"

Join us.

Barr faltered, his intent no longer sure.

Join us.

Like the voices from a past vision, the words echoed in his mind. But this voice was different. It whispered all around the words and slithered in between, distracting his every thought with the insistence of its plea.

Join us.

But it wasn't the joining of scattered parts, nor the piecing together of fragmented lives.

Join us.

It was a surrender to its will, a submission of mind and body, a yielding that promised to rid the flesh of any spirit, until nothing but the whispers remained.

Join us!

Aren growled, and all but one of the red masked priests backed away. The one who stood firm met the hound's warning gaze with eyes that flared a greenish hue. It was then that Aren noticed it.

That scent. I know that scent...

"No," Barr said and thrust the voice from his mind.

Anger welled up within him at what Khulfa had tried to do, at the insidious smile that marred the priest's face. That anger burned through him with a deadly intent, searing the edge of his senses in a fiery blaze. Like rings of flaming light, it expanded out and coruscated up the length of his body, forming a barrier no thoughts could transgress. The force with which Barr protected himself, thrusting Khulfa from his mind, was of such an intensity that the priest looked to have suffered a physical blow.

Regaining his composure, Khulfa raised a brow in surprise. His smile was that of a remonstrating parent.

"Do you wish to join us now? As you can see, the entire assemblage waits on your every word." His nostrils flared with warning. "Choose them wisely."

Barr tossed him the medallion. "Is it yours?"

"It has my blessing." Khulfa ran a hand over its surface and nodded. "Yes, it's faint, but I can still feel Revyn's favor upon it. Have you sought out this temple to return what's his? Or does such a darkness dwell in your heart that you'd seek to do us harm?"

"What I seek is the one who killed my father. A wolf, like yourself, wearing *that* medallion, took my father's life seven years ago."

Admit it! Barr wanted to scream at him, needing to hear the words. More than simple vengeance, he wanted Khulfa to confess. He leaned forward with the desire to pummel the truth free, but the one masked priest held him back.

Khulfa managed to look saddened. "I sense your anger, and I feel for your loss. Such is the way of our people. We must feed to maintain the magic that fuels our existence. We are, however, not an uncivil-"

"*Is* that or is it *not* your medallion?" Barr demanded.

"I told you, it bears the blessing I placed upon it," he answered and waved an arm across the chamber, "but all who worship the God of Change possess such a piece. It's my gift to those who are worthy of him."

"Barr," Ealdan said, "is it possible some other wolf took your father? That all you sense in that medallion is this priest's blessing?"

"It was him," Barr insisted. "He just won't admit it."

Khulfa shook his head. "I haven't left this temple in over a century. You may or may not find truth in my words, but I didn't kill your father. Those I feed on are brought to me, as willing sacrifices, in honor of Revyn." The priest held out both hands, as if showing they were free of blood somehow proved his innocence. "I couldn't have killed anyone outside these walls."

"Liar!" Barr roared and shoved the red-mask aside.

"No," the masked priest said calmly, "he speaks the truth."

That's it, Aren said, *the scent! I just wasn't sure until now!* Then he narrowed his gaze and growled out a feral warning.

Barr knew that voice as well, knew the hate that it harbored. Eyes wide with disbelief, breath stolen by the crushing revelation, he felt the world fall away and leave nothing but betrayal.

It can't be, Barr cried inwardly, struggling to come to grips. *How can it be you? How can you be one of them! You murdered your own people...*

Ceiran removed his mask.

"That medallion is mine," the elf sneered. "Thank you for returning it."

It was Ceiran? Idelle asked, her voice near to tears. *All that time, and no one knew. Why would he do such a thing?*

Barr could only shake his head, incredulous and confused.

"Finally speechless? You seemed to have much to say the last time we spoke."

Slowly, it all began to make sense. The wolf that had plagued the elves for so long, his father's death and Tuvrin finding him, the troll Chamal so close to Alixhir...

He wasn't following us in the forest. He was coming here, to the temple, Barr reasoned. *All along, it's been him.*

He's killed countless people, his own people! Tuvrin's family... And I almost caught him, he thought, recalling the hunt that ended in his being accused of Harduen's murder. *He slaughtered them all.*

"It all makes sense now," Barr said, "how you killed Harduen without a second thought and were in league with orcs. You're no elf." With a glance toward Ealdan and Dar-Paj, Ceiran grinned as if it were a compliment. "What exactly were you planning, you and that tribe?"

"Let us just say," he replied, "that I was not the only one with plans for your exile." His eyes hardened at the word. "And now I can repay you for what *you* have done. Did you know that after you left Geilon-Rai, I was exiled as well?" The mask twisted in his hands and dropped to the floor. "Because of you, I am no longer welcome in the land of my people!"

"You hunt them like animals," Barr scoffed. "They stopped being your people the moment you killed one. How many elves have you fed on? Or was it simply for sport? I can understand your hatred of humans, but how could you kill your own, the ones you were sworn to protect?" Barr spat at the Narohk's feet and drew both kyan. "Come on then, wolf, draw your sword. I have a promise to keep."

"Guards!" Khulfa shouted. "Seize them!"

Ealdan and Dar-Paj rushed past to deal with Khulfa and the other seven in red masks. More than twice the height of a tall man, its edge rounded the entire length, the platform was not meant to be climbed upon. Steps at either end were the quickest way up, and many of the guards below moved with all speed to use them. With a wave of one hand, Barr conjured a wall of flame on the steps to his left. The fire stretched up with a vigorous hunger, blackening the ceiling with its touch.

No one will get passed, Aren promised and went to help the others keep the dais cleared.

"You cannot win," Ceiran told Barr smugly and drew his sword. "What could you possibly be thinking, coming into a temple full of warrior priests? Did you think you could just walk in, have your revenge and then scamper back to your little hole? If you throw down your kyan, I will see that you die quickly." He cut the air with his own ironwood blade. "The alternative will take much longer."

A crossbow fired from behind Barr, out of the throng clamoring to reach the dais, and came flying towards his back. He turned his body sideways as it grew near, giving Ceiran no time to see or dodge the wooden shaft. It struck him through the thigh, just above the knee, and imbedded its pronged tip deep into muscle. The Narohk roared in pain and cursed the guard that had fired it, nearly forgetting that Barr stood before him. At least until the ironwood blades cut across his chest with incredible speed. Four gashes showed through Ceiran's tattered robes, and the intake of breath as he stumbled back was more from surprise than any pain.

"I warned you last time we spoke," Barr said evenly, "that if we crossed swords again, I'd do much worse than break your wrist." A stab to the shoulder and a cut to the sword arm. "I spared your life once before. I won't make that mistake again."

Anger and indignation shook the slender elf with a terrible roar. He struck out in rapid succession, a series of thrusts and powerful swings. The ironwood long sword crashed against Barr's kyan with growing strength in each hit, trembling his arms from the exertion to throw the blade off. Whatever happened to Ceiran since last they had fought, he was far stronger and faster than Barr recalled. The elf's sword flashed out and caught the edge of a shoulder, as Barr did his best to turn away.

The sight of blood only fuelled Ceiran's rage. As if renewed by the strike, flesh wound or no, he came on with relentless endurance. Spittle fell from his lips with each growl and great swing. There was little for Barr to do but stay on the defensive and turn aside what he could. A swing cut harmlessly against his wrist, through the leather sleeve and over Aislin's polished surface. Yet another came close to taking an ear. Still, Ceiran was beginning to tire, all his wild effort put to naught, and it was only a matter of time before he slipped and left an opening.

The moment Barr had been waiting for presented itself, and he reacted without hesitation. He sliced across Ceiran's abdomen, low enough to double the elf over. Clutching at his stomach, trying to keep the wound from bursting forth, Ceiran began to utter a string of words with both eyes tightly closed. A tingle of magic ran down Barr's neck, set the hair on end in a shiver that told him Ceiran could weave. A beryl nimbus formed around the Narohk, a glowing light that grew brightest at the point of his torn flesh.

"Oh, no you don't." Barr sheathed his kyan and held out both hands toward the elf. "Here's a little trick I learned as a Sage."

Ceiran dropped to his knees and gave an agonizing scream, as the *furie* was torn from his body. It left him in waves of visible light, an incandescence of shimmering blue mist that seeped from his eyes and chest. The mist rippled like a living thing, filling the space between them. It billowed out like a cloud, toward Barr's open hands, and an aura of power began to take shape all around him. It built in intensity, like a growing surge deep within him, desperate to break free. As Ceiran's skin turned a sickly brown and withered like dried leaves in a hungry fire, Barr fairly glowed with the additional *furie*.

Unfortunately for the guard who managed to climb upon the dais, that gathered storm of magic found a means for its release.

With one hand thrust towards the guard, Barr let it all go, while still drawing what little *furie* Ceiran had left. A single blast of searing heat, like a massive wall of fiery pearl, shot across the platform and took the soldier full on. It flashed through his body with a spark of brilliant white, turning him utterly to cinder, then continued on and dissipated over the open-mouthed priests below. As if a gust of wind had struck, the body-shaped pile of gray blew apart in a spray of ash and debris.

The release left Barr aching and Ceiran near death. The elf's skin looked like ancient parchment stretched taut over thin bones, brown and weathered, splotchy and weak. His fingers were like claws, twisted and decrepit, and his body shook with its new frailty. Shocks of wispy gray hair fell away from his head, littering the floor in aged clumps. The faint bout of whimpering that passed his drawn lips was too feeble and incoherent for Barr to grasp.

He reached down and took up the Narohk's sword.

"I keep my promises," Barr told him and drew the blade across the elf's distended belly, time and again. "For all the Sylvannis that you slaughtered. For Tuvrin and his family. For Harduen. And finally, for my father." Barr drove the blade through Ceiran's chest, through his rotted heart and the stone platform beneath.

"Pa'chuk nam inwah." *Their blood be avenged.*

A guard cried out as Aren's jaws clamped over the man's thigh, snapping the bone and twisting it with a *pop!* More of the helmed swordsmen were charging the dais, waving their massive axes overhead. Another went down with a swipe of Aren's paw, but two moved past to Barr's unprotected back.

Behind you! Aren warned.

The double-edged blade came crashing down, just as Barr turned sideways to avoid it. Wind from its passing sent his hair blowing back, and the axe struck deep into the floor by his feet. The second guard was already swinging, leaving Barr only enough time to throw up an arm in defense. The edge of his axe clanged against Aislin, sending an odd tingle down the length of Barr's arm but failing to mar the silvery gold surface.

As he drove an elbow into the first man and spun away from the second, a strange thing occurred at the end of Barr's arm. Aislin began to ripple, like the waves of an argent water or a distant memory of the Denshyar, then slid along his skin and covered his hand.

What was once an ornate bracer was now an equally magnificent looking sword. Barr drove Aislin's pommel, the likeness of a maiden's hand grasping a sphere, right into the face one attacker. He smashed the guard's gilded mask, including the fragile nose beneath it, and threw him off the platform. The instant Barr thought to draw a kyan, Aislin shrank in on itself, to the size and shape of a Maurdon blade. He was amazed that any weapon could contain such an unusual magic.

Then he was dodging yet another attack.

* * *

He had a dagger in hand and into the air, before the priest could utter another word. It struck deep into a shoulder, just a moment before Markus took him down with one hooked arm. Khulfa tried to speak, but the pommel of another knife smashed soundly against his forehead.

If any of them start throwing magic about, this fight will shortly be over.

Have no fear of that, Revyn cooed in his mind.

Markus slashed across the chest of a red-mask and saw Dar-Paj throw a punch that sent another careening through the air. The priest crashed against the stone wall with a sickly wet thud and slipped downward into an unmoving heap. Guards were rushing for the steps, to gain access to the dais. More knives shot out and took down two more masks.

They will think you abandoned them, he pointed out and picked up a sword. *Why not kill a few, while you are feeling so generous, and make this a bit easier?*

They will believe this boy weaver somehow affected their magic, and easing your efforts does not suit my purpose at this time.

There was no way they could hope to defeat so many, even if the shapelings didn't change form and leap up onto the dais. All Markus could do was trust that Revyn still needed him or that Barr was even stronger than he let on. For now, he focused on surviving. Thousands of years might have passed since he fought alongside his luminarron, but he still wielded a sword like he was born to it.

For all his frail looks, Dar-Paj was a force all his own. Markus could almost admire him, despite the odd coloring, nearly laughed when the apprentice hefted one of the priests and threw the man with enough strength to take down another four.

None of them are shifting, he noted, crushing a pair of hands on the edge of the platform. *I would think a wolf or a chaodyn could easily leap up here.*

True, Revyn said, clearly amused, *if they were able.*

"I could use some help over here!" Dar-Paj called out, kicking two down the steps.

Markus finished off the last of the masked priests, a female orc with painted markings all about her thick skin. She had tried to summon fire to burn him, but he was quicker than her magic. Once she was dead at his feet, he turned to lend a hand. That was when he noticed the gold apprentice was wounded, bleeding from at least a handful of cuts. Rather than risk being skewered along with him, Markus stayed back and fought off any that made it past. Throwing a knife when he could, careful not to kill his human shield, he was quite happy that the two of them did so well against so many.

We cannot keep this up forever.

Neither will you have to! The god sounded unusually excited. *Look! He has Aislin!*

With a sharp glance Barr's way, he caught sight of the Emblem, the mithrinum sword that would lead him to the others. A smile creased his lips and bubbled over into laughter. Fighting with renewed vigor, Markus raged forward and cut a bloody swathe through the guards. It felt like the old times, when his army ravaged the known lands.

And soon, he would have it all again.

* * *

He was a young boy once more, playing along the shore, when his friend turned with a puzzled look.

"Are you cross with me?"

Barr held the sword in both hands. "No, I – Aislin?"

The barn was on fire, and thick smoke rose up all around them. His mother was frantic, yelling over the crackle of flames.

"We must leave! Don't worry, I'll keep you safe!"

It was confusing, the bits and pieces of vision Aislin used to communicate. Aren nudged his side, pulling him out of his reverie and back to the frenzied din of battle. Ealdan and Dar-Paj were fighting for their lives, trying to keep at bay the mass of shapeling guards and priests. He was almost surprised they were still alive, as if at some point he was contented with the thought they would all die. Barr swallowed hard and resolved it not to be so.

Stay back, he told Aren.

About to jump into the crowd, the hound stopped short of the platform's edge and backed away instead.

What are you –

Cracks ran along the side walls and erupted across the floor of the temple. Each and every shapeling gave pause in their endeavor, filling the massive chamber with a preternatural calm, a dampened silence that rang out in the ear. Hair prickled and skin crawled at the building of will, before the assembled mass of shapelings dropped to all fours. Clutching their middles, crying out in quiet pain, they fought vainly against the unseen force. It began as a blue mist, seeping up from their bodies, but grew in full force to a gathering storm.

A hand out toward them, Barr tightened his grip, and with a fist he wrenched the *furie* from them all. It flew through the air like a visible wind and enveloped him with its ferocity, with a heat that blurred his vision. The flurry of swirling light then pulsed and grew calm, settled inward and took root in the sword. Barr could feel the power thrum in his hand, knew it was there for him to use.

Guards and priests alike began to flee. Barr had only taken enough to show that he could take it all, if he chose, and they wisely heeded the warning.

Are you alright? Idelle asked.

Barr looked over at Ceiran's remains. *We're fine now. We did what we came to do.*

"That was incredible," Ealdan said, as he and Dar-Paj stumbled over. Both of them looked exhausted and spattered with blood, though only Dar seemed to have suffered any visible wounds. "Interesting sword. Did you find it on one of them?"

"We need to leave," Dar-Paj said. "Immediately. None of us are safe, so long as they still live."

"I was just thinking that myself." Barr leveled a gaze at the altar. "How can I let this place stand? Or let any of them live? They're no different from Ceiran, monsters every one of them."

"Can you do that?" Ealdan asked. "Kill them all, I mean. There are so many. And we are in a temple, after all. Would you risk the wrath of a god?"

It looks like they're all fleeing, Idelle said. *They're pouring out of the temple and running south. Should I follow?*

Aren said, *I'm ready to fight, whatever you decide.*

"They will return," Dar-Paj warned, "and in greater numbers. I know you want to destroy this place and rid the world of these shapelings... but this is not the time."

Am I wrong? Wouldn't the world be better off without them? Barr looked down at Aislin, felt it tremble in his palm. *How many deaths would I prevent in doing so?*

Part of me agrees with you, Idelle said, *but who are we to make that sort of decision? Can you really kill off an entire people because of what they may or may not do? How long has this land been here? How long have they been neighbors to Alixhir? It just seems strange there's so many, and yet Ceiran was the only wolf that we knew of. It could be that the others don't hunt as he did.*

I don't know anymore. It just sickens me to think that Ceiran was the wolf, living among those that he hunted. If even one of these others is like him, how can I live with myself, knowing I let them survive?

The same way you would, knowing you killed the ones who might be innocent.

"We could always come back," Ealdan offered.

"Alright. Let's get out of here. Do you need me to heal you, Dar?"

"No, not right now. The sooner we are away from this place, the better I will feel."

They made their way back down the hall, toward the temple entrance. Not a shapeling could be seen. When they stepped outside and descended the steps, Aislin began to thrum stronger, vibrating up the length of his arm. When they reached the bottom steps, Dar stopped short and peered off into the distance.

"What is it?" Barr asked, unable to see anything. "I can feel something's wrong, but I don't know what it is. What do you see?"

He pointed north, as the dark outline of riders broke through the fog.

"Guardians."

– 26 –

The whole village was bustling about, some running frantically to avoid that which they had never seen but feared worse than death. When the hooded men arrived, buildings burned and people died. It was a fact of life that all had to cope with, but the Guardians had never come to Gwynneth before.

Deirth stood rooted to the spot, the bucket of water now at his feet and forming a muddied puddle. The fire, he thought. They know... They've come for me!

It felt as if stones weighed him down, so hard was it to lift each foot and run for the fields. There were few places to hide in Gwynneth, but Deirth knew his way around the forest. Once beyond the fields, few would have the skill to track and find him.

The Last Incarnation

How could she tell? *he asked himself, recalling Myrna and the barn. He had showed her something he kept secret from all others, even his family, and what did she do?* She told them! But it was an accident. I didn't mean for it to happen!
The colorful fires that came to each finger had gotten away from him. He didn't mean to catch the bail on fire and had quickly put out what small bits of hay took to the flame. It was all very harmless, a trick he had hoped would win her favor. Of all the girls in Gwynneth, Myrna was the prettiest.
And Deirth had thought she fancied him.
With the sickly grip of betrayal wrapped about his heart, he cursed himself and cried, as he ran for the trees. Da always warned I'd show off one too many times. *He stopped at the edge of the woods and turned back for what he expected to be his last glimpse of home. However, no Guardians rode on his trail, nor did angry shouting erupt in a heated search for him. All Deirth could see was old Lady Evams being dragged from her home, to the center of town.*
The midwife?
She was tied to the maypole, as the rest of the village quietly watched on. Most looked shocked that a woman who had delivered their children could be a turner, while others were simply fearful of the men who had come to cleanse her by fire. The midwife's pleas fell on deaf ears, for no one moved to help. Deirth wanted to run back and stop them, to show they had the wrong person.
It was me! *he yelled, waving his arms.* I was the one, not Lady Evams! It was me!
But he had run so far that his cries went unheard...

* * *

"Barr!" Dar-Paj shook him. "Snap out of it! Are you alright? We have to get out of here." The apprentice looked over a shoulder, as if he could hear something approach. "None of us are in any shape to deal with Guardians, let alone more shapelings. We must run for the woods and hide."

Guardians? Barr shook his head to clear the vision. *I'm more tired than I thought. I should've been able to break that vision on my own.*

Hurry! Idelle shouted. *More shapelings are coming your way, and the others are starting to turn around!*

They ran from the steps and headed east into the thickening fog. Barr hoped those riders weren't truly Guardians, but fervently wished even more they had no reason to give chase. Exhaustion settled over him, like a crashing wave of utter weariness. Considering what he had done in the temple, it was a wonder he remained conscious at all.

What would Guardians be doing in the middle of Lumintor? He looked down at the humming sword in his hand but discarded the idea. Enchanted weapons were not enough to draw their attention, were they? His kyan certainly hadn't, when they were in Alixhir. *They must have heard the battle, but still... How could they have gotten here so fast?*

We're not even sure they're Guardians, Aren said. *For all we know, it's just more shapelings. If they come, we deal with them.*

I'm trying, Idelle said, *but I can't see them anymore.*

Turning north and heading for the sparse trees, Barr thought he heard something and pulled up short. A nod from Dar-Paj showed he had heard it as well.

"I am out of knives," Ealdan whispered. "Could I use your new sword there? You still have the others."

A memory flashed before Barr's eyes, of a woman in a frantic state. "No!" the image pleaded and was gone.

"You can use this," he said and offered a kyan.

Ealdan frowned and waved it off. "I think I can do better than a wooden sword."

With a shrug, Barr sheathed it again. Deciding it was safe to move, he signaled the others to follow and ran with as much speed as he was able. Even wounded, Dar-Paj had no trouble keeping up. It was Ealdan that began to wheeze and fall behind, holding his side as if he were injured as well. Barr slowed down and felt much better when they reached a spot among the trees he recognized.

His relief, however, was short lived.

The twelve horsemen appeared before them, riding through the fog at a casual gait, as if they knew precisely where it was they were going.

"Stay back," Barr told his friends.

They looked incredibly daunting astride their Norian warhorses, massive steeds that were bred for combat. The iron shod hooves were as deadly a weapon as any found on the field. Those of the twelve who wore armor had tight fitting black plate that seem molded to their frame. The ripples of each muscle were shaped into the dark metal, as were the contours of each helm fashioned to depict the face of the rider. It left one wondering if the horns of one or the pointed fangs of another were true features belonging to the man underneath. With a shield that ran from toe to shoulder and weapons that ranged from a forked sword to a wicked cross between mace and axe, the warrior Guardians looked a nightmare incarnate.

The other magic hunters were shrouded in mystery, concealed beneath the heavy gray-lined black robes of a Justiciar. They bore no shield nor martial weapons, but the crackling blue light that shone from their cowls, as if their eyes were ablaze with *furie*, bespoke a far more dangerous foe. As different in size and shape as they all were, they did have one thing in common.

Each of them wore the insignia of a Guardian.

The riders stopped, side by side, and stood waiting for some unspoken command. Barr stood his ground, with Aren beside him, and felt Aislin begin to tremble even more. Ealdan and Dar-Paj backed away into the fog, but the Guardians made no move to follow. It was clear they had come for Barr, which was just as well. He could face them without worrying about his friends.

"You will surrender your weapon," the lead Guardian commanded in a hollow, ringing voice beneath his helm.

Though his body ached with exhaustion, Barr steeled his resolve and fought down the overwhelming urge to run away. He had been raised all his life to fear the very men before him, to hide who he was because of what they might do. They were the reason he and his father had left Alixhir, to live all alone in the forest. No amount of running or hiding would put them off now. He had no choice but to face them. It wrenched at his gut, but he summoned the *furie* to erect a shield.

"And if I don't?"

One in flowing robes answered, in a similarly hollow voice, "You will be held accountable for your crimes. Throw down your weapon, or face the consequences." All twelve moved to encircle Barr. "No harm will come to you and yours, if you yield. Throw down the sword and step away."

* * *

Dar-Paj wanted to stay and do what he could, but he realized Barr needed room to weave. Ealdan pulled at his elbow, drawing him away and into the concealment of fog all around them. Dar could hear the jangle of spurs, the breath of each horse, and none of them made a move to follow after.

"We can slip around," Ealdan whispered. "It is not us that they want. Look, they do not care that we are gone. We can use their voices as a mark, sneak around and attack them from behind."

Ealdan pulled him even further away.

"We have no weapons. They are trained soldiers and weavers. What can we do against them?"

"It does not matter," Ealdan said from behind.

A hand closed over Dar's mouth, as the biting cold of a knife plunged deep into his back. It became unbearably difficult to breath, as if a fire burned in his chest and stole away all his air. His legs grew weak and fell out beneath him, as the knife was pushed deeper still and twisted inside. Down on his knees, body arched against the pain, Dar had no breath to shout out a warning.

"I believe this is where we part company." Ealdan's laugh was less than mirthful. "It was fun while it lasted, though."

Traitor! Dar-Paj screamed in his mind and felt the tips of his fingers going numb. Paralyzed, barely able to draw breath, all he could feel was the cold of Ealdan's knife. *I should have known...*

The blade was pulled free, and Dar fell onto his back. A puddle of sticky wetness reached up toward his neck, gumming his hair with its chill. Ealdan knelt over him and wiped the dust from Dar's robe, then straightened its folds until satisfied.

"I thought you should look your best," he said with a smile, "you know, considering this is your final curtain call. Of course, I do have to make certain. All sorts of things can go wrong when you start getting sloppy. And with that said..."

Ealdan plunged the knife into Dar's chest, directly through the heart, then wiped the blood from his hands with a perfumed kerchief. Without another word, he stood up and walked away, leaving the frilly cloth and the knife imbedded deep inside. Dar-Paj fought just to breathe, as blood poured from his body, and cried out in his mind words he longed to give voice.

Barr... betrayed...

* * *

"You're less than half a mile from a shapeling temple, and you come after me?" Barr switched Aislin to his left hand. "I don't know who you are, but you're definitely not Guardians. You want my sword? Fine then. Come take it."

With a flick of his right hand, he let loose the *furie* around Aren and himself, surrounding them in a small shield, to protect them from weapons. He hoped it would give enough time to gather more strength. Calling upon what was left of his reserves and coupling it with the magic stored in Aislin, Barr dropped to one knee and slammed his open palm to the ground. The resounding shockwave that followed stretched out from his body. It rippled the cold earth with a visible ring that expanded with the force of storm. It passed harmlessly over Aren, but took the riders full on, toppling them end over end through the air with their horses.

With every ounce of will he could muster, Barr closed his grip on the land and took from it with a desperate vie for survival, a fraught need that knew no restraint. The ground blackened around him in a growing sphere of ashen death, throwing up the debris of spent soil and roots. Barr did his best not to harm Aren, or any of his friends, but he wasn't sure if he could safeguard their lives.

The sphere grew ever further, picking up speed as it went, and washed over the twelve in a flurry of cinders. Though the riders seemed unaffected, getting to their feet amidst the turmoil, the horses were not nearly so lucky. Barely a whinny could be heard, as their bodies were devoured, drained of all *furie* by a ravenous force. It went on without stopping, well beyond their shriveled corpses, tearing all life from the land. The sphere nearly reached the temple steps and consumed a number of shapelings before coming to a halt.

Barr stood ablaze with the stolen *furie*.

Swooping down like the shadow of death, Idelle took hold of one rider and threw him at another. The two crashed together, rolled into a heap and got back up with no sign of any damage. Aren growled and leapt, taking one by the shoulder and crushed both armor and man. The warriors drew their weapons, while those in heavy robes conjured a blackness to each hand. Like tiny suns of black light with a violet corona, the gathered *furie* burned in their grasp.

Now! Aren roared, tearing through another, snapping metal and bone with his teeth.

Palm held out, Barr let loose a blast of pent up *furie*. It struck against one of the soldiers, like heat from a furnace, and stopped him dead in his tracks. It ate away at the edges of his bubbling armor and snatched off what remained of his helm. It was what laid beneath that gave Barr pause and allowed the others time to attack.

They're not alive! Barr said in disbelief, despite the skeletal head and fiery eyes that looked back at him.

He dodged their attacks as best he could, and what he couldn't turn aside struck against the barrier with a flash of blue light. Moving with the learned grace of many lifetimes on the field, Barr still took numerous blows. He returned their attacks with Aislin, slicing through armor and the rotting limbs that laid beneath. He scarcely believed what he saw, that lifeless corpses could somehow move with such strength and great speed, let alone weave a dark magic he had never before seen.

Bolt after bolt tore through the air, leaving streamers of shadow in their wake. He was able to deflect most with Aislin, but they were attacking from all sides with an unrelenting fervor. Each time one struck his shield, its magic was diminished. Barr let loose the unspent *furie* in blasts of scorching heat, eating away at their long dead bodies but doing nothing to stop them. Pushed beyond his limits, exhausted past all measure, he knew with a terrible certainty that these creatures would outlast him.

You can do this! Idelle reassured, flying down to take one by the shoulders. *Keep trying!*

A knife flew through the air and sliced one of her wings, tearing muscle and fragile bones apart. She cried out and tumbled to the ground, throwing up a cloud of debris. When the two finally came to a stop, the armored Guardian crawled over and pummeled her frail body, over and over again.

"No!" Barr roared and sent a blast toward the soldier that flung him off Idelle and burst the armor from his decayed body. "Idelle!"

Aren yelped and went down, as a bolt crashed along his side. It scorched hair and singed flesh with a black fire that would not abate. Barr wanted to cry out, torn between helping them both, when the blade of an edged mace caught him across the shoulder. He dropped to one knee from the terrible force and watched with growing horror as more fiery darkness was hurled at Aren. The hound tried to stand, but a knife flew through the fog and struck deep in his hind.

Ealdan?

His shield was beginning to waver, when the mace struck again. Barr flung that one away with a blast of fire, but four more quickly came to take his place. Soon they were all around him, raining savage blows and throwing magic. Violet and ebon *furie* ran the length of his body, burst his protective barrier into cascading motes of fading light. Burned and broken, with smoky tendrils rising up from every inch of his skin, Barr reached out with his will to try and steal their *furie*. He was met with a steadfast resolve. Breathless and near death, awash in pain from his wounds and the silence in his mind, his anguish was further pushed at the sound of a familiar voice.

"I will take that," Ealdan said and wrenched Aislin from his grasp. "You have no idea how long I have waited for this moment. If I had known you had it with you, we could have avoided all this nonsense. I would have just killed you in your sleep."

"Why?" Barr asked and coughed up dark blood. *Can you hear me? Idelle? Aren?* "It's just... a sword."

"Hardly. I believe this is yours, Feraesk." He handed Aislin to one of the armored Guardians. "You know what to do with it."

"I trusted you... and you betray me... for a sword?"

"Live and learn, I suppose." Ealdan knelt and drew a knife. "Well, not in your case. I am reminded of a famous saying. I believe it was mine, but who can tell with so much time gone by. In any case, it goes something along the lines of... Never leave an enemy behind. Sounds rather ominous, does it not?" Barr reached out a weak hand towards him. "Plucky until the end. Yes, well, no hard feelings, eh? Better luck next time, and all that."

Ealdan thrust the knife into Barr's chest.

J.A. Giunta

– 27 –

The glittering of stars winked in the blackness above, reflecting off the dark waters that stretched out beneath him. Immersed in its touch, absorbing its warmth, the water soothed the length of his body. He heard nothing but the labored rise and fall of his chest, saw no light but the stars overhead.

Where am I? he thought. *What happened?*

Luminous eyes opened before him, the vibrant blue irises encircled in a glittering black. They belonged to a woman kneeling by his side.

You are in the Mists, she said. Her voice was gentle, almost lilting, like the water that eased him. *This place is a part of Faeronthalsos.*

Aren? Idelle? Barr tried to sit up, but the pain in his chest was too great. *Where are my friends? Are they* alright? I saw both of them fall. Idelle was knocked from the air... just like in my dream. His thoughts began to scatter in the confusion of concern. No, no, no! I saw it all happen, and still I brought her to Lumintor. It's all my fault!

Calm, she told him. *Your thoughts must remain calm to be understood. All are here, and those that need it are healing. As you should be.*

Barr studied her face, so much like the forest spirit who had given him Aislin. Her skin was pale and fairly sparkled in the light, almost with an opalescent sheen. Her brow was as smooth and delicate as her prominent cheeks and rounded chin.

She's beautiful.

Her laughter was like the tinkling of bells. *It pleases me that you think so. You, too, are beautiful.* She stroked his cheek with the back of her slender fingers. *It has been a very long time, even for one such as I.*

Who are you?

I am called Daesidaoli, Matron of the Guiding Mists. Her eyes glimmered with the flicker of stars off the water. *This place is my domain, where my hand alone shapes time and space. I have frozen this moment, to tend to your wounds.* She placed a hand on his chest. *You would have died otherwise.*

Barr was captured by her eyes, by the inescapable feeling that he should know this woman.

I know your name, from a fire tale. An old woman...

I am that Daesidaoli. She looked deeply into his eyes, as if searching for an answer. *Do you yet understand, Barr of Darleman, Sage of the Illumin Valar? Do you know me yet, son of Nedryn, son of Daroth, son of Tuvrin?* A tear ran down her cheek. *Ah, my dear, dear Aoleontril.*

Daesidaoli, he thought wonderingly and wiped away her tears. *I'm certain we've met once before. I should know you, I'm sure of it.*

Yes, she agreed softly, *you should.*
It came to him then, sparked by something she had said. Son of Nedryn... the man from the fire tale, the one who had left his son to be raised by an old widow.
I was told my mother died when I was a small child. I never knew her. She said nothing, as he worked through what he felt and what he thought he knew. *If it's true, that Nedryn is my father, then how did Daroth end up with me?*
Nedryn left you with Lady Biryn, a widowed teacher in Devomshire. As much as she adored the child left in her care, she knew she could not raise him. Her time was drawing near. Barr could see the happiness in her eyes, the tearful joy of a mother. *It so happened that her only nephew came to pay her a visit between campaigns. His life as a mercenary did little for his purse and threatened each day to take him from this world, with no one to bear his memory or name. His aunt begged him to take the child and raise it as his own, to give up his sword for a family. Though he had no wife, Daroth was instantly taken with the child, with you Barr.* She kissed the back of his hand and smiled. *It is the faeron in you that affects humans so.*
I'm faeron, Barr said sleepily, clinging to his mother's voice with what strength he had left. *I have a mother...* The thought was comforting, settled in his middle with a warmth that called him to sleep. *I have family.*
Rest now, Daesi told him, *for tomorrow is a new day, with new beginnings, and there is much that needs to be done.*

* * *

Tempas stepped through the swirling clouds of the ether, his mind racing at the turn of events. The others were calling, meeting yet again, more talk when action was needed. He knew the answer would not be found in his brothers and sisters, made helpless as they were by their own foolish oath. No, if none of them were to put an end to Revyn's machinations, he would have to go about it himself.

With a thought, he joined them, traversing the ether in a single step.

"Still talking, I see," Tempas said evenly, gray eyes searching those of his siblings. "For my part, you have all heard what I think. I hold war dearer than all things. It is an art, a philosophy, a way of living and dying, but Revyn has now gone too far. He will bring about one final war that will leave Taellus barren of all children but his own." He tried not to be angry, but their complacence was a constant source of frustration. He slammed the butt of his spear into the polished marble floor, sending cracks along the image of his iron-toed boots. "We must put an end to this matter, while still we are able."

"You assume much." Saernol leaned against a pillar, awash in a gown of stars. "You have both my love and respect, but you are yet young. War was not always known to our children, though they often fought amongst one another. The very mortal you wish to strike down attributed much to your birth."

Nanindar showed his painted face from behind a column of jade. "And for this he should give thanks? And they call me the God of Fools..." Both thin and wiry, the god's ribs showed through his tight yellow tunic, as he laughed with a hearty guffaw. "Fool I may be and soon will you see, but ne'er did the one lead to two."

Saernol looked thin on patience, narrowing her dark eyes to ominous slits. Nanindar soon found amusement with balls of light and juggled them off to a cloudy corner.

The Last Incarnation

"I believe," Kraug added smoothly, "what our sister is trying to say is that we must consider many things and never forget what has come before." The short and stout god was as wide as he was tall, but he hefted an iron hammer easily the length of his arm – and of a weight that would have staggered ten men. "You were not yet among us, Tempas, when the Emblems were taken and hidden away."

It infuriated him, how they took every opportunity to remind him of his birth, that he might be a god but not born of the Father.

Curoch gave a nod of his burnished helm. "Revyn's punishment was accompanied by an oath from us all." The golden-haired deity paced about in his plate armor, looking more knight than god. He glanced over at their brother, the Watcher, seated quietly in the stone steps that surrounded them, hidden beneath his timeworn robes and shadowy features. "There must be a fair and just solution to this dilemma."

"I am sure," Tempas said with waning patience, "that Revyn suffers from no such constraint. He is driven by power alone and will stop at nothing, until every living creature is his own."

Herne arrived through a swirling of mist, with Unther quick on his steps. The two hunter gods wore the garb of their children, Herne in linen breeches and a homespun tunic, Unther in the dark leathers of a Maurdon. The bows they carried bore the trophy marks of a thousand hunts, each notch in the glossy ironwood forming wards and glyphs of power.

"What news?" Herne asked. Where normally there stood the sharp horns of a deer, dark hair fell forward as he bowed to Saernol.

With a wave of her delicate fingers, an image of Revyn's dark child appeared in her palm.

"As you can see," she explained, "Markus has taken the Emblem. This Barr has learned much in his short life but only now knows the sting of betrayal."

"An apt teacher, did he have." Unther shook leaves from his silvery hair. "Naught a well-placed arrow could not mend."

Stepping out from the shadow of a pillar, Celene clucked her tongue in remonstration at the comment. Though she seemed to follow their conversation with intent, she was keeping her own council. The same was true for Veralnon, remaining quiet in the back, like dark mountains brooding in the distance.

Tempas wondered aloud, "If we cannot act openly against this Markus and his revenants, what is to stop one of my children from killing him? A single vision or a dream –"

"And every Warmaster on Taellus," Kraug snapped, finishing the thought for him and biting off each word through his scraggly beard, "would abandon their oath to hunt him down. You would unleash a force nearly as devastating as that yet to come."

"Besides," Saernol pointed out, "we agreed that your Warmasters would remain forever in their cloisters, secluded from the world, in exchange for the knowledge and power you grant them. Teachers only, Tempas. An oath is an oath."

Yet more oaths that would lead to the end of us all, he bitterly thought.

Curoch said, "There may be another course, brother. Have you considered bestowing a gift to the mortal he has betrayed? It would serve the same purpose but from a different end."

"I would expect more from the Patron of Truth." Laeryk, the Watcher, stood and walked down the steps to join them. Apparently, he would be silent no more. "You

The Last Incarnation

worry the words of your oath, until it fits what end you desire. Nay, brother Curoch, hear me. I know you would never break the spirit of an oath, let alone its very words, but sparking such a thought in others smacks of an equal dishonor. I would agree that helping one another's children does not breach our oath to do no harm, *but* in this particular instance, where the fate of all children stands in the balance, you cannot aid one without hurting another. Our course, our *only* course, is clear. We must do nothing to interfere. All is in the capable hands of our children. We must trust that they can take care of themselves."

Tempas watched their reactions, and it seemed most reluctantly agreed. He might find an ally in one or two, but the brunt of any effort would be his own. He gave a smart salute and departed the divine throng. There was much to be done, and little time left for doing.

A single Warmaster, he vowed, making plans in his head. *Just one to right the wrongs of the world...*

* * *

Ealdan looked on Barr through narrowed eyes in the shifting visions of dream. No hard feelings, eh? The thief laughed, as the knife entered Barr's chest, again and again.

This isn't over! *Barr roared in his mind. The world changed to a land of wind and dead sand.* I will hunt you to the ends of the realm, *he promised, his eyes boring into Ealdan as the actor backed away.* No mountain holds enough rock, no ocean the water nor hole the darkness to keep me from finding you. Mark my words, thief. *Barr's voice was low and even, seemingly carried by wind alone.* Mark them. You will be dead by next moon, you and the twelve that helped you. Say whatever you will, think what you like, but never forget this. I am coming for you.

The image of Ealdan backed away into nothing, its face not so sure as it once was. What little wind still blew settled into the fading landscape, a shifting of sands to thick grass and blue sky. Still Barr fumed, but the cool earth between his toes soon eased the burning in his heart. With a tranquil mind, he could see the futility in blazing a path of anger that burned the angered as well. What he felt then had direction, but only a calm and steady determination would move him safely toward it.

It was as if he could see Ealdan, off in the distance, where sky and ground met in a haze. The actor-thief would occasionally look back over a shoulder, worried but not overly so. After all, there was a measure of safety in distance.

Worry, *Barr warned.* I'm nearer than you think.

About the Author

J.A. Giunta has been writing poetry and short stories for over ten years and had his first fantasy novel – *The Last Incarnation* – published in February of 2005. With a B.A. in English from Arizona State, he is both an avid reader and video-gamer. Though his current career is in software development, he hopes to someday write novels full-time.

He lives with his wife, Lori, and daughter, Ada Rose, in the perpetual summer that is central Arizona.

Visit him online at www.jagiunta.com.

Made in the USA
Middletown, DE
14 March 2023